DAME AGATHA ABROAD
A Doubleday Large Print
Lost Classics Omnibus

DAME AGATHA ABROAD:

MURDER ON THE ORIENT EXPRESS

MURDER IN MESOPOTAMIA

by
Agatha Christie

DOUBLEDAY LARGE PRINT
HOME LIBRARY EDITION

Garden City, New York

This Large Print Edition, prepared especially for
Doubleday Large Print Home Library, contains
the complete, unabridged text of the original
Publisher's Edition.

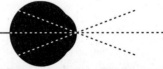

This Large Print Book carries the
Seal of Approval of N.A.V.H.

Contents

MURDER ON THE ORIENT EXPRESS

To M.E.L.M. Arpachiya, 1933

Contents

Part 3
Hercule Poirot Sits Back and Thinks

Cast of Characters

The Inspector   Hercule Poirot
The Belgian sleuth illustrates the efficiency of his methods when he comes face-to-face with a murderer on an international express.

The Director   M. Bouc
Representing Compagnie Internationale des Wagons Lits—shunts his friend Poirot onto the track of a discomfiting crime.

The Conductor   Pierre Michel
Fixes the criminal's wagon.

The Doctor   Dr. Constantine
Diagnoses that the right hand of the assassin did not know what the left hand was doing to the victim.

The Victim and the Suspects

Mary Debenham
An English governess whose manner was as calm and unruffled as her coiffure.

Colonel Arbuthnot
His French was limited, but his verbal defense in his duel with the Belgian is adroit.

Hector MacQueen
A secretary deluxe who speaks in many tongues.

M. Ratchett
This pseudophilanthropist was more malevolent than benevolent.

Antonio Foscarelli
Information gushed out of this swarthy, menacing Italian like the blood from the victim.

Edward Henry Masterman
A spare, neat, noncommunicative valet who has the haughtily disapproving face of the well-trained British servant.

Cyrus Hardman
An American commercial traveler who knows more than he tells and tells more than he knows.

Princess Dragomiroff
A Russian *grande dame* whose pearls were so large they were as improbable as her story.

Greta Ohlsson
This Swedish-trained nurse with the sheeplike face was the last suspect to see the victim alive.

Mrs. Hubbard
Stereotype of an American matron—she never stopped talking, but her acting spoke louder than her words.

Hildegarde Schmidt
Lady's-maid to the Russian princess, deeply involved in the murderous game of *chemin de fer*.

Count Andrenyi
More attached to the Hungarian Embassy than it is to him.

Countess Andrenyi
The youngest, prettiest snowbound suspect.

Part 1

The Facts

Chapter 1

An Important Passenger on the Taurus Express

It was five o'clock on a winter's morning in Syria. Alongside the platform at Aleppo stood the train grandly designated in railway guides as the Taurus Express. It consisted of a kitchen and dining-car, a sleeping-car and two local coaches.

By the step leading up into the sleeping-car stood a young French lieutenant, resplendent in uniform, conversing with a small man muffled up to the ears of whom nothing was visible but a pink-tipped nose and the two points of an upward-curled moustache.

It was freezingly cold, and this job of seeing off a distinguished stranger was not one to be envied, but Lieutenant Dubosc performed his part manfully. Graceful phrases fell from his lips in polished French. Not that he knew what it was all about. There had been rumours, of course, as there always were in such cases. The General's—*his* General's—temper had grown worse and worse. And then there had come this Belgian stranger—all the way from England, it seemed. There had been a week—a week of curious tensity. And then certain things had happened. A very distinguished officer had committed suicide, another had suddenly resigned, anxious faces had suddenly lost their anxiety, certain military precautions were relaxed. And the General, Lieutenant Dubosc's own particular General, had suddenly looked ten years younger.

Dubosc had overheard part of a conversation between him and the stranger. "You have saved us, *mon cher*," said the General emotionally, his great white moustache trembling as he spoke. "You have saved the honour of the French Army—you have averted much bloodshed! How can I thank you for acceding to my request? To have come so far—"

To which the stranger (by name M. Hercule Poirot) had made a fitting reply including the phrase—"But indeed, do I not remember that once you saved my life?" And then the General had made another fitting reply to that, disclaiming any merit for that past service; and with more mention of France, of Belgium, of glory, of honour and of such kindred things they had embraced each other heartily and the conversation had ended.

As to what it had all been about, Lieutenant Dubosc was still in the dark, but to him had been delegated the duty of seeing off M. Poirot by the Taurus Express, and he was carrying it out with all the zeal and ardour befitting a young officer with a promising career ahead of him.

"To-day is Sunday," said Lieutenant Dubosc. "To-morrow, Monday evening, you will be in Stamboul."

It was not the first time he had made this observation. Conversations on the platform, before the departure of a train, are apt to be somewhat repetitive in character.

"That is so," agreed M. Poirot.

"And you intend to remain there a few days, I think?"

"*Mais oui*. Stamboul, it is a city I have never visited. It would be a pity to pass through—*comme ça*." He snapped his fingers descriptively. "Nothing presses—I shall remain there as a tourist for a few days."

"La Sainte Sophie, it is very fine," said Lieutenant Dubosc, who had never seen it.

A cold wind came whistling down the platform. Both men shivered. Lieutenant Dubosc managed to cast a surreptitious glance at his watch. Five minutes to five— only five minutes more!

Fancying that the other man had noticed his glance, he hastened once more into speech.

"There are few people travelling this time of year," he said, glancing up at the windows of the sleeping-car above them.

"That is so," agreed M. Poirot.

"Let us hope you will not be snowed up in the Taurus!"

"That happens?"

"It has occurred, yes. Not this year, as yet."

"Let us hope, then," said M. Poirot. "The weather reports from Europe, they are bad."

"Very bad. In the Balkans there is much snow."

"In Germany, too, I have heard."

"*Eh bien*," said Lieutenant Dubosc hastily as another pause seemed to be about to occur. "Tomorrow evening at seven-forty you will be in Constantinople."

"Yes," said M. Poirot, and went on desperately, "La Sainte Sophie, I have heard it is very fine."

"Magnificent, I believe."

Above their heads the blinds of one of the sleeping-car compartments was pushed aside and a young woman looked out.

Mary Debenham had had little sleep since she left Baghdad on the preceding Thursday. Neither in the train to Kirkuk, nor in the Rest House at Mosul, nor last night on the train had she slept properly. Now, weary of lying wakeful in the hot stuffiness of her overheated compartment, she got up and peered out.

This must be Aleppo. Nothing to see, of course. Just a long, poorly lighted platform with loud, furious altercations in Arabic going on somewhere. Two men below her window were talking French. One was a French officer, the other was a little man with enormous moustaches. She smiled faintly. She had never seen anyone quite so heavily muffled up. It must be very cold outside. That was why they heated the train so terribly. She tried to force the window down lower, but it would not go.

The Wagon Lit conductor had come up to the two men. The train was about to depart, he said. Monsieur had better mount. The little man removed his hat. What an egg-shaped head he had! In spite of her pre-occupations Mary Debenham smiled. A ridiculous-looking little man. The sort of little man one could never take seriously.

Lieutenant Dubosc was saying his parting speech. He had thought it out beforehand and had kept it till the last minute. It was a very beautiful, polished speech.

Not to be outdone, M. Poirot replied in kind. . . .

"*En voiture, Monsieur,*" said the Wagon Lit conductor.

With an air of infinite reluctance M. Poirot climbed aboard the train. The conductor climbed after him. M. Poirot waved his hand. Lieutenant Dubosc came to the salute. The train, with a terrific jerk, moved slowly forward.

"*Enfin!*" murmured M. Hercule Poirot.

"*Brrrrrrrr,*" said Lieutenant Dubosc, realising to the full how cold he was.

* * *

"Voilà, Monsieur!" The conductor displayed to Poirot with a dramatic gesture the beauty of his sleeping compartment and the neat arrangement of his luggage. "The little valise of Monsieur, I have put it *here*."

His outstretched hand was suggestive. Hercule Poirot placed in it a folded note.

"Merci, Monsieur." The conductor became brisk and business-like. "I have the tickets of Monsieur. I will also take the passport, please. Monsieur breaks his journey in Stamboul, I understand?"

M. Poirot assented. "There are not many people travelling, I imagine?" he said.

"No, Monsieur. I have only two other passengers—both English. A Colonel from India and a young English lady from Baghdad. Monsieur requires anything?"

Monsieur demanded a small bottle of Perrier.

Five o'clock in the morning is an awkward time to board a train. There were still two hours before dawn. Conscious of an inadequate night's sleep, and of a delicate mission successfully accomplished, M. Poirot curled up in a corner and fell asleep.

When he awoke it was half-past nine and

he sallied forth to the restaurant car in search of hot coffee.

There was only one occupant at the moment, obviously the young English lady referred to by the conductor. She was tall, slim and dark—perhaps twenty-eight years of age. There was a kind of cool efficiency in the way she was eating her breakfast and in the way she called to the attendant to bring her more coffee, which bespoke a knowledge of the world and of travelling. She wore a dark-coloured travelling dress of some thin material eminently suitable for the heated atmosphere of the train.

M. Hercule Poirot, having nothing better to do, amused himself by studying her without appearing to do so.

She was, he judged, the kind of young woman who could take care of herself with perfect ease wherever she went. She had poise and efficiency. He rather liked the severe regularity of her features and the delicate pallor of her skin. He liked the burnished black head with its neat waves of hair, and her eyes—cool, impersonal and grey. But she was, he decided, just a little too efficient to be what he called *"jolie femme."*

Presently another person entered the restaurant car. This was a tall man of between forty and fifty, lean of figure, brown of skin, with hair slightly grizzled round the temples.

"The Colonel from India," said Poirot to himself.

The newcomer gave a little bow to the girl. "Morning, Miss Debenham."

"Good morning, Colonel Arbuthnot."

The Colonel was standing with a hand on the chair opposite her.

"Any objections?" he asked.

"Of course not. Sit down."

"Well, you know, breakfast isn't always a chatty meal."

"I should hope not. But I don't bite."

The Colonel sat down. "Boy," he called in peremptory fashion.

He gave an order for eggs and coffee.

His eyes rested for a moment on Hercule Poirot, but they passed on indifferently. Poirot, reading the English mind correctly, knew that he had said to himself: "Only some damned foreigner."

True to their nationality, the two English people were not chatty. They exchanged a few brief remarks and presently the girl rose and went back to her compartment.

At lunch time the other two again shared a table and again they both completely ignored the third passenger. Their conversation was more animated than at breakfast. Colonel Arbuthnot talked of the Punjab and occasionally asked the girl a few questions about Baghdad where, it became clear, she had been in a post as governess. In the course of conversation they discovered some mutual friends, which had the immediate effect of making them more friendly and less stiff. They discussed old Tommy Somebody and old Reggie Someone Else. The Colonel inquired whether she was going straight through to England or whether she was stopping in Stamboul.

"No, I'm going straight on."

"Isn't that rather a pity?"

"I came out this way two years ago and spent three days in Stamboul then."

"Oh! I see. Well, I may say I'm very glad you are going right through, because I am."

He made a kind of clumsy little bow, flushing a little as he did so.

He is susceptible, our Colonel, thought Hercule Poirot to himself with some amusement. "The train, it is as dangerous as a sea voyage!"

Miss Debenham said evenly that that would be very nice. Her manner was slightly repressive.

The Colonel, Hercule Poirot noticed, accompanied her back to her compartment. Later they passed through the magnificent scenery of the Taurus. As they looked down towards the Cilician Gates, standing in the corridor side by side, a sigh came suddenly from the girl. Poirot was standing near them and heard her murmur:

"It's so beautiful! I wish—I wish—"

"Yes?"

"I wish I could enjoy it!"

Arbuthnot did not answer. The square line of his jaw seemed a little sterner and grimmer.

"I wish to Heaven you were out of all this," he said.

"Hush, please. Hush."

"Oh! it's all right." He shot a slightly annoyed glance in Poirot's direction. Then he went on: "But I don't like the idea of your being a governess—at the beck and call of tyrannical mothers and their tiresome brats."

She laughed with just a hint of uncontrol in the sound.

"Oh! you mustn't think that. The down-trodden governess is quite an exploded myth. I can assure you that it's the parents who are afraid of being bullied by *me*."

They said no more. Arbuthnot was, perhaps, ashamed of his outburst.

"Rather an odd little comedy that I watch here," said Poirot to himself thoughtfully.

He was to remember that thought of his later.

They arrived at Konya that night about half-past eleven. The two English travellers got out to stretch their legs, pacing up and down the snowy platform.

M. Poirot was content to watch the teeming activity of the station through a window pane. After about ten minutes, however, he decided that a breath of air would not perhaps be a bad thing after all. He made careful preparations, wrapping himself in several coats and mufflers and encasing his neat boots in goloshes. Thus attired, he descended gingerly to the platform and began to pace its length. He walked out beyond the engine.

It was the voices which gave him the clue

to the two indistinct figures standing in the shadow of a traffic van. Arbuthnot was speaking.

"Mary—"

The girl interrupted him.

"Not now. Not now. When it's all over. When it's behind us—*then*—"

Discreetly M. Poirot turned away. He wondered. . . .

He would hardly have recognised the cool, efficient voice of Miss Debenham. . . .

"Curious," he said to himself.

The next day he wondered whether, perhaps, they had quarrelled. They spoke little to each other. The girl, he thought, looked anxious. There were dark circles under her eyes.

It was about half-past two in the afternoon when the train came to a halt. Heads were poked out of windows. A little knot of men was clustered by the side of the line looking and pointing at something under the dining-car.

Poirot leaned out and spoke to the Wagon Lit conductor who was hurrying past. The man answered, and Poirot drew back his head and, turning, almost collided with Mary Debenham who was standing just behind him.

"What is the matter?" she asked rather breathlessly in French. "Why are we stopping?"

"It is nothing, Mademoiselle. It is something that has caught fire under the dining-car. Nothing serious. It is put out. They are now repairing the damage. There is no danger, I assure you."

She made a little abrupt gesture, as though she were waving the idea of danger aside as something completely unimportant.

"Yes, yes, I understand that. But the *time!*"

"The time?"

"Yes, this will delay us."

"It is possible—yes," agreed Poirot.

"But we can't afford delay! This train is due in at 6.55, and one has to cross the Bosphorus and catch the Simplon Orient Express on the other side at nine o'clock. If there is an hour or two of delay we shall miss the connection."

"It is possible, yes," he admitted.

He looked at her curiously. The hand that

held the window bar was not quite steady;
her lips, too, were trembling.

"Does it matter to you very much, Mademoiselle?" he asked.

"Yes. Yes, it does. I—I *must* catch that train."

She turned away from him and went down the corridor to join Colonel Arbuthnot.

Her anxiety, however, was needless. Ten minutes later the train started again. It arrived at Haydapassar only five minutes late, having made up time on the journey.

The Bosphorus was rough and M. Poirot did not enjoy the crossing. He was separated from his travelling companions on the boat and did not see them again.

On arrival at the Galata Bridge he drove straight to the Tokatlian Hotel.

Chapter 2
The Tokatlian Hotel

At the Tokatlian, Hercule Poirot asked for a room with bath. Then he stepped over to the concierge's desk and inquired for letters.

There were three waiting for him and a telegram. His eyebrows rose a little at the sight of the telegram. It was unexpected.

He opened it in his usual neat, unhurried fashion. The printed words stood out clearly.

Development you predicted in Kassner case has come unexpectedly. Please return immediately.

"*Voilà ce qui est embêtant,*" muttered Poirot vexedly. He glanced up at the clock. "I shall have to go on to-night," he said to the concierge. "At what time does the Simplon Orient leave?"

"At nine o'clock, Monsieur."

"Can you get me a sleeper?"

"Assuredly, Monsieur. There is no difficulty this time of year. The trains are almost empty. First-class or second?"

"First."

"*Très bien, Monsieur.* How far are you going?"

"To London."

"*Bien, Monsieur.* I will get you a ticket to London and reserve your sleeping-car accommodation in the Stamboul-Calais coach."

Poirot glanced at the clock again. It was ten minutes to eight. "I have time to dine?"

"But assuredly, Monsieur."

The little Belgian nodded. He went over and cancelled his room order and crossed the hall to the restaurant.

As he was giving his order to the waiter, a hand was placed on his shoulder.

"Ah, *mon vieux*, but this is an unexpected pleasure!" said a voice behind him.

The speaker was a short, stout, elderly man, his hair cut *en brosse*. He was smiling delightedly.

Poirot sprang up.

"M. Bouc!"

"M. Poirot!"

M. Bouc was a Belgian, a director of the Compagnie Internationale des Wagons Lits, and his acquaintance with the former star of the Belgian police force dated back many years.

"You find yourself far from home, *mon cher*," said M. Bouc.

"A little affair in Syria."

"Ah! and you return home—when?"

"To-night."

"Splendid! I, too. That is to say, I go as far as Lausanne, where I have affairs. You travel on the Simplon Orient, I presume?"

"Yes. I have just asked them to get me a sleeper. It was my intention to remain here some days, but I have received a telegram recalling me to England on important business."

"Ah!" sighed M. Bouc. "*Les affaires—les affaires*! But you, you are at the top of the tree nowadays, *mon vieux*!"

"Some little success I have had, perhaps." Hercule Poirot tried to look modest but failed signally.

M. Bouc laughed.

"We will meet later," he said.

Hercule Poirot addressed himself to the task of keeping his moustaches out of the soup.

That difficult task accomplished, he glanced round him whilst waiting for the next course. There were only about half a dozen people in the restaurant, and of those half dozen there were only two that interested Hercule Poirot.

These two sat at a table not far away. The younger was a likeable-looking young man of thirty, clearly an American. It was, however, not he but his companion who had attracted the little detective's attention.

He was a man perhaps of between sixty and seventy. From a little distance he had the bland aspect of a philanthropist. His slightly bald head, his domed forehead, the smiling mouth that displayed a very white set of false teeth—all seemed to speak of a benevolent personality. Only the eyes belied this assumption. They were small, deep-set and crafty. Not only that. As the man, making some remark to his young companion, glanced across the room, his gaze stopped on Poirot for a moment and just for that second there was a strange malevolence, an unnatural tensity in the glance.

Then he rose.

"Pay the bill, Hector," he said.

His voice was slightly husky in tone. It had a queer, soft, dangerous quality.

When Poirot rejoined his friend in the lounge, the other two men were just leaving the hotel. Their luggage was being brought down. The younger was supervising the process. Presently he opened the glass door and said:

"Quite ready now, Mr. Ratchett."

The elder man grunted an assent and passed out.

"*Eh bien*," said Poirot. "What do you think of those two?"

"They are Americans," said M. Bouc.

"Assuredly they are Americans. I meant what did you think of their personalities?"

"The young man seemed quite agreeable."

"And the other?"

"To tell you the truth, my friend, I did not care for him. He produced on me an unpleasant impression. And you?"

Hercule Poirot was a moment in replying.

"When he passed me in the restaurant,"

he said at last, "I had a curious impression. It was as though a wild animal—an animal savage, but savage! you understand—had passed me by."

"And yet he looked altogether of the most respectable."

"*Précisément!* The body—the cage—is everything of the most respectable—but through the bars, the wild animal looks out."

"You are fanciful, *mon vieux*," said M. Bouc.

"It may be so. But I could not rid myself of the impression that evil had passed me by very close."

"That respectable American gentleman?"

"That respectable American gentleman."

"Well," said M. Bouc cheerfully, "it may be so. There is much evil in the world."

At that moment the door opened and the concierge came towards them. He looked concerned and apologetic.

"It is extraordinary, Monsieur," he said to Poirot. "There is not one first-class sleeping berth to be had on the train."

"*Comment?*" cried M. Bouc. "At this time of year? Ah, without doubt there is some party of journalists—of politicians—?"

"I don't know, sir," said the concierge,

turning to him respectfully. "But that's how it is."

"Well, well." M. Bouc turned to Poirot. "Have no fear, my friend. We will arrange something. There is always one compartment, the No. 16, which is not engaged. The conductor sees to that!" He smiled, then glanced up at the clock. "Come," he said, "it is time we started."

At the station M. Bouc was greeted with respectful empressement by the brown-uniformed Wagon Lit conductor.

"Good evening, Monsieur. Your compartment is the No. 1."

He called to the porters and they wheeled their load halfway along the carriage on which the tin plates proclaimed its destination:

ISTANBUL TRIESTE CALAIS

"You are full up to-night, I hear?"

"It is incredible, Monsieur. All the world elects to travel to-night!"

"All the same you must find room for this gentleman here. He is a friend of mine. He can have the No. 16."

"It is taken, Monsieur."

"What? The No. 16?"

A glance of understanding passed between them, and the conductor smiled. He was a tall sallow man of middle age.

"But yes, Monsieur. As I told you, we are full—full—everywhere."

"But what passes itself?" demanded M. Bouc angrily. "There is a conference somewhere? It is a party?"

"No, Monsieur. It is only chance. It just happens that many people have elected to travel to-night."

M. Bouc made a clicking sound of annoyance.

"At Belgrade," he said, "there will be the slip coach from Athens. There will also be the Bucharest-Paris coach. But we do not reach Belgrade until to-morrow evening. The problem is for to-night. There is no second-class berth free?"

"There is a second-class berth, Monsieur—"

"Well, then—"

"But it is a lady's berth. There is already a German woman in the compartment—a lady's maid."

"Là là, that is awkward," said M. Bouc.

"Do not distress yourself, my friend," said

Poirot. "I must travel in an ordinary carriage."

"Not at all. Not at all." He turned once more to the conductor. "Everyone has arrived?"

"It is true," said the man, "that there is one passenger who has not yet arrived." He spoke slowly, with hesitation.

"But speak then!"

"No. 7 berth—a second-class. The gentleman has not yet come, and it is four minutes to nine."

"Who is it?"

"An Englishman," the conductor consulted his list. "A M. Harris."

"A name of good omen," said Poirot. "I read my Dickens. M. Harris, he will not arrive."

"Put Monsieur's luggage in No. 7," said M. Bouc. "If this M. Harris arrives we will tell him that he is too late—that berths cannot be retained so long—we will arrange the matter one way or another. What do I care for a M. Harris?"

"As Monsieur pleases," said the conductor. He spoke to Poirot's porter, directing him where to go. Then he stood aside from the steps to let Poirot enter the train.

"Tout à fait au bout, Monsieur," he called. "The end compartment but one."

Poirot passed along the corridor, a somewhat slow progress, since most of the people travelling were standing outside their carriages.

His polite "Pardons" were uttered with the regularity of clockwork. At last he reached the compartment indicated. Inside it, reaching up to a suitcase, was the tall young American of the Tokatlian.

He frowned as Poirot entered.

"Excuse me," he said. "I think you've made a mistake." Then, laboriously in French: *"Je crois que vous avez un erreur."*

Poirot replied in English. "You are Mr. Harris?"

"No, my name is MacQueen. I—"

But at that moment the voice of the Wagon Lit conductor spoke from over Poirot's shoulder—an apologetic, rather breathless voice.

"There is no other berth on the train, Monsieur. The gentleman has to come in here."

He was hauling up the corridor window as he spoke and began to lift in Poirot's luggage.

Poirot noticed the apology in his tone with some amusement. Doubtless the man had been promised a good tip if he could keep the compartment for the sole use of the other traveller. However, even the most munificent of tips lose their effect when a Director of the Company is on board and issues his orders.

The conductor emerged from the compartment, having swung the suitcases up onto the racks.

"*Voilà, Monsieur,*" he said. "All is arranged. Yours is the upper berth, the No. 7. We start in one minute."

He hurried off down the corridor. Poirot reentered the compartment.

"A phenomenon I have seldom seen," he said cheerfully. "A Wagon Lit conductor himself puts up the luggage! It is unheard of!"

His fellow traveller smiled. He had evidently gotten over his annoyance—had probably decided that it was no good to take the matter otherwise than philosophically. "The train's remarkably full," he said.

A whistle blew, there was a long melancholy cry from the engine. Both men stepped out into the corridor.

Outside a voice shouted, *"En voiture!"*

"We're off," said MacQueen.

But they were not quite off. The whistle blew again.

"I say, sir," said the young man suddenly. "If you'd rather have the lower berth—easier and all that—well, that's all right by me."

A likeable young fellow.

"No, no," protested Poirot. "I would not deprive you—"

"That's all right—"

"You are too amiable—"

Polite protests on both sides.

"It is for one night only," explained Poirot. "At Belgrade—"

"Oh! I see. You're getting out at Belgrade—"

"Not exactly. You see—"

There was a sudden jerk. Both men swung round to the window, looking out at the long, lighted platform as it slid slowly past them.

The Orient Express had started on its three-day journey across Europe.

Chapter 3
Poirot Refuses a Case

M. Hercule Poirot was a little late in entering the luncheon-car on the following day. He had risen early, had breakfasted almost alone, and had spent the morning going over the notes of the case that was recalling him to London. He had seen little of his travelling companion.

M. Bouc, who was already seated, gesticulated a greeting and summoned his friend to the empty place opposite him. Poirot sat down and soon found himself in the favoured position of being at the table which was served first and with the choicest morsels. The food, too, was unusually good.

It was not till they were eating a delicate cream cheese that M. Bouc allowed his attention to wander to matters other than nourishment. He was at the stage of a meal when one becomes philosophic.

"Ah!" he sighed. "If I had but the pen of a Balzac! I would depict this scene." He waved a hand.

"It is an idea, that," said Poirot.

"Ah, you agree? It has not been done, I think? And yet—it lends itself to romance, my friend. All around us are people, of all classes, of all nationalities, of all ages. For three days these people, these strangers to one another, are brought together. They sleep and eat under one roof, they cannot get away from each other. At the end of three days they part, they go their several ways, never perhaps to see each other again."

"And yet," said Poirot, "suppose an accident—"

"Ah, no, my friend—"

"From your point of view it would be regrettable, I agree. But nevertheless let us just for one moment suppose it. Then, perhaps, all these here are linked together—by death."

"Some more wine," said M. Bouc, hastily

pouring it out. "You are morbid, *mon cher*. It is, perhaps the digestion."

"It is true," agreed Poirot, "that the food in Syria was not perhaps quite suited to my stomach."

He sipped his wine. Then, leaning back, he ran his eye thoughtfully round the dining-car. There were thirteen people seated there and, as M. Bouc had said, of all classes and nationalities. He began to study them.

At the table opposite them were three men. They were, he guessed, single travellers graded and placed there by the unerring judgment of the restaurant attendants. A big swarthy Italian was picking his teeth with gusto. Opposite him a spare neat Englishman had the expressionless disapproving face of the well-trained servant. Next to the Englishman was a big American in a loud suit—possibly a commercial traveller.

"You've got to put it over *big*," he was saying in a loud, nasal voice.

The Italian removed his toothpick to gesticulate with it freely.

"Sure," he said. "That whatta I say alla de time."

The Englishman looked out of the window and coughed.

Poirot's eye passed on.

At a small table, sitting very upright, was one of the ugliest old ladies he had ever seen. It was an ugliness of distinction—it fascinated rather than repelled. She sat very upright. Round her neck was a collar of very large pearls which, improbable though it seemed, were real. Her hands were covered with rings. Her sable coat was pushed back on her shoulders. A very small and expensive black toque was hideously unbecoming to the yellow, toad-like face beneath it.

She was speaking now to the restaurant attendant in a clear, courteous, but completely autocratic tone.

"You will be sufficiently amiable to place in my compartment a bottle of mineral water and a large glass of orange juice. You will arrange that I shall have chicken cooked without sauces for dinner this evening— also some boiled fish."

The attendant replied respectfully that it should be done.

She gave a slight gracious nod of the head and rose. Her glance caught Poirot's and swept over him with the nonchalance of the uninterested aristocrat.

"That is Princess Dragomiroff," said M.

Bouc in a low tone. "She is a Russian. Her husband realised all his money before the Revolution and invested it abroad. She is extremely rich. A cosmopolitan."

Poirot nodded. He had heard of Princess Dragomiroff.

"She is a personality," said M. Bouc. "Ugly as sin but she makes herself felt. You agree?"

Poirot agreed.

At another of the large tables Mary Debenham was sitting with two other women. One of them was tall and middle-aged, in a plaid blouse and tweed skirt. She had a mass of faded yellow hair unbecomingly arranged in a large bun, wore glasses, and had a long mild amiable face rather like a sheep. She was listening to the third woman, a stout, pleasant-faced, elderly person who was talking in a slow clear monotone which showed no signs of pausing for breath or coming to a stop.

"—and so my daughter said, 'Why,' she said, 'you just can't apply American methods in this country. It's natural to the folks here to be indolent,' she said. 'They just haven't got any hustle in them—' But all the same you'd be surprised to know what our college there is doing. They've got a fine staff of teachers. I guess there's nothing like education. We've got to apply our Western ideals and teach the East to recognise them. My daughter says—"

The train plunged into a tunnel. The calm, monotonous voice was drowned.

At the next table, a small one, sat Colonel Arbuthnot—alone. His gaze was fixed upon the back of Mary Debenham's head. They were not sitting together. Yet it could easily have been managed. Why?

Perhaps, Poirot thought, Mary Debenham had demurred. A governess learns to be careful. Appearances are important. A girl with her living to get has to be discreet.

His glance shifted to the other side of the carriage. At the far end, against the wall, was a middle-aged woman dressed in black with a broad, expressionless face. German or Scandinavian, he thought. Probably the German lady's-maid.

Beyond her were a couple leaning forward and talking animatedly together. The man wore English clothes of loose tweed, but he was not English. Though only the back of his head was visible to Poirot, the shape of it and the set of the shoulders betrayed him. A big man, well made. He turned his head suddenly and Poirot saw his profile. A very handsome man of thirty-odd with a big fair moustache.

The woman opposite him was a mere girl—twenty at a guess. A tight-fitting little black coat and skirt, white satin blouse, small chic black toque perched at the fashionable outrageous angle. She had a beautiful foreign-looking face, dead white skin, large brown eyes, jet black hair. She was smoking a cigarette in a long holder. Her manicured hands had deep red nails. She wore one large emerald set in platinum. There was coquetry in her glance and voice.

"Elle est jolie—et chic," murmured Poirot. "Husband and wife—eh?"

M. Bouc nodded. "Hungarian Embassy, I believe," he said. "A handsome couple."

There were only two more lunchers—Poirot's fellow traveller MacQueen and his employer, Mr. Ratchett. The latter sat facing Poirot, and for the second time Poirot studied that unprepossessing face, noting the false benevolence of the brow and the small, cruel eyes.

Doubtless M. Bouc saw a change in his friend's expression.

"It is at your wild animal you look?" he asked.

Poirot nodded.

As his coffee was brought to him, M. Bouc rose to his feet. Having started before Poirot he had finished some time ago.

"I return to my compartment," he said. "Come along presently and converse with me."

"With pleasure."

Poirot sipped his coffee and ordered a liqueur. The attendant was passing from table to table with his box of money, accepting payment for bills. The elderly American lady's voice rose shrill and plaintive.

"My daughter said: 'Take a book of food tickets and you'll have no trouble—no trouble at all.' Now, that isn't so. Seems they have to have a ten per cent tip, and then there's that bottle of mineral water—and a queer sort of water too. They didn't have any Evian or Vichy, which seems queer to me."

"It is—they must—how do you say?—serve the water of the country," explained the sheep-faced lady.

"Well, it seems queer to me." She looked distastefully at the heap of small change on the table in front of her. "Look at all this pe-culiar stuff he's given me. Dinars or some-thing. Just a lot of rubbish, it looks like! My daughter said—"

Mary Debenham pushed back her chair and left with a slight bow to the other two. Colonel Arbuthnot got up and followed her. Gathering up her despised money the American woman followed suit, followed by the other one like a sheep. The Hungarians had already departed. The restaurant car was empty save for Poirot and Ratchett and MacQueen.

Ratchett spoke to his companion, who got up and left the car. Then he rose himself, but instead of following MacQueen he dropped unexpectedly into the seat oppo-site Poirot.

"Can you oblige me with a light?" he said. His voice was soft—faintly nasal. "My name is Ratchett."

Poirot bowed slightly. He slipped his hand into his pocket and produced a matchbox which he handed to the other man, who took it but did not strike a light.

"I think," he went on, "that I have the pleasure of speaking to Mr. Hercule Poirot. Is that so?"

Poirot bowed again. "You have been correctly informed, Monsieur."

The detective was conscious of those strange shrewd eyes summing him up before the other spoke again.

"In my country," he said, "we come to the point quickly. Mr. Poirot, I want you to take on a job for me."

Hercule Poirot's eyebrows went up a trifle.

"My *clientèle*, Monsieur, is limited nowadays. I undertake very few cases."

"Why, naturally, I understand that. But this, Mr. Poirot, means big money." He repeated again in his soft, persuasive voice, "Big money."

Hercule Poirot was silent a minute or two. Then he said: "What is it you wish me to do for you, Monsieur—er—Ratchett?"

"Mr. Poirot, I am a rich man—a very rich man. Men in that position have enemies. I have an enemy."

"Only one enemy?"

"Just what do you mean by that question?" asked Ratchett sharply.

"Monsieur, in my experience when a man is in a position to have, as you say, enemies, then it does not usually resolve itself into one enemy only."

Ratchett seemed relieved by Poirot's answer. He said quickly:

"Why, yes, I appreciate that point. Enemy or enemies—it doesn't matter. What does matter is my safety."

"Safety?"

"My life has been threatened, Mr. Poirot. Now I'm a man who can take pretty good care of himself." From the pocket of his coat his hand brought a small automatic into sight for a moment. He continued grimly. "I don't think I'm the kind of man to be caught napping. But, as I look at it, I might as well make assurance doubly sure. I fancy you're the man for my money, Mr. Poirot. And remember—*big* money."

Poirot looked at him thoughtfully for some minutes. His face was completely expressionless. The other could have had no clue as to what thoughts were passing in that mind.

"I regret, Monsieur," he said at length, "that I cannot oblige you."

The other looked at him shrewdly. "Name your figure, then," he said.

Poirot shook his head.

"You do not understand, Monsieur. I have been very fortunate in my profession. I have made enough money to satisfy both my needs and my caprices. I take now only such cases as—interest me."

"You've got a pretty good nerve," said Ratchett. "Will twenty thousand dollars tempt you?"

"It will not."

"If you're holding out for more, you won't get it. I know what a thing's worth to me."

"I, also, M. Ratchett."

"What's wrong with my proposition?"

Poirot rose. "If you will forgive me for being personal—I do not like your face, M. Ratchett," he said.

And with that he left the restaurant car.

Chapter 4

A Cry in the Night

The Simplon Orient Express arrived at Belgrade at a quarter to nine that evening. It was not due to depart again until 9.15, so Poirot descended to the platform. He did not, however, remain there long. The cold was bitter, and though the platform itself was protected, heavy snow was falling outside. He returned to his compartment. The conductor, who was on the platform stamping his feet and waving his arms to keep warm, spoke to him.

"Your valises have been moved, Monsieur. To the compartment No. 1, the compartment of M. Bouc."

"But where is Monsieur Bouc, then?"

"He has moved into the coach from Athens which has just been put on."

Poirot went in search of his friend. M. Bouc waved his protestations aside.

"It is nothing. It is nothing. It is more convenient like this. You are going through to England, so it is better that you should stay in the through coach to Calais. Me, I am very well here. It is most peaceful. This coach is empty save for myself and one little Greek doctor. Ah! my friend, what a night! They say there has not been so much snow for years. Let us hope we shall not be held up. I am not too happy about it, I can tell you."

At 9.15 punctually the train pulled out of the station, and shortly afterwards Poirot got up, said good night to his friend, and made his way along the corridor back into his own coach which was in front next to the dining-car.

On this, the second day of the journey, barriers were breaking down. Colonel Arbuthnot was standing at the door of his compartment talking to MacQueen. When MacQueen saw Poirot he broke off something he was saying. He looked very much surprised.

"Why," he cried, "I thought you'd left us. You said you were getting off at Belgrade."

"You misunderstood me," said Poirot, smiling. "I remember now, the train started from Stamboul just as we were talking about it."

"But, man, your baggage. It's gone."

"It has been moved into another compartment, that is all."

"Oh! I see."

He resumed his conversation with Arbuthnot, and Poirot passed on down the corridor.

Two doors from his own compartment, the elderly American, Mrs. Hubbard, was standing talking to the sheep-like lady, who was a Swede. Mrs. Hubbard was pressing a magazine on the other.

"No, do take it, my dear," she said. "I've got plenty of other things to read. My, isn't the cold something frightful?" She nodded amicably to Poirot.

"You are most kind," said the Swedish lady.

"Not at all. I hope you'll sleep well and that your head will be better in the morning."

"It is the cold only. I make now myself a cup of tea."

"Have you got some aspirin? Are you sure

now? I've got plenty. Well, good night, my dear."

She turned to Poirot conversationally as the other woman departed.

"Poor creature, she's a Swede. As far as I can make out she's a kind of missionary. A teaching one. A nice creature, but doesn't talk much English. She was *most* interested in what I told her about my daughter."

Poirot, by now, knew all about Mrs. Hubbard's daughter. Everyone on the train who could understand English did! How she and her husband were on the staff of a big American college in Smyrna, and how this was Mrs. Hubbard's first journey to the East, and what she thought of the Turks and their slipshod ways and the condition of their roads.

The door next to them opened and the thin pale manservant stepped out. Inside, Poirot caught a glimpse of Mr. Ratchett sitting up in bed. He saw Poirot and his face changed, darkening with anger. Then the door was shut.

Mrs. Hubbard drew Poirot a little aside.

"You know, I'm dead scared of that man. Oh! not the valet—the other. His master. Master, indeed! There's something *wrong* about that man. My daughter always says I'm very intuitive. 'When Mamma gets a hunch, she's dead right,' that's what my daughter says. And I've got a hunch about that man. He's next door to me and I don't like it. I put my grips against the communicating door last night. I thought I heard him trying the handle. Do you know, I shouldn't be a bit surprised if that man turned out to be a murderer—one of these train robbers you read about. I daresay I'm foolish, but there it is. I'm absolutely scared to death of the man! My daughter said I'd have an easy journey, but somehow I don't feel happy about it. It may be foolish, but I feel as if anything might happen—anything at all. And how that nice young fellow can bear to be his secretary, I can't think."

Colonel Arbuthnot and MacQueen were coming towards them down the corridor.

"Come into my carriage," MacQueen was saying. "It isn't made up for the night yet. Now what I want to get right about your policy in India is this—"

The two men passed and went on down the corridor to MacQueen's carriage.

Mrs. Hubbard said good night to Poirot. "I

guess I'll go right to bed and read," she said. "Good night."

"Good night, Madame."

Poirot passed into his own compartment, which was the next one beyond Ratchett's. He undressed and got into bed, read for about half an hour and then turned out the light.

He awoke some hours later, awoke with a start. He knew what it was that had wakened him—a loud groan, almost a cry, somewhere close at hand. At the same moment the ting of a bell sounded sharply.

Poirot sat up and switched on the light. He noticed that the train was at a standstill—presumably at a station.

That cry had startled him. He remembered that it was Ratchett who had the next compartment. He got out of bed and opened the door just as the Wagon Lit conductor came hurrying along the corridor and knocked on Ratchett's door. Poirot kept his door open a crack and watched. The conductor tapped a second time. A bell rang and a light showed over another door farther down. The conductor glanced over his shoulder. At the same moment a voice from within the next compartment called out: *"Ce n'est rien. Je me suis trompé."*

"Bien, Monsieur." The conductor scurried off again, to knock at the door where the light was showing.

Poirot returned to bed, his mind relieved, and switched off the light. He glanced at his watch. It was just twenty-three minutes to one.

Chapter 5
The Crime

He found it difficult to go to sleep again at once. For one thing he missed the motion of the train. If it *was* a station outside, it was curiously quiet. By contrast the noises on the train seemed unusually loud. He could hear Ratchett moving about next door—a click as he pulled down the washbasin, the sound of the tap running, a splashing noise, then another click as the basin shut to again. Footsteps passed up the corridor outside, the shuffling footsteps of someone in bedroom slippers.

Hercule Poirot lay awake staring at the ceiling. Why was the station outside so silent? His throat felt dry. He had forgotten to ask for his usual bottle of mineral water. He looked at his watch again. Just after a

quarter past one. He would ring for the conductor and ask for some mineral water. His
finger went out to the bell, but he paused as
in the stillness he heard a ting. The man
couldn't answer every bell at once.

Ting. . . . Ting. . . . Ting. . . .

It sounded again and again. Where was
the man? Somebody was getting impatient.

Ti-i-i-ing!

Whoever it was, was keeping a finger
solidly on the push-button.

Suddenly with a rush, his footsteps echoing up the aisle, the man came. He knocked
at a door not far from Poirot's own.

Then came voices—the conductor's, deferential, apologetic; and a woman's, insis-
tent and voluble.

Mrs. Hubbard!

Poirot smiled to himself.

The altercation—if it was one—went on
for some time. Its proportions were ninety
per cent of Mrs. Hubbard's to a soothing ten
per cent of the conductor's. Finally the matter seemed to be adjusted. Poirot heard distinctly a *"Bonne nuit, Madame,"* and a closing door.

He pressed his own finger on the bell.

The conductor arrived promptly. He looked hot and worried.

"*De l'eau minérale, s'il vous plaît.*"

"*Bien, Monsieur.*" Perhaps a twinkle in Poirot's eye led him to unburden himself. "*La dame américaine—*"

"Yes?"

He wiped his forehead. "Imagine to yourself the time I have had with her! She insists—but *insists*—that there is a man in her compartment! Figure to yourself, Monsieur. In a space of this size." He swept a hand round. "Where would he conceal himself? I argue with her. I point out that it is impossible. She insists. She woke up, and there was a man there. And how, I ask, did he get out and leave the door bolted behind him? But she will not listen to reason. As though there were not enough to worry us already. This snow—"

"Snow?"

"But yes, Monsieur. Monsieur has not noticed? The train has stopped. We have run into a snowdrift. Heaven knows how long we shall be here. I remember once being snowed up for seven days."

"Where are we?"

"Between Vincovci and Brod."

"Là-là," said Poirot vexedly.

The man withdrew and returned with the water.

"Bon soir, Monsieur."

Poirot drank a glass of water and composed himself to sleep.

He was just dropping off when something again woke him. This time it was as though something heavy had fallen with a thud against the door.

He sprang up, opened it and looked out. Nothing. But to his right, some distance down the corridor, a woman wrapped in a scarlet kimono was retreating from him. At the other end, sitting on his little seat, the conductor was entering up figures on large sheets of paper. Everything was deathly quiet.

"Decidedly I suffer from the nerves," said Poirot and retired to bed again. This time he slept till morning.

When he awoke the train was still at a standstill. He raised a blind and looked out. Heavy banks of snow surrounded the train.

He glanced at his watch and saw that it was past nine o'clock.

At a quarter to ten, neat, spruce and dandified as ever, he made his way to the restaurant car, where a chorus of woe was going on.

Any barriers there might have been between the passengers had now quite broken down. All were united by a common misfortune. Mrs. Hubbard was loudest in her lamentations.

"My daughter said it would be the easiest way in the world. Just sit in the train until I got to Parrus. And now we may be here for days and days," she wailed. "And my boat sails day after to-morrow. How am I going to catch it now? Why, I can't even wire to cancel my passage. I'm just too mad to talk about it!"

The Italian said that he had urgent business himself in Milan. The large American said that that was "too bad, Ma'am," and soothingly expressed a hope that the train might make up time.

"My sister—her children wait me," said the Swedish lady, and wept. "I get no word to them. What they think? They will say bad things have happen to me."

"How long shall we be here?" demanded Mary Debenham. "Doesn't anybody *know*?"

Her voice sounded impatient, but Poirot noted that there were no signs of that almost feverish anxiety which she had displayed during the check to the Taurus Express.

Mrs. Hubbard was off again.

"There isn't anybody knows a thing on this train. And nobody's trying to *do* anything. Just a pack of useless foreigners. Why, if this were at home, there'd be someone at least *trying* to do something!"

Arbuthnot turned to Poirot and spoke in careful British French.

"Vous êtes un directeur de la ligne, je crois, Monsieur. Vous pouvez nous dire—"

Smiling, Poirot corrected him.

"No, no," he said in English. "It is not I. You confound me with my friend, M. Bouc."

"Oh! I'm sorry."

"Not at all. It is most natural. I am now in the compartment that he had formerly."

M. Bouc was not present in the restaurant car. Poirot looked about to notice who else was absent.

Princess Dragomiroff was missing, and the Hungarian couple. Also Ratchett, his valet, and the German lady's-maid.

The Swedish lady wiped her eyes.

"I am foolish," she said. "I am bad to cry. All is for the best, whatever happen."

This Christian spirit, however, was far from being shared.

"That's all very well," said MacQueen restlessly. "We may be here for days."

"What is this country anyway?" demanded Mrs. Hubbard tearfully.

On being told it was Jugo-Slavia, she said: "Oh! one of these Balkan things. What can you expect?"

"You are the only patient one, Mademoiselle," said Poirot to Miss Debenham.

She shrugged her shoulders slightly. "What can one do?"

"You are a philosopher, Mademoiselle."

"That implies a detached attitude. I think my attitude is more selfish. I have learned to save myself useless emotion."

She was speaking more to herself than to him. She was not even looking at him. Her gaze went past him, out of the window to where the snow lay in heavy masses.

"You are a strong character, Mademoiselle," said Poirot gently. "You are, I think, the strongest character amongst us."

"Oh! no. No, indeed. I know one far, far stronger than I am."

"And that is—?"

She seemed suddenly to come to herself,

to realise that she was talking to a stranger and foreigner, with whom, until this morning, she had exchanged only half a dozen sentences.

She laughed, a polite but estranging laugh.

"Well—that old lady, for instance. You have probably noticed her. A very ugly old lady but rather fascinating. She has only to lift a little finger and ask for something in a polite voice—and the whole train runs."

"It runs also for my friend M. Bouc," said Poirot. "But that is because he is a director of the line, not because he has a strong character."

Mary Debenham smiled.

The morning wore away. Several people, Poirot amongst them, remained in the dining-car. The communal life was felt, at the moment, to pass the time better. He heard a good deal more about Mrs. Hubbard's daughter, and he heard the lifelong habits of Mr. Hubbard, deceased, from his rising in the morning and commencing breakfast with a cereal to his final rest at night in the bed-socks that Mrs. Hubbard herself had been in the habit of knitting for him.

It was when he was listening to a confused account of the missionary aims of the
Swedish lady that one of the Wagon Lit conductors came into the car and stood at his
elbow.

"Pardon, Monsieur."

"Yes?"

"The compliments of M. Bouc, and he
would be glad if you would be so kind as to
come to him for a few minutes."

Poirot rose, uttered excuses to the
Swedish lady and followed the man out of
the dining-car. It was not his own conductor, but a big fair man.

He followed his guide down the corridor
of his own carriage and along the corridor of
the next one. The man tapped at a door,
then stood aside to let Poirot enter.

The compartment was not M. Bouc's
own. It was a second-class one—chosen
presumably because of its slightly larger
size. It certainly gave the impression of being crowded.

M. Bouc himself was sitting on the small
seat in the opposite corner. In the corner
next to the window, facing him, was a small
dark man looking out at the snow. Standing
up and quite preventing Poirot from ad-

vancing any farther were a big man in blue inform (the *chef de train*) and his own Wagon Lit conductor.

"Ah! my good friend," cried M. Bouc. "Come in. We have need of you."

The little man in the window shifted along the seat, and Poirot squeezed past the other two men and sat down facing his friend.

The expression on M. Bouc's face gave him, as he would have expressed it, furiously to think. It was clear that something out of the common had happened.

"What has occurred?" he asked.

"You may well ask that. First this snow—this stoppage. And now—"

He paused—and a sort of strangled gasp came from the Wagon Lit conductor.

"And now what?"

"And now a passenger lies dead in his berth—stabbed."

M. Bouc spoke with a kind of calm desperation.

"A passenger? Which passenger?"

"An American. A man called—called—" he consulted some notes in front of him. "Ratchett. That is right—Ratchett?"

"Yes, Monsieur." The Wagon Lit man gulped.

Poirot looked at him. He was as white as chalk.

"You had better let that man sit down," he said. "He may faint otherwise."

The *chef de train* moved slightly and the Wagon Lit man sank down in the corner and buried his face in his hands.

"*Brr!*" said Poirot. "This is serious!"

"Certainly it is serious. To begin with, a murder—that in itself is a calamity of the first water. But not only that, the circumstances are unusual. Here we are, brought to a standstill. We may be here for hours—and not only hours—days! Another circumstance—passing through most countries we have the police of that country on the train. But in Jugo-Slavia, no. You comprehend?"

"It is a position of great difficulty," said Poirot.

"There is worse to come. Dr. Constantine—I forgot, I have not introduced you. Dr. Constantine, M. Poirot."

The little dark man bowed, and Poirot returned the bow.

"Dr. Constantine is of the opinion that death occurred at about 1 A.M."

"It is difficult to speak exactly in these matters," said the doctor, "but I think I can say definitely that death occurred between midnight and two in the morning."

"When was this M. Ratchett last seen alive?" asked Poirot.

"He is known to have been alive at about twenty minutes to one, when he spoke to the conductor," said M. Bouc.

"That is quite correct," said Poirot. "I myself heard what passed. That is the last thing known?"

"Yes."

Poirot turned toward the doctor, who continued.

"The window of M. Ratchett's compartment was found wide open, leading one to suppose that the murderer escaped that way. But in my opinion that open window is a blind. Anyone departing that way would have left distinct traces in the snow. There were none."

"The crime was discovered—when?" asked Poirot.

"Michel!"

The Wagon Lit conductor sat up. His face still looked pale and frightened.

"Tell this gentleman exactly what occurred," ordered M. Bouc.

The man spoke somewhat jerkily.

"The valet of this M. Ratchett, he tapped several times at the door this morning. There was no answer. Then, half an hour ago, the restaurant car attendant came. He wanted to know if Monsieur was taking déjeuner. It was eleven o'clock, you comprehend.

"I open the door for him with my key. But there is a chain, too, and that is fastened. There is no answer and it is very still in there, and cold—but cold. With the window open and snow drifting in. I thought the gentleman had had a fit, perhaps. I got the chef de train. We broke the chain and went in. He was—Ah! c'était terrible!"

He buried his face in his hands again.

"The door was locked and chained on the inside," said Poirot thoughtfully. "It was not suicide—eh?"

The Greek doctor gave a sardonic laugh. "Does a man who commits suicide stab himself in ten—twelve—fifteen places?" he asked.

Poirot's eyes opened. "That is great ferocity," he said.

"It is a woman," said the *chef de train*, speaking for the first time. "Depend upon it, it was a woman. Only a woman would stab like that."

Dr. Constantine screwed up his face thoughtfully.

"She must have been a very strong woman," he said. "It is not my desire to speak technically—that is only confusing; but I can assure you that one or two of the blows were delivered with such force as to drive them through hard belts of bone and muscle."

"It was clearly not a scientific crime," said Poirot.

"It was most unscientific," returned Dr. Constantine. "The blows seem to have been delivered haphazard and at random. Some have glanced off, doing hardly any damage. It is as though somebody had shut his eyes and then in a frenzy struck blindly again and again."

"*C'est une femme,*" said the *chef de train* again. "Women are like that. When they are enraged they have great strength." He nodded so sagely that everyone suspected a personal experience of his own.

"I have, perhaps, something to contribute to your store of knowledge," said Poirot. "M. Ratchett spoke to me yesterday. He told me, as far as I was able to understand him, that he was in danger of his life."

" 'Bumped off'—that is the American expression, is it not?" asked M. Bouc. "Then it is not a woman. It is a 'gangster' or a 'gunman.' "

The *chef de train* looked pained at seeing his theory come to nought.

"If so," said Poirot, "it seems to have been done very amateurishly." His tone expressed professional disapproval.

"There is a large American on the train," said M. Bouc, pursuing his idea. "A common-looking man with terrible clothes. He chews the gum, which I believe is not done in good circles. You know whom I mean?"

The Wagon Lit conductor to whom he had appealed nodded.

"*Oui, Monsieur*, the No. 16. But it cannot have been he. I should have seen him enter or leave the compartment."

"You might not. You might not. But we will

go into that presently. The question is, what to do?" He looked at Poirot.

Poirot looked back at him.

"Come, my friend," said M. Bouc. "You comprehend what I am about to ask of you. I know your powers. Take command of this investigation! No, no, do not refuse. See, to us it is serious—I speak for the Compagnie Internationale des Wagons Lits. By the time the Jugo-Slavian police arrive, how simple if we can present them with the solution! Otherwise delays, annoyances, a million and one inconveniences. Perhaps, who knows, serious annoyance to innocent persons. Instead—*you* solve the mystery! We say, 'A murder has occurred—*this* is the criminal!' "

"And suppose I do not solve it?"

"Ah, *mon cher*!" M. Bouc's voice became positively caressing. "I know your reputation. I know something of your methods. This is the ideal case for you. To look up the antecedents of all these people, to discover their *bona fides*—all that takes time and endless inconvenience. But have I not heard you say often that to solve a case a man has only to lie back in his chair and think? Do that. Interview the passengers on the train, view the body, examine what clues there are, and then—well, I have faith in you! I am assured that it is no idle boast of yours. Lie back and think—use (as I have heard you say so often) the little grey cells of the mind—and you will *know*!"

He leaned forward, looking affectionately at the detective.

"Your faith touches me, my friend," said Poirot emotionally. "As you say, this cannot be a difficult case. I myself last night—but we will not speak of that now. In truth, this problem intrigues me. I was reflecting, not half an hour ago, that many hours of boredom lay ahead whilst we are stuck here. And now—a problem lies ready to my hand."

"You accept then?" said M. Bouc eagerly.

"*C'est entendu*. You place the matter in my hands."

"Good—we are all at your service."

"To begin with, I should like a plan of the Istanbul-Calais coach, with a note of the people who occupied the several compartments, and I should also like to see their passports and their tickets."

"Michel will get you those."

The Wagon Lit conductor left the compartment.

"What other passengers are there on the train?" asked Poirot.

"In this coach Dr. Constantine and I are the only travellers. In the coach from Bucharest is an old gentleman with a lame leg. He is well known to the conductor. Beyond that are the ordinary carriages, but these do not concern us, since they were locked after dinner had been served last night. Forward of the Istanbul-Calais coach there is only the dining-car."

"Then it seems," said Poirot slowly, "as though we must look for our murderer in the Istanbul-Calais coach." He turned to the doctor. "That is what you were hinting, I think?"

The Greek nodded. "At half an hour after midnight we ran into the snowdrift. No one can have left the train since then."

M. Bouc said solemnly, *"The murderer is with us—on the train now. . . ."*

Chapter 6
A Woman

"First of all," said Poirot, "I should like a word or two with young Mr. MacQueen. He may be able to give us valuable information."

"Certainly," said M. Bouc. He turned to the *chef de train*. "Get Mr. MacQueen to come here."

The *chef de train* left the carriage.

The conductor returned with a bundle of passports and tickets. M. Bouc took them from him.

"Thank you, Michel. It would be best now, I think, if you were to go back to your post. We will take your evidence formally later."

"Very good, Monsieur," said Michel, and in his turn left the carriage.

"After we have seen young MacQueen,"

said Poirot, "perhaps M. *le docteur* will come with me to the dead man's carriage."

"Certainly."

"After we have finished there—"

But at this moment the *chef de train* returned with Hector MacQueen.

M. Bouc rose. "We are a little cramped here," he said pleasantly. "Take my seat, Mr. MacQueen. M. Poirot will sit opposite you— so."

He turned to the *chef de train*. "Clear all the people out of the restaurant car," he said, "and let it be left free for M. Poirot. You will conduct your interviews there, *mon cher*?"

"It would be the most convenient, yes," agreed Poirot.

MacQueen had stood looking from one to the other, not quite following the rapid flow of French.

"*Qu'est-ce qu'il y a?*" he began laboriously. "*Pourquoi—?*"

With a vigorous gesture Poirot motioned him to the seat in the corner. He took it and began once more.

"*Pourquoi—?*" Then checking himself and relapsing into his own tongue: "What's up on the train? Has anything happened?"

He looked from one man to another.

Poirot nodded. "Exactly. Something has happened. Prepare yourself for a shock. *Your employer, M. Ratchett, is dead!*"

MacQueen's mouth pursed itself into a whistle. Except that his eyes grew a shade brighter, he showed no signs of shock or distress.

"So they got him after all," he said.

"What exactly do you mean by that phrase, Mr. MacQueen?"

MacQueen hesitated.

"You are assuming," said Poirot, "that M. Ratchett was murdered?"

"Wasn't he?" This time MacQueen did show surprise. "Why, yes," he said slowly. "That's just what I did think. Do you mean he just died in his sleep? Why, the old man was as tough as—as tough—"

He stopped, at a loss for a simile.

"No, no," said Poirot. "Your assumption was quite right. M. Ratchett was murdered. Stabbed. But I should like to know why you were so sure it *was* murder, and not just— death."

MacQueen hesitated. "I must get this clear," he said. "Who exactly are you? And where do you come in?"

"I represent the Compagnie Internationale des Wagons Lits." Poirot paused, then added, "I am a detective. My name is Hercule Poirot."

If he expected an effect he did not get one. MacQueen said merely, "Oh! yes?" and waited for him to go on.

"You know the name, perhaps?"

"Why, it does seem kind of familiar. Only I always thought it was a woman's dressmaker."

Hercule Poirot looked at him with distaste. "It is incredible!" he said.

"What's incredible?"

"Nothing. Let us advance with the matter in hand. I want you to tell me, M. MacQueen, all that you know about the dead man. You were not related to him?"

"No. I am—was—his secretary."

"For how long have you held that post?"

"Just over a year."

"Please give me all the information you can."

"Well, I met Mr. Ratchett just over a year ago when I was in Persia—"

Poirot interrupted.

"What were you doing there?"

"I had come over from New York to look

into an oil concession. I don't suppose you want to hear all about that. My friends and I had been let in rather badly over it. Mr. Ratchett was in the same hotel. He had just had a row with his secretary. He offered me the job and I took it. I was at a loose end and glad to find a well-paid job ready made, as it were."

"And since then?"

"We've travelled about. Mr. Ratchett wanted to see the world. He was hampered by knowing no languages. I acted more as a courier than as a secretary. It was a pleasant life."

"Now tell me as much as you can about your employer."

The young man shrugged his shoulders. A perplexed expression passed over his face.

"That's not so easy."

"What was his full name?"

"Samuel Edward Ratchett."

"He was an American citizen?"

"Yes."

"What part of America did he come from?"

"I don't know."

"Well, tell me what you do know."

"The actual truth is, Mr. Poirot, that I know nothing at all! Mr. Ratchett never spoke of himself or of his life in America."

"Why do you think that was?"

"I don't know. I imagined that he might be ashamed of his beginnings. Some men are."

"Does that strike you as a satisfactory solution?"

"Frankly, it doesn't."

"Has he any relatives?"

"He never mentioned any."

Poirot pressed the point.

"You must have formed *some* theory, Mr. MacQueen."

"Well, yes, I did. For one thing, I don't believe Ratchett was his real name. I think he left America definitely in order to escape someone or something. I think he was successful—until a few weeks ago."

"And then?"

"He began to get letters—threatening letters."

"Did you see them?"

"Yes. It was my business to attend to his correspondence. The first letter came a fortnight ago."

"Were these letters destroyed?"

"No, I think I've got a couple still in my

files—one I know Ratchett tore up in a rage. Shall I get them for you?"

"If you would be so good."

MacQueen left the compartment. He returned a few minutes later and laid down two sheets of rather dirty notepaper before Poirot.

The first letter ran as follows:

Thought you'd double-cross us and get away with it, did you? Not on your life. We're out to GET you, Ratchett, and we WILL get you!

There was no signature.

With no comment beyond raised eyebrows, Poirot picked up the second letter.

We're going to take you for a ride, Ratchett. Some time soon. We're going to GET you—see?

Poirot laid the letter down.

"The style is monotonous!" he said. "More so than the handwriting."

MacQueen stared at him.

"You would not observe," said Poirot pleasantly. "It requires the eye of one used to such things. This letter was not written by one person, M. MacQueen. Two or more persons wrote it—each writing one letter of a word at a time. Also, the letters are printed. That makes the task of identifying the handwriting much more difficult." He paused, then said: "Did you know that M. Ratchett had applied for help to me?"

"To *you*?"

MacQueen's astonished tone told Poirot quite certainly that the young man had not known of it.

The detective nodded. "Yes. He was alarmed. Tell me, how did he act when he received the first letter?"

MacQueen hesitated.

"It's difficult to say. He—he—passed it off with a laugh in that quiet way of his. But somehow"—he gave a slight shiver—"I felt that there was a good deal going on underneath the quietness."

Poirot nodded. Then he asked an unexpected question.

"Mr. MacQueen, will you tell me, quite honestly, exactly how you regarded your employer? Did you like him?"

Hector MacQueen took a moment or two before replying.

"No," he said at last. "I did not."

"Why?"

"I can't exactly say. He was always quite pleasant in his manner." He paused, then said: "I'll tell you the truth, Mr. Poirot. I disliked and distrusted him. He was, I am sure, a cruel and dangerous man. I must admit, though, that I have no reasons to advance for my opinion."

"Thank you, Mr. MacQueen. One further question: when did you last see Mr. Ratchett alive?"

"Last evening about"—he thought for a minute—"ten o'clock, I should say. I went into his compartment to take down some memoranda from him."

"On what subject?"

"Some tiles and antique pottery that he bought in Persia. What had been delivered was not what he had purchased. There has been a long, vexatious correspondence on the subject."

"And that was the last time Mr. Ratchett was seen alive?"

"Yes, I suppose so."

"Do you know when Mr. Ratchett received the last threatening letter?"

"On the morning of the day we left Constantinople."

"There is one more question I must ask
you, Mr. MacQueen. Were you on good
terms with your employer?"

The young man's eyes twinkled suddenly.

"This is where I'm supposed to go all
goosefleshy down the back. In the words of
a best seller, 'You've nothing on me.' Ratchett and I were on perfectly good terms."

"Perhaps, Mr. MacQueen, you will give
me your full name and your address in
America."

MacQueen gave his name—Hector Willard
MacQueen—and an address in New York.

Poirot leaned back against the cushions.

"That is all for the present, Mr. Mac-
Queen," he said. "I should be obliged if you
would keep the matter of Mr. Ratchett's
death to yourself for a little time."

"His valet, Masterman, will have to know."

"He probably knows already," said Poirot
drily. "If so, try to get him to hold his
tongue."

"That oughtn't to be difficult. He's a
Britisher and, as he calls it, he 'keeps to
himself.' He has a low opinion of Ameri-

cans, and no opinion at all of any other nationality."

"Thank you, Mr. MacQueen."

The American left the carriage.

"Well?" demanded M. Bouc. "You believe what he says, this young man?"

"He seems honest and straightforward. He did not pretend to any affection for his employer, as he probably would have done had he been involved in any way. It is true, Mr. Ratchett did not tell him that he had tried to enlist my services and failed, but I do not think that that is really a suspicious circumstance. I fancy Mr. Ratchett was a gentleman who kept his own counsel on every possible occasion."

"So you pronounce one person at least innocent of the crime," said M. Bouc jovially.

Poirot cast on him a look of reproach.

"Me, I suspect everybody till the last minute," he said. "All the same, I must admit that I cannot see this sober, long-headed MacQueen losing his head and stabbing his victim twelve or fourteen times. It is not in accord with his psychology—not at all."

"No," said M. Bouc thoughtfully. "That is

the act of a man driven almost crazy with a frenzied hate—it suggests rather the Latin temperament. Or else it suggests, as our friend the *chef de train* insisted—a woman."

Chapter 7
The Body

Followed by Dr. Constantine, Poirot made his way to the next coach and to the compartment occupied by the murdered man. The conductor came and unlocked the door for them with his key.

The two men passed inside. Poirot turned inquiringly to his companion.

"How much has been disarranged in this compartment?"

"Nothing has been touched. I was careful not to move the body in making my examination."

Poirot nodded. He looked round him.

The first thing that struck the senses was the intense cold. The window was pushed down as far as it would go, and the blind was drawn up.

"Brrr," observed Poirot.

The other smiled appreciatively.

"I did not like to close it," he said.

Poirot examined the window carefully.

"You are right," he announced. "Nobody left the carriage this way. Possibly the open window was intended to suggest that somebody did; but if so, the snow has defeated the murderer's intention."

He examined the frame of the window carefully. Taking a small case from his pocket he blew a little powder over the frame.

"No fingerprints at all," he said. "That means it has been wiped. Well, if there had been fingerprints they would have told us very little. They would have been those of Mr. Ratchett or his valet or the conductor. Criminals do not make mistakes of that kind nowadays.

"And that being so," he added cheerfully, "we might as well shut the window. Positively it is the cold storage in here!"

He suited the action to the word and then turned his attention for the first time to the motionless figure lying in the bunk.

Ratchett lay on his back. His pyjama

jacket, stained with rusty patches, had been unbuttoned and thrown back.

"I had to see the nature of the wounds, you see," explained the doctor.

Poirot nodded. He bent over the body. Finally he straightened himself with a slight grimace.

"It is not pretty," he said. "Someone must have stood there and stabbed him again and again. How many wounds are there exactly?"

"I make it twelve. One or two are so slight as to be practically scratches. On the other hand, at least three would be capable of causing death."

Something in the doctor's tone caught Poirot's attention. He looked at him sharply. The little Greek was standing staring down at the body with a puzzled frown.

"Something strikes you as odd, does it not?" he asked gently. "Speak, my friend. There is something here that puzzles you?"

"You are right," acknowledged the other.

"What is it?"

"You see these two wounds—here and here—" He pointed. "They are deep. Each cut must have severed blood vessels—and yet the edges do not gape. They have not bled as one would have expected."

"Which suggests?"

"That the man was already dead—some little time dead—when they were delivered. But that is surely absurd."

"It would seem so," said Poirot thoughtfully. "Unless our murderer figured to himself that he had not accomplished his job properly and came back to make quite sure—but that is manifestly absurd! Anything else?"

"Well, just one thing."

"And that?"

"You see this wound here—under the right arm—near the right shoulder. Take this pencil of mine. Could you deliver such a blow?"

Poirot poised his hand.

"Précisément," he said. "I see. With the *right* hand it is exceedingly difficult, almost impossible. One would have to strike backhanded, as it were. But if the blow were struck with the *left* hand—"

"Exactly, M. Poirot. That blow was almost certainly struck with the *left* hand."

"So that our murderer is left-handed? No, it is more difficult than that, is it not?"

"As you say, M. Poirot. Some of these other blows are just as obviously right-handed."

"Two people. We are back at two people again," murmured the detective. He asked abruptly: "Was the electric light on?"

"It is difficult to say. You see, it is turned off by the conductor every morning about ten o'clock."

"The switches will tell us," said Poirot.

He examined the switch of the top light and also the roll-back, bed-head light. The former was turned off. The latter was closed.

"*Eh bien,*" he said thoughtfully. "We have here a hypothesis of the First and the Second Murderer, as the great Shakespeare would put it. The First Murderer stabbed his victim and left the compartment, turning off the light. The Second Murderer came in in the dark, did not see that his or her work had been done, and stabbed at least twice at a dead body. *Que pensez-vous de ça?*"

"Magnificent!" said the little doctor with enthusiasm.

The other's eyes twinkled.

"You think so? I am glad. It sounded to me a little like the nonsense."

"What other explanation can there be?"

"That is just what I am asking myself. Have we here a coincidence, or what? Are there any other inconsistencies, such as would point to two people being concerned?"

"I think I can say yes. Some of these blows, as I have already said, point to a weakness—a lack of strength or a lack of determination. They are feeble, glancing blows. But this one here—and this one—" Again he pointed. "Great strength was needed for those blows. They have penetrated the muscle."

"They were, in your opinion, delivered by a man?"

"Most certainly."

"They could not have been delivered by a woman?"

"A young, vigorous, athletic woman might have struck them, especially if she were in the grip of a strong emotion; but it is in my opinion highly unlikely."

Poirot was silent a moment or two.

The other asked anxiously, "You understand my point?"

"Perfectly," said Poirot. "The matter begins to clear itself up wonderfully! The murderer was a man of great strength—he was feeble—it was a woman—it was a right-handed person—it was a left-handed person. *Ah! c'est rigolo, tout ça!*" He spoke with sudden anger. "And the victim—what does he do in all this? Does he cry out? Does he struggle? Does he defend himself?"

He slipped his hand under the pillow and drew out the automatic pistol which Ratchett had shown him the day before.

"Fully loaded, you see," he said.

They looked round them. Ratchett's day clothing was hanging from the hooks on the wall. On the small table formed by the lid of the wash basin were various objects. False teeth in a glass of water. Another glass, empty. A bottle of mineral water. A large flask. An ashtray containing the butt of a cigar and some charred fragments of paper; also two burnt matches.

The doctor picked up the empty glass and sniffed it.

"Here is the explanation of the victim's inertia," he said quietly.

"Drugged?"

"Yes."

Poirot nodded. He picked up the two matches and scrutinised them carefully.

"You have a clue then?" demanded the little doctor eagerly.

"Those two matches are of different shapes," said Poirot.

"One is flatter than the other. You see?"

"It is the kind you get on the train," said the doctor. "In paper covers."

Poirot was feeling in the pockets of Ratchett's clothing.

Presently he pulled out a box of matches. He compared them carefully with the burnt ones.

"The rounder one is a match struck by Mr. Ratchett," he said. "Let us see if he had also the flatter kind."

But a further search showed no other matches.

Poirot's eyes were darting about the compartment. They were bright and sharp like a bird's. One felt that nothing could escape their scrutiny.

With a little exclamation he bent and picked up something from the floor.

It was a small square of cambric, very dainty. In the corner was an embroidered initial—H.

"A woman's handkerchief," said the doctor. "Our friend the *chef de train* was right. There is a woman concerned in this."

"And most conveniently she leaves her handkerchief behind!" said Poirot. "Exactly as it happens in the books and on the films—and to make things even easier for us, it is marked with an initial."

"What a stroke of luck for us!" exclaimed the doctor.

"Is it not?" said Poirot.

Something in his tone surprised the doctor, but before he could ask for elucidation Poirot had made another dive onto the floor.

This time he held out on the palm of his hand—a pipe cleaner.

"It is perhaps the property of Mr. Ratchett?" suggested the doctor.

"There was no pipe in any of his pockets, and no tobacco or tobacco pouch."

"Then it is a clue."

"Oh! decidedly. And again dropped most conveniently. A masculine clue, this time, you note! One cannot complain of having no clues in this case. There are clues here in abundance. By the way, what have you done with the weapon?"

"There was no sign of any weapon. The

murderer must have taken it away with him."

"I wonder why," mused Poirot.

"Ah!" The doctor had been delicately exploring the pyjama pockets of the dead man.

"I overlooked this," he said. "I unbuttoned the jacket and threw it straight back."

From the breast pocket he brought out a gold watch. The case was dented savagely, and the hands pointed to a quarter past one.

"You see?" cried Constantine eagerly. "This gives us the hour of the crime. It agrees with my calculations. Between midnight and two in the morning is what I said, and probably about one o'clock, though it is difficult to be exact in these matters. *Eh bien*, here is confirmation. A quarter past one. That was the hour of the crime."

"It is possible, yes. It is certainly possible."

The doctor looked at him curiously. "You will pardon me, M. Poirot, but I do not quite understand you."

"I do not understand myself," said Poirot. "I understand nothing at all. And, as you perceive, it worries me."

He sighed and bent over the little table examining the charred fragment of paper. He murmured to himself, "What I need at this moment is an old-fashioned woman's hatbox."

Dr. Constantine was at a loss to know what to make of this singular remark. In any case Poirot gave him no time for questions. Opening the door into the corridor, he called for the conductor.

The man arrived at a run.

"How many women are there in this coach?"

The conductor counted on his fingers.

"One, two, three—six, Monsieur. The old American lady, a Swedish lady, the young English lady, the Countess Andrenyi, and Madame la Princesse Dragomiroff and her maid."

Poirot considered.

"They all have hatboxes, yes?"

"Yes, Monsieur."

"Then bring me—let me see—yes, the Swedish lady's and that of the lady's-maid. Those two are the only hope. You will tell them it is a customs regulation—something—anything that occurs to you."

"That will be all right, Monsieur. Neither lady is in her compartment at the moment."

"Then be quick."

The conductor departed. He returned with the two hatboxes. Poirot opened that of the maid, and tossed it aside. Then he opened the Swedish lady's and uttered an exclamation of satisfaction. Removing the hats carefully, he disclosed round humps of wire netting.

"Ah, here is what we need! About fifteen years ago hatboxes were made like this. You skewered through the hat with a hatpin on to this hump of wire netting."

As he spoke he was skillfully removing two of the attached humps. Then he repacked the hatbox and told the conductor to return both boxes where they belonged.

When the door was shut once more he turned to his companion.

"See you, my dear doctor, me, I am not one to rely upon the expert procedure. It is the psychology I seek, not the fingerprint or the cigarette ash. But in this case I would welcome a little scientific assistance. This compartment is full of clues, but can I be sure that those clues are really what they seem to be?"

"I do not quite understand you, M. Poirot."

"Well, to give you an example—we find a woman's handkerchief. Did a woman drop it? Or did a man, committing the crime, say to himself: 'I will make this look like a woman's crime. I will stab my enemy an unnecessary number of times, making some of the blows feeble and ineffective, and I will drop this handkerchief where no one can miss it'? That is one possibility. Then there is another. Did a woman kill him, and did she deliberately drop a pipe cleaner to make it look like a man's work? Or are we seriously to suppose that two people, a man and a woman, were separately concerned, and that each was so careless as to drop a clue to his or her identity? It is a little too much of a coincidence, that!"

"But where does the hatbox come in?" asked the doctor, still puzzled.

"Ah! I am coming to that. As I say, these clues—the watch stopped at a quarter past one, the handkerchief, the pipe cleaner—they may be genuine, or they may be faked. As to that I cannot yet tell. But there is one clue here which—though again I may be wrong—I believe has not been faked. I mean this flat match, *M. le docteur. I believe that that match was used by the murderer, not by Mr. Ratchett.* It was used to burn an incriminating paper of some kind. Possibly a note. If so, there was something in that note, some mistake, some error, that left a possible clue to the assailant. I am going to try to discover what that something was."

He went out of the compartment and returned a few moments later with a small spirit stove and a pair of curling-tongs.

"I use them for the moustaches," he said, referring to the latter.

The doctor watched him with great interest. Poirot flattened out the two humps of wire, and with great care wriggled the charred scrap of paper on to one of them. He clapped the other on top of it and then, holding both pieces together with the tongs, held the whole thing over the flame of the spirit-lamp.

"It is a very makeshift affair, this," he said over his shoulder. "Let us hope that it will answer our purpose."

The doctor watched the proceedings attentively. The metal began to glow. Suddenly he saw faint indications of letters.

Words formed themselves slowly—words of fire.

It was a very tiny scrap. Only three words and part of another showed.

—*member little Daisy Armstrong*

"Ah!" Poirot gave a sharp exclamation.

"It tells you something?" asked the doctor.

Poirot's eyes were shining. He laid down the tongs carefully.

"Yes," he said. *"I know the dead man's real name. I know why he had to leave America."*

"What was his name?"

"Cassetti."

"Cassetti?" Constantine knitted his brows. "It brings back to me something. Some years ago. I cannot remember. . . . It was a case in America, was it not?"

"Yes," said Poirot. "A case in America."

Further than that Poirot was not disposed to be communicative. He looked round him as he went on:

"We will go into all that presently. Let us first make sure that we have seen all there is to be seen here."

Quickly and deftly he went once more through the pockets of the dead man's clothes but found nothing there of interest. He tried the communicating door which led through to the next compartment, but it was bolted on the other side.

"There is one thing that I do not understand," said Dr. Constantine. "If the murderer did not escape through the window, and if this communicating door was bolted on the other side, and if the door into the corridor was not only locked on the inside but chained, how then did the murderer leave the compartment?"

"That is what the audience says when a person bound hand and foot is shut into a cabinet—and disappears."

"You mean—?"

"I mean," explained Poirot, "that if the murderer intended us to believe that he had escaped by way of the window, he would naturally make it appear that the other two exits were impossible. Like the 'disappearing person' in the cabinet, it is a trick. It is our business to find out how the trick is done."

He locked the communicating door on their side—"In case," he said, "the excellent

Mrs. Hubbard should take it into her head to acquire first-hand details of the crime to write to her daughter."

He looked round once more.

"There is nothing more to do here, I think. Let us rejoin M. Bouc."

Chapter 8

The Armstrong Kidnapping Case

They found M. Bouc finishing an omelet.

"I thought it best to have lunch served immediately in the restaurant car," he said. "Afterwards it will be cleared and M. Poirot can conduct his examination of the passengers there. In the meantime I have ordered them to bring us three some food here."

"An excellent idea," said Poirot.

None of the three men was hungry, and the meal was soon eaten; but not till they were sipping their coffee did M. Bouc mention the subject that was occupying all their minds.

"*Eh bien?*" he asked.

"*Eh bien*, I have discovered the identity of the victim. I know why it was imperative he should leave America."

"Who was he?"

"Do you remember reading of the Armstrong baby? This is the man who murdered little Daisy Armstrong. Cassetti."

"I recall it now. A shocking affair—though I cannot remember the details."

"Colonel Armstrong was an Englishman—a V.C. He was half American, his mother having been a daughter of W. K. Van der Halt, the Wall Street millionaire. He married the daughter of Linda Arden, the most famous tragic American actress of her day. They lived in America and had one child—a girl whom they idolized. When she was three years old she was kidnapped, and an impossibly high sum demanded as the price of her return. I will not weary you with all the intricacies that followed. I will come to the moment when, after the parents had paid over the enormous sum of two hundred thousand dollars, the child's dead body was discovered; it had been dead for at least a fortnight. Public indignation rose to fever point. And there was worse to follow. Mrs. Armstrong was expecting another baby. Following the shock of the discovery, she gave birth prematurely to a dead child, and herself died. Her broken-hearted husband shot himself."

"*Mon Dieu*, what a tragedy. I remember now," said M. Bouc. "There was also another death, if I remember rightly?"

"Yes, an unfortunate French or Swiss nursemaid. The police were convinced that she had some knowledge of the crime. They refused to believe her hysterical denials. Finally, in a fit of despair the poor girl threw herself from a window and was killed. It was proved afterwards that she had been absolutely innocent of any complicity in the crime."

"It is not good to think of," said M. Bouc.

"About six months later, this man Cassetti was arrested as the head of the gang who had kidnapped the child. They had used the same methods in the past. If the police seemed likely to get on their trial, they killed their prisoner, hid the body, and continued to extract as much money as possible before the crime was discovered.

"Now, I will make clear to you this, my friend. Cassetti was the man! But by means of the enormous wealth he had piled up, and owing to the secret hold he had over various persons, he was acquitted on some technical inaccuracy. Notwithstanding that, he would have been lynched by the populace had he not been clever enough to give them the slip. It is now clear to me what happened. He changed his name and left America. Since then he has been a gentleman of leisure, travelling abroad and living on his *rentes*."

"*Ah! quel animal!*" M. Bouc's tone was redolent of heartfelt disgust. "I cannot regret that he is dead—not at all!"

"I agree with you."

"*Tout de même*, it is not necessary that he should be killed on the Orient Express. There are other places."

Poirot smiled a little. He realised that M. Bouc was biased in the matter.

"The question we have now to ask ourselves is this," he said. "Is this murder the work of some rival gang whom Cassetti had double-crossed in the past, or is it an act of private vengeance?"

He explained his discovery of the few words on the charred fragment of paper.

"If I am right in my assumption, then, the letter was burnt by the murderer. Why? Because it mentioned the name 'Armstrong,' which is the clue to the mystery."

"Are there any members of the Armstrong family living?"

"That, unfortunately, I do not know. I think I remember reading of a younger sister of Mrs. Armstrong's."

Poirot went on to relate the joint conclusions of himself and Dr. Constantine. M. Bouc brightened at the mention of the broken watch.

"That seems to give us the time of the crime very exactly."

"Yes," said Poirot. "It is very convenient."

There was an indescribable something in his tone that made both the other two look at him curiously.

"You say that you yourself heard Ratchett speak to the conductor at twenty minutes to one?" asked M. Bouc.

Poirot related just what had occurred.

"Well," said M. Bouc, "that proves at least that Cassetti—or Ratchett, as I shall continue to call him—was certainly alive at twenty minutes to one."

"Twenty-three minutes to one, to be precise."

"Then at twelve thirty-seven, to put it formally, Mr. Ratchett was alive. That is one fact, at least."

Poirot did not reply. He sat looking thoughtfully in front of him.

There was a tap on the door and the restaurant attendant entered.

"The restaurant car is free now, Monsieur," he said.

"We will go there," said M. Bouc, rising.

"I may accompany you?" asked Constantine.

"Certainly, my dear doctor. Unless M. Poirot has any objection?"

"Not at all. Not at all," said Poirot.

After a little politeness in the matter of precedence—*"Après vous, Monsieur"*— *"Mais non, après vous"*—they left the compartment.

Part 2

The Evidence

Chapter 1
The Evidence of the Wagon Lit Conductor

In the restaurant car all was in readiness.

Poirot and M. Bouc sat together on one side of a table. The doctor sat across the aisle.

On the table in front of Poirot was a plan of the Istanbul-Calais coach with the names of the passengers marked in red ink. The passports and tickets were in a pile at one side. There was writing paper, ink, pen, and pencils.

"Excellent," said Poirot. "We can open our Court of Inquiry without more ado. First, I think, we should take the evidence of the Wagon Lit conductor. You probably know something about the man. What character has he? Is he a man on whose word you would place reliance?"

"I should say so, most assuredly. Pierre Michel has been employed by the company for over fifteen years. He is a Frenchman— lives near Calais. Thoroughly respectable and honest. Not, perhaps, remarkable for brains."

Poirot nodded comprehendingly. "Good," he said. "Let us see him."

Pierre Michel had recovered some of his assurance, but he was still extremely nervous.

"I hope Monsieur will not think that there has been any negligence on my part," he said anxiously, his eyes going from Poirot to M. Bouc. "It is a terrible thing that has happened. I hope Monsieur does not think that it reflects on me in any way?"

Having soothed the man's fears, Poirot began his questions. He first elicited Michel's name and address, his length of service, and the length of time he had been on this particular route. These particulars he already knew, but the routine questions served to put the man at his ease.

"And now," went on Poirot, "let us come to the events of last night. M. Ratchett retired to bed—when?"

"Almost immediately after dinner, Monsieur. Actually before we left Belgrade. So he did on the previous night. He had directed me to make up the bed while he was at dinner, and I did so."

"Did anybody go into his compartment afterwards?"

"His valet, Monsieur, and the young American gentleman, his secretary."

"Anyone else?"

"No, Monsieur, not that I know of."

"Good. And that is the last you saw or heard of him?"

"No, Monsieur. You forget he rang his bell about twenty to one—soon after we had stopped."

"What happened exactly?"

"I knocked at the door, but he called out and said he had made a mistake."

"In English or in French?"

"In French."

"What were his words exactly?"

"Ce n'est rien. Je me suis trompé."

"Quite right," said Poirot. "That is what I heard. And then you went away?"

"Yes, Monsieur."

"Did you go back to your seat?"

"No, Monsieur, I went first to answer another bell that had just rung."

"Now, Michel, I am going to ask you an important question. Where were you at a quarter past one?"

"I, Monsieur? I was at my little seat at the end—facing up the corridor."

"You are sure?"

"*Mais oui*—at least—"

"Yes?"

"I went into the next coach, the Athens coach, to speak to my colleague there. We spoke about the snow. That was at some time soon after one o'clock. I cannot say exactly."

"And you returned—when?"

"One of my bells rang, Monsieur—I remember—I told you. It was the American lady. She had rung several times."

"I recollect," said Poirot. "And after that?"

"After that, Monsieur? I answered your bell and brought you some mineral water. Then, about half an hour later, I made up the bed in one of the other compartments—that of the young American gentleman, Mr. Ratchett's secretary."

"Was Mr. MacQueen alone in his compartment when you went to make up his bed?"

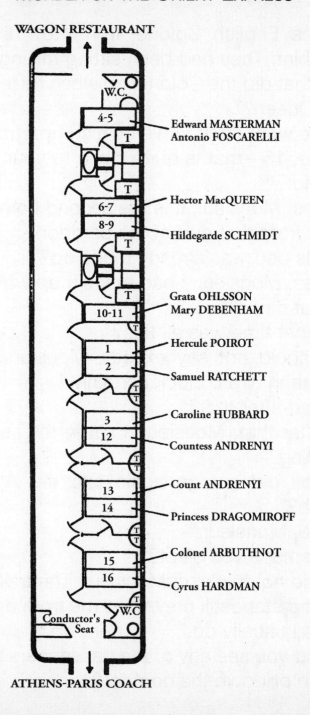

"The English Colonel from No. 15 was with him. They had been sitting talking."

"What did the Colonel do when he left Mr. MacQueen?"

"He went back to his own compartment."

"No. 15—that is quite close to your seat, is it not?"

"Yes, Monsieur, it is the second compartment from that end of the corridor."

"His bed was already made up?"

"Yes, Monsieur. I had made it up while he was at dinner."

"What time was all this?"

"I could not say exactly, Monsieur. Not later than two o'clock certainly."

"And after that?"

"After that, Monsieur, I sat in my seat till morning."

"You did not go again into the Athens coach?"

"No, Monsieur."

"Perhaps you slept?"

"I do not think so, Monsieur. The train being at a standstill prevented me from dozing off as I usually do."

"Did you see any of the passengers moving up or down the corridor?"

The man reflected. "One of the ladies went to the toilet at the far end, I think."

"Which lady?"

"I do not know, Monsieur. It was far down the corridor and she had her back to me. She had on a kimono of scarlet with dragons on it."

Poirot nodded. "And after that?"

"Nothing, Monsieur, until the morning."

"You are sure?"

"Ah, pardon—you yourself, Monsieur, opened your door and looked out for a second."

"Good, my friend," said Poirot. "I wondered whether you would remember that. By the way, I was awakened by what sounded like something heavy falling against my door. Have you any idea what that could have been?"

The man stared at him. "There was nothing, Monsieur. Nothing, I am positive of it."

"Then I must have had the *cauchemar*," said Poirot philosophically.

"Unless," put in M. Bouc, "it was something in the compartment next door that you heard."

Poirot took no notice of the suggestion.

Perhaps he did not wish to before the Wagon Lit conductor.

"Let us pass to another point," he said. "Supposing that last night an assassin joined the train. Is it quite certain that he could not have left it after committing the crime?"

Pierre Michel shook his head.

"Nor that he can be concealed on it somewhere?"

"It has been well searched," said M. Bouc. "Abandon that idea, my friend."

"Besides," said Michel, "no one could get on to the sleeping-car without my seeing them."

"When was the last stop?"

"Vincovci."

"What time was that?"

"We should have left there at 11.58, but owing to the weather we were twenty minutes late."

"Someone might have come along from the ordinary part of the train?"

"No, Monsieur. After the service of dinner, the door between the ordinary carriages and the sleeping-cars is locked."

"Did you yourself descend from the train at Vincovci?"

"Yes, Monsieur. I got down onto the platform as usual and stood by the step up into the train. The other conductors did the same."

"What about the forward door—the one near the restaurant car?"

"It is always fastened on the inside."

"It is not so fastened now."

The man looked surprised; then his face cleared. "Doubtless one of the passengers opened it to look out on the snow."

"Probably," said Poirot.

He tapped thoughtfully on the table for a minute or two.

"Monsieur does not blame me?" said the man timidly.

Poirot smiled on him kindly.

"You have had the evil chance, my friend," he said. "Ah! one other point while I remember it. You said that another bell rang just as you were knocking at M. Ratchett's door. In fact I heard it myself. Whose was it?"

"It was the bell of Madame la Princesse Dragomiroff. She desired me to summon her maid."

"And you did so?"

"Yes, Monsieur."

Poirot studied the plan in front of him thoughtfully. Then he inclined his head.

"That is all," he said, "for the moment."

"Thank you, Monsieur."

The man rose. He looked at M. Bouc.

"Do not distress yourself," said the latter kindly. "I cannot see that there has been any negligence on your part."

Gratified, Pierre Michel left the compartment.

Chapter 2

The Evidence of the Secretary

For a minute or two Poirot remained lost in thought.

"I think," he said at last, "that it would be well to have a further word with Mr. Mac-Queen, in view of what we now know."

The young American appeared promptly.

"Well," he said, "how are things going?"

"Not too badly. Since our last conversation, I have learnt something—the identity of Mr. Ratchett."

Hector MacQueen leaned forward interestedly. "Yes?" he said.

" 'Ratchett,' as you suspected, was merely an alias. The man 'Ratchett' was Cassetti, who ran the celebrated kidnapping stunts—including the famous affair of little Daisy Armstrong."

An expression of utter astonishment appeared on MacQueen's face. Then it darkened. "The damned skunk!" he exclaimed.

"You had no idea of this, Mr. MacQueen?"

"No, sir," said the young American decidedly. "If I had, I'd have cut off my right hand before it had a chance to do secretarial work for him!"

"You feel strongly about the matter, Mr. MacQueen?"

"I have a particular reason for doing so. My father was the district attorney who handled the case, Mr. Poirot. I saw Mrs. Armstrong more than once—she was a lovely woman. So gentle and heartbroken." His face darkened. "If ever a man deserved what he got, Ratchett—or Cassetti—is the man. I'm rejoiced at his end. Such a man wasn't fit to live!"

"You almost feel as though you would have been willing to do the good deed yourself?"

"I do. I—" He paused, then added rather guiltily, "Seems I'm kind of incriminating myself."

"I should be more inclined to suspect you, Mr. MacQueen, if you displayed an inordinate sorrow at your employer's decease."

"I don't think I could do that even to save

myself from the chair," said MacQueen
grimly. Then he added: "If I'm not being un-
duly curious, just how did you figure this
out? Cassetti's identity, I mean."

"By a fragment of a letter found in his
compartment."

"But surely—I mean—that was rather
careless of the old man?"

"That depends," said Poirot, "on the point
of view."

The young man seemed to find this remark rather baffling. He stared at Poirot as
though trying to make him out.

"The task before me," said Poirot, "is to
make sure of the movements of everyone
on the train. No offence need be taken, you
understand. It is only a matter of routine."

"Sure. Get right on with it and let me clear
my character if I can."

"I need hardly ask you the number of your
compartment," said Poirot, smiling, "since I
shared it with you for a night. It is the second-
class compartment Nos. 6 and 7, and after
my departure you had it to yourself."

"That's right."

"Now, Mr. MacQueen, I want you to describe your movements last night from the
time of leaving the dining-car."

"That's quite easy. I went back to my compartment, read a bit, got out on the platform at Belgrade, decided it was too cold, and got in again. I talked for a while to a young English lady who is in the compartment next to mine. Then I fell into conversation with that Englishman, Colonel Arbuthnot—as a matter of fact I think you passed us as we were talking. Then I went in to Mr. Ratchett and, as I told you, took down some memoranda of letters he wanted written. I said good night to him and left him. Colonel Arbuthnot was still standing in the corridor. His compartment was already made up for the night, so I suggested that he should come along to mine. I ordered a couple of drinks and we got right down to it. Discussed world politics and the Government of India and our own troubles with Prohibition and the Wall Street crisis. I don't as a rule cotton to Britishers—they're a stiff-necked lot—but I liked this one."

"Do you know what time it was when he left you?"

"Pretty late. Nearly two o'clock, I should say."

"You noticed that the train had stopped?"

"Oh, yes. We wondered a bit. Looked out

and saw the snow lying very thick, but we didn't think it was serious."

"What happened when Colonel Arbuthnot finally said good night?"

"He went along to his compartment and I called to the conductor to make up my bed."

"Where were you whilst he was making it?"

"Standing just outside the door in the corridor smoking a cigarette."

"And then?"

"And then I went to bed and slept till morning."

"During the evening did you leave the train at all?"

"Arbuthnot and I thought we'd get out at—what was the name of the place?—Vincovci—to stretch our legs a bit. But it was bitterly cold—a blizzard on. We soon hopped back again."

"By which door did you leave the train?"

"By the one nearest to our compartment."

"The one next to the dining-car?"

"Yes."

"Do you remember if it was bolted?"

MacQueen considered.

"Why, yes, I seem to remember it was. At

least there was a kind of bar that fitted across the handle. Is that what you mean?"

"Yes. On getting back into the train did you replace that bar?"

"Why, no—I don't think I did. I got in last. No, I don't seem to remember doing so." He added suddenly, "Is that an important point?"

"It may be. Now, I presume, Monsieur, that while you and Colonel Arbuthnot were sitting talking the door of your compartment into the corridor was open?"

Hector MacQueen nodded.

"I want you, if you can, to tell me if anyone passed along that corridor *after* the train left Vincovci up to the time you parted company for the night."

MacQueen drew his brows together.

"I think the conductor passed along once," he said, "coming from the direction of the dining-car. And a woman passed the other way, going towards it."

"Which woman?"

"I couldn't say. I didn't really notice. You see I was arguing a point with Arbuthnot. I just seem to remember a glimpse of some scarlet silk affair passing the door. I didn't look, and anyway I wouldn't have seen the person's face. As you know, my carriage faces the dining-car end of the train, so a woman going along the corridor in that direction would have her back to me as soon as she'd passed."

Poirot nodded. "She was going to the toilet, I presume?"

"I suppose so."

"And you saw her return?"

"Well, no, now that you mention it, I didn't notice her returning, but I suppose she must have done so."

"One more question. Do you smoke a pipe, Mr. MacQueen?"

"No, sir, I do not."

Poirot paused a moment. "I think that is all at present. I should now like to see the valet of Mr. Ratchett. By the way, did both you and he always travel second-class?"

"He did. But I usually went first—if possible in the compartment adjoining Mr. Ratchett's. Then he had most of his baggage put in my compartment and yet could get at both it and me easily whenever he chose. But on this occasion all the first-class berths were booked except the one that he took."

"I comprehend. Thank you, Mr. Mac-Queen."

Chapter 3

The Evidence of the Valet

The American was succeeded by the pale Englishman with the inexpressive face whom Poirot had already noticed on the day before. He stood waiting very correctly. Poirot motioned to him to sit down.

"You are, I understand, the valet of M. Ratchett."

"Yes, sir."

"Your name?"

"Edward Henry Masterman."

"Your age?"

"Thirty-nine."

"And your home address?"

"21 Friar Street, Clerkenwell."

"You have heard that your master has been murdered?"

"Yes, sir. A very shocking occurrence."

"Will you now tell me, please, at what hour you last saw M. Ratchett?"

The valet considered.

"It must have been about nine o'clock, sir, last night. That or a little after."

"Tell me in your own words exactly what happened."

"I went in to Mr. Ratchett as usual, sir, and attended to his wants."

"What were your duties exactly?"

"To fold or hang up his clothes, sir, put his dental plate in water and see that he had everything he wanted for the night."

"Was his manner much the same as usual?"

The valet considered a moment.

"Well, sir, I think he was upset."

"In what way—upset?"

"Over a letter he'd been reading. He asked me if it was I who had put it in his compartment. Of course I told him I hadn't done any such thing, but he swore at me and found fault with everything I did."

"Was that unusual?"

"Oh, no, sir. He lost his temper easily—as I say, it just depended what had happened to upset him."

"Did your master ever take a sleeping draught?"

Dr. Constantine leaned forward a little.

"Always when travelling by train, sir. He said he couldn't sleep otherwise."

"Do you know what drug he was in the habit of taking?"

"I couldn't say, I'm sure, sir. There was no name on the bottle—just *'The Sleeping Draught to be taken at bedtime.'* "

"Did he take it last night?"

"Yes, sir. I poured it into a glass and put it on top of the toilet table ready for him."

"You didn't actually see him drink it?"

"No, sir."

"What happened next?"

"I asked if there was anything further, and also asked what time he would like to be called in the morning. He said he didn't want to be disturbed till he rang."

"Was that usual?"

"Quite usual, sir. When he was ready to get up he used to ring the bell for the conductor and then send him for me."

"Was he usually an early or a late riser?"

"It depended, sir, on his mood. Sometimes he'd get up for breakfast, sometimes he wouldn't get up till just on lunch time."

"So that you weren't alarmed when the morning wore on and no summons came?"

"No, sir."

"Did you know that your master had enemies?"

"Yes, sir." The man spoke quite unemotionally.

"How did you know?"

"I had heard him discussing some letters, sir, with Mr. MacQueen."

"Had you an affection for your employer, Masterman?"

Masterman's face became, if possible, even more inexpressive than it was normally.

"I should hardly like to say that, sir. He was a generous employer."

"But you didn't like him?"

"Shall we put it that I don't care very much for Americans, sir?"

"Have you ever been in America?"

"No, sir."

"Do you remember reading in the paper of the Armstrong kidnapping case?"

A little colour came into the man's cheeks.

"Yes, indeed, sir. A little baby girl, wasn't it? A very shocking affair."

"Did you know that your employer, Mr. Ratchett, was the principal instigator in that affair?"

"No, indeed, sir." The valet's tone held positive warmth and feeling for the first time. "I can hardly believe it, sir."

"Nevertheless, it is true. Now, to pass to your own movements last night. A matter of routine, you understand. What did you do after leaving your master?"

"I told Mr. MacQueen, sir, that the master wanted him. Then I went to my own compartment and read."

"Your compartment was—"

"The end second-class one, sir. Next to the dining-car." Poirot was looking at his plan.

"I see—and you had which berth?"

"The lower one, sir."

"That is No. 4?"

"Yes, sir."

"Is there anyone in with you?"

"Yes, sir. A big Italian fellow."

"Does he speak English?"

"Well, a kind of English, sir." The valet's tone was deprecating. "He's been in America—Chicago, I understand."

"Do you and he talk together much?"

"No, sir. I prefer to read."

Poirot smiled. He could visualize the scene—the large, voluble Italian, and the snub direct administered by the gentleman's gentleman.

"And what, may I ask, are you reading?" he inquired.

"At present, sir, I am reading *Love's Captive*, by Mrs. Arabella Richardson."

"A good story?"

"I find it highly enjoyable, sir."

"Well, let us continue. You returned to your compartment and read *Love's Captive* till—when?"

"At about ten thirty, sir, this Italian wanted to go to bed. So the conductor came and made the beds up."

"And then you went to bed and to sleep?"

"I went to bed, sir, but I didn't sleep."

"Why didn't you sleep?"

"I had the toothache, sir."

"Oh, là-là—that is painful."

"Most painful, sir."

"Did you do anything for it?"

"I applied a little oil of cloves, sir, which relieved the pain a little, but I was still not able to get to sleep. I turned the light on above my head and continued to read—to take my mind off, as it were."

"And did you not go to sleep at all?"

"Yes, sir, I dropped off about four in the morning."

"And your companion?"

"The Italian fellow? Oh, he just snored."

"He did not leave the compartment at all during the night?"

"No, sir."

"Did you?"

"No, sir."

"Did you hear anything during the night?"

"I don't think so, sir. Nothing unusual, I mean. The train being at a standstill made it all very quiet."

Poirot was silent a moment or two. Then he spoke.

"Well, I think there is very little more to be said. You cannot throw any light upon the tragedy?"

"I'm afraid not. I'm sorry, sir."

"As far as you know, was there any quarrel or bad blood between your master and Mr. MacQueen?"

"Oh! no, sir. Mr. MacQueen was a very pleasant gentleman."

"Where were you in service before you came to Mr. Ratchett?"

"With Sir Henry Tomlinson, sir, in Grosvenor Square."

"Why did you leave him?"

"He was going to East Africa, sir, and did not require my services any longer. But I am sure he will speak for me, sir. I was with him some years."

"And you have been with Mr. Ratchett—how long?"

"Just over nine months, sir."

"Thank you, Masterman. By the way, are you a pipesmoker?"

"No, sir. I only smoke cigarettes—gaspers, sir."

"Thank you, that will do."

Poirot gave him a nod of dismissal.

The valet hesitated a moment.

"You'll excuse me, sir, but the elderly American lady is in what I might describe as a state, sir. She's saying she knows all about the murderer. She's in a very excitable condition, sir."

"In that case," said Poirot, smiling, "we had better see her next."

"Shall I tell her, sir? She's been demanding to see someone in authority for a long

time. The conductor's been trying to pacify
her."

"Send her to us, my friend," said Poirot.
"We will listen to her story now."

Chapter 4
The Evidence of the American Lady

Mrs. Hubbard arrived in the dining-car in such a state of breathless excitement that she was hardly able to articulate her words.

"Now just tell me this—who's in authority here? I've got some very important information, *very* important indeed, and I'm going to tell it to someone in authority just as soon as I can. If you gentlemen—"

Her wavering glance fluctuated between the three men. Poirot leaned forward.

"Tell it to me, Madame," he said. "But first, pray be seated."

Mrs. Hubbard plumped heavily down on to the seat opposite to him.

"What I've got to tell you is just this. There was a murder on the train last night, and the murderer was *right there in my compartment!*"

She paused to give dramatic emphasis to her words.

"You are sure of this, Madame?"

"Of course I'm sure! The idea! I know what I'm talking about. I'll tell you everything there is to tell. I'd gotten into bed and gone to sleep, and suddenly I woke up—everything was dark—and I knew there was a man in my compartment. I was just so scared I couldn't scream, if you know what I mean. I just lay there and thought, 'Mercy, I'm going to be killed!' I just can't describe to you how I felt. These nasty trains, I thought, and all the outrages I'd read of. And I thought, 'Well, anyway, he won't get my jewellery'—because, you see, I'd put that in a stocking and hidden it under my pillow—which isn't any too comfortable, by the way; kinda bumpy, if you know what I mean. But that's neither here nor there. Where was I?"

"You realised, Madame, that there was a man in your compartment."

"Yes, well, I just lay there with my eyes closed, and wondered what I'd do. And I thought, well, I'm just thankful that my daughter doesn't know the plight I'm in.

And then, somehow, I got my wits about me and I felt about with my hand and I pressed the bell for the conductor. I pressed it and I pressed it, but nothing happened—and I can tell you, I thought my heart was going to stop beating. 'Mercy,' I said to myself, 'maybe they've murdered every single soul on the train.' It was at a standstill anyhow and there was a nasty quiet feel in the air. But I just went on pressing that bell and oh! the relief when I heard footsteps coming running down the corridor and a knock on the door! 'Come in,' I screamed, and I switched on the lights at the same time. And would you believe it, there wasn't a *soul* there!"

This seemed to Mrs. Hubbard to be a dramatic climax rather than an anticlimax.

"And what happened next, Madame?"

"Why, I told the man what had happened and he didn't seem to believe me. Seemed to imagine I'd dreamed the whole thing. I made him look under the seat, though he said there wasn't room for a man to squeeze himself in there. It was plain enough that the man had got away—but there *had* been a man there, and it just made me mad the way the conductor tried to soothe me down! I'm not one to imagine things, Mr.—I don't think I know your name?"

"Poirot, Madame; and this is M. Bouc, a director of the company, and Dr. Constantine."

Mrs. Hubbard murmured, "Pleased to meet you, I'm sure," to all three of them in an abstracted manner and then plunged once more into her recital.

"Now I'm just not going to pretend I was as bright as I might have been. I got it into my head that it was the man from next door—the poor fellow who's been killed. I told the conductor to look at the door between the compartments, and sure enough it wasn't bolted. Well, I soon saw to that. I told him to bolt it then and there, and after he'd gone out I got up and put a suitcase against it to make sure."

"What time was this, Mrs. Hubbard?"

"Well, I'm sure I can't tell you. I never looked to see. I was so upset."

"And what is your theory now?"

"Why, I should say it was just as plain as plain could be. The man in my compartment was the murderer. Who else could he be?"

"And you think he went back into the adjoining compartment?"

"How do I know where he went? I had my eyes tight shut."

"He might have slipped out through the door into the corridor."

"Well, I couldn't say. You see, I had my eyes tight shut."

Mrs. Hubbard sighed convulsively.

"Mercy, I was scared! If my daughter only knew—"

"You do not think, Madame, that what you heard was the noise of someone moving about next door—in the murdered man's compartment?"

"No, I do not, Mr.—what is it?—Poirot. The man was *right there in the same compartment with me*. And what's more I've got proof of it."

Triumphantly, she hauled a large handbag into view and proceeded to burrow in its interior.

She took out in turn two large clean handkerchiefs, a pair of horn-rimmed glasses, a bottle of aspirin, a packet of Glauber's Salts, a celluloid tube of bright green peppermints, a bunch of keys, a pair of scissors, a book of American Express cheques, a snapshot of an extraordinarily plain-looking child, some letters, five strings of pseudo-Oriental beads, and a small metal object—a button.

"You see this button? Well, it's not one of my buttons. It's not off anything I've got. I found it this morning when I got up."

As she placed it on the table, M. Bouc leaned forward and gave an exclamation. "But this is a button from the tunic of a Wagon Lit attendant!"

"There may be a natural explanation for that," said Poirot.

He turned gently to the lady.

"This button, Madame, may have dropped from the conductor's uniform, either when he searched your cabin or when he was making the bed up last night."

"I just don't know what's the matter with all you people. Seems as though you don't want to do anything but make objections. Now listen here. I was reading a magazine last night before I went to sleep. Before I turned the light out, I placed that magazine on a little case that was standing on the floor near the window. Have you got that?"

They assured her that they had.

"Very well then. The conductor looked

under the seat from near the door, and then he came in and bolted the door between me and the next compartment, but he never went near the window. Well, this morning that button was lying right on top of the magazine. What do you call that, I should like to know?"

"That, Madame, I call evidence," said Poirot.

The answer seemed to appease the lady.

"It makes me madder than a hornet to be disbelieved," she explained.

"You have given us most interesting and valuable evidence," said Poirot soothingly. "Now may I ask you a few questions?"

"Why, certainly."

"How was it, since you were nervous of this man Ratchett, that you hadn't already bolted the door between the compartments?"

"I had," returned Mrs. Hubbard promptly.

"Oh, you had?"

"Well, as a matter of fact I asked that Swedish creature—a pleasant soul—if it was bolted, and she said it was."

"How was it you couldn't see for yourself?"

"Because I was in bed and my sponge-bag was hanging on the door-handle."

"What time was it when you asked her to do this for you?"

"Now let me think. It must have been round about half-past ten or a quarter to eleven. She'd come along to see if I had an aspirin. I told her where to find it and she got it out of my grip."

"You yourself were in bed?"

"Yes."

Suddenly she laughed. "Poor soul—she was so upset! You see, she'd opened the door of the next compartment by mistake."

"Mr. Ratchett's?"

"Yes. You know how difficult it is as you come along the train and all the doors are shut. She opened his by mistake. She was very distressed about it. He'd laughed, it seemed, and I guess he said something not quite nice. Poor thing, she certainly was upset. 'Oh! I make mistake,' she said. 'I ashamed make mistake. Not nice man,' she said. 'He say, "You too old." ' "

Dr. Constantine sniggered, and Mrs. Hubbard immediately froze him with a glance.

"He wasn't a nice kind of man," she said,

"to say a thing like that to a lady. It's not right to laugh at such things."

Dr. Constantine hastily apologised.

"Did you hear any noise from Mr. Ratchett's compartment after that?" asked Poirot.

"Well—not exactly."

"What do you mean by that, Madame?"

"Well—" She paused. "He snored."

"Ah!—he snored, did he?"

"Terribly. The night before, it kept me awake."

"You didn't hear him snore after you had had the scare about a man being in your compartment?"

"Why, Mr. Poirot, how could I? He was dead."

"Ah, yes, truly," said Poirot. He appeared confused.

"Do you remember the affair of the Armstrong kidnapping, Mrs. Hubbard?" he asked.

"Yes, indeed I do. And how the wretch that did it escaped scot-free! My, I'd have liked to get my hands on him."

"He has not escaped. He is dead. He died last night."

"You don't mean—?" Mrs. Hubbard half rose from her chair in excitement.

"But yes, I do. Ratchett was the man."

"*Well*! Well, to think of that! I must write and tell my daughter. Now, didn't I tell you last night that that man had an evil face? I was right, you see. My daughter always says: 'When Mamma's got a hunch you can bet your bottom dollar it's O.K.'"

"Were you acquainted with any of the Armstrong family, Mrs. Hubbard?"

"No. They moved in a very exclusive circle. But I've always heard that Mrs. Armstrong was a perfectly lovely woman and that her husband worshipped her."

"Well, Mrs. Hubbard, you have helped us very much—very much indeed. Perhaps you will give me your full name?"

"Why, certainly. Caroline Martha Hubbard."

"Will you write your address down here?"

Mrs. Hubbard did so, without ceasing to speak. "I just can't get over it. Cassetti—on this train. I had a hunch about that man, didn't I, Mr. Poirot?"

"Yes, indeed, Madame. By the way, have you a scarlet silk dressing gown?"

"Mercy, what a funny question! Why, no. I've got two dressing gowns with me—a pink flannel one that's kind of cosy for on board ship, and one my daughter gave me as a present—a kind of local affair in purple silk. But what in creation do you want to know about my dressing gowns for?"

"Well, you see, Madame, someone in a scarlet kimono entered either your or Mr. Ratchett's compartment last night. It is, as you said just now, very difficult when all the doors are shut to know which compartment is which."

"Well, no one in a scarlet dressing gown came into my compartment."

"Then she must have gone into Mr. Ratchett's."

Mrs. Hubbard pursed her lips together and said grimly: "That wouldn't surprise me any."

Poirot leaned forward. "So you heard a woman's voice next door?"

"I don't know how you guessed that, Mr. Poirot. I don't really. But—well—as a matter of fact, I *did*."

"But when I asked you just now if you heard anything next door, you only said you heard Mr. Ratchett snoring."

"Well, that was true enough. He *did* snore part of the time. As for the other—" Mrs.

Hubbard got rather embarrassed. "It isn't a very nice thing to speak about."

"What time was it when you heard a woman's voice?"

"I can't tell you. I just woke up for a minute and heard a woman talking, and it was plain enough where she was. So I just thought, 'Well, *that's* the kind of man he is! I'm not surprised'—and then I went to sleep again. And I'm sure I should never have mentioned anything of the kind to three strange gentlemen if you hadn't dragged it out of me."

"Was it before the scare about the man in your compartment, or after?"

"Why, that's like what you said just now! He wouldn't have had a woman talking to him if he were dead, would he?"

"*Pardon.* You must think me very stupid, Madame."

"I guess even you get kinda muddled now and then. I just can't get over its being that monster Cassetti. What my daughter will say—"

Poirot managed adroitly to help the good lady to replace the contents of her handbag, and he then shepherded her towards the door.

At the last moment, he said:

"You have dropped your handkerchief, Madame."

Mrs. Hubbard looked at the little scrap of cambric he held out to her.

"That's not mine, Mr. Poirot. I've got mine right here."

"*Pardon*. I thought as it had the initial H on it—"

"Well, now, that's funny, but it's certainly not mine. Mine are marked C.M.H., and they're sensible things—not expensive Paris fal-lals. What good is a handkerchief like that to anybody's nose?"

None of the three men seemed to have an answer to this question and Mrs. Hubbard sailed out triumphantly.

Chapter 5

The Evidence of the Swedish Lady

M. Bouc was handling the button that Mrs. Hubbard had left behind her.

"This button. I cannot understand it. Does it mean that after all, Pierre Michel is involved in some way?" he asked. He paused, then continued, as Poirot did not reply. "What have you to say, my friend?"

"That button, it suggests possibilities," said Poirot thoughtfully. "Let us interview next the Swedish lady before we discuss the evidence that we have heard."

He sorted through the pile of passports in front of him.

"Ah! here we are. Greta Ohlsson, age forty-nine."

M. Bouc gave directions to the restaurant attendant, and presently the lady with the yellowish grey bun of hair and the long, mild, sheep-like face was ushered in. She peered short-sightedly at Poirot through her glasses, but was quite calm.

It transpired that she understood and spoke French, so the conversation took place in that language. Poirot first asked her the questions to which he already knew the answers—her name, age, and address. He then asked her her occupation.

She was, she told him, matron in a missionary school near Stamboul. She was a trained nurse.

"You know, of course, of what took place last night, Mademoiselle?"

"Naturally. It is very dreadful. And the American lady tells me that the murderer was actually in her compartment."

"I hear, Mademoiselle, that you were the last person to see the murdered man alive?"

"I do not know. It may be so. I opened the door of his compartment by mistake. I was much ashamed. It was a most awkward mistake."

"You actually saw him?"

"Yes. He was reading a book. I apologised quickly and withdrew."

"Did he say anything to you?"

A slight flush showed on the worthy lady's cheek.

"He laughed and said a few words. I—I did not quite catch them."

"And what did you do after that, Mademoiselle?" asked Poirot, passing from the subject tactfully.

"I went in to the American lady, Mrs. Hubbard. I asked her for some aspirin and she gave it to me."

"Did she ask you whether the communicating door between her compartment and that of Mr. Ratchett was bolted?"

"Yes."

"And was it?"

"Yes."

"And after that?"

"After that I went back to my own compartment, took the aspirin, and lay down."

"What time was all this?"

"When I got into bed it was five minutes to eleven. I know because I looked at my watch before I wound it up."

"Did you go to sleep quickly?"

"Not very quickly. My head got better, but I lay awake some time."

"Had the train come to a stop before you went to sleep?"

"I do not think so. We stopped, I think, at a station just as I was getting drowsy."

"That would be Vincovci. Now your compartment, Mademoiselle, is this one?" He indicated it on the plan.

"That is so, yes."

"You had the upper or the lower berth?"

"The lower berth, No. 10."

"And you had a companion?"

"Yes, a young English lady. Very nice, very amiable. She had travelled from Baghdad."

"After the train left Vincovci, did she leave the compartment?"

"No, I am sure she did not."

"Why are you sure if you were asleep?"

"I sleep very lightly. I am used to waking at a sound. I am sure that if she had come down from the berth above I should have awakened."

"Did you yourself leave the compartment?"

"Not until this morning."

"Have you a scarlet silk kimono, Mademoiselle?"

"No, indeed. I have a good comfortable dressing gown of Jaeger material."

"And the lady with you, Miss Debenham? What colour is her dressing gown?"

"A pale mauve aba such as you buy in the East."

Poirot nodded. Then he asked in a friendly tone: "Why are you taking this journey? A holiday?"

"Yes, I am going home for a holiday. But first I am going to Lausanne to stay with a sister for a week or so."

"Perhaps you will be so amiable as to write me down the name and address of your sister?"

"With pleasure."

She took the paper and pencil he gave her and wrote down the name and address as requested.

"Have you ever been in America, Mademoiselle?"

"No. I very nearly went once. I was to go with an invalid lady, but the plan was cancelled at the last moment. I much regretted this. They are very good, the Americans. They give much money to found schools and hospitals. And they are very practical."

"Do you remember hearing of the Armstrong kidnapping case?"

"No, what was that?"

Poirot explained.

Greta Ohlsson was indignant. Her yellow bun of hair quivered with her emotion.

"That there are in the world such evil men! It tries one's faith. The poor mother—my heart aches for her."

The amiable Swede departed, her kindly face flushed, her eyes suffused with tears.

Poirot was writing busily on a sheet of paper.

"What is it you write there, my friend?" asked M. Bouc.

"*Mon cher*, it is my habit to be neat and orderly. I make here a little chronological table of events."

He finished writing and passed the paper to M. Bouc.

9.15   Train leaves Belgrade.

about 9.40   Valet leaves Ratchett with sleeping draught beside him.

about 10.00   MacQueen leaves Ratchett.

about 10.40   Greta Ohlsson sees Ratchett (last seen alive). N.B. He was awake reading a book.

0.10   Train leaves Vincovci (late).

0.30   Train runs into a snowdrift.

0.37   Ratchett's bell rings. Conductor

answers it. Ratchett says: *"Ce n'est rien. Je me suis trompé."*

about 1.17 Mrs. Hubbard thinks man is in her carriage. Rings for conductor.

M. Bouc nodded approval.

"That is very clear," he said.

"There is nothing there that strikes you as at all odd?"

"No, it seems all quite clear and aboveboard. It seems quite plain that the crime was committed at 1.15. The evidence of the watch shows us that, and Mrs. Hubbard's story fits in. For my mind, I will make a guess at the identity of the murderer. I say, my friend, that it is the big Italian. He comes from America—from Chicago—and remember an Italian's weapon is the knife, and he stabs not once but several times."

"That is true."

"Without a doubt, that is the solution of the mystery. Doubtless he and this Ratchett were in this kidnapping business together. Cassetti is an Italian name. In some way Ratchett did on him what they call the double-cross. The Italian tracks him down, sends him warning letters first, and finally revenges himself upon him in a brutal way. It was all quite simple."

Poirot shook his head doubtfully.

"It is hardly so simple as that, I fear," he murmured.

"Me, I am convinced it is the truth," said M. Bouc, becoming more and more enamoured of his theory.

"And what about the valet with the toothache who swears that the Italian never left the compartment?"

"That is the difficulty."

Poirot twinkled.

"Yes, it is annoying, that. Unlucky for your theory, and extremely lucky for our Italian friend that M. Ratchett's valet should have had the toothache."

"It will be explained," said M. Bouc with magnificent certainty.

Poirot shook his head again.

"No, it is hardly so simple as that," he murmured again.

Chapter 6

The Evidence of the Russian Princess

"Let us hear what Pierre Michel has to say about this button," he said.

The Wagon Lit conductor was recalled. He looked at them inquiringly.

M. Bouc cleared his throat.

"Michel," he said, "here is a button from your tunic. It was found in the American lady's compartment. What have you to say for yourself about it?"

The conductor's hand went automatically to his tunic.

"I have lost no button, Monsieur," he said. "There must be some mistake."

"That is very odd."

"I cannot account for it, Monsieur." The man seemed astonished, but not in any way guilty or confused.

M. Bouc said meaningly: "Owing to the circumstances in which it was found, it seems fairly certain that this button was dropped by the man who was in Mrs. Hubbard's compartment last night when she rang the bell."

"But, Monsieur, there was no one there. The lady must have imagined it."

"She did not imagine it, Michel. The assassin of M. Ratchett passed that way—*and dropped that button*."

As the significance of M. Bouc's words became plain to him, Pierre Michel flew into a violent state of agitation.

"It is not true, Monsieur; it is not true!" he cried. "You are accusing me of the crime. Me, I am innocent. I am absolutely innocent! Why should I want to kill a Monsieur whom I have never seen before?"

"Where were you when Mrs. Hubbard's bell rang?"

"I told you, Monsieur, in the next coach talking to my colleague."

"We will send for him."

"Do so, Monsieur, I implore you, do so."

The conductor of the next coach was summoned. He immediately confirmed Pierre Michel's statement. He added that the conductor from the Bucharest coach had also been there. The three of them had been discussing the situation caused by the snow. They had been talking some ten minutes when Michel fancied he heard a bell. As he opened the doors connecting the two coaches, they had all heard it plainly—a bell ringing repeatedly. Michel had run posthaste to answer it.

"So you see, Monsieur, I am not guilty," cried Michel anxiously.

"And this button from a Wagon Lit tunic, how do you explain it?"

"I cannot, Monsieur. It is a mystery to me. All my buttons are intact."

Both of the other conductors also declared that they had not lost a button; also that they had not been inside Mrs. Hubbard's compartment at any time.

"Calm yourself, Michel," said M. Bouc, "and cast your mind back to the moment when you ran to answer Mrs. Hubbard's bell. Did you meet anyone at all in the corridor?"

"No, Monsieur."

"Did you see anyone going away from you down the corridor in the other direction?"

"Again, no, Monsieur."

"Odd," said M. Bouc.

"Not so very," said Poirot. "It is a question of time. Mrs. Hubbard wakes to find someone in her compartment. For a minute or two she lies paralysed, her eyes shut. Probably it was then that the man slipped out into the corridor. Then she starts ringing the bell. But the conductor does not come at once. It is only the third or fourth peal that he hears. I should say myself that there was ample time—"

"For what? For what, *mon cher*? Remember, there are thick drifts of snow all round the train."

"There are two courses open to our mysterious assassin," said Poirot slowly. "He could retreat into either of the toilets or—he could disappear into one of the compartments."

"But they were all occupied."

"Yes."

"You mean that he could retreat into his own compartment?"

Poirot nodded.

"It fits—it fits," murmured M. Bouc. "During that ten minutes' absence of the conductor, the murderer comes from his own compartment, goes into Ratchett's, kills him, locks and chains the door on the inside, goes out through Mrs. Hubbard's compartment, and is back safely in his own compartment by the time the conductor arrives."

Poirot murmured: "It is not quite so simple as that, my friend. Our friend the doctor here will tell you so."

With a gesture M. Bouc signified that the three conductors might depart.

"We have still to see eight passengers," said Poirot. "Five first-class passengers—Princess Dragomiroff, Count and Countess Andrenyi, Colonel Arbuthnot, and Mr. Hardman. Three second-class passengers—Miss Debenham, Antonio Foscarelli, and the lady's-maid, Fräulein Schmidt."

"Whom will you see first—the Italian?"

"How you harp on your Italian! No, we will start at the top of the tree. Perhaps Madame la Princesse will be so good as to spare us a few moments of her time. Convey that message to her, Michel."

"*Oui, Monsieur,*" said the conductor, who was just leaving the car.

"Tell her we can wait on her in her compartment if she does not wish to put herself to the trouble of coming here," called M. Bouc.

But Princess Dragomiroff declined to take this course. She appeared in the dining-car, inclined her head slightly and sat down opposite Poirot.

Her small toad-like face looked even yellower than the day before. She was certainly ugly, and yet, like the toad, she had eyes like jewels, dark and imperious, revealing latent energy and an intellectual force that could be felt at once.

Her voice was deep, very distinct, with a slight grating quality in it.

She cut short a flowery phrase of apology from M. Bouc.

"You need not offer apologies, Messieurs. I understand a murder has taken place. Naturally you must interview all the passengers. I shall be glad to give you all the assistance in my power."

"You are most amiable, Madame," said Poirot.

"Not at all. It is a duty. What do you wish to know?"

"Your full Christian names and address, Madame. Perhaps you would prefer to write them yourself?"

Poirot proffered a sheet of paper and pencil, but the Princess waved them aside.

"You can write it," she said. "There is nothing difficult. Natalia Dragomiroff, 17 Avenue Kléber, Paris."

"You are travelling home from Constantinople, Madame?"

"Yes. I have been staying at the Austrian Embassy. My maid is with me."

"Would you be so good as to give me a brief account of your movements last night from dinner onwards?"

"Willingly. I directed the conductor to make up my bed whilst I was in the dining-car. I retired to bed immediately after dinner. I read until the hour of eleven, when I turned out my light. I was unable to sleep owing to certain rheumatic pains from which I suffer. At about a quarter to one I rang for my maid. She massaged me and then read aloud till I felt sleepy. I cannot say exactly when she left me. It may have been half an hour afterward, it may have been later."

"The train had stopped then?"

"The train had stopped."

"You heard nothing—nothing unusual during the time, Madame?"

"I heard nothing unusual."

"What is your maid's name?"

"Hildegarde Schmidt."

"She has been with you long?"

"Fifteen years."

"You consider her trustworthy?"

"Absolutely. Her people come from an estate of my late husband's in Germany."

"You have been in America, I presume, Madame?"

The abrupt change of subject made the old lady raise her eyebrows. "Many times."

"Were you at any time acquainted with a family of the name of Armstrong—a family in which a tragedy occurred?"

With some emotion in her voice the old lady said: "You speak of friends of mine, Monsieur."

"You knew Colonel Armstrong well, then?"

"I knew him slightly, but his wife, Sonia Armstrong, was my god-daughter. I was on terms of friendship with her mother, the actress Linda Arden. Linda Arden was a great genius, one of the greatest tragic actresses in the world. As Lady Macbeth, as Magda, there was no one to touch her. I was not only an admirer of her art, I was a personal friend."

"She is dead?"

"No, no, she is alive, but she lives in complete retirement. Her health is very delicate, and she has to lie on a sofa most of the time."

"There was, I think, a second daughter?"

"Yes, much younger than Mrs. Armstrong."

"And she is alive?"

"Certainly."

"Where is she?"

The old woman bent an acute glance at him.

"I must ask you the reason for these questions. What have they to do with the matter in hand—the murder on this train?"

"They are connected in this way, Madame: the man who was murdered was the man responsible for the kidnapping and murder of Mrs. Armstrong's child."

"Ah!"

The straight brows came together. Princess Dragomiroff drew herself a little more erect.

"In my view, then, this murder is an entirely admirable happening! You will pardon my slightly biased point of view."

"It is most natural, Madame. And now to

return to the question you did not answer. Where is the younger daughter of Linda Arden, the sister of Mrs. Armstrong?"

"I honestly cannot tell you, Monsieur. I have lost touch with the younger generation. I believe she married an Englishman some years ago and went to England, but at the moment I cannot recollect the name."

She paused a minute and then said:

"Is there anything further you want to ask me, gentlemen?"

"Only one thing, Madame, a somewhat personal question. The colour of your dressing gown."

She raised her eyebrows slightly. "I must suppose you have a reason for such a question. My dressing gown is of black satin."

"There is nothing more, Madame. I am much obliged to you for answering my questions so promptly."

She made a slight gesture with her heavily beringed hand. Then as she rose, and the others rose with her, she stopped.

"You will excuse me, Monsieur," she said, "but may I ask your name? Your face is somehow familiar to me."

"My name, Madame, is Hercule Poirot—at your service."

She was silent a minute, then: "Hercule Poirot," she said. "Yes. I remember now. This is Destiny."

She walked away, very erect, a little stiff in her movements.

"Voilà une grande dame," said M. Bouc. "What do you think of her, my friend?"

But Hercule Poirot merely shook his head.

"I am wondering," he said, "what she meant by Destiny."

Chapter 7

The Evidence of Count and Countess Andrenyi

Count and Countess Andrenyi were next summoned. The Count, however, entered the dining-car alone.

There was no doubt that he was a fine-looking man seen face-to-face. He was at least six feet in height, with broad shoulders and slender hips. He was dressed in very well-cut English tweeds and might have been taken for an Englishman had it not been for the length of his moustache and something in the line of the cheekbone.

"Well, Messieurs," he said, "what can I do for you?"

"You understand, Monsieur," said Poirot, "that in view of what has occurred I am obliged to put certain questions to all the passengers."

"Perfectly, perfectly," said the Count easily. "I quite understand your position. Not, I fear, that my wife and I can do much to assist you. We were asleep and heard nothing at all."

"Are you aware of the identity of the deceased, Monsieur?"

"I understood it was the big American—a man with a decidedly unpleasant face. He sat at that table at meal times." He indicated with a nod of his head the table at which Ratchett and MacQueen had sat.

"Yes, yes, Monsieur, you are perfectly correct. I meant—did you know the name of the man?"

"No." The Count looked thoroughly puzzled by Poirot's queries.

"If you want to know his name," he said, "surely it is on his passport?"

"The name on his passport is Ratchett," said Poirot. "But that, Monsieur, is not his real name. He is the man Cassetti, who was responsible for a celebrated kidnapping outrage in America."

He watched the Count closely as he spoke, but the latter seemed quite unaffected by this piece of news. He merely opened his eyes a little.

"Ah!" he said. "That certainly should throw light upon the matter. An extraordinary country, America."

"You have been there, perhaps, Monsieur le Comte?"

"I was in Washington for a year."

"You knew, perhaps, the Armstrong family?"

"Armstrong—Armstrong—it is difficult to recall. One met so many." He smiled, shrugged his shoulders. "But to come back to the matter in hand, gentlemen," he said. "What more can I do to assist you?"

"You retired to rest—when, Monsieur le Comte?"

Hercule Poirot's eyes stole to his plan. Count and Countess Andrenyi occupied compartment Nos. 12 and 13 adjoining.

"We had one compartment made up for the night whilst we were in the dining-car. On returning we sat in the other for a while—"

"Which number would that be?"

"No. 13. We played piquet together. At about eleven o'clock my wife retired for the night. The conductor made up my compartment and I also went to bed. I slept soundly until morning."

"Did you notice the stopping of the train?"

"I was not aware of it till this morning."

"And your wife?"

The Count smiled. "My wife always takes a sleeping draught when travelling by train. She took her usual dose of trional."

He paused. "I am sorry I am not able to assist you in any way."

Poirot passed him a sheet of paper and a pen.

"Thank you, Monsieur le Comte. It is a formality, but will you just let me have your name and address?"

The Count wrote slowly and carefully.

"It is just as well that I should write this for you," he said pleasantly. "The spelling of my country estate is a little difficult for those unacquainted with the language."

He passed the paper across to Poirot and rose.

"It will be quite unnecessary for my wife to come here," he said. "She can tell you nothing more than I have."

A little gleam came into Poirot's eye.

"Doubtless, doubtless," he said. "But all the same I think I should like to have just one little word with Madame la Comtesse."

"I assure you it is quite unnecessary." The Count's voice rang out authoritatively.

Poirot blinked gently at him.

"It will be a mere formality," he said. "But, you understand, it is necessary for my report."

"As you please."

The Count gave way grudgingly. He made a short foreign bow and left the dining-car.

Poirot reached out a hand to a passport. It set out the Count's names and titles. He passed on to the further information. "*Accompanied by*, wife; *Christian name*, Elena Maria; *maiden name*, Goldenberg; *age*, twenty." A spot of grease had been dropped on it at some time by a careless official.

"A diplomatic passport," said M. Bouc. "We must be careful, my friend, to give no offence. These people can have nothing to do with the murder."

"Be easy, *mon vieux*, I will be most tactful. A mere formality."

His voice dropped as the Countess Andrenyi entered the dining-car. She looked timid and extremely charming.

"You wish to see me, Messieurs?"

"A mere formality, Madame la Comtesse." Poirot rose gallantly, bowed her into the seat opposite him. "It is only to ask you if you saw or heard anything last night that may throw light upon this matter."

"Nothing at all, Monsieur. I was asleep."

"You did not hear, for instance, a commotion going on in the compartment next to yours? The American lady who occupies it had quite an attack of hysterics and rang for the conductor."

"I heard nothing, Monsieur. You see, I had taken a sleeping draught."

"Ah! I comprehend. Well, I need not detain you further." Then, as she rose swiftly— "Just one little minute. These particulars— your maiden name, age and so on—they are correct?"

"Quite correct, Monsieur."

"Perhaps you will sign this memorandum to that effect, then."

She signed quickly, in a graceful slanting handwriting—*Elena Andrenyi*.

"Did you accompany your husband to America, Madame?"

"No, Monsieur." She smiled, flushed a little. "We were not married then; we have been married only a year."

"Ah, yes, thank you, Madame. By the way, does your husband smoke?"

She stared at him as she stood poised for departure.

"Yes."

"A pipe?"

"No. Cigarettes and cigars."

"Ah! Thank you."

She lingered, her eyes watching him curiously. Lovely eyes they were, dark and almond—shaped with very long black lashes that swept the exquisite pallor of her cheeks. Her lips, very scarlet in the foreign fashion, were parted just a little. She looked exotic and beautiful.

"Why did you ask me that?"

"Madame," Poirot waved an airy hand, "detectives have to ask all sorts of questions. For instance, perhaps you will tell me the colour of your dressing gown?"

She stared at him. Then she laughed. "It is corn-coloured chiffon. Is that really important?"

"Very important, Madame."

She asked curiously: "Are you really a detective, then?"

"At your service, Madame."

"I thought there were no detectives on the train when it passed through Jugo-Slavia—not until one got to Italy."

"I am not a Jugo-Slavian detective, Madame. I am an international detective."

"You belong to the League of Nations?"

"I belong to the world, Madame," said Poirot dramatically. He went on: "I work mainly in London. You speak English?" he added in that language.

"I speak a leetle, yes." Her accent was charming. Poirot bowed once more.

"We will not detain you further, Madame. You see, it was not so very terrible."

She smiled, inclined her head and departed.

"Elle est jolie femme," said M. Bouc appreciatively. He sighed. "Well, that did not advance us much."

"No," said Poirot. "Two people who saw nothing and heard nothing."

"Shall we now see the Italian?"

Poirot did not reply for a moment. He was studying a grease spot on a Hungarian diplomatic passport.

Chapter 8
The Evidence of Colonel Arbuthnot

Poirot roused himself with a slight start. His eyes twinkled a little as they met the eager ones of M. Bouc.

"Ah! my dear old friend," he said, "you see I have become what they call the snob! The first class, I feel it should be attended to before the second class. Next, I think, we will interview the good-looking Colonel Arbuthnot."

Finding the Colonel's French to be of a severely limited description, Poirot conducted his interrogatory in English.

Arbuthnot's name, age, home address and exact military standing were all ascertained. Poirot proceeded:

"It is that you come home from India on

what is called the leave—what we can call
en permission?"

Colonel Arbuthnot, uninterested in what a
pack of foreigners called anything, replied
with true British brevity, "Yes."

"But you do not come home on the
P. & O. boat?"

"No."

"Why not?"

"I chose to come by the overland route
for reasons of my own."

("And that," his manner seemed to say,
"is one for you, you interfering little jack-
anapes.")

"You came straight through from India?"

The Colonel replied drily: "I stopped for
one night to see Ur of the Chaldees, and for
three days in Baghdad with the A.O.C., who
happens to be an old friend of mine."

"You stopped three days in Baghdad. I
understand that the young English lady,
Miss Debenham, also comes from Baghdad. Perhaps you met her there?"

"No, I did not. I first met Miss Debenham
when she and I shared the railway convoy
car from Kirkuk to Nissibin."

Poirot leaned forward. He became persuasive and a little more foreign than he need have been.

"Monsieur, I am about to appeal to you. You and Miss Debenham are the only two English people on the train. It is necessary that I should ask you each your opinion of the other."

"Highly irregular," said Colonel Arbuthnot coldly.

"Not so. You see, this crime, it was most probably committed by a woman. The man was stabbed no fewer than twelve times. Even the *chef de train* said at once, 'It is a woman.' Well, then, what is my first task? To give all the women travelling on the Istanbul-Calais coach what Americans call the 'once-over.' But to judge an English-woman is difficult. They are very reserved, the English. So I appeal to you, Monsieur, in the interest of justice. What sort of person is this Miss Debenham? What do you know about her?"

"Miss Debenham," said the Colonel with some warmth, "is a lady."

"Ah!" said Poirot with every appearance of being much gratified. "So you do not think that she is likely to be implicated in this crime?"

"The idea is absurd," said Arbuthnot. "The man was a perfect stranger—she had never seen him before."

"Did she tell you so?"

"She did. She commented at once upon his somewhat unpleasant appearance. If a woman *is* concerned, as you seem to think (to my mind without any evidence but on a mere assumption), I can assure you that Miss Debenham could not possibly be implicated."

"You feel warmly in the matter," said Poirot with a smile.

Colonel Arbuthnot gave him a cold stare. "I really don't know what you mean," he said.

The stare seemed to abash Poirot. He dropped his eyes and began fiddling with the papers in front of him.

"All this is by the way," he said. "Let us be practical and come to facts. This crime, we have reason to believe, took place at a quarter past one last night. It is part of the necessary routine to ask everyone on the train what he or she was doing at that time."

"Quite so. At a quarter past one, to the best of my belief, I was talking to the young

American fellow—secretary to the dead man."

"Ah! were you in his compartment, or was he in yours?"

"I was in his."

"That is the young man of the name of MacQueen?"

"Yes."

"He was a friend or acquaintance of yours?"

"No, I never saw him before this journey. We fell into casual conversation yesterday and both became interested. I don't as a rule like Americans—haven't any use for 'em—"

Poirot smiled, remembering MacQueen's strictures on "Britishers."

"—but I liked this young fellow. He'd got hold of some tomfool idiotic ideas about the situation in India. That's the worst of Americans—they're so sentimental and idealistic. Well, he was interested in what I had to tell him. I've had nearly thirty years' experience of the country. And I was interested in what he had to tell me about the working of Prohibition in America. Then we got down to world politics in general. I was quite surprised to look at my watch and find it was a quarter to two."

"That is the time you broke up this conversation?"

"Yes."

"What did you do then?"

"Walked along to my own compartment and turned in."

"Your bed was made up ready?"

"Yes."

"That is the compartment—let me see— No. 15—the one next but one to the end away from the dining-car?"

"Yes."

"Where was the conductor when you went to your compartment?"

"Sitting at the end at a little table. As a matter of fact MacQueen called him just as I went in to my own compartment."

"Why did he call him?"

"To make up his bed, I suppose. The compartment hadn't been made up for the night."

"Now, Colonel Arbuthnot, I want you to think carefully. During the time you were talking to Mr. MacQueen, did anyone pass along the corridor outside the door?"

"A good many people, I should think. I wasn't paying attention."

"Ah! but I am referring to—let us say, the last hour and a half of your conversation. You got out at Vincovci, didn't you?"

"Yes, but only for about a minute. There was a blizzard on. The cold was something frightful. Made one quite thankful to get back to the fug, though as a rule I think the way these trains are overheated is something scandalous."

M. Bouc sighed. "It is very difficult to please everybody," he said. "The English they open everything—then others they come along and shut everything. It is very difficult."

Neither Poirot nor Colonel Arbuthnot paid any attention to him.

"Now, Monsieur, cast your mind back," said Poirot encouragingly. "It was cold outside. You have returned to the train. You sit down again, you smoke—perhaps a cigarette—perhaps a pipe—"

He paused for the fraction of a second.

"A pipe for me. MacQueen smoked cigarettes."

"The train starts again. You smoke your pipe. You discuss the state of Europe—of the world. It is late now. Most people have retired for the night. Does anyone pass the door? Think."

Arbuthnot frowned in the effort of remembrance.

"Difficult to say," he said. "You see I wasn't paying any attention."

"But you have the soldier's observation for detail. You notice without noticing, so to speak."

The Colonel thought again, but shook his head.

"I couldn't say. I don't remember anyone passing except the conductor. Wait a minute—and there was a woman, I think."

"You saw her? Was she old—young?"

"Didn't see her. Wasn't looking that way. Just a rustle and a sort of smell of scent."

"Scent? A *good* scent?"

"Well, rather fruity, if you know what I mean. I mean you'd smell it a hundred yards away. But mind you," the Colonel went on hastily, "this may have been earlier in the evening. You see, as you said just now, it was just one of those things you notice without noticing, so to speak. Some time that evening I said to myself—'Woman—scent—got it on pretty thick.' But *when* it was I can't be sure, except that—why, yes, it must have been after Vincovci."

"Why?"

"Because I remember—sniffing, you know—just when I was talking about the utter washout Stalin's Five Year Plan was turning out. I know the idea *woman* brought the idea of the position of women in Russia into my mind. And I know we hadn't got on to Russia until pretty near the end of our talk."

"You can't pin it down more definitely than that?"

"N-no. It must have been roughly within the last half-hour."

"It was after the train had stopped?"

The other nodded. "Yes, I'm almost sure it was."

"Well, we will pass from that. Have you ever been in America, Colonel Arbuthnot?"

"Never. Don't want to go."

"Did you ever know a Colonel Armstrong?"

"Armstrong—Armstrong—I've known two or three Armstrongs. There was Tommy Armstrong in the 60th—you don't mean him? And Selby Armstrong—he was killed on the Somme."

"I mean the Colonel Armstrong who married an American wife and whose only child was kidnapped and killed."

"Ah, yes, I remember reading about that—shocking affair. I don't think I actually ever came across the fellow, though of course I knew of him. Toby Armstrong. Nice fellow. Everybody liked him. He had a very distinguished career. Got the V.C."

"The man who was killed last night was the man responsible for the murder of Colonel Armstrong's child."

Arbuthnot's face grew rather grim. "Then in my opinion the swine deserved what he got. Though I would have preferred to see him properly hanged—or electrocuted, I suppose, over there."

"In fact, Colonel Arbuthnot, you prefer law and order to private vengeance?"

"Well, you can't go about having blood feuds and stabbing each other like Corsicans or the Mafia," said the Colonel. "Say what you like, trial by jury is a sound system."

Poirot looked at him thoughtfully for a minute or two.

"Yes," he said. "I am sure that would be your view. Well, Colonel Arbuthnot, I do not think there is anything more I have to ask you. There is nothing you yourself can recall last night that in any way struck you—or shall we say strikes you now, looking back—as suspicious?"

Arbuthnot considered for a moment or two.

"No," he said. "Nothing at all. Unless—" he hesitated.

"But yes, continue, I pray of you."

"Well, it's nothing really," said the Colonel slowly. "But you said *anything*."

"Yes, yes. Go on."

"Oh! it's nothing. A mere detail. But as I got back to my compartment I noticed that the door of the one beyond mine—the end one, you know—"

"Yes, No. 16."

"Well, the door of it was not quite closed. And the fellow inside peered out in a furtive sort of way. Then he pulled the door to quickly. Of course I know there's nothing in that—but it just struck me as a bit odd. I mean, it's quite usual to open a door and stick your head out if you want to see anything. But it was the furtive way he did it that caught my attention."

"Ye-es," said Poirot doubtfully.

"I told you there was nothing to it," said Arbuthnot, apologetically. "But you know what it is—early hours of the morning—everything very still. The thing had a sinister look—like a detective story. All nonsense really."

He rose. "Well, if you don't want me any more—"

"Thank you, Colonel Arbuthnot, there is nothing else."

The soldier hesitated for a minute. His first natural distaste for being questioned by "foreigners" had evaporated.

"About Miss Debenham," he said rather awkwardly. "You can take it from me that she's all right. She's a *pukka sahib*."

Flushing a little, he withdrew.

"What," asked Dr. Constantine with interest, "does a *pukka sahib* mean?"

"It means," said Poirot, "that Miss Debenham's father and brothers were at the same kind of school as Colonel Arbuthnot was."

"Oh!" said Dr. Constantine, disappointed. "Then it has nothing to do with the crime at all."

"Exactly," said Poirot.

He fell into a reverie, beating a light tattoo on the table. Then he looked up.

"Colonel Arbuthnot smokes a pipe," he said. "In the compartment of Mr. Ratchett I found a pipe-cleaner. Mr. Ratchett smoked only cigars."

"You think—?"

"He is the only man so far who admits to smoking a pipe. And he knew of Colonel Armstrong—perhaps actually did know him, though he won't admit it."

"So you think it possible—?"

Poirot shook his head violently.

"That is just it—it is *im*possible—quite im-possible—that an honourable, slightly stu-pid, upright Englishman should stab an en-emy twelve times with a knife! Do you not feel, my friends, how impossible it is?"

"That is the psychology," said M. Bouc.

"And one must respect the psychology. This crime has a signature, and it is certainly not the signature of Colonel Arbuthnot. But now to our next interview."

This time M. Bouc did not mention the Italian. But he thought of him.

Chapter 9

The Evidence of Mr. Hardman

The last of the first-class passengers to be interviewed, Mr. Hardman, was the big flamboyant American who had shared a table with the Italian and the valet.

He wore a somewhat loud check suit, a pink shirt, and a flashy tie-pin, and was rolling something round his tongue as he entered the dining-car. He had a big, fleshy, coarse-featured face, with a good-humoured expression.

"Morning, gentlemen," he said. "What can I do for you?"

"You have heard of this murder, Mr.—er—Hardman?"

"Sure." He shifted the chewing gum deftly.

"We are of necessity interviewing all the passengers on the train."

"That's all right by me. Guess that's the only way to tackle the job."

Poirot consulted the passport lying in front of him.

"You are Cyrus Bethman Hardman, United States subject, forty-one years of age, travelling salesman for typewriting ribbons?"

"O.K. That's me."

"You are travelling from Stamboul to Paris?"

"That's so."

"Reason?"

"Business."

"Do you always travel first-class, Mr. Hardman?"

"Yes, sir. The firm pays my travelling expenses." He winked.

"Now, Mr. Hardman, we come to the events of last night."

The American nodded.

"What can you tell us about the matter?"

"Exactly nothing at all."

"Ah, that is a pity. Perhaps, Mr. Hardman, you will tell us exactly what you did last night from dinner onwards?"

For the first time the American did not seem ready with his reply. At last he said:

"Excuse me, gentlemen, but just who are you? Put me wise."

"This is M. Bouc, a director of the Compagnie des Wagons Lits. This gentleman is the doctor who examined the body."

"And you yourself?"

"I am Hercule Poirot. I am engaged by the company to investigate this matter."

"I've heard of you," said Mr. Hardman. He reflected a minute or two longer. "Guess I'd better come clean."

"It will certainly be advisable for you to tell us all you know," said Poirot drily.

"You'd have said a mouthful if there was anything I *did* know. But I don't. I know nothing at all—just as I said. But I *ought* to know something. That's what makes me sore. I *ought* to."

"Please explain, Mr. Hardman."

Mr. Hardman sighed, removed the chewing gum, and dived into a pocket. At the same time his whole personality seemed to undergo a change. He became less of a stage character and more of a real person. The resonant nasal tones of his voice became modified.

"That passport's a bit of bluff," he said. "That's who I really am."

Poirot scrutinised the card flipped across to him. M. Bouc peered over his shoulder.

MR. CYRUS B. HARDMAN
MCNEIL'S DETECTIVE AGENCY
NEW YORK CITY

Poirot knew the name as that of one of the best-known and most reputable private detective agencies in New York.

"Now, Mr. Hardman," he said, "let us hear the meaning of this."

"Sure. Things came about this way. I'd come over to Europe trailing a couple of crooks—nothing to do with this business. The chase ended in Stamboul. I wired the Chief and got his instructions to return, and I would have been making my tracks back to little old New York when I got this."

He pushed across a letter.

THE TOKATLIAN HOTEL

Dear Sir: You have been pointed out to me as an operative of the McNeil Detective Agency. Kindly report at my suite at four o'clock this afternoon.
S. E. Ratchett

"Eh bien?"

"I reported at the time stated, and Mr. Ratchett put me wise to the situation. He showed me a couple of letters he'd got."

"He was alarmed?"

"Pretended not to be, but he was rattled, all right. He put up a proposition to me. I was to travel by the same train as he did to Parrus and see that nobody got him. Well, gentlemen, I *did* travel by the same train, and in spite of me, somebody *did* get him. I certainly feel sore about it. It doesn't look any too good for me."

"Did he give you any indication of the line you were to take?"

"Sure. He had it all taped out. It was his idea that I should travel in the compartment alongside his. Well, that blew up right at the start. The only place I could get was berth No. 16, and I had a job getting that. I guess the conductor likes to keep that compartment up his sleeve. But that's neither here nor there. When I looked all round the situation, it seemed to me that No. 16 was a pretty good strategic position. There was only the dining-car in front of the Stamboul sleeping-car, and the door onto the platform at the front end was barred at night. The only way a thug could come was through the rear-end door to the platform, or along the train from the rear, and in either case he'd have to pass right by my compartment."

"You had no idea, I suppose, of the identity of the possible assailant?"

"Well, I knew what he looked like. Mr. Ratchett described him to me."

"What?"

All three men leaned forward eagerly.

Hardman went on.

"A small man—dark—with a womanish kind of voice. That's what the old man said. Said, too, that he didn't think it would be the first night out. More likely the second or third."

"He knew something," said M. Bouc.

"He certainly knew more than he told his secretary," commented Poirot thoughtfully. "Did he tell you anything about this enemy of his? Did he, for instance, say *why* his life was threatened?"

"No, he was kinda reticent about that part of it. Just said the fellow was out for his blood and meant to get it."

"A small man—dark—with a womanish voice," repeated Poirot thoughtfully. Then, fixing a sharp glance on Hardman, he asked: "You knew who he really was, of course?"

"Which, Mister?"

"Ratchett. You recognised him?"

"I don't get you."

"Ratchett was Cassetti, the Armstrong murderer."

Mr. Hardman gave vent to a prolonged whistle.

"That certainly is some surprise!" he said. "Yes, *sir!* No, I didn't recognise him. I was away out West when that case came on. I suppose I saw photos of him in the papers, but I wouldn't recognise my own mother when a newspaper photographer got through with her. Well, I don't doubt that a few people had it in for Cassetti all right."

"Do you know of anyone connected with the Armstrong case who answers to that description: small—dark—womanish voice?"

Hardman reflected a minute or two. "It's hard to say. Pretty nearly everyone connected with that case is dead."

"There was the girl who threw herself out of the window, remember."

"Sure. That's a good point, that. She was a foreigner of some kind. Maybe she had

some Wop relations. But you've got to remember that there were other cases besides the Armstrong one. Cassetti had been
running this kidnapping stunt for some time.
You can't concentrate on that only."

"Ah, but we have reason to believe that
this crime is connected with the Armstrong
case."

Mr. Hardman cocked an inquiring eye.
Poirot did not respond. The American shook
his head.

"I can't call to mind anybody answering
that description in the Armstrong case," he
said slowly. "But of course I wasn't in it and
didn't know much about it."

"Well, continue your narrative, Mr. Hardman."

"There's very little to tell. I got my sleep in
the daytime and stayed awake on the watch
at night. Nothing suspicious happened the
first night. Last night was the same, as far
as I was concerned. I had my door a little
ajar and watched. No stranger passed."

"You are sure of that, Mr. Hardman?"

"I'm plumb certain. Nobody got on that
train from outside, and nobody came along
the train from the rear carriages. I'll take my
oath on that."

"Could you see the conductor from your position?"

"Sure. He sits on that little seat almost flush with my door."

"Did he leave that seat at all after the train stopped at Vincovci?"

"That was the last station? Why, yes, he answered a couple of bells—that would be just after the train came to a halt for good. Then, after that, he went past me into the rear coach—was there about a quarter of an hour. There was a bell ringing like mad and he came back running. I stepped out into the corridor to see what it was all about— felt a mite nervous, you understand—but it was only the American dame. She was raising hell about something or other. I grinned. Then he went on to another compartment and came back and got a bottle of mineral water for someone. After that he settled down in his seat till he went up to the far end to make somebody's bed up. I don't think he stirred after that until about five o'clock this morning."

"Did he doze off at all?"

"That I can't say. He may have."

Poirot nodded. Automatically his hands

straightened the papers on the table. He picked up the official card once more.

"Be so good as just to initial this," he said.

The other complied.

"There is no one, I suppose, who can confirm your story of your identity, Mr. Hardman?"

"On this train? Well, not exactly. Unless it might be young MacQueen. I know him well enough—I've seen him in his father's office in New York. But that's not to say he'll remember me from a crowd of other operatives. No, Mr. Poirot, you'll have to wait and cable New York when the snow lets up. But it's O.K. I'm not telling the tale. Well, so long, gentlemen. Pleased to have met you, Mr. Poirot."

Poirot proffered his cigarette case. "But perhaps you prefer a pipe?"

"Not me." He helped himself, then strode briskly off.

The three men looked at each other.

"You think he is genuine?" asked Dr. Constantine.

"Yes, yes. I know the type. Besides, it is a story that would be very easy to disprove."

"He has given us a piece of very interesting evidence," said M. Bouc.

"Yes, indeed."

"A small man—dark—with a high-pitched voice," said M. Bouc thoughtfully.

"A description which applies to no one on the train," said Poirot.

Chapter 10
The Evidence of the Italian

"And now," said Poirot with a twinkle in his eye, "we will delight the heart of M. Bouc and see the Italian."

Antonio Foscarelli came into the dining-car with a swift, cat-like tread. His face beamed. It was a typical Italian face, sunny-looking and swarthy.

He spoke French well and fluently with only a slight accent.

"Your name is Antonio Foscarelli?"

"Yes, Monsieur."

"You are, I see, a naturalised American subject?"

The American grinned. "Yes, Monsieur. It is better for my business."

"You are an agent for Ford motor cars?"

"Yes, you see—"

A voluble exposition followed. At the end of it anything that the three men did not know about Foscarelli's business methods, his journeys, his income, and his opinion of the United States and most European countries seemed a negligible factor. This was not a man who had to have information dragged from him. It gushed out.

His good-natured, childish face beamed with satisfaction as, with a last eloquent gesture, he paused and wiped his forehead with a handkerchief.

"So you see," he said. "I do big business. I am up to date. I understand salesmanship!"

"You have been in the United States, then, for the last ten years on and off."

"Yes, Monsieur. Ah! well do I remember the day I first took the boat—to go to America, so far away! My mother, my little sister—"

Poirot cut short the flood of reminiscence.

"During your sojourn in the United States, did you ever come across the deceased?"

"Never. But I know the type. Oh! yes." He snapped his fingers expressively. "It is very respectable, very well-dressed, but underneath it is all wrong. Out of my experience I should say he was the big crook. I give you my opinion for what it is worth."

"Your opinion is quite right," said Poirot drily. "Ratchett was Cassetti, the kidnapper."

"What did I tell you? I have learned to be very acute—to read the face. It is necessary. Only in America do they teach you the proper way to sell. I—"

"You remember the Armstrong case?"

"I do not quite remember. The name, yes? It was a little girl, a baby, was it not?"

"Yes, a very tragic affair."

The Italian seemed the first person to demur to this view.

"Ah! well, these things they happen," he said philosophically, "in a great civilisation such as America—"

Poirot cut him short. "Did you ever come across any members of the Armstrong family?"

"No, I do not think so. It is difficult to say. I will give you some figures. Last year alone, I sold—"

"Monsieur, pray confine yourself to the point."

The Italian's hands flung themselves out

in a gesture of apology. "A thousand pardons."

"Tell me, if you please, your exact movements last night from dinner onwards."

"With pleasure. I stay here as long as I can. It is more amusing. I talk to the American gentleman at my table. He sells typewriter ribbons. Then I go back to my compartment. It is empty. The miserable John Bull who shares it with me is away attending to his master. At last he comes back—very long face as usual. He will not talk—says yes and no. A miserable race, the English—not sympathetic. He sits in the corner, very stiff, reading a book. Then the conductor comes and makes our beds."

"Nos. 4 and 5," murmured Poirot.

"Exactly—the end compartment. Mine is the upper berth. I get up there. I smoke and read. The little Englishman has, I think, the toothache. He gets out a little bottle of stuff that smells very strong. He lies in bed and groans. Presently I sleep. Whenever I wake I hear him groaning."

"Do you know if he left the carriage at all during the night?"

"I do not think so. That, I should hear. The light from the corridor—one wakes up automatically thinking it is the customs examination at some frontier."

"Did he ever speak of his master? Ever express any animus against him?"

"I tell you he did not speak. He was not sympathetic. A fish."

"You smoke, you say—a pipe, cigarettes, cigar?"

"Cigarettes only."

Poirot proffered one, which he accepted.

"Have you ever been in Chicago?" inquired M. Bouc.

"Oh! yes—a fine city—but I know best New York, Cleveland, Detroit. You have been to the States? No? You should go. It—"

Poirot pushed a sheet of paper across to him.

"If you will sign this, and put your permanent address, please."

The Italian wrote with a flourish. Then he rose, his smile as engaging as ever.

"That is all? You do not require me further? Good day to you, Messieurs. I wish we could get out of the snow. I have an appointment in Milan." He shook his head sadly. "I shall lose the business." He departed.

Poirot looked at his friend.

"He has been a long time in America," said M. Bouc, "and he is an Italian, and Italians use the knife! And they are great liars! I do not like Italians."

"*Ça se voit*," said Poirot with a smile. "Well, it may be that you are right, but I will point out to you, my friend, that there is absolutely no evidence against the man."

"And what about the psychology? Do not Italians stab?"

"Assuredly," said Poirot. "Especially in the heat of a quarrel. But this—this is a different kind of crime. I have the little idea, my friend, that this is a crime very carefully planned and staged. It is a far-sighted, long-headed crime. It is not—how shall I express it?—a *Latin* crime. It is a crime that shows traces of a cool, resourceful, deliberate brain—I think an Anglo-Saxon brain."

He picked up the last two passports.

"Let us now," he said, "see Miss Mary Debenham."

Chapter 11

The Evidence of Miss Debenham

When Mary Debenham entered the dining-car she confirmed Poirot's previous estimate of her. She was very neatly dressed in a little black suit with a French grey shirt, and the smooth waves of her dark head were neat and unruffled. Her manner was as calm and unruffled as her hair.

She sat down opposite Poirot and M. Bouc and looked at them inquiringly.

"Your name is Mary Hermione Debenham and you are twenty-six years of age?" began Poirot.

"Yes."

"English?"

"Yes."

"Will you be so kind, Mademoiselle, as to

write down your permanent address on this piece of paper?"

She complied. Her writing was clear and legible.

"And now, Mademoiselle, what have you to tell us of the affair last night?"

"I am afraid I have nothing to tell you. I went to bed and slept."

"Does it distress you very much, Mademoiselle, that a crime has been committed on this train?"

The question was clearly unexpected. Her grey eyes widened a little.

"I don't quite understand you?"

"It was a perfectly simple question that I asked you, Mademoiselle. I will repeat it. Are you very much distressed that a crime should have been committed on this train?"

"I have not really thought about it from that point of view. No, I cannot say that I am at all distressed."

"A crime—it is all in the day's work to you, eh?"

"It is naturally an unpleasant thing to have happen," said Mary Debenham quietly.

"You are very Anglo-Saxon, Mademoiselle. *Vous n'éprouvez pas d'émotion.*"

She smiled a little. "I am afraid I cannot

have hysterics to prove my sensibility. After all, people die every day."

"They die, yes. But murder is a little more rare."

"Oh! certainly."

"You were not acquainted with the dead man?"

"I saw him for the first time when lunching here yesterday."

"And how did he strike you?"

"I hardly noticed him."

"He did not impress you as an evil personality?"

She shrugged her shoulders slightly. "Really, I cannot say I thought about it."

Poirot looked at her keenly.

"You are, I think, a little bit contemptuous of the way I prosecute my inquiries," he said with a twinkle. "Not so, you think, would an English inquiry be conducted. There everything would be cut and dried—it would be all kept to the facts—a well-ordered business. But I, Mademoiselle, have my little originalities. I look first at my witness, I sum up his or her character, and I frame my questions accordingly. Just a little minute ago I am asking questions of a gentleman who wants to tell me all his ideas on every subject. Well, him I keep strictly to the point. I want him to answer yes or no. This or that. And then you come. I see at once that you will be orderly and methodical. You will confine yourself to the matter in hand. Your answers will be brief and to the point. And because, Mademoiselle, human nature is perverse, I ask of you quite different questions. I ask what you feel, what you think. It does not please you, this method?"

"If you will forgive my saying so, it seems somewhat of a waste of time. Whether or not I liked Mr. Ratchett's face does not seem likely to be helpful in finding out who killed him."

"Do you know who the man Ratchett really was, Mademoiselle?"

She nodded. "Mrs. Hubbard has been telling everyone."

"And what do you think of the Armstrong affair?"

"It was quite abominable," said the girl crisply.

Poirot looked at her thoughtfully.

"You are travelling from Baghdad, I believe, Miss Debenham?"

"Yes."

"To London?"

"Yes."

"What have you been doing in Baghdad?"

"I have been acting as governess to two children."

"Are you returning to your post after your holiday?"

"I am not sure."

"Why is that?"

"Baghdad is rather out of things. I think I should prefer a post in London if I can hear of a suitable one."

"I see. I thought, perhaps, you might be going to be married."

Miss Debenham did not reply. She raised her eyes and looked Poirot full in the face. The glance said plainly: "You are impertinent."

"What is your opinion of the lady who shares your compartment—Miss Ohlsson?"

"She seems a pleasant, simple creature."

"What colour is her dressing gown?"

Mary Debenham stared. "A kind of brownish colour—natural wool."

"Ah! I may mention without indiscretion, I hope, that I noticed the colour of your dressing gown on the way from Aleppo to Stamboul. A pale mauve, I believe."

"Yes, that is right."

"Have you any other dressing gown, Mademoiselle? A scarlet dressing gown, for example?"

"No, that is not mine."

Poirot leant forward. He was like a cat pouncing on a mouse.

"Whose, then?"

The girl drew back a little, startled. "I don't know. What do you mean?"

"You do not say, 'No, I have no such thing.' You say, 'That is not mine.' Meaning that such a thing *does* belong to someone else."

She nodded.

"Somebody else on this train?"

"Yes."

"Whose is it?"

"I told you just now: I don't know. I woke up this morning about five o'clock with the feeling that the train had been standing still for a long time. I opened the door and looked out into the corridor, thinking we might be at a station. I saw someone in a scarlet kimono some way down the corridor."

"And you don't know who it was? Was she fair, or dark, or grey-haired?"

"I can't say. She had on a shingle cap and I only saw the back of her head."

"And in build?"

"Tallish and slim, I should judge, but it's difficult to say. The kimono was embroidered with dragons."

"Yes, yes, that is right—dragons." He was silent a minute. He murmured to himself: "I cannot understand. I cannot understand. None of this makes sense."

Then, looking up, he said: "I need not keep you further, Mademoiselle."

"Oh!" She seemed rather taken aback but rose promptly.

In the doorway, however, she hesitated a minute and then came back.

"The Swedish lady—Miss Ohlsson, is it?—seems rather worried. She says you told her she was the last person to see this man alive. She thinks, I believe, that you suspect her on that account. Can't I tell her that she has made a mistake? Really, you know, she is the kind of creature who wouldn't hurt a fly." She smiled a little as she spoke.

"What time was it that she went to fetch the aspirin from Mrs. Hubbard?"

"Just after half-past ten."

"She was away—how long?"

"About five minutes."

"Did she leave the compartment again during the night?"

"No."

Poirot turned to the doctor. "Could Ratchett have been killed as early as that?"

The doctor shook his head.

"Then I think you can reassure your friend, Mademoiselle."

"Thank you." She smiled suddenly at him, a smile that invited sympathy. "She's like a sheep, you know. She gets anxious and bleats."

She turned and went out.

Chapter 12

The Evidence of the German Lady's-maid

M. Bouc was looking at his friend curiously.

"I do not quite understand you, *mon vieux*. You were trying to do—what?"

"I was searching for a flaw, my friend."

"A flaw?"

"Yes—in the armour of a young lady's self-possession. I wished to shake her *sang-froid*. Did I succeed? I do not know. But I know this: she did not expect me to tackle the matter as I did."

"You suspect her," said M. Bouc slowly. "But why? She seems a very charming young lady—the last person in the world to be mixed up in a crime of this kind."

"I agree," said Constantine. "She is cold. She has not emotions. She would not stab a man—she would sue him in the law courts."

Poirot sighed.

"You must, both of you, get rid of your obsession that this is an unpremeditated and sudden crime. As for the reasons why I suspect Miss Debenham, there are two. One is because of something that I overheard, and that you do not as yet know."

He retailed to them the curious interchange of phrases he had overheard on the journey from Aleppo.

"That is curious, certainly," said M. Bouc when he had finished. "It needs explaining. If it means what you suspect it means, then they are both of them in it together—she and the stiff Englishman."

Poirot nodded.

"And that is just what is not borne out by the facts," he said. "See you, if they were both in this together, what should we expect to find? That each of them would provide an alibi for the other. Is not that so? But no— that does not happen. Miss Debenham's alibi is provided by a Swedish woman whom she has never seen before, and Colonel Arbuthnot's alibi is vouched for by MacQueen, the dead man's secretary. No, that solution of the puzzle is too easy."

"You said there was another reason for your suspicions of her," M. Bouc reminded him.

Poirot smiled.

"Ah! but that is only psychological. I ask myself, is it possible for Miss Debenham to have planned this crime? Behind this business, I am convinced, there is a cool, intelligent, resourceful brain. Miss Debenham answers to that description."

M. Bouc shook his head. "I think you are wrong, my friend. I do not see that young English girl as a criminal."

"Ah! Well," said Poirot, picking up the last passport. "To the final name on our list. Hildegarde Schmidt, lady's-maid."

Summoned by the attendant, Hildegarde Schmidt came into the restaurant car and stood waiting respectfully.

Poirot motioned her to sit down.

She did so, folding her hands and waiting placidly till he questioned her. She seemed a placid creature altogether—eminently respectable, perhaps not overintelligent.

Poirot's methods with Hildegarde Schmidt

were a complete contrast to his handling of
Mary Debenham.

He was at his kindest and most genial,
setting the woman at her ease. Then, having
got her to write down her name and address, he slid gently into his questions.

The interview took place in German.

"We want to know as much as possible
about what happened last night," he said.
"We know that you cannot give us much information bearing on the crime itself, but
you may have seen or heard something
that, while conveying nothing to you, may
be valuable to us. You understand?"

She did not seem to. Her broad, kindly
face remained set in its expression of placid
stupidity as she answered:

"I do not know anything, Monsieur."

"Well, for instance you know that your
mistress sent for you last night."

"That, yes."

"Do you remember the time?"

"I do not, Monsieur. I was asleep, you
see, when the attendant came and told
me."

"Yes, yes. Was it usual for you to be sent
for in this way?"

"It was not unusual, Monsieur. The gracious lady often required attention at night. She did not sleep well."

"*Eh bien*, then, you received the summons and you got up. Did you put on a dressing gown?"

"No, Monsieur, I put on a few clothes. I would not like to go in to her Excellency in my dressing gown."

"And yet it is a very nice dressing gown—scarlet, is it not?"

She stared at him. "It is a dark blue flannel dressing gown, Monsieur."

"Ah! continue. A little pleasantry on my part, that is all. So you went along to Madame la Princesse. And what did you do when you got there?"

"I gave her massage, Monsieur, and then I read aloud. I do not read aloud very well, but her Excellency says that is all the better—so it sends her better to sleep. When she became sleepy, Monsieur, she told me to go, so I closed the book and I returned to my own compartment."

"Do you know what time that was?"

"No, Monsieur."

"Well, how long had you been with Madame la Princesse?"

"About half an hour, Monsieur."

"Good, continue."

"First, I fetched her Excellency an extra rug from my compartment. It was very cold in spite of the heating. I arranged the rug over her, and she wished me good night. I poured her out some mineral water. Then I turned out the light and left her."

"And then?"

"There is nothing more, Monsieur. I returned to my carriage and went to sleep."

"And you met no one in the corridor?"

"No, Monsieur."

"You did not, for instance, see a lady in a scarlet kimono with dragons on it?"

Her mild eyes bulged at him. "No, indeed, Monsieur. There was nobody about except the attendant. Everyone was asleep."

"But you did see the conductor?"

"Yes, Monsieur."

"What was he doing?"

"He came out of one of the compartments, Monsieur."

"What?" M. Bouc leaned forward. "Which one?"

Hildegarde Schmidt looked frightened again, and Poirot cast a reproachful glance at his friend.

"Naturally," he said. "The conductor often

MURDER ON THE ORIENT EXPRESS   225

has to answer bells at night. Do you remember which compartment it was?"

"It was about the middle of the coach, Monsieur. Two or three doors from Madame la Princesse."

"Ah! tell us, if you please, exactly where this was and what happened?"

"He nearly ran into me, Monsieur. It was when I was returning from my compartment to that of the Princess with the rug."

"And he came out of a compartment and almost collided with you. In which direction was he going?"

"Towards me, Monsieur. He apologised and passed on down the corridor towards the dining-car. A bell began ringing, but I do not think he answered it." She paused and then said: "I do not understand. How is it—?"

Poirot spoke reassuringly.

"It is just a question of time," he said. "All a matter of routine. This poor conductor, he seems to have had a busy night—first waking you and then answering bells."

"It was not the same conductor who woke me, Monsieur. It was another one."

"Ah! another one! Had you seen him before?"

"No, Monsieur."

"Ah!—do you think you would recognise him if you saw him?"

"I think so, Monsieur."

Poirot murmured something in M. Bouc's ear. The latter got up and went to the door to give an order.

Poirot was continuing his questions in an easy, friendly manner.

"Have you ever been to America, Fräulein Schmidt?"

"Never, Monsieur. It must be a fine country."

"You have heard, perhaps, who this man who was killed really was—that he was responsible for the death of a little child?"

"Yes, I have heard, Monsieur. It was abominable—wicked. The good God should not allow such things. We are not so wicked as that in Germany."

Tears had come into the woman's eyes. Her strong, motherly soul was moved.

"It was an abominable crime," said Poirot gravely.

He drew a scrap of cambric from his pocket and handed it to her.

"Is this your handkerchief, Fräulein Schmidt?"

There was a moment's silence as the woman examined it. She looked up after a minute. The colour had mounted a little in her face.

"Ah! no, indeed. It is not mine, Monsieur."

"It has the initial H, you see. That is why I thought it was yours."

"Ah! Monsieur, it is a lady's handkerchief, that. A very expensive handkerchief. Embroidered by hand. It comes from Paris, I should say."

"It is not yours and you do not know whose it is?"

"I? Oh! no, Monsieur."

Of the three listening, only Poirot caught the nuance of hesitation in the reply.

M. Bouc whispered in his ear. Poirot nodded and said to the woman:

"The three sleeping-car attendants are coming in. Will you be so kind as to tell me which is the one you met last night as you were going with the rug to the Princess?"

The three men entered. Pierre Michel, the big blond conductor of the Athens-Paris coach, and the stout burly conductor of the Bucharest one.

Hildegarde Schmidt looked at them and immediately shook her head.

"No, Monsieur," she said. "None of these is the man I saw last night."

"But these are the only conductors on the train. You must be mistaken."

"I am quite sure, Monsieur. These are all tall, big men. The one I saw was small and dark. He had a little moustache. His voice when he said *'Pardon'* was weak, like a woman's. Indeed, I remember him very well, Monsieur."

Chapter 13
Summary of the Passengers' Evidence

"A small dark man with a womanish voice," said M. Bouc.

The three conductors and Hildegarde Schmidt had been dismissed.

M. Bouc made a despairing gesture. "But I understand nothing—but nothing of all this! The enemy that this Ratchett spoke of, he was then on the train after all? But where is he now? How can he have vanished into thin air? My head, it whirls. Say something, then, my friend, I implore you. Show me how the impossible can be possible!"

"It is a good phrase that," said Poirot. "The impossible cannot have happened, therefore the impossible must be possible in spite of appearances."

"Explain to me, then, quickly, what actually happened on the train last night."

"I am not a magician, *mon cher*. I am, like you, a very puzzled man. This affair advances in a very strange manner."

"It does not advance at all. It stays where it was."

Poirot shook his head. "No, that is not true. We are more advanced. We know certain things. We have heard the evidence of the passengers."

"And what has that told us? Nothing at all."

"I would not say that, my friend."

"I exaggerate, perhaps. The American Hardman, and the German maid—yes, they have added something to our knowledge. That is to say, they have made the whole business more unintelligible than it was."

"No, no, no," said Poirot soothingly.

M. Bouc turned upon him. "Speak, then, let us hear the wisdom of Hercule Poirot."

"Did I not tell you that I was, like you, a very puzzled man? But at least we can face our problem. We can arrange such facts as we have with order and method."

"Pray continue, Monsieur," said Dr. Constantine.

Poirot cleared his throat and straightened a piece of blotting paper.

"Let us review the case as it stands at this moment. First, there are certain indisputable facts. This man, Ratchett or Cassetti, was stabbed in twelve places and died last night. That is fact one."

"I grant it you—I grant it, *mon vieux*," said M. Bouc with a gesture of irony.

Hercule Poirot was not at all put out. He continued calmly.

"I will pass over for the moment certain rather peculiar appearances which Dr. Constantine and I have already discussed together. I will come to them presently. The next fact of importance, to my mind, is the *time* of the crime."

"That, again, is one of the few things we do know," said M. Bouc. "The crime was committed at a quarter past one this morning. Everything goes to show that that was so."

"Not *everything*. You exaggerate. There is, certainly, a fair amount of evidence to support that view."

"I am glad you admit that at least."

Poirot went on calmly, unperturbed by the interruption.

"We have before us three possibilities.

"(1)—that the crime was committed, as you say, at a quarter past one. This is supported by the evidence of the watch, by the evidence of Mrs. Hubbard, and by the evidence of the German woman, Hildegarde Schmidt. It agrees with the evidence of Dr. Constantine.

"(2)—that the crime was committed *later*, and that the evidence of the watch was deliberately faked in order to mislead.

"(3)—that the crime was committed *earlier*, and the evidence faked for the same reason as above.

"Now if we accept possibility (1) as the most likely to have occurred, and the one supported by most evidence, we must also accept certain facts arising from it. If the crime was committed at a quarter past one, the murderer cannot have left the train, and the questions arise: Where is he? And *who* is he?

"To begin with, let us examine the evidence carefully. We first hear of the existence of this man—the small dark man with a womanish voice—from the man Hardman. He says that Ratchett told him of this person and employed him to watch out for the man. There is no *evidence* to support this; we have only Hardman's word for it. Let us next examine the question: Is Hardman the person he pretends to be—an operative of a New York detective agency?

"What to my mind is so interesting in this case is that we have none of the facilities afforded to the police. We cannot investigate the *bona fides* of any of these people. We have to rely solely on deduction. That, to me, makes the matter very much more interesting. There is no routine work. It is all a matter of the intellect. I ask myself: Can we accept Hardman's account of himself? I make my decision and I answer 'Yes.' I am of the opinion that we *can* accept Hardman's account of himself."

"You rely on the intuition? What the Americans call 'the hunch'?" asked Dr. Constantine.

"Not at all. I regard the probabilities. Hardman is travelling with a false passport—that will at once make him an object of suspicion. The first thing that the police will do when they do arrive upon the scene is to detain Hardman and cable as to whether his account of himself is true. In the case of many of the passengers, to establish their *bona fides* will be difficult; in most cases it will probably not be attempted, especially since there seems nothing in the way of suspicion attaching to them. But in Hardman's case it is simple. Either he is the person he represents himself to be, or he is not. Therefore I say that all will prove to be in order."

"You acquit him of suspicion?"

"Not at all. You misunderstand me. For all I know, any American detective might have his own private reasons for wishing to murder Ratchett. No, what I am saying is that I think we *can* accept Hardman's own account of *himself*. This story, then, that he tells of Ratchett's seeking him out and employing him is not unlikely, and is most probably—though not of course certainly—true. If we are going to accept it as true, we must see if there is any confirmation of it. We find it in rather an unlikely place—in the evidence of Hildegarde Schmidt. Her description of the man she saw in Wagon Lit uniform tallies exactly. Is there any further confirmation of these two stories? There is. There is the button that Mrs. Hubbard found in her compartment. And there is also another corroborating statement which you may not have noticed."

"What is that?"

"The fact that both Colonel Arbuthnot and Hector MacQueen mention that the conductor passed their carriage. They attached no importance to the fact, but, Messieurs, *Pierre Michel has declared that he did not leave his seat except on certain specified occasions*—none of which would take him down to the far end of the coach past the compartment in which Arbuthnot and MacQueen were sitting.

"Therefore this story, the story of a small dark man with a womanish voice dressed in Wagon Lit uniform, rests on the testimony, direct or indirect, of four witnesses."

"One small point," said Dr. Constantine. "If Hildegarde Schmidt's story is true, how is it that the real conductor did not mention having seen her when he came to answer Mrs. Hubbard's bell?"

"That is explained, I think. When he arrived to answer Mrs. Hubbard, the maid was in with her mistress. When she finally returned to her own compartment, the conductor was in with Mrs. Hubbard."

M. Bouc had been waiting with difficulty until they had finished.

"Yes, yes, my friend," he said impatiently to Poirot. "But whilst I admire your caution, your method of advancing a step at a time, I submit that you have not yet touched the point at issue. We are all agreed that this person exists. The point is, *where did he go*?"

Poirot shook his head reprovingly.

"You are in error. You are inclined to put the cart before the horse. Before I ask myself, *'Where did this man vanish to?'* I ask myself, *'Did such a man really exist?'* Because, you see, if the man were an invention—a fabrication—how much easier to make him disappear! So I try to establish first that there really *is* such a flesh-and-blood person."

"And having arrived at the fact that there is—*eh bien*, where is he now?"

"There are only two answers to that, *mon cher*. Either he is still hidden on the train in a place of such extraordinary ingenuity that we cannot even think of it; or else he is, as one might say, *two persons*. That is, he is both himself—the man feared by M. Ratchett—and a passenger on the train so well disguised that M. Ratchett did not recognise him."

"It is an idea, that," said M. Bouc, his face lighting up. Then it clouded over again. "But there is one objection—"

Poirot took the words out of his mouth.

"The height of the man. It is that you would say? With the exception of Mr. Ratchett's valet, all the passengers are big men—the Italian, Colonel Arbuthnot, Hector MacQueen, Count Andrenyi. Well, that leaves us the valet—not a very likely supposition. But there is another possibility. Remember the 'womanish' voice. That gives us a choice of alternatives. The man may be disguised as a woman, or, alternatively, he may actually *be* a woman. A tall woman dressed in men's clothes would look small."

"But surely Ratchett would have known—"

"Perhaps he *did* know. Perhaps, already, this woman had attempted his life, wearing a man's clothes the better to accomplish her purpose. Ratchett may have guessed that she would use the same trick again, so he tells Hardman to look for a man. But he mentions, however, a womanish voice."

"It is a possibility," said M. Bouc. "But—"

"Listen, my friend, I think that I should now tell you of certain inconsistencies noticed by Dr. Constantine."

He retailed at length the conclusions that he and the doctor had arrived at together from the nature of the dead man's wounds. M. Bouc groaned and held his head again.

"I know," said Poirot sympathetically. "I know exactly how you feel. The head spins, does it not?"

"The whole thing is a fantasy!" cried M. Bouc.

"Exactly. It is absurd—improbable—it cannot be. So I myself have said. And yet, my friend, *there it is*! One cannot escape from the facts."

"It is madness!"

"Is it not? It is so mad, my friend, that sometimes I am haunted by the sensation that really it must be very simple. . . . But that is only one of my 'little ideas'!"

"Two murderers," groaned M. Bouc. "And on the Orient Express—"

The thought almost made him weep.

"And now let us make the fantasy more fantastic," said Poirot cheerfully. "Last night on the train, there are two mysterious strangers. There is the Wagon Lit attendant answering to the description given us by M. Hardman, and seen by Hildegarde Schmidt, Colonel Arbuthnot and M. Mac-Queen. There is also a woman in a red kimono—a tall slim woman, seen by Pierre Michel, Miss Debenham, M. MacQueen and myself (and smelt, I may say, by Colonel Arbuthnot!). Who was she? No one on the train admits to having a scarlet kimono. She, too, has vanished. Was she one and the same with the spurious Wagon Lit attendant? Or was she some quite distinct personality? Where are they, these two? And incidentally, where are the Wagon Lit uniform and the scarlet kimono?"

"Ah! that is something definite." M. Bouc sprang up eagerly. "We must search all the passengers' luggage. Yes, that will be something."

Poirot rose also. "I will make a prophecy," he said.

"You know where they are?"

"I have a little idea."

"Where, then?"

"You will find the scarlet kimono in the baggage of one of the men, and you will find the uniform of the Wagon Lit conductor in the baggage of Hildegarde Schmidt."

"Hildegarde Schmidt? You think—"

"Not what you are thinking. I will put it like this. If Hildegarde Schmidt is guilty, the uniform may be found in her baggage. But if she is innocent, it *certainly* will be."

"But how—" began M. Bouc and stopped. "What is this noise that approaches?" he cried. "It resembles a locomotive in motion."

The noise drew nearer. It consisted of shrill cries and protests in a woman's voice. The door at the end of the dining-car burst open. Mrs. Hubbard burst in.

"It's too horrible!" she cried. "It's just too horrible. In my sponge-bag. My sponge-bag! A great knife—all over blood!"

And suddenly toppling forward, she fainted heavily on M. Bouc's shoulder.

Chapter 14

The Evidence of the Weapon

With more vigour than chivalry, M. Bouc deposited the fainting lady with her head on the table. Dr. Constantine yelled for one of the restaurant attendants, who came at a run.

"Keep her head so," said the doctor. "If she revives give her a little cognac. You understand?"

Then he hurried off after the other two. His interest lay wholly in the crime—swooning middle-aged ladies did not interest him at all.

It is possible that Mrs. Hubbard revived rather more quickly by these methods than she might otherwise have done. A few minutes later she was sitting up, sipping cognac from a glass proffered by the attendant, and talking once more.

"I just can't tell you how terrible it was! I don't suppose anybody on this train can understand my feelings. I've always been very, very sensitive ever since I was a child. The mere sight of blood—*ugh*! Why, even now I get faint when I think about it!"

The attendant proffered the glass again. *"Encore un peu, Madame?"*

"D'you think I'd better? I'm a lifelong teetotaller. I never touch spirits or wine at any time. All my family are abstainers. Still, perhaps as this is only medicinal—"

She sipped once more.

In the meantime Poirot and M. Bouc, closely followed by Dr. Constantine, had hurried out of the restaurant car and along the corridor of the Stamboul coach towards Mrs. Hubbard's compartment.

Every traveller on the train seemed to be congregated outside the door. The conductor, a harassed look on his face, was keeping them back.

"Mais il n'y a rien à voir," he said, and repeated the sentiment in several other languages.

"Let me pass if you please," said M. Bouc.

Squeezing his rotundity past the obstructing passengers he entered the compartment, Poirot close behind him.

"I am glad you have come, Monsieur," said the conductor with a sigh of relief. "Everyone has been trying to enter. The American lady—such screams as she gave—*ma foi*, I thought she too had been murdered! I came at a run, and there she was screaming like a mad woman; and she cried out that she must fetch you, and she departed screeching at the top of her voice and telling everybody whose carriage she passed what had occurred."

He added, with a gesture of the hand: "*It* is in there, Monsieur. I have not touched it."

Hanging on the handle of the door that gave access to the next compartment was a large-checked rubber sponge-bag. Below it on the floor, just where it had fallen from Mrs. Hubbard's hand, was a straight-bladed dagger—a cheap affair, sham Oriental with an embossed hilt and a tapering blade. The blade was stained with patches of what looked like rust.

Poirot picked it up delicately.

"Yes," he murmured. "There is no mistake. Here is our missing weapon all right—eh, doctor?"

The doctor examined it.

"You need not be so careful," said Poirot. "There will be no fingerprints on it save those of Mrs. Hubbard."

Constantine's examination did not take long.

"It is the weapon all right," he said. "It would account for any of the wounds."

"I implore you, my friend, do not say that!"

The doctor looked astonished.

"Already we are heavily overburdened by coincidence. Two people decided to stab M. Ratchett last night. It is too much of a good thing that both of them should select the same weapon."

"As to that, the coincidence is not perhaps so great as it seems," said the doctor. "Thousands of these sham Eastern daggers are made and shipped to the bazaars of Constantinople."

"You console me a little, but only a little," said Poirot.

He looked thoughtfully at the door in front of him, then, lifting off the sponge-bag, he tried the handle. The door did not budge. About a foot above the handle was the door bolt. Poirot drew it back and tried again, but still the door remained fast.

"We locked it from the other side, you remember," said the doctor.

"That is true," said Poirot absently. He seemed to be thinking about something else. His brow was furrowed as though in perplexity.

"It agrees, does it not?" said M. Bouc. "The man passes through this carriage. As he shuts the communicating door behind him he feels the sponge-bag. A thought comes to him and he quickly slips the bloodstained knife inside. Then, all unwitting that he has awakened Mrs. Hubbard, he slips out through the other door into the corridor."

"As you say," murmured Poirot. "That is how it must have happened." But the puzzled look did not leave his face.

"But what is it?" demanded M. Bouc. "There is something, is there not, that does not satisfy you?"

Poirot darted a quick look at him.

"The same point does not strike you? No, evidently not. Well, it is a small matter."

The conductor looked into the carriage. "The American lady is coming back."

Dr. Constantine looked rather guilty. He had, he felt, treated Mrs. Hubbard rather cavalierly. But she had no reproaches for him. Her energies were concentrated on another matter.

"I'm going to say one thing right out," she said breathlessly as she arrived in the doorway. "I'm not going on any longer in this compartment! Why, I wouldn't sleep in it tonight if you paid me a million dollars."

"But, Madame—"

"I know what you are going to say, and I'm telling you right now that I won't do any such thing! Why, I'd rather sit up all night in the corridor." She began to cry. "Oh, if my daughter could only know—if she could see me now, why—"

Poirot interrupted firmly.

"You misunderstand, Madame. Your demand is most reasonable. Your baggage shall be changed at once to another compartment."

Mrs. Hubbard lowered her handkerchief. "Is that so? Oh! I feel better right away. But surely it's all full, unless one of the gentlemen—"

M. Bouc spoke.

"Your baggage, Madame, shall be moved out of this coach altogether. You shall have a compartment in the next coach, which was put on at Belgrade."

"Why, that's splendid. I'm not an extra nervous woman, but to sleep in that compartment next door to a dead man!" She shivered. "It would drive me plumb crazy."

"Michel," called M. Bouc. "Move this baggage into a vacant compartment in the Athens-Paris coach."

"Yes, Monsieur. The same one as this—the No. 3?"

"No," said Poirot before his friend could reply. "I think it would be better for Madame to have a different number altogether. The No. 12, for instance."

"*Bien, Monsieur.*"

The conductor seized the luggage. Mrs. Hubbard turned gratefully to Poirot.

"That's very kind and delicate of you. I appreciate it, I assure you."

"Do not mention it, Madame. We will come with you and see you comfortably installed."

Mrs. Hubbard was escorted by the three

men to her new home. She looked round her happily. "This is fine."

"It suits you, Madame? It is, you see, exactly like the compartment you have left."

"That's so—only it faces the other way. But that doesn't matter, for these trains go first one way and then the other. I said to my daughter, 'I want a carriage facing the engine,' and she said, 'Why, Mamma, that'll be no good to you, for if you go to sleep one way, when you wake up, the train's going the other!' And it was quite true what she said. Why, last evening we went into Belgrade one way and out the other."

"At any rate, Madame, you are quite happy and contented now?"

"Well, no, I wouldn't say that. Here we are stuck in a snowdrift and nobody doing anything about it, and my boat sailing the day after to-morrow."

"Madame," said M. Bouc, "we are all in the same case—every one of us."

"Well, that's true," admitted Mrs. Hubbard. "But nobody else has had a murderer walking right through her compartment in the middle of the night."

"What still puzzles me, Madame," said Poirot, "is how the man got into your compartment if the communicating door was bolted as you say. You are sure that it *was* bolted?"

"Why, the Swedish lady tried it before my eyes."

"Let us just reconstruct that little scene. You were lying in your bunk—so—and you could not see for yourself, you say?"

"No, because of the sponge-bag. Oh! my, I shall have to get a new sponge-bag. It makes me feel sick at my stomach to look at this one."

Poirot picked up the sponge-bag and hung it on the handle of the communicating door into the next carriage.

"*Précisément*. I see," he said. "The bolt is just underneath the handle—the sponge-bag masks it. You could not see from where you were lying whether the bolt was turned or not."

"Why, that's just what I've been telling you!"

"And the Swedish lady, Miss Ohlsson, stood so, between you and the door. She tried it and told you it was bolted."

"That's so."

"All the same, Madame, she may have made an error. You see what I mean." Poirot seemed anxious to explain. "The bolt is just a projection of metal—so. When it is turned to the right, the door is locked. When it is left straight, the door is unlocked. Possibly she merely tried the door, and as it was locked on the other side she may have assumed that it was locked on your side."

"Well, I guess that would be rather stupid of her."

"Madame, the most kind, the most amiable, are not always the cleverest."

"That's so, of course."

"By the way, Madame, did you travel out to Smyrna this way?"

"No. I sailed right to Stamboul, and a friend of my daughter's, Mr. Johnson (a perfectly lovely man, I'd like to have you know him), met me and showed me all round Stamboul. But it was a very disappointing city—all tumbling down; and as for those mosques, and putting on those great shuffling things over your shoes—where was I?"

"You were saying that Mr. Johnson met you."

"That's so, and he saw me on board a French Messageries boat for Smyrna, and my daughter's husband was waiting right on the quay. What he'll say when he hears about all this! My daughter said this would be just the safest, easiest way imaginable. 'You just sit in your carriage,' she said, 'and you land right in Parrus, and there the American Express will meet you.' And, oh, dear, what am I to do about cancelling my steamship passage? I ought to let them know. I can't possibly make it now. This is just too terrible—"

Mrs. Hubbard showed signs of tears once more.

Poirot, who had been fidgeting slightly, seized his opportunity.

"You have had a shock, Madame. The restaurant attendant shall be instructed to bring you along some tea and some biscuits."

"I don't know that I'm so set on tea," said Mrs. Hubbard tearfully. "That's more an English habit."

"Coffee, then, Madame. You need some stimulant."

"That cognac's made my head feel mighty funny. I think I would like some coffee."

"Excellent. You must revive your forces."

"My, what a funny expression!"

"But first, Madame, a little matter of routine. You permit that I make a search of your baggage?"

"What for?"

"We are about to commence a search of all the passengers' luggage. I do not want to remind you of an unpleasant experience, but your sponge-bag—remember."

"Mercy! Perhaps you'd better! I just couldn't bear to get any more surprises of that kind."

The examination was quickly over. Mrs. Hubbard was travelling with the minimum of luggage—a hatbox, a cheap suitcase, and a well-burdened travelling bag. The contents of all three were simple and straightforward, and the examination would not have taken more than a couple of minutes had not Mrs. Hubbard delayed matters by insisting on due attention being paid to photographs of "my daughter" and of two rather ugly children—"my daughter's children. Aren't they cunning?"

Chapter 15

The Evidence of the Passengers' Luggage

Having delivered himself of various polite insincerities, and having told Mrs. Hubbard that he would order coffee to be brought to her, Poirot was able to take his leave accompanied by his two friends.

"Well, we have made a start and drawn a blank," observed M. Bouc. "Whom shall we tackle next?"

"It would be simplest, I think, just to proceed along the train, carriage by carriage. That means that we start with No. 16—the amiable Mr. Hardman."

Mr. Hardman, who was smoking a cigar, welcomed them affably.

"Come right in, gentlemen. That is, if it's humanly possible. It's just a mite cramped in here for a party."

M. Bouc explained the object of their visit, and the big detective nodded comprehendingly.

"That's O.K. To tell the truth I've been wondering you didn't get down to it sooner. Here are my keys, gentlemen, and if you like to search my pockets too, why, you're welcome. Shall I reach the grips down for you?"

"The conductor will do that. Michel!"

The contents of Mr. Hardman's two "grips" were soon examined and passed. They contained, perhaps, an undue proportion of spirituous liquor. Mr. Hardman winked.

"It's not often they search your grips at the frontiers—not if you fix the conductor. I handed out a wad of Turkish notes right away, and there's been no trouble so far."

"And at Paris?"

Mr. Hardman winked again. "By the time I get to Paris," he said, "what's left over of this little lot will go into a bottle labelled hairwash."

"You are not a believer in Prohibition, Monsieur Hardman," said M. Bouc with a smile.

"Well," said Hardman, "I can't say Prohibition has ever worried me any."

"Ah!" said M. Bouc. "The speakeasy." He pronounced the word with care, savouring it. "Your American terms are so quaint, so expressive," he said.

"Me, I would much like to go to America," said Poirot.

"You'd learn a few go-ahead methods over there," said Hardman. "Europe needs waking up. She's half asleep."

"It is true that America is the country of progress," agreed Poirot. "There is much that I admire about Americans. Only—I am perhaps old-fashioned—but me, I find the American women less charming than my own country-women. The French or the Belgian girl, coquettish, charming—I think there is no one to touch her."

Hardman turned away to peer out at the snow for a minute.

"Perhaps you're right, M. Poirot," he said. "But I guess every nation likes its own girls best." He blinked as though the snow hurt his eyes.

"Kind of dazzling, isn't it?" he remarked. "Say, gentlemen, this business is getting on my nerves. Murder and the snow and all.

And nothing *doing*. Just hanging about and killing time. I'd like to get busy after someone or something."

"The true Western spirit of hustle," said Poirot with a smile.

The conductor replaced the bags and they moved on to the next compartment. Colonel Arbuthnot was sitting in a corner smoking a pipe and reading a magazine.

Poirot explained their errand. The Colonel made no demur. He had two heavy leather suitcases.

"The rest of my kit has gone by long sea," he explained.

Like most Army men the Colonel was a neat packer. The examination of his baggage took only a few minutes. Poirot noted a packet of pipe cleaners.

"You always use the same kind?" he asked.

"Usually. If I can get 'em."

"Ah!" Poirot nodded. These pipe cleaners corresponded exactly with the one he had found on the floor of the dead man's compartment.

Dr. Constantine remarked as much when they were out in the corridor again.

"Tout de même," murmured Poirot, "I can

hardly believe it. It is not *dans son caractére*, and when you have said that, you have said everything."

The door of the next compartment was closed. It was that occupied by Princess Dragomiroff. They knocked on the door and the Princess's deep voice called *"Entrez!"*

M. Bouc was spokesman. He was very deferential and polite as he explained their errand.

The Princess listened to him in silence, her small toadlike face quite impassive.

"If it is necessary, Messieurs," she said quietly when he had finished, "that is all there is to it. My maid has the keys. She will attend to it with you."

"Does your maid always carry your keys, Madame?" asked Poirot.

"Certainly, Monsieur."

"And if, during the night at one of the frontiers, the customs officials should require a piece of luggage to be opened?"

The old lady shrugged her shoulders. "It is very unlikely. But in such a case, the conductor would fetch her."

"You trust her, then, implicitly, Madame?"

"I have told you so already," said the

Princess quietly. "I do not employ people whom I do not trust."

"Yes," said Poirot thoughtfully. "Trust is indeed something in these days. It is perhaps better to have a homely woman whom one can trust than a more *chic* maid—for example, some smart Parisienne."

He saw the dark intelligent eyes come slowly round and fasten themselves upon his face. "What exactly are you implying, M. Poirot?"

"Nothing, Madame. I? Nothing."

"But yes. You think, do you not, that I should have a smart Frenchwoman to attend to my toilet?"

"It would be perhaps more usual, Madame." She shook her head. "Schmidt is devoted to me." Her voice dwelt lingeringly on the words. "Devotion—*c'est impayable*."

The German woman had arrived with the keys. The Princess spoke to her in her own language, telling her to open the valises and help the gentlemen in their search. She herself remained in the corridor looking out at the snow, and Poirot remained with her, leaving M. Bouc to the task of searching the luggage.

She regarded him with a grim smile.

"Well, Monsieur, do you not wish to see what my valises contain?"

He shook his head. "Madame, it is a formality, that is all."

"Are you so sure?"

"In your case, yes."

"And yet I knew and loved Sonia Armstrong. What do you think, then? That I would not soil my hands with killing such *canaille* as that man Cassetti? Well, perhaps you are right."

She was silent a minute or two. Then she said:

"With such a man as that, do you know what I should have liked to do? I should have liked to call to my servants: 'Flog this man to death and fling him out on the rubbish heap!' That is the way things were done when I was young, Monsieur."

Still he did not speak, just listened attentively.

She looked at him with a sudden impetuosity. "You do not say anything, M. Poirot. What is it that you are thinking, I wonder?"

He looked at her with a very direct glance. "I think, Madame, that your strength is in your will—not in your arm."

She glanced down at her thin, black-clad

arms ending in those claw-like yellow hands with the rings on the fingers.

"It is true," she said. "I have no strength in these—none. I do not know whether I am sorry or glad."

Then she turned abruptly back towards her carriage where the maid was busily packing up the cases.

The Princess cut short M. Bouc's apologies.

"There is no need for you to apologise, Monsieur," she said. "A murder has been committed. Certain actions have to be performed. That is all there is to it."

"*Vous êtes bien aimable, Madame.*"

She inclined her head slightly as they departed.

The doors of the next two carriages were shut. M. Bouc paused and scratched his head.

"*Diable!*" he said. "This may be awkward. These are diplomatic passports. Their luggage is exempt."

"From customs examination, yes. But a murder is different."

"I know. All the same—we do not want to have complications."

"Do not distress yourself, my friend. The

Count and Countess will be reasonable. See how amiable Princess Dragomiroff was about it."

"She is truly *grande dame*. These two are also of the same position, but the Count impressed me as a man of somewhat truculent disposition. He was not pleased when you insisted on questioning his wife. And this will annoy him still further. Suppose—eh?—we omit them. After all, they can have nothing to do with the matter. Why should I stir up needless trouble for myself?"

"I do not agree with you," said Poirot. "I feel sure that Count Andrenyi will be reasonable. At any rate let us make the attempt."

And before M. Bouc could reply, he rapped sharply on the door of No. 13.

A voice from within cried, *"Entrez!"*

The Count was sitting in the corner near the door reading a newspaper. The Countess was curled up in the opposite corner near the window. There was a pillow behind her head and she seemed to have been asleep.

"Pardon, Monsieur le Comte," began Poirot. "Pray forgive this intrusion. It is that we are making a search of all the baggage on the train. In most cases a mere formality.

But it has to be done. M. Bouc suggests that, as you have a diplomatic passport, you might reasonably claim to be exempt from such a search."

The Count considered for a moment.

"Thank you," he said. "But I do not think that I care to have an exception made in my case. I should prefer that our baggage should be examined like that of the other passengers."

He turned to his wife. "You do not object, I hope, Elena?"

"Not at all," said the Countess without hesitation.

A rapid and somewhat perfunctory search followed. Poirot seemed to be trying to mask an embarrassment by making various small pointless remarks, such as:

"Here is a label all wet on your suitcase, Madame," as he lifted down a blue morocco case with initials on it and a coronet.

The Countess did not reply to this observation. She seemed, indeed, rather bored by the whole proceeding, remaining curled up in her corner and staring dreamily out through the window whilst the men searched her luggage in the compartment next door.

Poirot finished his search by opening the little cupboard above the washbasin and taking a rapid glance at its contents—a sponge, face cream, powder and a small bottle labelled TRIONAL.

Then with polite remarks on either side, the search party withdrew.

Mrs. Hubbard's compartment, that of the dead man, and Poirot's own came next.

They now came to the second-class carriages. The first one, Nos. 10 and 11, was occupied by Mary Debenham, who was reading a book, and Greta Ohlsson, who was fast asleep but woke with a start at their entrance.

Poirot repeated his formula. The Swedish lady seemed agitated, Mary Debenham calmly indifferent. He addressed himself to the Swedish lady.

"If you permit, Mademoiselle, we will examine your baggage first, and then perhaps you would be so good as to see how the American lady is getting on. We have moved her into one of the carriages in the next coach, but she is still very much upset as the result of her discovery. I have ordered coffee to be sent to her, but I think she is of those to whom someone to talk to is a necessity of the first order."

The good lady was instantly sympathetic. She would go immediately. It must have been indeed a terrible shock to the nerves, and already the poor lady was upset by the journey and leaving her daughter. Ah, yes, certainly she would go at once—her case was not locked—and she would take with her some sal ammoniac.

She bustled off. Her possessions were soon examined. They were meagre in the extreme. She had evidently not yet noticed the missing wires from the hatbox.

Miss Debenham had put her book down. She was watching Poirot. When he asked her, she handed over her keys. Then, as he lifted down a case and opened it, she said:

"Why did you send her away, M. Poirot?"

"I, Mademoiselle? Why, to minister to the American lady."

"An excellent pretext—but a pretext all the same."

"I don't understand you, Mademoiselle."

"I think you understand me very well." She smiled. "You wanted to get me alone. Wasn't that it?"

"You are putting words into my mouth, Mademoiselle."

"And ideas into your head? No, I don't think so. The ideas are already there. That is right, isn't it?"

"Mademoiselle, we have a proverb—"

"*Qui s'excuse s'accuse*—is that what you were going to say? You must give me the credit for a certain amount of observation and common sense. For some reason or other you have got it into your head that I know something about this sordid business—this murder of a man I never saw before."

"You are imagining things, Mademoiselle."

"No, I am not imagining things at all. But it seems to me that a lot of time is wasted by not speaking the truth—by beating about the bush instead of coming straight out with things."

"And you do not like the waste of time. No, you like to come straight to the point. You like the direct method. *Eh bien*, I will give it to you, the direct method. I will ask you the meaning of certain words that I overheard on the journey from Syria. I had got out of the train to do what the English call 'stretch the legs' at the station of Konya. Your voice and the Colonel's, Mademoiselle, they came to me out of the night. You said to him, *'Not now. Not now. When it's all over. When it's behind us.'* What did you mean by those words, Mademoiselle?"

She asked very quietly, "Do you think I meant—murder?"

"It is I who am asking you, Mademoiselle."

She sighed—was lost a minute in thought. Then, as though rousing herself, she said:

"Those words had a meaning, Monsieur, but not one that I can tell you. I can only give you my solemn word of honour that I had never set eyes on this man Ratchett in my life until I saw him on this train."

"And—you refuse to explain those words?"

"Yes, if you like to put it that way—I refuse. They had to do with—with a task I had undertaken."

"A task that is now ended?"

"What do you mean?"

"It is ended, is it not?"

"Why should you think so?"

"Listen, Mademoiselle, I will recall to you

another incident. There was a delay to the train on the day we were to reach Stamboul. You were very agitated, Mademoiselle. You, so calm, so self-controlled. You lost that calm."

"I did not want to miss my connection."

"So you said. But, Mademoiselle, the Orient Express leaves Stamboul every day of the week. Even if you had missed the connection it would only have been a matter of twenty-four hours' delay."

Miss Debenham for the first time showed signs of losing her temper.

"You do not seem to realise that one may have friends awaiting one's arrival in London, and that a day's delay upsets arrangements and causes a lot of annoyance."

"Ah, it is like that? There are friends awaiting your arrival? You do not want to cause them inconvenience?"

"Naturally."

"And yet—it is curious—"

"What is curious?"

"On this train—again we have a delay. And this time a more serious delay, since there is no possibility of sending a telegram to your friends or of getting them on the long—the long—"

"Long distance? The telephone, you mean."

"Ah, yes, the portmanteau call, as you say in England."

Mary Debenham smiled a little in spite of herself. "Trunk call," she corrected. "Yes, as you say, it is extremely annoying not to be able to get any word through, either by telephone or by telegraph."

"And yet, Mademoiselle, *this* time your manner is quite different. You no longer betray the impatience. You are calm and philosophical."

Mary Debenham flushed and bit her lip. She no longer felt inclined to smile.

"You do not answer, Mademoiselle?"

"I am sorry. I did not know that there was anything to answer."

"Your change of attitude, Mademoiselle."

"Don't you think that you are making rather a fuss about nothing, M. Poirot?"

Poirot spread out his hands in an apologetic gesture.

"It is perhaps a fault with us detectives. We expect the behaviour to be always consistent. We do not allow for changes of mood."

Mary Debenham made no reply.

"You know Colonel Arbuthnot well, Mademoiselle?"

He fancied that she was relieved by the change of subject.

"I met him for the first time on this journey."

"Have you any reason to suspect that he may have known this man Ratchett?"

She shook her head decisively. "I am quite sure he didn't."

"Why are you sure?"

"By the way he spoke."

"And yet, Mademoiselle, we found a pipe-cleaner on the floor of the dead man's compartment. And Colonel Arbuthnot is the only man on the train who smokes a pipe."

He watched her narrowly, but she displayed neither surprise nor emotion, merely said:

"Nonsense. It's absurd. Colonel Arbuthnot is the last man in the world to be mixed up in a crime—especially a theatrical kind of crime like this."

It was so much what Poirot himself thought that he found himself on the point of agreeing with her. He said instead:

"I must remind you that you do not know him very well, Mademoiselle."

She shrugged her shoulders. "I know the type well enough."

He said very gently:

"You still refuse to tell me the meaning of those words: 'When it's behind us'?"

She replied coldly, "I have nothing more to say."

"It does not matter," said Hercule Poirot. "I shall find out."

He bowed and left the compartment, closing the door after him.

"Was that wise, my friend?" asked M. Bouc. "You have put her on her guard—and through her you have put the Colonel on his guard also."

"*Mon ami*, if you wish to catch a rabbit you put a ferret into the hole, and if the rabbit is there—he runs. That is all I have done."

They entered the compartment of Hildegarde Schmidt.

The woman was standing in readiness, her face respectful but unemotional.

Poirot took a quick glance through the contents of the small case on the seat. Then he motioned to the attendant to get down the bigger suitcase from the rack.

"The keys?" he said.

"It is not locked, Monsieur."

Poirot undid the hasps and lifted the lid.

"Aha!" he said, and turning to M. Bouc, "You remember what I said? Look here a little moment!"

On the top of the suitcase was a hastily rolled-up brown Wagon Lit uniform.

The stolidity of the German woman underwent a sudden change.

"*Ach!*" she cried. "That is not mine. I did not put it there. I have never looked in that case since we left Stamboul. Indeed, indeed, it is true!" She looked from one to another of the men pleadingly.

Poirot took her gently by the arm and soothed her.

"No, no, all is well. We believe you. Do not be agitated. I am sure you did not hide the uniform there as I am sure that you are a good cook. See. You *are* a good cook, are you not?"

Bewildered, the woman smiled in spite of herself. "Yes, indeed, all my ladies have said so. I—"

She stopped, her mouth open, looking frightened again.

"No, no," said Poirot. "I assure you all is well. See, I will tell you how this happened.

This man, the man you saw in Wagon Lit uniform, comes out of the dead man's compartment. He collides with you. That is bad luck for him. He has hoped that no one will see him. What to do next? He must get rid of his uniform. It is now not a safeguard, but a danger."

His glance went to M. Bouc and Dr. Constantine, who were listening attentively.

"There is the snow, you see. The snow which confuses all his plans. Where can he hide these clothes? All the compartments are full. No, he passes one whose door is open, showing it to be unoccupied. It must be the one belonging to the woman with whom he has just collided. He slips in, removes the uniform and jams it hurriedly into a suitcase on the rack. It may be some time before it is discovered."

"And then?" said M. Bouc.

"That we must discuss," said Poirot with a warning glance.

He held up the tunic. A button, the third down, was missing. Poirot slipped his hand into the pocket and took out a conductor's pass-key, used to unlock the doors of the compartments.

"Here is the explanation of how one man

was able to pass through locked doors," said M. Bouc. "Your questions to Mrs. Hubbard were unnecessary. Locked or not locked, the man could easily get through the communicating door. After all, if a Wagon Lit uniform, why not a Wagon Lit key?"

"Why not indeed?" returned Poirot.

"We might have known it, really. You remember that Michel said that the door into the corridor of Mrs. Hubbard's compartment was locked when he came in answer to her bell."

"That is so, Monsieur," said the conductor. "That is why I thought the lady must have been dreaming."

"But now it is easy," continued M. Bouc. "Doubtless he meant to relock the communicating door also, but perhaps he heard some movement from the bed and it startled him."

"We have now," said Poirot, "only to find the scarlet kimono."

"True. And these last two compartments are occupied by men."

"We will search all the same."

"Oh! assuredly. Besides, I remember what you said."

Hector MacQueen acquiesced willingly in the search.

"I'd just as soon you did," he said with a rueful smile. "I feel I'm definitely the most suspicious character on the train. You've only got to find a will in which the old man left me all his money, and that'll just about fix things."

M. Bouc bent a suspicious glance upon him.

"That's only my fun," added MacQueen hastily. "He'd never have left me a cent, really. I was just useful to him—languages and so on. You're likely to be out of luck, you know, if you don't speak anything but good American. I'm no linguist myself, but I know what I call Shopping and Hotel—snappy bits in French and German and Italian."

His voice was a little louder than usual. It was as though he were slightly uneasy over the search in spite of his expressed willingness.

Poirot emerged. "Nothing," he said. "Not even a compromising bequest!"

MacQueen sighed. "Well, that's a load off my mind," he said humorously.

They moved on to the last compartment.

The examination of the luggage of the big Italian and of the valet yielded no result.

The three men stood at the end of the coach looking at each other.

"What next?" said M. Bouc.

"We will go back to the dining-car," said Poirot. "We know now all that we can know. We have the evidence of the passengers, the evidence of their baggage, the evidence of our eyes. . . . We can expect no further help. It must be our part now to use our brains."

He felt in his pocket for his cigarette case. It was empty.

"I will join you in a moment," he said. "I shall need the cigarettes. This is a very difficult, a very curious, affair. Who wore that scarlet kimono? Where is it now? I wish I knew. There is something in this case— some factor—that escapes me! It is difficult because it has been *made* difficult. But we will discuss it. Pardon me a moment."

He went hurriedly along the corridor to his own compartment. He had, he knew, a further supply of cigarettes in one of his valises.

He got it down and snapped back the lock.

Then he sat back on his heels and stared.

Neatly folded on the top of the case was a thin scarlet silk kimono embroidered with dragons.

"So," he murmured. "It is like that. A defiance. Very well, I take it up."

Part 3

Hercule Poirot Sits Back and Thinks

Chapter 1

Which of Them?

M. Bouc and Dr. Constantine were talking together when Poirot entered the dining-car. M. Bouc was looking depressed.

"Le voilà," said the latter when he saw Poirot. Then he added, as his friend sat down, "If you solve this case, *mon cher*, I shall indeed believe in miracles!"

"It worries you, this case?"

"Naturally it worries me. I cannot make head or tail of it."

"I agree," said the doctor. He looked at Poirot with interest. "To be frank," he said, "I cannot see what you are going to do next."

"No?" said Poirot thoughtfully.

He took out his cigarette case and lit one of his tiny cigarettes. His eyes were dreamy.

"That, to me, is the interest of this case,"

he said. "We are cut off from all the normal routes of procedure. Are these people whose evidence we have taken speaking the truth, or lying? We have no means of finding out—except such means as we can devise ourselves. It is an exercise, this, of the brain."

"That is all very fine," said M. Bouc. "But what have you to go upon?"

"I told you just now. We have the evidence of the passengers and the evidence of our own eyes."

"Pretty evidence—that of the passengers! It told us just nothing at all."

Poirot shook his head.

"I do not agree, my friend. The evidence of the passengers gave us several points of interest."

"Indeed," said M. Bouc sceptically. "I did not observe it."

"That is because you did not listen."

"Well, tell me, what did I miss?"

"I will just take one instance—the first evidence we heard, that of the young Mac-Queen. He uttered, to my mind, one very significant phrase."

"About the letters?"

"No, not about the letters. As far as I can remember, his words were: *'We travelled about. Mr. Ratchett wanted to see the world. He was hampered by knowing no languages. I acted more as a courier than a secretary.' "*

He looked from the doctor's face to that of M. Bouc.

"What? You still do not see? That is inexcusable—for you had a second chance again just now when he said, *'You're likely to be out of luck if you don't speak anything but good American.' "*

"You mean—?" M. Bouc still looked puzzled.

"Ah, it is that you want it given to you in words of one syllable. Well, here it is! *M. Ratchett spoke no French.* Yet, when the conductor came in answer to his bell last night, it was a voice speaking in *French* that told him that it was a mistake and that he was not wanted. It was, moreover, a perfectly idiomatic phrase that was used, not one that a man knowing only a few words of French would have selected. *'Ce n'est rien. Je me suis trompé.' "*

"It is true," cried Constantine excitedly. "We should have seen that! I remember your laying stress on the words when you repeated them to us. Now I understand your reluctance to rely upon the evidence of the dented watch. Already, at twenty-three minutes to one, Ratchett was dead—"

"And it was his murderer speaking!" finished M. Bouc impressively.

Poirot raised a deprecating hand.

"Let us not go too fast. And do not let us assume more than we actually know. It is safe, I think, to say that at that time—twenty-three minutes to one—*some other person* was in Ratchett's compartment, and that that person either was French or could speak the French language fluently."

"You are very cautious, *mon vieux*."

"One should advance only a step at a time. We have no actual *evidence* that Ratchett was dead at that time."

"There is the cry that awakened you."

"Yes, that is true."

"In one way," said M. Bouc thoughtfully, "this discovery does not affect things very much. You heard someone moving about next door. That someone was not Ratchett, but the other man. Doubtless he is washing blood from his hands, clearing up after the crime, burning the incriminating letter. Then he waits till all is still, and, when he thinks it is safe and the coast is clear, he locks and chains Ratchett's door on the inside, unlocks the communicating door through into Mrs. Hubbard's compartment and slips out that way. In fact, it is exactly as we thought, *with the difference that Ratchett was killed about half an hour earlier* and the watch put on to a quarter past one to create an alibi."

"Not such a famous alibi," said Poirot. "The hands of the watch pointed to 1.15—the exact time when the intruder actually left the scene of the crime."

"True," said M. Bouc, a little confused. "What then does the watch convey to you?"

"If the hands were altered—I say *if*—then the time at which they were set *must* have a significance. The natural reaction would be to suspect anyone who had a reliable alibi for the time indicated—in this case, 1.15."

"Yes, yes," said the doctor. "That reasoning is good."

"We must also pay a little attention to the time the intruder *entered* the compartment. When had he an opportunity of doing so? Unless we are to assume the complicity of the real conductor, there was only one time when he could have done so—during the time the train stopped at Vincovci. After the train left Vincovci the conductor was sitting facing the corridor, and whereas any one of the passengers would pay little attention to a Wagon Lit attendant, the *one* person who *would* notice an impostor is the real conductor. But during the halt at Vincovci the conductor is out on the platform. The coast is clear."

"And by our former reasoning, it *must* be one of the passengers," said M. Bouc. "We come back to where we were. Which of them?"

Poirot smiled.

"I have made a list," he said. "If you like to see it, it will perhaps refresh your memory."

The doctor and M. Bouc pored over the list together. It was written out neatly in a methodical manner in the order in which the passengers had been interviewed.

Hector MacQueen—American subject, Berth No. 6, Second Class.

> *Motive:* Possibly arising out of association with dead man?
> *Alibi:* From midnight to A.M. (Midnight to 1.30 vouched for by Col. Arbuthnot, and 1.15 to 2 vouched for by conductor.)
> *Evidence against him:* None.
> *Suspicious circumstances:* None.

Conductor Pierre Michel—French subject.

Motive: None.

Alibi: From midnight to 2 A.M. (Seen by H. P. in corridor at same time as voice spoke from Ratchett's compartment at 12.37. From 1 A.M. to 1.16 vouched for by other two conductors.)

Evidence against him: None.

Suspicious circumstances: The Wagon Lit uniform found is a point in his favour since it seems to have been intended to throw suspicion on him.

Edward Masterman—English subject, Berth No. 4, Second Class.

Motive: Possibly arising out of connection with deceased, whose valet he was.

Alibi: From midnight to 2 A.M. (Vouched for by Antonio Foscarelli.)

Evidence against him or suspicious circumstances: None, except that he is the only man of the right height or size to have worn the Wagon Lit uniform. On the other hand, it is unlikely that he speaks French well.

Mrs. Hubbard—American subject, Berth No. 3, First Class.

Motive: None.

Alibi: From midnight to 2 A.M.—None.

Evidence against her or suspicious circumstances: Story of man in her compartment is substantiated by the evidence of Hardman and that of the woman Schmidt.

Greta Ohlsson—Swedish subject, Berth No. 10, Second Class.

Motive: None.

Alibi: From midnight to 2 A.M. (Vouched for by Mary Debenham.)

NOTE: Was last to see Ratchett alive.

Princess Dragomiroff—Naturalised French subject, Berth No. 14, First Class.

Motive: Was intimately acquainted with Armstrong family, and godmother to Sonia Armstrong.

Alibi: From midnight to 2 A.M. (Vouched for by conductor and maid.)

Evidence against her or suspicious circumstances: None.

Count Andrenyi—Hungarian subject, Diplomatic passport, Berth No. 13, First Class.

Motive: None.

Alibi: Midnight to 2 A.M. (Vouched for by conductor—this does not cover period from 1 to 1.15.)

Countess Andrenyi—As above, Berth 12.

Motive: None.

Alibi: Midnight to 2 A.M. Took trional and slept. (Vouched for by husband. Trional bottle in her cupboard.)

Colonel Arbuthnot—British subject, Berth No. 15, First Class.

Motive: None.

Alibi: Midnight to 2 A.M. Talked with MacQueen till 1.30. Went to own compartment and did not leave it. (Substantiated by MacQueen and conductor.)

Evidence against him or suspicious circumstances: Pipe cleaner.

Cyrus Hardman—American subject, Berth No. 16.

Motive: None known.

Alibi: Midnight to 2 A.M. Did not leave compartment. (Substantiated by conductor except for period 1 to 1.15.)
Evidence against him or suspicious circumstances: None.

Antonio Foscarelli—American subject (Italian by birth), Berth No. 5, Second Class.
Motive: None known.
Alibi: Midnight to 2 A.M. (Vouched for by Edward Masterman.)
Evidence against him or suspicious circumstances: None, except that weapon used might be said to suit his temperament (Vide M. Bouc.)

Mary Debenham—British subject, Berth No. 11, Second Class.
Motive: None.
Alibi: Midnight to 2 A.M. (Vouched for by Greta Ohlsson.)
Evidence against her or suspicious circumstances: Conversation overhead by H. P., and her refusal to explain it.

Hildegarde Schmidt—German subject, Berth No. 8, Second Class.

Motive: None.

Alibi: Midnight to 2 A.M. (Vouched for by conductor and her mistress.) Went to bed. Was aroused by conductor at 12.38 approx. and went to mistress.

NOTE:—The evidence of the passengers is supported by the statement of the conductor that no one entered or left Mr. Ratchett's compartment from midnight to 1 o'clock (when he himself went into the next coach) and from 1.15 to 2 o'clock.

"That document, you understand," said Poirot, "is a mere *précis* of the evidence we heard, arranged in that way for convenience."

With a grimace, M. Bouc handed it back. "It is not illuminating," he said.

"Perhaps you may find this more to your taste," said Poirot, with a slight smile as he handed him a second sheet of paper.

Chapter 2
Ten Questions

On the paper was written:

Things Needing Explanation
1. The handkerchief marked with the initial H. Whose is it?
2. The pipe-cleaner. Was it dropped by Colonel Arbuthnot? Or by someone else?
3. Who wore the scarlet kimono?
4. Who was the man or woman masquerading in Wagon Lit uniform?
5. Why do the hands of the watch point to 1.15?
6. Was the murder committed at that time?
7. Was it earlier?
8. Was it later?

9. Can we be sure that Ratchett was stabbed by more than one person?

10. What other explanation of his wounds can there be?

"Well, let us see what we can do," said M. Bouc, brightening a little at this challenge to his wits. "The handkerchief, to begin with. Let us by all means be orderly and methodical."

"Assuredly," said Poirot, nodding his head in a satisfied fashion.

M. Bouc continued somewhat didactically.

"The initial H is connected with three people—Mrs. Hubbard, Miss Debenham, whose second name is Hermione, and the maid, Hildegarde Schmidt."

"Ah! And of those three?"

"It is difficult to say. But I *think* I should vote for Miss Debenham. For all one knows she may be called by her second name and not her first. Also there is already some suspicion attaching to her. That conversation you overheard, *mon cher*, was certainly a little curious, and so is her refusal to explain it."

"As for me, I plump for the American,"

said Dr. Constantine. "It is a very expensive handkerchief, that; and Americans, as all the world knows, do not care what they pay."

"So you both eliminate the maid?" asked Poirot.

"Yes. As she herself said, it is the handkerchief of a member of the upper classes."

"And the second question—the pipe-cleaner. Did Colonel Arbuthnot drop it, or somebody else?"

"That is more difficult. The English, they do not stab. You are right there. I incline to the view that someone else dropped the pipe-cleaner—and did so to incriminate the long-legged Englishman."

"As you said, M. Poirot," put in the doctor, "*two* clues is too much carelessness. I agree with M. Bouc. The handkerchief was a genuine oversight—hence none of the women will admit that it is hers. The pipe-cleaner is a faked clue. In support of that theory, you notice that Colonel Arbuthnot shows no embarrassment and admits freely to smoking a pipe and using that type of cleaner."

"You reason well," said Poirot.

"Question No. 3—Who wore the scarlet

kimono?" went on M. Bouc. "As to that, I will confess I have not the slightest idea. Have you any views on the subject, Dr. Constantine?"

"None."

"Then we confess ourselves beaten there. The next question has, at any rate, possibilities. Who was the man or the woman masquerading in Wagon Lit uniform? Well, one can list with certainty a number of people that it could not have been. Hardman, Colonel Arbuthnot, Foscarelli, Count Andrenyi and Hector MacQueen are all too tall. Mrs. Hubbard, Hildegarde Schmidt and Greta Ohlsson are too broad. That leaves the valet, Miss Debenham, Princess Dragomiroff and Countess Andrenyi—and none of them sounds likely! Greta Ohlsson in one case, and Antonio Foscarelli in the other, both swear that Miss Debenham and the valet never left their compartments. Hildegarde Schmidt swears that the Princess was in hers, and Count Andrenyi has told us that his wife took a sleeping draught. Therefore it seems impossible that it can be anybody—which is absurd!"

"As our old friend Euclid says," murmured Poirot.

"It must be one of those four," said Dr. Constantine. "Unless it is someone from outside who has found a hiding-place—and that we agreed was impossible."

M. Bouc had passed on to the next question on the list.

"No. 5—Why do the hands of the broken watch point to 1.15? I can see two explanations of that. Either it was done by the murderer to establish an alibi, and afterwards, when he meant to leave the compartment, he was prevented by hearing people moving about; or else—wait—I have an idea coming—"

The other two waited respectfully while M. Bouc struggled in mental agony.

"I have it," he said at last. "It was *not* the Wagon Lit murderer who tampered with the watch! It was the person we have called the Second Murderer—the left-handed person—in other words the woman in the scarlet kimono. She arrives later and moves back the hands of the watch in order to make an alibi for herself."

"Bravo," said Dr. Constantine. "It is well imagined, that."

"In fact," said Poirot, "she stabbed him in the dark, not realizing that he was dead already, but somehow deduced that he had a watch in his pyjama pocket, took it out, put back the hands blindly, and gave it the requisite dent."

M. Bouc looked at him coldly. "Have you anything better to suggest, yourself?" he asked.

"At the moment—no," admitted Poirot. "All the same," he went on, "I do not think you have either of you appreciated the most interesting point about that watch."

"Does question No. 6 deal with it?" asked the doctor. "To that question—Was the murder committed at that time, 1.15?—I answer *No*."

"I agree," said M. Bouc. " 'Was it earlier?' is the next question. I say—Yes! You, too, doctor?"

The doctor nodded. "Yes, but the question 'Was it later?' can also be answered in the affirmative. I agree with your theory, M. Bouc, and so, I think, does M. Poirot, although he does not wish to commit himself. The First Murderer came earlier than 1.15, but the Second Murderer came *after* 1.15. And as regards the question of left-handedness, ought we not to take steps to ascertain which of the passengers is left-handed?"

"I have not completely neglected that point," said Poirot. "You may have noticed that I made each passenger write either a signature or an address. That is not conclusive, because some people do certain actions with the right hand and others with the left. Some write right-handed, but play golf left-handed. Still, it is something. Every person questioned took the pen in his or her right hand—with the exception of Princess Dragomiroff, who refused to write."

"Princess Dragomiroff—impossible," said M. Bouc.

"I doubt if she would have had the strength to inflict that left-handed blow," said Dr. Constantine dubiously. "That particular wound had been inflicted with considerable force."

"More force than a woman could use?"

"No, I would not say that. But I think more force than an elderly woman could display, and Princess Dragomiroff's physique is particularly frail."

"It might be a question of the influence of mind over body," said Poirot. "Princess Dragomiroff has great personality and immense willpower. But let us pass from that for the moment."

"To questions Nos. 9 and 10? Can we be sure that Ratchett was stabbed by more than one person, and what other explanation of the wounds can there be? In my opinion, medically speaking, there can be *no other* explanation of those wounds. To suggest that one man struck first feebly and then with violence, first with the right hand and then with the left, and after an interval of perhaps half an hour inflicted fresh wounds on a dead body—well, it does not make sense."

"No," said Poirot. "It does not make sense. And you think that two murderers do make sense?"

"As you yourself have said, what other explanation can there be?"

Poirot stared straight ahead of him. "That is what I ask myself," he said. "That is what I never cease to ask myself."

He leaned back in his seat.

"From now on, it is all here." He tapped himself on the forehead. "We have thrashed it all out. The facts are all in front of us—neatly arranged with order and method. The passengers have sat here, one by one, giving their evidence. We know all that can be known—*from outside.* . . ."

He gave M. Bouc an affectionate smile.

"It has been a little joke between us, has it not—this business of sitting back and *thinking* out the truth? Well, I am about to put my theory into practice—here before your eyes. You two must do the same. Let us all three close our eyes and *think.* . . .

"One or more of those passengers killed Ratchett. *Which of them?*"

Chapter 3
Certain Suggestive Points

It was quite a quarter of an hour before anyone spoke. M. Bouc and Dr. Constantine had started by trying to obey Poirot's instructions. They had endeavored to see through a maze of conflicting particulars to a clear and outstanding solution.

M. Bouc's thoughts had run something as follows:

"Assuredly I must think. But as far as that goes I have already thought. . . . Poirot obviously thinks that this English girl is mixed up in the matter. I cannot help feeling that that is most unlikely. . . . The English are extremely cold. Probably it is because they have no figures. . . . But that is not the point. It seems that the Italian could not have done it—a pity. I suppose the English valet is not lying when he said the other never left the compartment? But why should he? It is not easy to bribe the English; they are so unapproachable. The whole thing is most unfortunate. I wonder when we shall get out of this. There must be *some* rescue work in progress. They are so slow in these countries . . . it is hours before anyone thinks of doing anything. And the police of these countries, they will be most trying to deal with—puffed up with importance, touchy, on their dignity. They will make a grand affair of all this. It is not often that such a chance comes their way. It will be in all the newspapers. . . ."

And from there on, M. Bouc's thoughts went along a well-worn course which they had already traversed some hundred times.

Dr. Constantine's thoughts ran thus:

"He is queer, this little man. A genius? Or a crank? Will he solve this mystery? Impossible—I can see no way out of it. It is all too confusing. . . . Everyone is lying, perhaps. . . . But even then, that does not help one. If they are all lying, it is just as confusing as if they were speaking the truth. Odd about those wounds. I cannot understand it. . . . It would be easier to understand if he had been shot—after all, the term 'gunman' must mean that they shoot with a gun. A curious country, America. I should like to go there. It is so progressive. When I get home I must get hold of Demetrius Zagone—he has been to America, he has all the modern ideas. . . . I wonder what Zia is doing at this moment. If my wife ever finds out—"

His thoughts went on to entirely private matters. . . .

Hercule Poirot sat very still.

One might have thought he was asleep.

And then, suddenly, after a quarter of an hour's complete immobility his eyebrows began to move slowly up his forehead. A little sigh escaped him. He murmured beneath his breath.

"But after all, why not? And if so—why, if so, that would explain everything."

His eyes opened. They were green like a cat's. He said softly: "*Eh bien*. I have thought. And you?"

Lost in their reflections, both men started violently.

"I have thought also," said M. Bouc, just a shade guiltily. "But I have arrived at no conclusion. The elucidation of crime is your *métier*, not mine, my friend."

"I, too, have reflected with great earnestness," said the doctor, unblushingly recalling his thoughts from certain pornographic details. "I have thought of many possible theories, but not one that really satisfies me."

Poirot nodded amiably. His nod seemed to say:

"Quite right. That is the proper thing to say. You have given me the cue I expected."

He sat very upright, threw out his chest, caressed his moustaches and spoke in the manner of a practised speaker addressing a public meeting.

"My friends, I have reviewed the facts in my mind, and have also gone over to myself the evidence of the passengers—with this result: I see, nebulously as yet, a certain explanation that would cover the facts as we know them. It is a very curious explanation, and I cannot be sure as yet that it is the true one. To find out definitely I shall have to make certain experiments.

"I would like first to mention certain points which appear to me suggestive. Let us start with a remark made to me by M. Bouc in this very place on the occasion of our first lunch together on the train. He commented on the fact that we were surrounded by people of all classes, of all ages, of all nationalities. That is a fact somewhat rare at this time of year. The Athens-Paris and the Bucharest-Paris coaches, for instance, are almost empty. Remember also, the passenger who failed to turn up. He is, I think, significant. Then there are some minor points that strike me as suggestive—for instance, the position of Mrs. Hubbard's sponge-bag, the name of Mrs. Armstrong's mother, the detective methods of M. Hardman, the suggestion of M. MacQueen that Ratchett himself destroyed the charred note we found, Princess Dragomiroff's Christian name, and a grease spot on a Hungarian passport."

The two men stared at him.

"Do they suggest anything to you, those points?" asked Poirot.

"Not a thing," said M. Bouc frankly.

"And M. *le docteur*?"

"I do not understand in the least what you are talking of."

M. Bouc, meanwhile, seizing upon the one tangible thing his friend had mentioned, was sorting through the passports. With a grunt he picked up that of Count and Countess Andrenyi and opened it.

"Is this what you mean? This dirty mark?"

"Yes. It is a fairly fresh grease spot. You notice where it occurs?"

"At the beginning of the description of the Count's wife—her Christian name, to be exact. But I confess that I still do not see the point."

"I am going to approach it from another angle. Let us go back to the handkerchief found at the scene of the crime. As we stated not long ago, three people are associated with the letter H: Mrs. Hubbard, Miss Debenham and the maid, Hildegarde Schmidt. Now let us regard that handkerchief from another point of view. It is, my friends, an extremely expensive handkerchief—an *objet de luxe*, handmade, embroidered in Paris. Which of the passengers, apart from the initial, was likely to own such a handkerchief? Not Mrs. Hubbard, a worthy woman with no pretensions to reckless extravagance in dress. Not Miss Debenham—that class of Englishwoman has a dainty linen handkerchief, not an expensive wisp of cambric costing perhaps two hundred francs. And certainly not the maid. But there *are* two women on the train who would be likely to own such a handkerchief. Let us see if we can connect them in any way with the letter H. The two women I refer to are Princess Dragomiroff—"

"Whose Christian name is Natalia," put in M. Bouc ironically.

"Exactly. And her Christian name, as I said just now, is decidedly suggestive. The other woman is Countess Andrenyi. And at once something strikes us—"

"*You!*"

"*Me*, then. Her Christian name on her passport is disfigured by a blob of grease. Just an accident, anyone would say. But consider that Christian name. Elena. Suppose that, instead of Elena, it were *Helena*. That capital H could be turned into a capital E and then run over the small e next to it quite easily—and then a spot of grease dropped to cover up the alteration."

"Helena!" cried M. Bouc. "It is an idea, that."

"Certainly it is an idea! I look about for any confirmation, however slight, of my idea—and I find it. One of the luggage labels on the Countess's baggage is slightly damp. It is one that happens to run over the first initial on top of the case. That label has been soaked off and put on again in a different place."

"You begin to convince me," said M. Bouc. "But the Countess Andrenyi— surely—"

"Ah, now, *mon vieux*, you must turn yourself round and approach an entirely different angle of the case. How was this murder intended to appear to everybody? Do not forget that the snow has upset all the murderer's original plans. Let us imagine, for a little minute, that there is no snow, that the train proceeded on its normal course. What, then, would have happened?

"The murder, let us say, would still have been discovered in all probability at the Italian frontier early this morning. Much of the same evidence would have been given to the Italian police. The threatening letters would have been produced by M. Mac-Queen; M. Hardman would have told his story; Mrs. Hubbard would have been eager to tell how a man passed through her compartment; the button would have been found. I imagine that two things only would have been different. The man would have passed through Mrs. Hubbard's compartment just before one o'clock—and the Wagon Lit uniform would have been found cast off in one of the toilets."

"You mean?"

"I mean that the murder was *planned to look like an outside job*. It would have been presumed that the assassin had left the train at Brod where it is timed to arrive at 0.58. Somebody would probably have passed a strange Wagon Lit conductor in the corridor. The uniform would be left in a conspicuous place so as to show clearly just how the trick had been played. No suspicion would have attached to the passengers. That, my friends, was how the affair was intended to appear to the outside world.

"But the accident to the train changes everything. Doubtless we have here the reason why the man remained in the compartment with his victim so long. He was waiting for the train to go on. But at last he realised that *the train was not going on*. Different plans would have to be made. The murderer would now be *known* to be still on the train."

"Yes, yes," said M. Bouc impatiently. "I

see all that. But where does the handkerchief come in?"

"I am returning to it by a somewhat circuitous route. To begin with, you must realise that the threatening letters were in the nature of a blind. They might have been lifted bodily out of an indifferently written American crime novel. They are not *real*. They are, in fact, simply intended for the police. What we have to ask ourselves is: 'Did they deceive Ratchett?' On the face of it, the answer seems to be No. His instructions to Hardman seem to point to a definite 'private' enemy, of whose identity he was well aware. That is, if we accept Hardman's story as true. But Ratchett certainly received *one* letter of a very different character—the one containing a reference to the Armstrong baby, a fragment of which we found in his compartment. In case Ratchett had not realised it sooner, this was to make sure that he understood the reason of the threats against his life. That letter, as I have said all along, was *not* intended to be found. The murderer's first care was to destroy it. This, then, was the second hitch in his plans. The first was the snow, the second was our reconstruction of that fragment.

"That the note was destroyed so carefully can mean only one thing. *There must be on the train someone so intimately connected with the Armstrong family that the finding of that note would immediately direct suspicion upon that person.*

"Now we come to the other two clues that we found. I pass over the pipe-cleaner. We have already said a good deal about that. Let us pass on to the handkerchief. Taken at its simplest it is a clue which directly incriminates someone whose initial is H, and it was dropped there unwittingly by that person."

"Exactly," said Dr. Constantine. "She finds out that she has dropped the handkerchief and immediately takes steps to conceal her Christian name."

"How fast you go! You arrive at a conclusion much sooner than I would permit myself to do."

"Is there any other alternative?"

"Certainly there is. Suppose, for instance, that you have committed a crime and wish to cast the blame for it on someone else. Well, there is on the train a certain person connected intimately with the Armstrong family—a woman. Suppose, then, that you leave there a handkerchief belonging to that woman. She will be questioned, her connection with the Armstrong family will be brought out—*et voilà*: motive—*and* an incriminating article of evidence."

"But in such a case," objected the doctor, "the person indicated, being innocent, would not take steps to conceal her identity."

"Ah, really? That is what you think? That is, truly, the opinion of the police court. But I know human nature, my friend, and I tell you that, suddenly confronted with the possibility of being tried for murder, the most innocent person will lose his head and do the most absurd things. No, no, the grease spot and the changed label do not prove guilty— they only prove that the Countess Andrenyi is anxious for some reason to conceal her identity."

"What do you think her connection with the Armstrong family can be? She has never been in America, she says."

"Exactly, and she speaks English with a foreign accent, and she has a very foreign appearance which she exaggerates. But it should not be difficult to guess who she is. I mentioned just now the name of Mrs. Armstrong's mother. It was 'Linda Arden,' and she was a very celebrated actress—among other things a Shakespearean actress. Think of *As You Like It*, with the Forest of Arden and Rosalind. It was there she got the inspiration for her acting name. 'Linda Arden,' the name by which she was known all over the world, was not her real name. It may have been Goldenberg; it is quite likely that she had Central European blood in her veins—a strain of Jewish, perhaps. Many nationalities drift to America. I suggest to you, gentlemen, that that young sister of Mrs. Armstrong's, little more than a child at the time of the tragedy, was Helena Goldenberg, the younger daughter of Linda Arden, and that she married Count Andrenyi when he was an attaché in Washington."

"But Princess Dragomiroff says that the girl married an Englishman."

"Whose name she cannot remember! I ask you, my friends, is that really likely? Princess Dragomiroff loved Linda Arden as great ladies do love great artists. She was godmother to one of the actress's daughters. Would she forget so quickly the married name of the other daughter? It is not likely. No, I think we can safely say that

Princess Dragomiroff was lying. She knew Helena was on the train, she had seen her. She realised at once, as soon as she heard who Ratchett really was, that Helena would be suspected. And so, when we question her as to the sister, she promptly lies—is vague, cannot remember, but 'thinks Helena married an Englishman'—a suggestion as far away from the truth as possible."

One of the restaurant attendants came through the door at the end and approached them. He addressed M. Bouc.

"The dinner, Monsieur, shall I serve it? It is ready some little time."

M. Bouc looked at Poirot. The latter nodded. "By all means, let dinner be served."

The attendant vanished through the doors at the other end. His bell could be heard ringing and his voice upraised:

"*Premier service. Le dîner est servi. Premier dîner*—First service."

Chapter 4

The Grease Spot on a Hungarian Passport

Poirot shared a table with M. Bouc and the doctor.

The company assembled in the restaurant car was a very subdued one. They spoke little. Even the loquacious Mrs. Hubbard was unnaturally quiet. She murmured as she sat:

"I don't feel as though I had the heart to eat anything," and then partook of everything offered her, encouraged by the Swedish lady who seemed to regard her as a special charge.

Before the meal was served, Poirot had caught the chief attendant by the sleeve and murmured something to him. Constantine made a pretty good guess as to what the instructions had been when he noticed that the Count and Countess Andrenyi were always served last and that at the end of the meal there was a delay in making out their bill. It therefore came about that the Count and Countess were the last left in the restaurant car.

When they rose at length and moved in the direction of the door, Poirot sprang up and followed them.

"Pardon, Madame, you have dropped your handkerchief."

He was holding out to her the tiny monogrammed square.

She took it, glanced at it, then handed it back to him.

"You are mistaken, Monsieur, that is not my handkerchief."

"Not your handkerchief? Are you sure?"

"Perfectly sure, Monsieur."

"And yet, Madame, it has your initial—the initial H."

The Count made a sudden movement. Poirot ignored him. His eyes were fixed on the Countess's face.

Looking steadily at him she replied:

"I do not understand, Monsieur. My initials are E. A."

"I think not. Your name is Helena—not

Elena. Helena Goldenberg, the younger daughter of Linda Arden—Helena Goldenberg, the sister of Mrs. Armstrong."

There was a dead silence for a minute or two. Both the Count and the Countess had gone deadly white.

Poirot said in a gentler tone: "It is of no use denying. That is the truth, is it not?"

The Count burst out furiously, "I demand, Monsieur, by what right you—"

She interrupted him, putting up a small hand towards his mouth.

"No, Rudolph. Let me speak. It is useless to deny what this gentleman says. We had better sit down and talk the matter out."

Her voice had changed. It still had the southern richness of tone, but it had become suddenly more clear cut and incisive. It was, for the first time, a definitely American voice.

The Count was silenced. He obeyed the gesture of her hand and they both sat down opposite Poirot.

"Your statement, Monsieur, is quite true," said the Countess. "I am Helena Goldenberg, the younger sister of Mrs. Armstrong."

"You did not acquaint me with that fact this morning, Madame la Comtesse."

"No."

"In fact, all that your husband and you told me was a tissue of lies."

"Monsieur!" cried the Count angrily.

"Do not be angry, Rudolph. M. Poirot puts the fact rather brutally, but what he says is undeniable."

"I am glad you admit the fact so freely, Madame. Will you now tell me your reasons for that, and also for altering your Christian name on your passport?"

"That was my doing entirely," put in the Count.

Helena said quietly: "Surely, M. Poirot, you can guess my reason—our reason. This man who was killed is the man who murdered my baby niece, who killed my sister, who broke my brother-in-law's heart. Three of the people I loved best and who made up my home—my world!"

Her voice rang out passionately. She was a true daughter of that mother the emotional force of whose acting had moved huge audiences to tears.

She went on more quietly.

"Of all the people on the train I alone had probably the best motive for killing him."

"And you did not kill him, Madame?"

"I swear to you, M. Poirot—and my husband knows and will swear also—that much as I may have been tempted to do so, I never lifted a hand against that man."

"I, too, gentlemen," said the Count. "I give you my word of honour that last night Helena never left her compartment. She took a sleeping draught exactly as I said. She is utterly and entirely innocent."

Poirot looked from one to the other of them.

"On my word of honour," repeated the Count.

Poirot shook his head slightly.

"And yet you took it upon yourself to alter the name in the passport?"

"Monsieur Poirot," the Count said earnestly and passionately, "consider my position. Do you think I could stand the thought of my wife dragged through a sordid police case? She was innocent, I knew it, but what she said was true—because of her connection with the Armstrong family she would have been immediately suspected. She would have been questioned—arrested, perhaps. Since some evil chance had taken us on the same train as this man Ratchett, there was, I felt sure, but one thing for it. I admit, Monsieur, that I lied to you—all, that is, save in one thing. My wife never left her compartment last night."

He spoke with an earnestness that it was hard to gainsay.

"I do not say that I disbelieve you, Monsieur," said Poirot slowly. "Your family is, I know, a proud and ancient one. It would be bitter indeed for you to have your wife dragged into an unpleasant police case. With that I can sympathise. But how then do you explain the presence of your wife's handkerchief actually in the dead man's compartment?"

"That handkerchief is not mine, Monsieur," said the Countess.

"In spite of the initial H?"

"In spite of the initial. I have handkerchiefs not unlike that, but not one that is exactly of that pattern. I know, of course, that I cannot hope to make you believe me, but I assure you that it is so. That handkerchief is not mine."

"It may have been placed there by someone in order to incriminate you?"

She smiled a little. "You are enticing me to admit that, after all, it is mine? But indeed,

M. Poirot, it isn't." She spoke with great earnestness.

"Then why, if the handkerchief was not yours, did you alter the name in the passport?"

The Count answered this.

"Because we heard that a handkerchief had been found with the initial H on it. We talked the matter over together before we came to be interviewed. I pointed out to Helena that if it were seen that her Christian name began with an H she would immediately be subjected to much more rigorous questioning. And the thing was so simple— to alter Helena to Elena was easily done."

"You have, M. le Comte, the makings of a very fine criminal," remarked Poirot dryly. "A great natural ingenuity, and an apparently remorseless determination to mislead justice."

"Oh, no, no." The girl leaned forward. "M. Poirot, he's explained to you how it was." She broke from French into English. "I was scared—absolutely dead scared, you understand. It had been so awful—that time—and to have it all raked up again. And to be suspected and perhaps thrown into prison. I was just scared stiff, M. Poirot. Can't you understand at all?"

Her voice was lovely—deep—rich—pleading, the voice of the daughter of Linda Arden the actress.

Poirot looked gravely at her.

"If I am to believe you, Madame—and I do not say that I will *not* believe you—then you must help me."

"Help you?"

"Yes. The reason for the murder lies in the past—in that tragedy which broke up your home and saddened your young life. Take me back into the past, Mademoiselle, that I may find there the link that explains the whole thing."

"What can there be to tell you? They are all dead." She repeated mournfully: "All dead—all dead—Robert, Sonia—darling, darling Daisy. She was so sweet—so happy—she had such lovely curls. We were all just crazy about her."

"There was another victim, Madame. An indirect victim, you might say."

"Poor Susanne? Yes, I had forgotten about her. The police questioned her. They were convinced that she had something to do with it. Perhaps she had—but if so only innocently. She had, I believe, chatted idly with someone, giving information as to the time of Daisy's outings. The poor thing got terribly wrought up—she thought she was being held responsible." She shuddered. "She threw herself out of the window. Oh! it was horrible."

She buried her face in her hands.

"What nationality was she, Madame?"

"She was French."

"What was her last name?"

"It's absurd, but I can't remember—we all called her Susanne. A pretty, laughing girl. She was devoted to Daisy."

"She was the nursery-maid, was she not?"

"Yes."

"Who was the nurse?"

"She was a trained hospital nurse. Stengelberg her name was. She too was devoted to Daisy—and to my sister."

"Now, Madame, I want you to think carefully before you answer this question. Have you, since you were on this train, seen anyone that you recognised?"

She stared at him. "I? No, no one at all."

"What about Princess Dragomiroff?"

"Oh! her. I know her, of course. I thought you meant anyone—anyone from—from that time."

"So I did, Madame. Now think carefully.

Some years have passed, remember. The person might have altered his or her appearance."

Helena pondered deeply. Then she said: "No—I am sure—there is no one."

"You yourself—you were a young girl at the time—did you have no one to superintend your studies or to look after you?"

"Oh! yes, I had a dragon—a sort of governess to me and secretary to Sonia combined. She was English—or rather Scotch; a big red-haired woman."

"What was her name?"

"Miss Freebody."

"Young or old?"

"She seemed frightfully old to me. I suppose she couldn't have been more than forty. Susanne, of course, used to look after my clothes and maid me."

"And there were no other inmates of the house?"

"Only servants."

"And you are certain, quite certain, Madame, that you have recognised no one on the train?"

She replied earnestly: "No one, Monsieur. No one at all."

Chapter 5

The Christian Name of Princess Dragomiroff

When the Count and Countess had departed, Poirot looked across at the other two.

"You see," he said, "we make progress."

"Excellent work," said M. Bouc cordially. "On my part, I should never have dreamed of suspecting Count and Countess Andrenyi. I will admit I thought them quite *hors de combat*. I suppose there is no doubt that she committed the crime? It is rather sad. Still, they will not guillotine her. There are extenuating circumstances. A few years' imprisonment—that will be all."

"In fact you are quite certain of her guilt."

"My dear friend—surely there is no doubt of it? I thought your reassuring manner was only to smooth things over till we are dug out of the snow and the police take charge."

"You do not believe the Count's positive assertion—on his word of honor—that his wife is innocent?"

"*Mon cher*—naturally—what else *could* he say? He adores his wife. He wants to save her! He tells his lie very well—quite in the grand *seigneur* manner. But what else than a lie could it be?"

"Well, you know, I had the preposterous idea that it might be the truth."

"No, no. The handkerchief, remember. The handkerchief clinches the matter."

"Oh, I am not so sure about the handkerchief. You remember, I always told you that there were two possibilities as to the ownership of the handkerchief."

"All the same—"

M. Bouc broke off. The door at the end had opened, and Princess Dragomiroff entered the dining-car. She came straight to them and all three men rose to their feet.

She spoke to Poirot, ignoring the others.

"I believe, Monsieur," she said, "that you have a handkerchief of mine."

Poirot shot a glance of triumph at the other two.

"Is this it, Madame?"

He produced the little square of fine cambric.

"That is it. It has my initial in the corner."

"But, Madame la Princesse, that is the letter H," said M. Bouc. "Your Christian name—pardon me—is Natalia."

She gave him a cold stare.

"That is correct, Monsieur. My handkerchiefs are always initialed in the Russian characters. H is N in Russian."

M. Bouc was somewhat taken aback. There was something about this indomitable old lady which made him feel flustered and uncomfortable.

"You did not tell us that this handkerchief was yours at the inquiry this morning."

"You did not ask me," said the Princess dryly.

"Pray be seated, Madame," said Poirot.

She sighed. "I may as well, I suppose." She sat down.

"You need not make a long business of this, Messieurs.

"Your next question will be—How did my handkerchief come to be lying by a murdered man's body? My reply to that is that I have no idea."

"You have really no idea?"

"None whatever."

"You will excuse me, Madame, but how much can we rely upon the truthfulness of your replies?"

Poirot said the words very softly.

Princess Dragomiroff answered contemptuously. "I suppose you mean because I did not tell you that Helena Andrenyi was Mrs. Armstrong's sister?"

"In fact you deliberately lied to us in the matter."

"Certainly. I would do the same again. Her mother was my friend. I believe, Messieurs, in loyalty—to one's friends and one's family and one's caste."

"You do not believe in doing your utmost to further the ends of justice?"

"In this case I consider that justice—strict justice—has been done."

Poirot leaned forward.

"You see my difficulty, Madame. In this matter of the handkerchief, even, am I to believe you? Or are you shielding your friend's daughter?"

"Oh! I see what you mean." Her face broke into a grim smile. "Well, Messieurs, this statement of mine can be easily proved.

I will give you the address of the people in Paris who make my handkerchiefs. You have only to show them the one in question and they will inform you that it was made to my order over a year ago. The handkerchief is mine, Messieurs."

She rose.

"Have you anything further you wish to ask me?"

"Your maid, Madame, did she recognise this handkerchief when we showed it to her this morning?"

"She must have done so. She saw it and said nothing? Ah, well, that shows that she too can be loyal."

With a slight inclination of her head she passed out of the dining-car.

"So that was it," murmured Poirot softly. "I noticed just a trifling hesitation when I asked the maid if she knew to whom the handkerchief belonged. She was uncertain whether or not to admit that it was her mistress's. But how does that fit in with that strange central idea of mine? Yes, it might well be."

"Ah!" said M. Bouc with a characteristic gesture. "She is a terrible old lady, that!"

"Could she have murdered Ratchett?" asked Poirot of the doctor.

He shook his head.

"Those blows—the ones delivered with great force penetrating the muscle—never, never could anyone with so frail a physique inflict them."

"But the feebler ones?"

"The feebler ones, yes."

"I am thinking," said Poirot, "of the incident this morning when I said to her that the strength was in her will rather than in her arm. It was in the nature of a trap, that remark. I wanted to see if she would look down at her right or her left arm. She did neither. She looked at them both. But she made a strange reply. She said, 'No, I have no strength in these. I do not know whether to be sorry or glad.' A curious remark that. It confirms me in my belief about the crime."

"It did not settle the point about the left-handedness."

"No. By the way, did you notice that Count Andrenyi keeps his handkerchief in his right-hand breast pocket?"

M. Bouc shook his head. His mind reverted to the astonishing revelations of the last half-hour. He murmured:

"Lies—and again lies. It amazes me, the number of lies we had told to us this morning."

"There are more still to discover," said Poirot cheerfully.

"You think so?"

"I shall be very much disappointed if it is not so."

"Such duplicity is terrible," said M. Bouc. "But it seems to please you," he added reproachfully.

"It has this advantage," said Poirot. "If you confront anyone who has lied with the truth, he will usually admit it—often out of sheer surprise. It is only necessary to guess *right* to produce your effect.

"That is the only way to conduct this case. I select each passenger in turn, consider his or her evidence, and say to myself, '*If* so and so is lying, on what *point* is he lying, and what is the *reason* for the lie?' And I answer, 'If he is lying—if, you mark—it could only be for such a reason and on such a point.' We have done that once very successfully with Countess Andrenyi. We shall now proceed to try the same method on several other persons."

"And supposing, my friend, that your guess happens to be wrong?"

"Then one person, at any rate, will be completely freed from suspicion."

"Ah!—a process of elimination."

"Exactly."

"And whom do we tackle next?"

"We are going to tackle that *pukka sahib*, Colonel Arbuthnot."

Chapter 6

A Second Interview with Colonel Arbuthnot

Colonel Arbuthnot was clearly annoyed at being summoned to the dining-car for a second interview. His face wore a most forbidding expression as he sat down and said:

"Well?"

"All my apologies for troubling you a second time," said Poirot. "But there is still some information that I think you might be able to give us."

"Indeed? I hardly think so."

"To begin with, you see this pipe cleaner?"

"Yes."

"Is it one of yours?"

"Don't know. I don't put a private mark on them, you know."

"Are you aware, Colonel Arbuthnot, that

you are the only man amongst the passengers in the Stamboul-Calais carriage who smokes a pipe?"

"In that case it probably is one of mine."

"Do you know where it was found?"

"Not the least idea."

"It was found by the body of the murdered man."

Colonel Arbuthnot raised his eyebrows.

"Can you tell us, Colonel Arbuthnot, how it is likely to have got there?"

"If you mean, did I drop it there myself, no, I didn't."

"Did you go into Mr. Ratchett's compartment at any time?"

"I never even spoke to the man."

"You never spoke to him and you did not murder him?"

The Colonel's eyebrows went up again sardonically.

"If I had, I should hardly be likely to acquaint you with the fact. As a matter of fact I *didn't* murder the fellow."

"Ah, well," murmured Poirot. "It is of no consequence."

"I beg your pardon?"

"I said that it was of no consequence."

"Oh!" Arbuthnot looked taken aback. He eyed Poirot uneasily.

"Because, you see," continued the little man, "the pipe cleaner, it is of no importance. I can myself think of eleven other excellent explanations of its presence."

Arbuthnot stared at him.

"What I really wished to see you about was quite another matter," went on Poirot. "Miss Debenham may have told you, perhaps, that I overheard some words spoken to you at the station of Konya?"

Arbuthnot did not reply.

"She said, *'Not now. When it's all over. When it's behind us!'* Do you know to what those words referred?"

"I am sorry, M. Poirot, but I must refuse to answer that question."

"Pourquoi?"

The Colonel said stiffly, "I suggest that you ask Miss Debenham herself for the meaning of those words."

"I have done so."

"And she refused to tell you?"

"Yes."

"Then I should think it would have been perfectly plain—even to you—that my lips are sealed."

"You will not give away a lady's secret?"

"You can put it that way, if you like."

"Miss Debenham told me that they referred to a private matter of her own."

"Then why not accept her word for it?"

"Because, Colonel Arbuthnot, Miss Debenham is what one might call a highly suspicious character."

"Nonsense," said the Colonel with warmth.

"It is not nonsense."

"You have nothing whatever against her."

"Not the fact that Miss Debenham was companion governess in the Armstrong household at the time of the kidnapping of little Daisy Armstrong?"

There was a minute's dead silence.

Poirot nodded his head gently.

"You see," he said. "We know more than you think. If Miss Debenham is innocent, why did she conceal that fact? Why did she tell me that she had never been in America?"

The Colonel cleared his throat. "Aren't you possibly making a mistake?"

"I am making no mistake. Why did Miss Debenham lie to me?"

Colonel Arbuthnot shrugged his shoulders. "You had better ask her. I still think that you are wrong."

Poirot raised his voice and called. One of the restaurant attendants came from the far end of the car.

"Go and ask the English lady in No. 11 if she will be good enough to come here."

"Bien, Monsieur."

The man departed. The four men sat in silence. Colonel Arbuthnot's face looked as though it were carved out of wood, rigid and impassive.

The man returned.

"The lady is just coming, Monsieur."

"Thank you."

A minute or two later Mary Debenham entered the dining-car.

Chapter 7

The Identity of Mary Debenham

She wore no hat. Her head was thrown back as though in defiance. The sweep of her hair back from her face, the curve of her nostril suggested the figurehead of a ship plunging gallantly into a rough sea. In that moment she was beautiful.

Her eyes went to Arbuthnot for a minute—just a minute.

She said to Poirot, "You wished to see me?"

"I wished to ask you, Mademoiselle, why you lied to us this morning?"

"Lied to you? I don't know what you mean."

"You concealed the fact that at the time of the Armstrong tragedy you were actually living in the house. You told me that you had never been in America."

He saw her flinch for a moment and then recover herself.

"Yes," she said. "That is true."

"No, Mademoiselle, it was false."

"You misunderstood me. I mean that it is true that I lied to you."

"Ah, you admit it?"

Her lips curved into a smile. "Certainly, since you have found me out."

"You are at least frank, Mademoiselle."

"There does not seem anything else for me to be."

"Well, of course, that is true. And now, Mademoiselle, may I ask you the reason for these evasions?"

"I should have thought the reason leapt to the eye, M. Poirot?"

"It does not leap to mine, Mademoiselle."

She said in a quiet even voice with a trace of hardness in it, "I have my living to get."

"You mean—?"

She raised her eyes and looked him full in the face.

"How much do you know, M. Poirot, of the fight to get and keep decent employment? Do you think that a girl who had been detained in connection with a murder case, whose name and perhaps photograph were reproduced in the English papers—do you think that any nice ordinary middle-class Englishwoman would want to engage that girl as governess to her daughters?"

"I do not see why not—if no blame attached to you."

"Oh, blame—it is not *blame*—it is the publicity! So far, M. Poirot, I have succeeded in life. I have had well-paid, pleasant posts. I was not going to risk the position I had attained when no good end could have been served."

"I will venture to suggest, Mademoiselle, that I would have been the best judge of that, not you."

She shrugged her shoulders.

"For instance, you could have helped me in the matter of identification."

"What do you mean?"

"Is it possible, Mademoiselle, that you did not recognise in the Countess Andrenyi Mrs. Armstrong's young sister whom you taught in New York?"

"Countess Andrenyi? No." She shook her head. "It may seem extraordinary to you—but I did not recognise her. She was not grown up, you see, when I knew her. That was over three years ago. It is true that the Countess reminded me of someone; it puzzled me. But she looks so foreign—I never connected her with the little American schoolgirl. I only glanced at her casually when coming into the restaurant car, and I noticed her clothes more than her face." She smiled faintly. "Women do! And then—well—I had my own preoccupations."

"You will not tell me your secret, Mademoiselle?"

Poirot's voice was very gentle and persuasive.

She said in a low voice, "I can't—I can't."

And suddenly, without warning, she broke down, dropping her face down upon her outstretched arms and crying as though her heart would break.

The Colonel sprang up and stood awkwardly beside her.

"I—look here—"

He stopped and turning round scowled fiercely at Poirot.

"I'll break every bone in your damned body, you dirty little whipper-snapper," he said.

"Monsieur," protested M. Bouc.

Arbuthnot had turned back to the girl. "Mary—for God's sake—"

She sprang up. "It's nothing. I'm all right. You don't need me any more, do you, M. Poirot? If you do, you must come and find me. Oh, what an idiot—what an idiot I'm making of myself!" She hurried out of the car.

Arbuthnot, before following her, turned once more on Poirot.

"Miss Debenham's got nothing to do with this business—nothing, do you hear? And if she's worried and interfered with, you'll have me to deal with." He strode out.

"I like to see an angry Englishman," said Poirot. "They are very amusing. The more emotional they feel, the less command they have of language."

But M. Bouc was not interested in the emotional reactions of Englishmen. He was overcome by admiration of his friend.

"Mon cher, vous être épatant!" he cried. "Another miraculous guess."

"It is incredible how you think of these things," said Dr. Constantine admiringly.

"Oh, I claim no credit this time. It was not a guess. Countess Andrenyi practically told me."

"*Comment?* Surely not?"

"You remember, I asked her about her governess or companion? I had already decided in my mind that *if* Mary Debenham were mixed up in the matter, she must have figured in the household in some such capacity."

"Yes, but the Countess Andrenyi described a totally different person."

"Exactly. A tall middle-aged woman with red hair—in fact, the exact opposite in every respect of Miss Debenham, so much so as to be quite remarkable. But then she had to invent a name quickly, and there it was that the unconscious association of ideas gave her away. She said Miss Freebody, you remember."

"Yes?"

"*Eh bien*, you may not know it, but there is a shop in London that was called until recently Debenham & Freebody. With the name Debenham running in her head, the Countess clutches at another name quickly, and the first that comes is Freebody. Naturally I understood immediately."

"That is yet another lie. Why did she do it?"

"Possibly more loyalty. It makes things a little difficult."

"Ma foi!" said M. Bouc with violence. "But does everybody on this train tell lies?"

"That," said Poirot, "is what we are about to find out."

Chapter 8
Further Surprising Revelations

"Nothing would surprise me now," said M. Bouc. "Nothing! Even if everybody in the train proved to have been in the Armstrong household, I should not express surprise."

"That is a very profound remark," said Poirot. "Would you like to see what your favorite suspect, the Italian, has to say for himself?"

"You are going to make another of these famous guesses of yours?"

"Precisely."

"It is really a *most* extraordinary case," said Constantine.

"No, it is most natural."

M. Bouc flung up his arms in comic despair. "If this is what you call natural, *mon ami*—" Words failed him.

Poirot had by this time requested the dining-car attendant to fetch Antonio Foscarelli.

The big Italian had a wary look in his eye as he came in. He shot nervous glances from side to side like a trapped animal.

"What do you want?" he said. "I have nothing more to tell you—nothing, do you hear? *Per Dio*—" He struck his hand on the table.

"Yes, you have something more to tell us," said Poirot firmly. "The truth!"

"The truth?" He shot an uneasy glance at Poirot. All the assurance and geniality had gone out of his manner.

"*Mais oui*. It may be that I know it already. But it will be a point in your favour if it comes from you spontaneously."

"You talk like the American police. 'Come clean'—that is what they say—'come clean.' "

"Ah! so you have had experience of the New York police?"

"No, no, never. They could not prove a thing against me—but it was not for want of trying."

Poirot said quietly: "That was in the Armstrong case, was it not? You were the chauffeur?"

His eyes met those of the Italian. The bluster went out of the big man. He was like a pricked balloon.

"Since you know—why ask me?"

"Why did you lie this morning?"

"Business reasons. Besides, I do not trust the Jugo-Slav police. They hate the Italians. They would not have given me justice."

"Perhaps it is exactly justice that they *would* have given you!"

"No, no, I had nothing to do with this business last night. I never left my carriage. The long-faced Englishman, he can tell you so. It was not I who killed this pig—this Ratchett. You cannot prove anything against me."

Poirot was writing something on a sheet of paper. He looked up and said quietly: "Very good. You can go."

Foscarelli lingered uneasily. "You realise that it was not I? That I could have had nothing to do with it?"

"I said that you could go."

"It is a conspiracy. You are going to frame me? All for a pig of a man who should have gone to the chair! It was an infamy that he did not. If it had been me—if I had been arrested—"

"But it was not you. You had nothing to do with the kidnapping of the child."

"What is that you are saying? Why, that little one—she was the delight of the house. Tonio, she called me. And she would sit in the car and pretend to hold the wheel. All the household worshipped her! Even the police came to understand that. Ah, the beautiful little one!"

His voice had softened. The tears came into his eyes. Then he wheeled round abruptly on his heel and strode out of the dining-car.

"Pietro," called Poirot.

The dining-car attendant came at a run.

"The No. 10—the Swedish lady."

"Bien, Monsieur."

"Another?" cried M. Bouc. "Ah, no—it is not possible. I tell you it is not possible."

"Mon cher—we have to *know*. Even if in the end everybody on the train proves to have had a motive for killing Ratchett, we have to know. Once we know, we can settle once for all where the guilt lies."

"My head is spinning," groaned M. Bouc. Greta Ohlsson was ushered in sympathetically by the attendant. She was weeping bitterly.

She collapsed on the seat facing Poirot and wept steadily into a large handkerchief.

"Now do not distress yourself, Mademoiselle. Do not distress yourself." Poirot patted her on the shoulder. "Just a few little words of truth, that is all. You were the nurse who was in charge of little Daisy Armstrong?"

"It is true—it is true," wept the wretched woman. "Ah, she was an angel—a little sweet trustful angel. She knew nothing but kindness and love—and she was taken away by that wicked man—cruelly treated—and her poor mother—and the other little one who never lived at all. You cannot understand—you cannot know—if you had been there as I was—if you had seen the whole terrible tragedy! I ought to have told you the truth about myself this morning. But I was afraid—afraid. I did so rejoice that that evil man was dead—that he could not any more kill or torture little children. Ah! I cannot speak—I have no words. . . ."

She wept with more vehemence than ever.

Poirot continued to pat her gently on the

shoulder. "There—there—I comprehend—I comprehend everything—everything, I tell you. I will ask you no more questions. It is enough that you have admitted what I know to be the truth. I understand, I tell you."

By now inarticulate with sobs, Greta Ohlsson rose and groped her way blindly towards the door. As she reached it she collided with a man coming in.

It was the valet—Masterman.

He came straight up to Poirot and spoke in his usual quiet, unemotional voice.

"I hope I'm not intruding, sir. I thought it best to come along at once, sir, and tell you the truth. I was Colonel Armstrong's batman in the War, sir, and afterwards I was his valet in New York. I'm afraid I concealed that fact this morning. It was very wrong of me, sir, and I thought I'd better come and make a clean breast of it. But I hope, sir, that you're not suspecting Tonio in any way. Old Tonio, sir, wouldn't hurt a fly. And I can swear positively that he never left the carriage all last night. So, you see, sir, he couldn't have done it. Tonio may be a foreigner, sir, but he's a very gentle creature. Not like those nasty murdering Italians one reads about."

He stopped.

Poirot looked steadily at him. "Is that all you have to say?"

"That is all, sir."

He paused; then, as Poirot did not speak, he made an apologetic little bow and after a momentary hesitation left the dining-car in the same quiet unobtrusive fashion as he had come.

"This," said Dr. Constantine, "is more wildly improbable than any *roman policier* I have ever read."

"I agree," said M. Bouc. "Of the twelve passengers in that coach, nine have been proved to have had a connection with the Armstrong case. What next, I ask you? Or should I say, who next?"

"I can almost give you the answer to your question," said Poirot. "Here comes our American sleuth, Mr. Hardman."

"Is he, too, coming to confess?"

Before Poirot could reply the American had reached their table. He cocked an alert eye at them and sitting down he drawled out: "Just exactly what's up on this train? It seems bughouse to me."

Poirot twinkled at him.

"Are you quite sure, Mr. Hardman, that

you yourself were not the gardener at the Armstrong home?"

"They didn't have a garden," replied Mr. Hardman literally.

"Or the butler?"

"Haven't got the fancy manners for a place like that. No, I never had any connection with the Armstrong house—but I'm beginning to believe I'm about the only one on this train who hadn't! Can you beat it? That's what I say—can you beat it?"

"It is certainly a little surprising," said Poirot mildly.

"*C'est rigolo*," burst from M. Bouc.

"Have you any ideas of your own about the crime, Mr. Hardman?" inquired Poirot.

"No, sir. It's got me beat. I don't know how to figure it out. They can't *all* be in it— but which one is the guilty party is beyond me. How did you get wise to all this? That's what I want to know."

"I just guessed."

"Then, believe me, you're a pretty slick guesser. Yes, I'll tell the world you're a slick guesser."

Mr. Hardman leaned back and looked at Poirot admiringly.

"You'll excuse me," he said, "but no one

would believe it to look at you. I take off my hat to you. I do indeed."

"You are too kind, M. Hardman."

"Not at all. I've got to hand it to you."

"All the same," said Poirot, "the problem is not yet quite solved. Can we say with authority that we know who killed M. Ratchett?"

"Count me out," said Mr. Hardman. "I'm not saying anything at all. I'm just full of natural admiration. What about the other two you haven't had a guess at yet? The old American dame, and the lady's-maid? I suppose we can take it that they're the only innocent parties on the train?"

"Unless," said Poirot, smiling, "we can fit them into our little collection as—shall we say—housekeeper and cook in the Armstrong household?"

"Well, nothing in the world would surprise me now," said Mr. Hardman with quiet resignation. "Bughouse—that's what this business is—bughouse!"

"Ah! *mon cher*, that would be indeed stretching coincidence a little too far," said M. Bouc. "They cannot all be in it."

Poirot looked at him. "You do not understand," he said. "You do not understand at all. Tell me, do you know who killed Ratchett?"

"Do you?" countered M. Bouc.

Poirot nodded. "Oh, yes," he said. "I have known for some time. It is so clear that I wonder you have not seen it also." He looked at Hardman and asked: "And you?"

The detective shook his head. He stared at Poirot curiously. "I don't know," he said. "I don't know at all. Which of them was it?"

Poirot was silent a minute. Then he said:

"If you will be so good, M. Hardman, assemble everyone here. There are two possible solutions of this case. I want to lay them both before you all."

Chapter 9
Poirot Propounds Two Solutions

The passengers came crowding into the restaurant car and took their seats round the tables. They all bore more or less the same expression, one of expectancy mingled with apprehension. The Swedish lady was still weeping, and Mrs. Hubbard was comforting her.

"Now you must just take a hold on yourself, my dear. Everything's going to be perfectly all right. You mustn't lose your grip on yourself. If one of us is a nasty murderer, we know quite well it isn't you. Why, anyone would be crazy even to think of such a thing. You sit here, and I'll stay right by you—and don't you worry any." Her voice died away as Poirot stood up.

The Wagon Lit conductor was hovering in

the doorway. "You permit that I stay, Monsieur?"

"Certainly, Michel."

Poirot cleared his throat.

"*Messieurs et mesdames*, I will speak in English since I think all of you know a little of that language. We are here to investigate the death of Samuel Edward Ratchett—*alias* Cassetti. There are two possible solutions of the crime. I shall put them both before you, and I shall ask M. Bouc and Dr. Constantine here to judge which solution is the right one.

"Now you all know the facts of the case. Mr. Ratchett was found stabbed this morning. He was last known to be alive at 12.37 last night when he spoke to the Wagon Lit conductor through the door. A watch in his pyjama pocket was found to be badly dented, and it had stopped at a quarter past one. Dr. Constantine, who examined the body when found, puts the time of death as having been between midnight and two in the morning. At half an hour after midnight, as you all know, the train ran into a snowdrift. After that time *it was impossible for anyone to leave the train*.

"The evidence of Mr. Hardman, who is a member of a New York detective agency"—

(Several heads turned to look at Mr. Hardman.)—"shows that no one could have passed his compartment (No. 16 at the extreme end) without being seen by him. We are therefore forced to the conclusion that the murderer is to be found among the occupants of one particular coach—the Stamboul-Calais coach.

"That, I will say, *was* our theory."

"*Comment?*" ejaculated M. Bouc, startled.

"But I will put before you an alternative theory. It is very simple. Mr. Ratchett had a certain enemy whom he feared. He gave Mr. Hardman a description of this enemy and told him that the attempt, if made at all, would most probably be made on the second night out from Stamboul.

"Now I put it to you, ladies and gentlemen, that Mr. Ratchett knew a good deal more than he told. The enemy, as Mr. Ratchett expected, joined the train *at Belgrade or else at Vincovci* by the door left open by Colonel Arbuthnot and Mr. MacQueen, who had just descended to the platform. He was provided with a suit of Wagon Lit uniform, which he wore over his ordinary clothes, and a pass-key which enabled him

to gain access to Mr. Ratchett's compartment in spite of the door's being locked. Mr.
Ratchett was under the influence of a sleeping draught. This man stabbed him with
great ferocity and left the compartment
through the communicating door leading to
Mrs. Hubbard's compartment—"

"That's so," said Mrs. Hubbard, nodding
her head.

"He thrust the dagger he had used into
Mrs. Hubbard's sponge-bag in passing.
Without knowing it, he lost a button of his
uniform. Then he slipped out of the compartment and along the corridor. He hastily
thrust the uniform into a suitcase in an
empty compartment, and a few minutes
later, dressed in ordinary clothes, he left the
train just before it started off, using the
same means for egress—the door near the
dining-car."

Everybody gasped.

"What about that watch?" demanded Mr.
Hardman.

"There you have the explanation of the
whole thing. *Mr. Ratchett had omitted to put
his watch back an hour as he should have
done at Tzaribrod*. His watch still registered
Eastern European time, which is one hour

ahead of Central European time. It was a quarter past *twelve* when Mr. Ratchett was stabbed—not a quarter past one."

"But it is absurd, that explanation!" cried M. Bouc. "What of the voice that spoke from the compartment at twenty-three minutes to one? It was either the voice of Ratchett—or else that of his murderer."

"Not necessarily. It might have been—well—a third person. One who had gone in to speak to Ratchett and found him dead. He rang the bell to summon the conductor; then, as you express it, the wind rose in him—he was afraid of being accused of the crime, and he spoke pretending to be Ratchett."

"C'est possible," admitted M. Bouc grudgingly.

Poirot looked at Mrs. Hubbard. "Yes, Madame, you were going to say—"

"Well, I don't quite know what I was going to say. Do you think I forgot to put my watch back too?"

"No, Madame. I think you heard the man pass through—but unconsciously. Later you had a nightmare of a man being in your compartment and woke up with a start and rang for the conductor."

"Well, I suppose that's possible," admitted Mrs. Hubbard.

Princess Dragomiroff was looking at Poirot with a very direct glance. "How do you explain the evidence of my maid, Monsieur?"

"Very simply, Madame. Your maid recognised the handkerchief I showed her as yours. She somewhat clumsily tried to shield you. She did encounter the man, but earlier—while the train was at Vincovci station. She pretended to have seen him at a later hour, with a confused idea of giving you a water-tight alibi."

The Princess bowed her head. "You have thought of everything, Monsieur. I—I admire you."

There was a silence.

Then everyone jumped as Dr. Constantine suddenly hit the table a blow with his fist.

"But no," he said. "No, no, and again no! That is an explanation that will not hold water. It is deficient in a dozen minor points. The crime was not committed so—M. Poirot must know that perfectly well."

Poirot turned a curious glance on him. "I see," he said, "that I shall have to give you my second solution. But do not abandon this one too abruptly. You may agree with it later."

He turned back again to face the others.

"There is another possible solution of the crime. This is how I arrived at it.

"When I had heard all the evidence, I leaned back and shut my eyes, and began to *think*. Certain points presented themselves to me as worthy of attention. I enumerated these points to my two colleagues. Some I have already elucidated—such as a grease spot on a passport, and so on. I will run over the points that remain. The first and most important is a remark made to me by M. Bouc in the restaurant car at lunch on the first day after leaving Stamboul—to the effect that the company assembled was interesting because it was so varied—representing as it did all classes and nationalities.

"I agreed with him, but when this particular point came into my mind, I tried to imagine whether such an assembly was ever likely to be collected under any other conditions. And the answer I made to myself was—only in America. In America there might be a household composed of just such varied nationalities—an Italian chauffeur, an English governess, a Swedish nurse, a German lady's-maid, and so on. That led me to my scheme of 'guessing'— that is, casting each person for a certain part in the Armstrong drama much as a producer casts a play. Well, that gave me an extremely interesting and satisfactory result.

"I had also examined in my own mind each separate person's evidence, with some curious results. Take first the evidence of Mr. MacQueen. My first interview with him was entirely satisfactory. But in my second he made rather a curious remark. I had described to him the finding of a note mentioning the Armstrong case. He said, 'But surely—' and then paused and went on, 'I mean—that was rather careless of the old man.'

"Now I could feel that that was not what he had started out to say. *Supposing what he had meant to say was 'But surely that was burnt!'* In which case, *MacQueen knew of the note and of its destruction*—in other words, he was either the murderer or an accomplice of the murderer. Very good.

"Then the valet. He said his master was in the habit of taking a sleeping draught when travelling by train. That might be true, but *would Ratchett have taken one last night?*

The automatic under his pillow gave the lie to that statement. Ratchett intended to be on the alert last night. Whatever narcotic was administered to him must have been given without his knowledge. By whom? Obviously by MacQueen or the valet.

"Now we come to the evidence of Mr. Hardman. I believed all that he told me about his own identity, but when it came to the actual methods he had employed to guard Mr. Ratchett, his story was neither more nor less than absurd. The only way to have protected Ratchett effectively was to pass the night actually in his compartment or in some spot where he could watch the door. The one thing that his evidence *did* show plainly was that *no one in any other part of the train could possibly have murdered Ratchett*. It drew a clear circle round the Stamboul-Calais carriage. That seemed to me a rather curious and inexplicable fact, and I put it aside to think over.

"You probably all know by now of the few words I overheard between Miss Debenham and Colonel Arbuthnot. The interesting thing to my mind was the fact that Colonel Arbuthnot called her *Mary* and was clearly on terms of intimacy with her. But the

Colonel was supposed to have met her only a few days previously. And I know Englishmen of the Colonel's type—even if he had fallen in love with the young lady at first sight, he would have advanced slowly and with decorum, not rushing things. Therefore I concluded that Colonel Arbuthnot and Miss Debenham were in reality well acquainted and were for some reason pretending to be strangers. Another small point was Miss Debenham's easy familiarity with the term 'long distance' for a telephone call. Yet Miss Debenham had told me that she had never been in the States.

"To pass to another witness. Mrs. Hubbard had told us that lying in bed she had been unable to see whether the communicating door was bolted or not, and so had asked Miss Ohlsson to see for her. Now—though her statement would have been perfectly true if she had been occupying compartment No. 2, 4, 12 or any *even* number, in which the bolt is directly under the handle of the door—in the *uneven* numbers such as compartment No. 3 the bolt is well *above* the handle and could not therefore be masked by the sponge-bag in the least. I was forced to the conclusion that Mrs. Hubbard was inventing an incident that had never occurred.

"And here let me say just a word or two about *times*. To my mind the really interesting point about the dented watch is the place where it was found—in Ratchett's pyjama pocket, a singularly uncomfortable and unlikely place to keep one's watch, especially as there is a watch 'hook' provided just by the head of the bed. I felt sure, therefore, that the watch had been deliberately placed in the pocket—faked. The crime, then, was not committed at a quarter past one.

"Was it then committed earlier? To be exact, at twenty-three minutes to one? My friend M. Bouc advanced as an argument in favour of it the loud cry which awoke me from sleep. But if Ratchett had been heavily drugged, *he could not have cried out*. If he had been capable of crying out, he would have been capable of making some kind of struggle to defend himself, and there were no signs of any such struggle.

"I remembered that MacQueen had called attention, not once but twice (and the second time in a very blatant manner), to the fact that Ratchett could speak no French. I came to the conclusion that the whole business at twenty-three minutes to one was a comedy played for my benefit! Anyone might see through the watch business—it is a common enough device in detective stories. They assumed that I *should* see through it and that, pluming myself on my own cleverness, I would go on to assume that since Ratchett spoke no French, the voice I heard at twenty-three minutes to one could not have been his, and that Ratchett must have been already dead. But I am convinced that at twenty-three minutes to one Ratchett was still lying in his drugged sleep.

"But the device has succeeded! I have opened my door and looked out. I have actually heard the French phrase used. If I am so unbelievably dense as not to realise the significance of that phrase, it must be brought to my attention. If necessary, MacQueen can come right out in the open. He can say, 'Excuse me, M. Poirot, *that can't have been Mr. Ratchett speaking*. He couldn't speak French.'

"Now, what was the real time of the crime? And who killed him?

"In my opinion—and this is only an opinion—Ratchett was killed at some time very close upon two o'clock, the latest hour the doctor gives us as possible.

"As to who killed him—"

He paused, looking at his audience. He could not complain of any lack of attention. Every eye was fixed upon him. In the stillness you could have heard a pin drop.

He went on slowly:

"I was particularly struck by the extraordinary difficulty of proving a case against any one person on the train, and by the rather curious coincidence that in each case the testimony giving an alibi came from what I might describe as an 'unlikely' person. Thus, Mr. MacQueen and Colonel Arbuthnot provided alibis for each other—two persons between whom it seemed most unlikely there should have been any prior acquaintanceship. The same thing happened with the English valet and the Italian, and with the Swedish lady and the English girl. I said to myself: This is extraordinary—they cannot *all* be in it!

"And then, Messieurs, I saw light. They *were* all in it. For so many people connected with the Armstrong case to be travelling by the same train through coincidence was not only unlikely: it was *impossible*. It must be not chance, but *design*. I remembered a remark of Colonel Arbuthnot's about trial by jury. A jury is composed of twelve people—there were twelve passengers—Ratchett was stabbed twelve times. And the thing that had worried me all along—the extraordinary crowd travelling in the Stamboul-Calais coach at a slack time of year—this was explained.

"Ratchett had escaped justice in America. There was no question as to his guilt. I visualised a self-appointed jury of twelve people who had condemned him to death and who by the exigencies of the case had themselves been forced to be his executioners. And immediately, on that assumption, the whole case fell into beautiful shining order.

"I saw it as a perfect mosaic, each person playing his or her allotted part. It was so arranged that, if suspicion should fall on any one person, the evidence of one or more of the others would clear the accused person and confuse the issue. Hardman's evidence was necessary in case some outsider should be suspected of the crime and be unable to prove an alibi. The passengers in the Stamboul carriage were in no danger. Every minute detail of their evidence was worked out beforehand. The whole thing was a very cleverly planned jigsaw puzzle, so arranged that every fresh piece of knowledge that came to light made the solution of the whole more difficult. As my friend M. Bouc remarked, the case seemed fantastically impossible! That was exactly the impression intended to be conveyed.

"Did this solution explain everything? Yes, it did. The nature of the wounds—each inflicted by a different person. The artificial threatening letters—artificial since they were unreal, written only to be produced as evidence. (Doubtless there *were* real letters, warning Ratchett of his fate, which MacQueen destroyed, substituting for them these others.) Then Hardman's story of being called in by Ratchett—a lie, of course, from beginning to end. The description of the mythical 'small dark man with a womanish voice'—a convenient description since it had the merit of not incriminating any of the actual Wagon Lit conductors and would apply equally well to a man or a woman.

"The idea of stabbing is at first sight a curious one, but on reflection nothing else would fit the circumstances so well. A dagger was a weapon that could be used by everyone—strong or weak—and it made no noise. I fancy, though I may be wrong, that each person in turn entered Ratchett's darkened compartment through that of Mrs. Hubbard—and struck! They themselves would never know which blow actually killed him.

"The final letter which Ratchett had probably found on his pillow was carefully burnt. With no clue pointing to the Armstrong case there would be absolutely no reason for suspecting any of the passengers on the train. It would be put down as an outside job, and the 'small dark man with the womanish voice' would actually have been seen by one or more of the passengers leaving the train at Brod!

"I do not know exactly what happened when the conspirators discovered that this part of their plan was impossible owing to the accident to the train. There was, I imagine, a hasty consultation, and then they decided to go through with it. It was true that now one and all of the passengers were bound to come under suspicion, but that possibility had already been foreseen and provided for. The only additional thing to be done was to confuse the issue even further. Two so-called 'clues' were dropped in the dead man's compartment—one incriminating Colonel Arbuthnot (who had the strongest alibi and whose connection with the Armstrong family was probably the hardest to prove); and the second clue, the handkerchief, incriminating Princess Dragomiroff who, by virtue of her social position, her particularly frail physique and the alibi given her by her maid and the conductor, was practically in an unassailable position.

"Further to confuse the issue, a red herring was drawn across the trail—the mythical woman in the red kimono. Again I am to bear witness to this woman's existence. There is a heavy bang at my door. I get up and look out—and see the scarlet kimono disappearing in the distance. A judicious selection of people—the conductor, Miss Debenham and MacQueen—will also have seen her. It was, I think, someone with a sense of humour who thoughtfully placed the scarlet kimono on the top of my suitcase whilst I was interviewing people in the dining-car. Where the garment came from in the first place, I do not know. I suspect it is the property of Countess Andrenyi, since her luggage contained only a chiffon negligee so elaborate as to be rather a teagown than a dressing gown.

"When MacQueen first learned that the letter which had been so carefully burnt had in part escaped destruction, and that the word Armstrong was exactly the word remaining, he must at once have communicated his news to the others. It was at this minute that the position of Countess Andrenyi became acute, and her husband immediately took steps to alter the passport. It was their second piece of bad luck!

"They one and all agreed to deny utterly any connection with the Armstrong family. They knew I had no immediate means of finding out the truth, and they did not believe that I should go into the matter unless my suspicions were aroused against one particular person.

"Now there was one further point to consider. Allowing that my theory of the crime was the correct one, and I believed that it *must* be the correct one, then obviously the Wagon Lit conductor himself must be privy to the plot. But if so, that gave us thirteen persons, not twelve. Instead of the usual formula 'Of so many people one is guilty,' I was faced with the problem that of thirteen persons one and one only was innocent. Which was that person?

"I came to a very odd conclusion. I came to the conclusion that the person who had taken no part in the crime was the person who would be considered the most likely to do so. I refer to Countess Andrenyi. I was impressed by the earnestness of her husband when he swore to me solemnly on his honour that his wife never left her compartment that night. I decided that Count Andrenyi took, so to speak, his wife's place.

"If so, then Pierre Michel was definitely one of the twelve. But how could one explain his complicity? He was a decent man who had been many years in the employ of the company—not the kind of man who could be bribed to assist in a crime. Then Pierre Michel must be involved in the Armstrong case. But that seemed very improbable. Then I remembered that the dead nursery-maid had been French. Supposing that that unfortunate girl had been Pierre Michel's daughter. That would explain everything—it would also explain the place chosen for the staging of the crime. Were there any others whose part in the drama was not clear? Colonel Arbuthnot I put down as a friend of the Armstrongs. They had probably been through the War together. The maid, Hildegarde Schmidt—I could guess her place in the Armstrong household. I am, perhaps, over greedy, but I sense a good cook instinctively. I laid a trap for her—she fell into it. I said I knew she was a good cook. She answered: 'Yes, indeed, all my ladies have said so.' But if you are employed as a *lady's-maid* your employers seldom have a chance of learning whether or not you are a good cook.

"Then there was Hardman. He seemed quite definitely not to belong to the Armstrong household. I could only imagine that he had been in love with the French girl. I spoke to him of the charm of foreign women—and again I obtained the reaction I was looking for. Sudden tears came into his eyes, which he pretended were dazzled by the snow.

"There remains Mrs. Hubbard. Now Mrs. Hubbard, let me say, played the most important part in the drama. By occupying the compartment communicating with that of

Ratchett she was more open to suspicion than anyone else. In the nature of things she could not have an alibi to fall back upon. To play the part she played—the perfectly natural, slightly ridiculous American fond mother—an artist was needed. But there *was* an artist connected with the Armstrong family: Mrs. Armstrong's mother—Linda Arden, the actress. . . ."

He stopped.

Then in a soft rich dreamy voice, quite unlike the one she had used throughout the journey, Mrs. Hubbard said:

"I always fancied myself in comedy parts."

She went on, still dreamily:

"That slip about the sponge-bag was silly. It shows that you should always rehearse properly. We tried it on the way out—I was in an even-number compartment then, I suppose. I never thought of the bolts being in different places."

She shifted her position a little and looked straight at Poirot.

"You know all about it, M. Poirot. You're a very wonderful man. But even you can't quite imagine what it was like—that awful day in New York. I was just crazy with grief;

so were the servants. And Colonel Arbuthnot was there too. He was John Armstrong's best friend."

"He saved my life in the War," said Arbuthnot.

"We decided then and there (perhaps we were mad—I don't know) that the sentence of death that Cassetti had escaped had got to be carried out. There were twelve of us— or rather eleven; Susanne's father was over in France, of course. First we thought we'd draw lots as to who should do it, but in the end we decided on this way. It was the chauffeur, Antonio, who suggested it. Mary worked out all the details later with Hector MacQueen. He'd always adored Sonia—my daughter—and it was he who explained to us exactly how Cassetti's money had managed to get him off.

"It took a long time to perfect our plan. We had first to track Ratchett down. Hardman managed that in the end. Then we had to try and get Masterman and Hector into his employment—or at any rate one of them. Well, we managed that. Then we had a consultation with Susanne's father. Colonel Arbuthnot was very keen on having twelve of us. He seemed to think it made it more in order.

He didn't like the stabbing idea much, but he agreed that it did solve most of our difficulties. Well, Susanne's father was willing. Susanne had been his only child. We knew from Hector that Ratchett would be coming back from the East sooner or later by the Orient Express. With Pierre Michel actually working on that train, the chance was too good to be missed. Besides, it would be a good way of not incriminating any outsiders.

"My daughter's husband had to know, of course, and he insisted on coming on the train with her. Hector wangled it so that Ratchett selected the right day for travelling, when Michel would be on duty. We meant to engage every carriage in the Stamboul-Calais coach, but unfortunately there was one carriage we couldn't get. It had been reserved long beforehand for a director of the company. 'Mr. Harris,' of course, was a myth. But it would have been awkward to have any stranger in Hector's compartment. And then, at the last minute, *you* came. . . ."

She stopped.

"Well," she said, "you know everything now, M. Poirot. What are you going to do about it? If it must all come out, can't you lay the blame upon me and me only? I would have stabbed that man twelve times willingly. It wasn't only that he was responsible for my daughter's death and her child's and that of the other child who might have been alive and happy now. It was more than that: there had been other children kidnapped before Daisy, and there might be others in the future. Society had condemned him— we were only carrying out the sentence. But it's unnecessary to bring all these others into it. All these good faithful souls—and poor Michel—and Mary and Colonel Arbuthnot— they love each other. . . ."

Her voice was wonderful, echoing through the crowded space—that deep, emotional, heart-stirring voice that had thrilled many a New York audience.

Poirot looked at his friend.

"You are a director of the company, M. Bouc," he said. "What do you say?"

M. Bouc cleared his throat.

"In my opinion, M. Poirot," he said, "the first theory you put forward was the correct one—decidedly so. I suggest that that is the solution we offer to the Jugo-Slavian police when they arrive. You agree, Doctor?"

"Certainly I agree," said Dr. Constantine.

"As regards the medical evidence, I think—er—that I made one or two fantastic suggestions."

"Then," said Poirot, "having placed my solution before you, I have the honour to retire from the case. . . ."

MURDER IN MESOPOTAMIA

Dedicated to
MY MANY ARCHÆOLOGICAL FRIENDS
IN IRAQ AND SYRIA

Contents

FOREWORD
By Giles Reilly, M.D.

The events chronicled in this narrative took place some four years ago. Circumstances have rendered it necessary, in my opinion, that a straightforward account of them should be given to the public. There have been the wildest and most ridiculous rumours suggesting that important evidence was suppressed and other nonsense of that kind. Those misconstructions have appeared more especially in the American press.

For obvious reasons it was desirable that the account should not come from the pen of one of the expedition staff, who might reasonably be supposed to be prejudiced.

I therefore suggested to Miss Amy Leatheran that she should undertake the task. She is obviously the person to do it. She has a professional character of the highest, she is not biased by having any previous connection with the University of Pittstown Expedition to Iraq and she was an observant and intelligent eye-witness.

It was not very easy to persuade Miss Leatheran to undertake this task—in fact, persuading her was one of the hardest jobs of my professional career—and even after it was completed she displayed a curious reluctance to let me see the manuscript. I discovered that this was partly due to some critical remarks she had made concerning my daughter Sheila. I soon disposed of that, assuring her that as children criticize their parents freely in print nowadays, parents are only too delighted when their offspring come in for their share of abuse! Her other objection was extreme modesty about her literary style. She hoped I would "put the grammar right and all that." I have, on the contrary, refused to alter so much as a single word. Miss Leatheran's style in my opinion is vigorous, individual and entirely apposite. If she calls Hercule Poirot "Poirot" in one paragraph and "Mr. Poirot" in the next, such a variation is both interesting and suggestive. At one moment she is, so to speak, "remembering her manners" (and hospital nurses are great sticklers for etiquette) and at the next her interest in what she is telling is that of a pure human being—cap and cuffs forgotten!

The only thing I have done is to take the liberty of writing a first chapter—aided by a letter kindly supplied by one of Miss Leatheran's friends. It is intended to be in the nature of a frontispiece—that is, it gives a rough sketch of the narrator.

Chapter 1
Foreword

In the hall of the Tigris Palace Hotel in Baghdad a hospital nurse was finishing a letter. Her fountain-pen drove briskly over the paper.

". . . Well, dear, I think that's really all my news. I must say it's been nice to see a bit of the world—though England for me every time, thank you! The dirt and the mess in Baghdad you wouldn't believe—and not romantic at all like you'd think from the Arabian Nights! Of course, it's pretty just on the river, but the town itself is just awful—and no proper shops at all. Major Kelsey took me through the bazaars, and of course there's no denying they're quaint—but just a lot of rubbish and hammering

away at copper pans till they make your head ache—and not what I'd like to use myself unless I was sure about the cleaning. You've got to be so careful of verdigris with copper pans.

"I'll write and let you know if anything comes of the job that Dr. Reilly spoke about. He said this American gentleman was in Baghdad now and might come and see me this afternoon. It's for his wife—she has 'fancies,' so Dr., Reilly said. He didn't say any more than that, and of course, dear, one knows what that usually means (but I hope not actually D.T.'s!). Of course, Dr. Reilly didn't say anything—but he had a look—if you know what I mean. This Dr. Leidner is an archaeologist and is digging up a mound out in the desert somewhere for some American museum.

"Well, dear, I will close now. I thought what you told me about little Stubbins was simply killing! Whatever did Matron say?

"No more now.

"Yours ever,
"Amy Leatheran."

Enclosing the letter in an envelope, she addressed it to Sister Curshaw, St. Christopher's Hospital, London.

As she put the cap on her fountain pen, one of the native boys approached her.

"A gentleman come see you. Dr. Leidner."

Nurse Leatheran turned. She saw a man of middle height with slightly stooping shoulders, a brown beard and gentle tired eyes.

Dr. Leidner saw a woman of thirty-five of erect, confident bearing. He saw a good-humoured face with slightly prominent blue eyes and glossy brown hair. She looked, he thought, just what a hospital nurse for a nervous case ought to look. Cheerful, robust, shrewd and matter of fact.

Nurse Leatheran, he thought, would do.

Chapter 2
Introducing Amy Leatheran

I don't pretend to be an author or to know anything about writing. I'm doing this simply because Dr. Reilly asked me to, and somehow when Dr. Reilly asks you to do a thing you don't like to refuse.

"Oh, but, doctor," I said, "I'm not literary—not literary at all."

"Nonsense!" he said. "Treat it as case notes, if you like."

Well, of course, you *can* look at it that way.

Dr. Reilly went on. He said that an unvarnished plain account of the Tell Yarimjah business was badly needed.

"If one of the interested parties writes it, it won't carry conviction. They'll say it's biased one way or another."

And of course that was true, too. I was in
it all and yet an outsider, so to speak.

"Why don't you write it yourself, doctor?"
I asked.

"I wasn't on the spot—you were. Besides," he added with a sigh, "my daughter
won't let me."

The way he knuckles under to that chit of
a girl of his is downright disgraceful. I had
half a mind to say so, when I saw that his
eyes were twinkling. That was the worst of
Dr. Reilly. You never knew whether he was
joking or not. He always said things in the
same slow melancholy way—but half the
time there was a twinkle underneath it.

"Well," I said doubtfully. "I suppose I
could."

"Of course you could."

"Only I don't quite know how to set about
it."

"There's a good precedent for that. Begin
at the beginning, go on to the end and then
leave off."

"I don't even know quite where and what
the beginning was," I said doubtfully.

"Believe me, nurse, the difficulty of beginning will be nothing to the difficulty of knowing how to stop. At least that's the way it is

with me when I have to make a speech. Some one's got to catch hold of my coat-tails and pull me down by main force."

"Oh, you're joking, doctor."

"It's profoundly serious I am. Now what about it?"

Another thing was worrying me. After hesitating a moment or two I said:

"You know, doctor, I'm afraid I might tend to be—well, a little *personal* sometimes."

"God bless my soul, woman, the more personal you are the better! This is a story of human beings—not dummies! Be personal—be prejudiced—be catty—be anything you please! Write the thing your own way. We can always prune out the bits that are libellous afterwards! You go ahead. You're a sensible woman, and you'll give a sensible common-sense account of the business."

So that was that, and I promised to do my best.

And here I am beginning, but as I said to the doctor, it's difficult to know just where to start.

I suppose I ought to say a word or two about myself. I'm thirty-two and my name is Amy Leatheran. I took my training at St.

Christopher's and after that did two years' maternity. I did a certain amount of private work and I was for four years at Miss Bendix's Nursing Home in Devonshire Place. I came out to Iraq with a Mrs. Kelsey. I'd attended her when her baby was born. She was coming out to Baghdad with her husband and had already got a children's nurse booked who had been for some years with friends of hers out there. Their children were coming home and going to school, and the nurse had agreed to go to Mrs. Kelsey when they left. Mrs. Kelsey was delicate and nervous about the journey out with so young a child, so Major Kelsey arranged that I should come out with her and look after her and the baby. They would pay my passage home unless we found some one needing a nurse for the return journey.

Well, there is no need to describe the Kelseys—the baby was a little love and Mrs. Kelsey quite nice, though rather the fretting kind. I enjoyed the voyage very much. I'd never been on a long trip on the sea before.

Dr. Reilly was on board the boat. He was a black-haired, long-faced man who said all sorts of funny things in a low, sad voice. I think he enjoyed pulling my leg and used to make the most extraordinary statements to see if I would swallow them. He was the civil surgeon at a place called Hassanieh—a day and a half's journey from Baghdad.

I had been about a week in Baghdad when I ran across him and he asked when I was leaving the Kelseys. I said that it was funny his asking that because as a matter of fact the Wrights (the other people I mentioned) were going home earlier than they had meant to and their nurse was free to come straightaway.

He said that he had heard about the Wrights and that that was why he had asked me.

"As a matter of fact, nurse, I've got a possible job for you."

"A case?"

He screwed his face up as though considering.

"You could hardly call it a case. It's just a lady who has—shall we say—fancies?"

"Oh!" I said.

(One usually knows what *that* means—drink or drugs!)

Dr. Reilly didn't explain further. He was very discreet.

"Yes," he said. "A Mrs. Leidner. Husband's an American—an American Swede to be exact. He's the head of a large American dig."

And he explained how this expedition was excavating the site of a big Assyrian city something like Nineveh. The expedition house was not actually very far from Hassanieh, but it was a lonely spot and Dr. Leidner had been worried for some time about his wife's health.

"He's not been very explicit about it, but it seems she has these fits of recurring nervous terrors."

"Is she left alone all day amongst natives?" I asked.

"Oh, no, there's quite a crowd—seven or eight. I don't fancy she's ever alone in the house. But there seems to be no doubt that she's worked herself up into a queer state. Leidner has any amount of work on his shoulders, but he's crazy about his wife and it worries him to know she's in this state. He felt he'd be happier if he knew that some responsible person with expert knowledge was keeping an eye on her."

"And what does Mrs. Leidner herself think about it?"

Dr. Reilly answered gravely.

"Mrs. Leidner is a very lovely lady. She's seldom of the same mind about anything two days on end. But on the whole she favours the idea." He added, "She's an odd woman. A mass of affectation and, I should fancy, a champion liar—but Leidner seems honestly to believe that she is scared out of her life by something or other."

"What did she herself say to you, doctor?"

"Oh, she hasn't consulted me! She doesn't like me anyway—for several reasons. It was Leidner who came to me and propounded this plan. Well, nurse, what do you think of the idea? You'd see something of the country before you go home—they'll be digging for another two months. And excavation is quite interesting work."

After a moment's hesitation while I turned the matter over in my mind:

"Well," I said. "I really think I might try it."

"Splendid," said Dr. Reilly, rising. "Leidner's in Baghdad now. I'll tell him to come round and see if he can fix things up with you."

Dr. Leidner came to the hotel that afternoon. He was a middle-aged man with a rather nervous, hesitating manner. There was something gentle and kindly and rather helpless about him.

He sounded very devoted to his wife, but he was very vague about what was the matter with her.

"You see," he said, tugging at his beard in a rather perplexed manner that I later came to know to be characteristic of him, "my wife is really in a very nervous state. I—I'm quite worried about her."

"She is in good physical health?" I asked.

"Yes—oh, yes, I think so. No, I should not think there was anything the matter with her physically. But she—well—imagines things, you know."

"What kind of things?" I asked.

But he shied off from the point, merely murmuring perplexedly:

"She works herself up over nothing at all. . . . I really can see no foundations for these fears."

"Fears of what, Dr. Leidner?"

He said vaguely, "Oh, just—nervous terrors, you know."

Ten to one, I thought to myself, it's drugs. And he doesn't realize it! Lots of men don't. Just wonder why their wives are so jumpy and have such extraordinary changes of mood.

I asked whether Mrs. Leidner herself approved of the idea of my coming.

His face lighted up.

"Yes. I was surprised. Most pleasurably surprised. She said it was a very good idea. She said she would feel very much safer."

The word struck me oddly. *Safer.* A very queer word to use. I began to surmise that Mrs. Leidner might be a mental case.

He went on with a kind of boyish eagerness.

"I'm sure you'll get on very well with her. She's really a very charming woman." He smiled disarmingly. "She feels you'll be the greatest comfort to her. I felt the same as soon as I saw you. You look, if you will allow me to say so, so splendidly healthy and full of common sense. I'm sure you're just the person for Louise."

"Well, we can but try, Dr. Leidner," I said cheerfully. "I'm sure I hope I can be of use to your wife. Perhaps she's nervous of natives."

"Oh, dear me, no." He shook his head, amused at the idea. "My wife likes Arabs very much—she appreciates their simplicity and their sense of humour. This is only her second season—we have been married less than two years—but she already speaks quite a fair amount of Arabic."

I was silent for a moment or two, then I had one more try.

"Can't you tell me at all what it is your wife is afraid of, Dr. Leidner?" I asked.

He hesitated. Then he said slowly, "I hope—I believe—that she will tell you that herself."

And that's all I could get out of him.

Chapter 3
Gossip

It was arranged that I should go to Tell Yarimjah the following week.

Mrs. Kelsey was settling into her house at Alwiyah, and I was glad to be able to take a few things off her shoulders.

During that time I heard one or two allusions to the Leidner expedition. A friend of Mrs. Kelsey's, a young squadron-leader, pursed his lips in surprise as he exclaimed:

"Lovely Louise. So that's her latest!" He turned to me. "That's our nickname for her, nurse. She's always known as Lovely Louise."

"Is she so very handsome then?" I asked.

"It's taking her at her own valuation. *She* thinks she is!"

"Now don't be spiteful, John," said Mrs.

Kelsey. "You know it's not only she who thinks so! Lots of people have been very smitten by her."

"Perhaps you're right. She's a bit long in the tooth, but she has a certain attraction."

"You were completely bowled over yourself," said Mrs. Kelsey, laughing.

The squadron-leader blushed and admitted rather shamefacedly:

"Well, she has a way with her. As for Leidner himself, he worships the ground she walks on—and all the rest of the expedition has to worship too! It's expected of them!"

"How many are there altogether?" I asked.

"All sorts and nationalities, nurse," said the squadron-leader cheerfully. "An English architect, a French Father from Carthage— he does the inscriptions—tablets and things, you know. And then there's Miss Johnson. She's English too—sort of general bottle-washer. And a little plump man who does the photography—he's an American. And the Mercados. Heaven knows what nationality they are. She's quite young—a snaky-looking creature—and oh! doesn't she hate Lovely Louise! And there are a couple of youngsters, and that's the lot. A few odd fish, but nice on the whole—don't you agree, Pennyman?"

He was appealing to an elderly man who was sitting thoughtfully twirling a pair of pince-nez.

The latter started and looked up.

"Yes—yes—very nice indeed. Taken individually, that is. Of course, Mercado is rather a queer fish—"

"He has such a very *odd* beard," put in Mrs. Kelsey. "A queer limp kind."

Major Pennyman went on without noticing her interruption.

"The young 'uns are both nice. The American's rather silent, and the English boy talks a bit too much. Funny, it's usually the other way round. Leidner himself is a delightful fellow—so modest and unassuming. Yes, individually they are all pleasant people. But somehow or other, I may have been fanciful, but the last time I went to see them I got a queer impression of something being wrong. I don't know what it was exactly. . . . Nobody seemed quite natural. There was a queer atmosphere of tension. I can explain best what I mean by saying that they all passed the butter to each other too politely."

Blushing a little, because I don't like airing my own opinions too much, I said:

"If people are too much cooped up together it's got a way of getting on their nerves. I know that myself from experience in hospital."

"That's true," said Major Kelsey, "but it's early in the season, hardly time for that particular irritation to have set in."

"An expedition is probably like our life here in miniature," said Major Pennyman. "It has its cliques and rivalries and jealousies."

"It sounds as though they'd got a good many newcomers this year," said Major Kelsey.

"Let me see." The squadron-leader counted them off on his fingers. "Young Coleman is new, so is Reiter. Emmott was out last year and so were the Mercados. Father Lavigny is a new-comer. He's come in place of Dr. Byrd, who was ill this year and couldn't come out. Carey, of course, is an old hand. He's been out ever since the beginning, five years ago. Miss Johnson's been out nearly as many years as Carey."

"I always thought they got on so well together at Tell Yarimjah," remarked Major Kelsey. "They seemed like a happy family—

which is really surprising when one considers what human nature is! I'm sure Nurse Leatheran agrees with me."

"Well," I said. "I don't know that you're not right! The rows I've known in hospital and starting often from nothing more than a dispute about a pot of tea."

"Yes, one tends to get petty in close communities," said Major Pennyman. "All the same I feel there must be something more to it in this case. Leidner is such a gentle, unassuming man, with really a remarkable amount of tact. He's always managed to keep his expedition happy and on good terms with each other. And yet I *did* notice that feeling of tension the other day."

Mrs. Kelsey laughed.

"And you don't see the explanation? Why, it leaps to the eye!"

"What do you mean?"

"*Mrs*. Leidner, of course."

"Oh, come, Mary," said her husband, "she's a charming woman—not at all the quarrelsome kind."

"I didn't say she was quarrelsome. She *causes* quarrels!"

"In what way? And why should she?"

"Why? Why? Because she's bored. She's

not an archaeologist, only the wife of one. She's bored shut away from any excitements and so she provides her own drama. She amuses herself by setting other people by the ears."

"Mary, you don't know in the least. You're merely imagining."

"Of course I'm imagining! But you'll find I'm right. Lovely Louise doesn't look like the Mona Lisa for nothing! She mayn't mean any harm, but she likes to see what will happen."

"She's devoted to Leidner."

"Oh! I dare say. I'm not suggesting vulgar intrigues. But she's an *allumeuse*, that woman."

"Women are so sweet to each other," said Major Kelsey.

"I know. Cat, cat, cat, that's what you men say. But we're usually right about our own sex."

"All the same," said Major Pennyman thoughtfully, "assuming all Mrs. Kelsey's uncharitable surmises to be true, I don't think it would quite account for that curious sense of tension—rather like the feeling there is before a thunderstorm. I had the impression very strongly that the storm might break any minute."

"Now don't frighten nurse," said Mrs. Kelsey. "She's going there in three days' time and you'll put her right off."

"Oh, you won't frighten me," I said, laughing.

All the same I thought a good deal about what had been said. Dr. Leidner's curious use of the word "safer" recurred to me. Was it his wife's secret fear, unacknowledged or expressed perhaps, that was reacting on the rest of the party? Or was it the actual tension (or perhaps the unknown cause of it) that was reacting on *her* nerves?

I looked up the word "allumeuse" that Mrs. Kelsey had used in a dictionary, but couldn't get any sense out of it.

"Well," I thought to myself, "I must wait and see."

Chapter 4
I Arrive in Hassanieh

Three days later I left Baghdad.

I was sorry to leave Mrs. Kelsey and the baby, who was a little love and was thriving splendidly, gaining her proper number of ounces every week. Major Kelsey took me to the station and saw me off. I should arrive at Kirkuk the following morning, and there some one was to meet me.

I slept badly. I never sleep very well in a train and I was troubled by dreams.

The next morning, however, when I looked out of the window it was a lovely day and I felt interested and curious about the people I was going to see.

As I stood on the platform hesitating and looking about me I saw a young man coming towards me. He had a round pink face, and really, in all my life, I have never seen any one who seemed so exactly like a young man out of one of Mr. P. G. Wodehouse's books.

"Hallo, 'allo, 'allo," he said. "Are you Nurse Leatheran? Well, I mean you must be—I can see that. Ha ha! My name's Coleman. Dr. Leidner sent me along. How are you feeling? Beastly journey and all that? Don't I know these trains! Well, here we are—had any breakfast? This your kit? I say, awfully modest, aren't you? Mrs. Leidner has four suitcases and a trunk—to say nothing of a hat-box and a patent pillow, and this, that and the other. Am I talking too much? Come along to the old bus."

There was what I heard called later a station wagon waiting outside. It was a little like a wagonette, a little like a lorry and a little like a car. Mr. Coleman helped me in, explaining that I had better sit next to the driver so as to get less jolting.

Jolting! I wonder the whole contraption didn't fall to pieces! And nothing like a road—just a sort of track all ruts and holes. Glorious East indeed! When I thought of our splendid arterial roads in England it made me quite homesick.

Mr. Coleman leaned forward from his seat behind me and yelled in my ear a good deal.

"Track's in pretty good condition," he shouted just after we had all been thrown up in our seats till we nearly touched the roof.

And apparently he was speaking quite seriously.

"Very good for you—jogs the liver," he said. "You ought to know that, nurse."

"A stimulated liver won't be much good to me if my head's split open," I observed tartly.

"You should come along here after it's rained! The skids are glorious. Most of the time one's going sideways."

To this I did not respond.

Presently we had to cross the river, which we did on the craziest ferry-boat you can imagine. To my mind it was a mercy we ever got across, but every one seemed to think it was quite usual.

It took us about four hours to get to Hassanieh, which, to my surprise, was quite a big place. Very pretty it looked, too, before we got there from the other side of the river—standing up quite white and fairy-like with minarets. It was a bit different, though, when one had crossed the bridge and come right into it. Such a smell, and everything ramshackle and tumble-down, and mud and mess everywhere.

Mr. Coleman took me to Dr. Reilly's house, where, he said, the doctor was expecting me to lunch.

Dr. Reilly was just as nice as ever, and his house was nice too, with a bathroom and everything spick and span. I had a nice bath, and by the time I got back into my uniform and came down I was feeling fine.

Lunch was just ready and we went in, the doctor apologizing for his daughter, whom he said was always late.

We'd just had a very good dish of eggs in sauce when she came in and Dr. Reilly said, "Nurse, this is my daughter Sheila."

She shook hands, hoped I'd had a good journey, tossed off her hat, gave a cool nod to Mr. Coleman and sat down.

"Well, Bill," she said. "How's everything?"

He began to talk to her about some party or other that was to come off at the club, and I took stock of her.

I can't say I took to her much. A thought too cool for my liking. An off-hand sort of girl, though good-looking. Black hair and blue eyes—a pale sort of face and the usual lip-sticked mouth. She'd a cool, sarcastic way of talking that rather annoyed me. I had a probationer like her under me once—a girl who worked well, I'll admit, but whose manner always riled me.

It looked to me rather as though Mr. Coleman was gone on her. He stammered a bit, and his conversation became slightly more idiotic than it was before, if that was possible! He reminded me of a large stupid dog wagging its tail and trying to please.

After lunch Dr. Reilly went off to the hospital, and Mr. Coleman had some things to get in the town, and Miss Reilly asked me whether I'd like to see round the town a bit or whether I'd rather stop in the house. Mr. Coleman, she said, would be back to fetch me in about an hour.

"Is there anything to see?" I asked.

"There are some picturesque corners," said Miss Reilly. "But I don't know that you'd care for them. They're extremely dirty."

The way she said it rather nettled me. I've never been able to see that picturesqueness excuses dirt.

In the end she took me to the club, which

was pleasant enough, overlooking the river, and there were English papers and magazines there.

When we got back to the house Mr. Coleman wasn't there yet, so we sat down and talked a bit. It wasn't easy somehow.

She asked me if I'd met Mrs. Leidner yet.

"No," I said. "Only her husband."

"Oh," she said. "I wonder what you'll think of her?"

I didn't say anything to that. And she went on:

"I like Dr. Leidner very much. Everybody likes him."

That's as good as saying, I thought, that you don't like his wife.

I still didn't say anything and presently she asked abruptly:

"What's the matter with her? Did Dr. Leidner tell you?"

I wasn't going to start gossiping about a patient before I got there even, so I said evasively:

"I understand she's a bit run down and wants looking after."

She laughed—a nasty sort of laugh—hard and abrupt.

"Good God," she said. "Aren't nine people looking after her already enough?"

"I suppose they've all got their work to do," I said.

"Work to do? Of course they've got work to do. But Louise comes first—she sees to that all right."

"No," I said to myself. "You *don't* like her."

"All the same," went on Miss Reilly, "I don't see what she wants with a professional hospital nurse. I should have thought amateur assistance was more in her line; not some one who'll jam a thermometer in her mouth, and count her pulse and bring everything down to hard facts."

Well, I must admit it, I was curious.

"You think there's nothing the matter with her?" I asked.

"Of course there's nothing the matter with her! The woman's as strong as an ox. 'Dear Louise hasn't slept.' 'She's got black circles under her eyes.' Yes—put there with a blue pencil! Anything to get attention, to have everybody hovering round her, making a fuss of her!"

There was something in that, of course. I had (what nurse hasn't?) come across many cases of hypochondriacs whose delight it is to keep a whole household dancing attendance. And if a doctor or a nurse were to say to them, "There's nothing on earth the matter with you!" well, to begin with they wouldn't believe it, and their indignation would be as genuine as indignation can be.

Of course it was quite possible that Mrs. Leidner might be a case of this kind. The husband, naturally, would be the first to be deceived. Husbands, I've found, are a credulous lot where illness is concerned. But all the same, it didn't quite square with what I'd heard. It didn't, for instance, fit in with that word "safer."

Funny how that word had got kind of stuck in my mind.

Reflecting on it, I asked:

"Is Mrs. Leidner a nervous woman? Is she nervous, for instance, of living out far from anywhere?"

"What is there to be nervous of? Good heavens, there are ten of them! And they've got guards too—because of the antiquities. Oh, no, she's not nervous—at least—"

She seemed struck by some thought and stopped—going on slowly after a minute or two.

"It's odd your saying that."

"Why?"

"Flight-Lieutenant Jervis and I rode over the other day. It was in the morning. Most of them were up on the dig. She was sitting writing a letter and I suppose she didn't hear us coming. The boy who brings you in wasn't about for once, and we came straight up on to the verandah. Apparently she saw Flight-Lieutenant Jervis's shadow thrown on the wall—and she fairly screamed! Apologized, of course. Said she thought it was a strange man. A bit odd, that. I mean, even if it was a strange man, why get the wind up?"

I nodded thoughtfully.

Miss Reilly was silent, then burst out suddenly.

"I don't know what's the matter with them there this year. They've all got the jumps. Johnson goes about so glum she can't open her mouth. David never speaks if he can help it. Bill, of course, never stops, and somehow his chatter seems to make the others worse. Carey goes about looking as though something would snap any minute. And they all watch each other as though— as though—Oh, I don't know, but it's *queer*."

It was odd, I thought, that two such dissimilar people as Miss Reilly and Major Pennyman should have been struck in the same manner.

Just then Mr. Coleman came bustling in. Bustling was just the word for it. If his tongue had hung out and he had suddenly produced a tail to wag you wouldn't have been surprised.

"Hallo-allo," he said. "Absolutely the world's best shopper—that's me. Have you shown nurse all the beauties of the town?"

"She wasn't impressed," said Miss Reilly dryly.

"I don't blame her," said Mr. Coleman heartily. "Of all the one-horse tumble-down places!"

"Not a lover of the picturesque or the antique, are you, Bill? I can't think why you are an archaeologist."

"Don't blame me for that. Blame my guardian. He's a learned bird—fellow of his college—browses among books in bedroom slippers—that kind of man. Bit of a shock for him to have a ward like me."

"I think it's frightfully stupid of you to be forced into a profession you don't care for," said the girl sharply.

"Not forced, Sheila, old girl, not forced. The old man asked if I had any special profession in mind, and I said I hadn't, and so he wangled a season out here for me."

"But haven't you any idea really what you'd *like* to do? You *must* have!"

"Of course I have. My idea would be to give work a miss altogether. What I'd like to do is to have plenty of money and go in for motor-racing."

"You're absurd!" said Miss Reilly.

She sounded quite angry.

"Oh, I realize that it's quite out of the question," said Mr. Coleman cheerfully. "So, if I've got to do something, I don't much care what it is so long as it isn't mugging in an office all day long. I was quite agreeable to seeing a bit of the world. Here goes, I said, and along I came."

"And a fat lot of use you must be, I expect!"

"There you're wrong. I can stand up on the dig and shout '*Y' Allah*' with anybody! And as a matter of fact I'm not so dusty at drawing. Imitating handwriting used to be my speciality at school. I'd have made a first-class forger. Oh, well, I may come to that yet. If my Rolls-Royce splashes you with mud as you're waiting for a bus, you'll know that I've taken to crime."

Miss Reilly said coldly:

"Don't you think it's about time you started instead of talking so much?"

"Hospitable, aren't we, nurse?"

"I'm sure Nurse Leatheran is anxious to get settled in."

"You're always sure of everything," retorted Mr. Coleman with a grin.

That was true enough, I thought. Cocksure little minx.

I said dryly:

"Perhaps we'd better start, Mr. Coleman."

"Right you are, nurse."

I shook hands with Miss Reilly and thanked her, and we set off.

"Damned attractive girl, Sheila," said Mr. Coleman. "But always ticking a fellow off."

We drove out of the town and presently took a kind of track between green crops. It was very bumpy and full of ruts.

After about half an hour Mr. Coleman pointed to a big mound by the riverbank ahead of us and said:

"Tell Yarimjah."

I could see little black figures moving about it like ants.

As I was looking they suddenly began to run all together down the side of the mound.

"Fidos," said Mr. Coleman. "Knocking off time. We knock off an hour before sunset."

The expedition house lay a little way back from the river.

The driver rounded a corner, bumped through an extremely narrow arch and there we were.

The house was built round a courtyard. Originally it had occupied only the south side of the courtyard with a few unimportant out-buildings on the east. The expedition had continued the building on the other two sides. As the plan of the house was to prove of special interest later, I append a rough sketch of it.

All the rooms opened on to the courtyard, and most of the windows—the exception being in the original south building where there were windows giving on the outside country as well. These windows, however, were barred on the outside. In the south-west corner a staircase ran up to a long flat roof with a parapet running the length of the south side of the building which was higher than the other three sides.

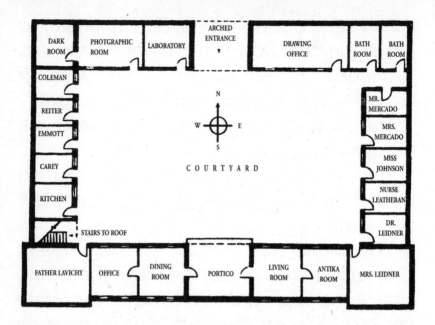

Mr. Coleman led me along the east side of the courtyard and round to where a big open verandah occupied the centre of the south side. He pushed open a door at one side of it and we entered a room where several people were sitting round a tea table.

"Toodle-oodle-oo!" said Mr. Coleman. "Here's Sairey Gamp."

The lady who was sitting at the head of the table rose and came to greet me.

I had my first glimpse of Louise Leidner.

Chapter 5
Tell Yarimjah

I don't mind admitting that my first impression on seeing Mrs. Leidner was one of downright surprise. One gets into the way of imagining a person when one hears them talked about. I'd got it firmly into my head that Mrs. Leidner was a dark, discontented kind of woman. The nervy kind, all on edge. And then, too, I'd expected her to be—well, to put it frankly—a bit vulgar.

She wasn't a bit like what I'd imagined her! To begin with, she was very fair. She wasn't a Swede, like her husband, but she might have been as far as looks went. She had that blonde Scandinavian fairness that you don't very often see. She wasn't a young woman. Midway between thirty and forty, I should say. Her face was rather haggard, and there was some grey hair mingled with the fairness. Her eyes, though, were lovely. They were the only eyes I've ever come across that you might truly describe as violet. They were very large, and there were faint shadows underneath them. She was very thin and fragile-looking, and if I say that she had an air of intense weariness and was at the same time very much alive, it sounds like nonsense—but that's the feeling I got. I felt, too, that she was a lady through and through. And that means something—even nowadays.

She put out her hand and smiled. Her voice was low and soft with an American drawl in it.

"I'm so glad you've come, nurse. Will you have some tea? Or would you like to go to your room first?"

I said I'd have tea, and she introduced me to the people sitting round the table.

"This is Miss Johnson—and Mr. Reiter. Mrs. Mercado. Mr. Emmott. Father Lavigny. My husband will be in presently. Sit down here between Father Lavigny and Miss Johnson."

I did as I was bid and Miss Johnson began talking to me, asking about my journey and so on.

I liked her. She reminded me of a matron I'd had in my probationer days whom we had all admired and worked hard for.

She was getting on for fifty, I should judge, and rather mannish in appearance, with iron-grey hair cropped short. She had an abrupt, pleasant voice, rather deep in tone. She had an ugly rugged face with an almost laughably turned-up nose which she was in the habit of rubbing irritably when anything troubled or perplexed her. She wore a tweed coat and skirt made rather like a man's. She told me presently that she was a native of Yorkshire.

Father Lavigny I found just a bit alarming. He was a tall man with a great black beard and pince-nez. I had heard Mrs. Kelsey say that there was a French monk there, and I now saw that Father Lavigny was wearing a monk's robe of some white woollen material. It surprised me rather, because I always understood that monks went into monasteries and didn't come out again.

Mrs. Leidner talked to him mostly in French, but he spoke to me in quite fair English. I noticed that he had shrewd, observant eyes which darted about from face to face.

Opposite me were the other three. Mr. Reiter was a stout, fair young man with glasses. His hair was rather long and curly, and he had very round blue eyes. I should think he must have been a lovely baby, but he wasn't much to look at now! In fact he was just a little like a pig. The other young man had very short hair cropped close to his head. He had a long, rather humorous face and very good teeth, and he looked very attractive when he smiled. He said very little, though, just nodded if spoken to or answered in monosyllables. He, like Mr. Reiter, was an American. The last person was Mrs. Mercado, and I couldn't have a good look at her because whenever I glanced in her direction I always found her staring at me with a kind of hungry stare that was a bit disconcerting to say the least of it. You might have thought a hospital nurse was a strange animal the way she was looking at me. No manners at all!

She was quite young—not more than about twenty-five—and sort of dark and slinky-looking, if you know what I mean. Quite nice-looking in a kind of way, but rather as though she might have what my mother used to call "a touch of the tarbrush." She had on a very vivid pullover and her nails matched it in colour. She had a thin bird-like eager face with big eyes and rather a tight, suspicious mouth.

The tea was very good—a nice strong blend—not like the weak China stuff that Mrs. Kelsey always had and that had been a sore trial to me.

There was toast and jam and a plate of rock buns and a cutting cake. Mr. Emmott was very polite passing me things. Quiet as he was he always seemed to notice when my plate was empty.

Presently Mr. Coleman bustled in and took the place beyond Miss Johnson. There didn't seem to be anything the matter with *his* nerves. He talked away nineteen to the dozen.

Mrs. Leidner sighed once and cast a wearied look in his direction but it didn't have any effect. Nor did the fact that Mrs. Mercado, to whom he was addressing most of his conversation, was far too busy watching me to do more than make perfunctory replies.

Just as we were finishing, Dr. Leidner and Mr. Mercado came in from the dig.

Dr. Leidner greeted me in his nice kind manner. I saw his eyes go quickly and anxiously to his wife's face and he seemed to be relieved by what he saw there. Then he sat down at the other end of the table and Mr. Mercado sat down in the vacant place by Mrs. Leidner. He was a tall, thin, melancholy man, a good deal older than his wife, with a sallow complexion and a queer, soft, shapeless-looking beard. I was glad when he came in, for his wife stopped staring at me and transferred her attention to him, watching him with a kind of anxious impatience that I found rather odd. He himself stirred his tea dreamily and said nothing at all. A piece of cake lay untasted on his plate.

There was still one vacant place, and presently the door opened and a man came in.

The moment I saw Richard Carey I felt he was one of the handsomest men I'd seen for a long time—and yet I doubt if that were really so. To say a man is handsome and at the same time to say he looks like a death's head sounds a rank contradiction, and yet it was true. His head gave the effect of having the skin stretched unusually tightly over the bones—but they were beautiful bones. The lean line of jaw and temple and forehead was so sharply outlined that he reminded me of a bronze statue. Out of this lean brown face looked two of the brightest and most intensely blue eyes I have ever seen. He stood about six foot and was, I should imagine, a little under forty years of age.

Dr. Leidner said:

"This is Mr. Carey, our architect, nurse."

He murmured something in a pleasant, inaudible English voice and sat down by Mrs. Mercado.

Mrs. Leidner said:

"I'm afraid the tea is a little cold, Mr. Carey."

He said: "Oh, that's quite all right Mrs. Leidner. My fault for being late. I wanted to finish plotting those walls."

Mrs. Mercado said, "Jam, Mr. Carey?"

Mr. Reiter pushed forward the toast.

And I remember Major Pennyman saying:

"I can explain best what I mean by saying that they all passed the butter to each other a shade too politely."

Yes, there was something a little too odd about it. . . .

A shade formal. . . .

You'd have said it was a party of strangers—not people who had known each other—some of them—for quite a number of years.

Chapter 6
First Evening

After tea Mrs. Leidner took me to show me my room.

Perhaps here I had better give a short description of the arrangement of the rooms. This was very simple and can easily be understood by a reference to the plan.

On either side of the big open porch were doors leading into the two principal rooms. That on the right led into the dining-room, where we had had tea. The one on the other side led into an exactly similar room (I have called it the living-room) which was used as a sitting-room and kind of informal work-room—that is, a certain amount of drawing (other than the strictly architectural) was done there, and the more delicate pieces of pottery were brought there to be pieced together. Through the living-room one passed into the antiquities-room where all the finds from the dig were brought in and stored on shelves and in pigeon-holes, and also laid out on big benches and tables. From the antika-room there was no exit save through the living-room.

Beyond the antika-room, but reached through a door which gave on the court-yard, was Mrs. Leidner's bedroom. This, like the other rooms on that side of the house, had a couple of barred windows looking out over the ploughed countryside. Round the corner next to Mrs. Leidner's room, but with no actual communicating door, was Dr. Leidner's room. This was the first of the rooms on the east side of the building. Next to it was the room that was to be mine. Next to me was Miss Johnson's, with Mr. and Mrs. Mercado's beyond. After that came two so-called bathrooms.

(When I once used that last term in the hearing of Dr. Reilly he laughed at me and said a bathroom was either a bathroom or not a bathroom! All the same, when you've got used to taps and proper plumbing, it seems strange to call a couple of mud-rooms with a tin hip-bath in each of them, and muddy water brought in kerosene tins, *bathrooms!*)

All this side of the building had been added by Dr. Leidner to the original Arab house. The bedrooms were all the same, each with a window and a door giving on to the courtyard.

Along the north side were the drawing office, the laboratory and the photographic rooms.

To return to the verandah, the arrangement of rooms was much the same on the other side. There was the dining-room leading into the office where the files were kept and the cataloguing and typing was done. Corresponding to Mrs. Leidner's room was that of Father Lavigny, who was given the largest bedroom; he used it also for the decoding—or whatever you call it—of tablets.

In the south-west corner was the staircase running up to the roof. On the west side were first the kitchen quarters and then four small bedrooms used by the young men—Carey, Emmott, Reiter and Coleman.

At the north-west corner was the photographic-room with the dark-room leading out of it. Next to that the laboratory. Then came the only entrance—the big arched doorway through which we had entered. Outside were sleeping quarters for the native servants, the guard-house for the soldiers, and stables, etc., for the water horses. The drawing-office was to the right of the archway occupying the rest of the north side.

I have gone into the arrangements of the house rather fully here because I don't want to have to go over them again later.

As I say, Mrs. Leidner herself took me round the building and finally established me in my bedroom, hoping that I should be comfortable and have everything I wanted.

The room was nicely though plainly furnished—a bed, a chest of drawers, a washstand and a chair.

"The boys will bring you hot water before lunch and dinner—and in the morning, of course. If you want it any other time, go outside and clap your hands, and when the boy comes say, *jib mai' har*. Do you think you can remember that?"

I said I thought so and repeated it a little haltingly.

"That's right. And be sure and shout it. Arabs don't understand anything said in an ordinary 'English' voice."

"Languages are funny things," I said. "It seems odd there should be such a lot of different ones."

Mrs. Leidner smiled.

"There is a church in Palestine in which the Lord's Prayer is written up in—ninety, I think it is—different languages."

"Well!" I said, "I must write and tell my old aunt that. She *will* be interested."

Mrs. Leidner fingered the jug and basin absently and shifted the soap-dish an inch or two.

"I do hope you'll be happy here," she said. "And not get too bored."

"I'm not often bored," I assured her. "Life's not long enough for that."

She did not answer. She continued to toy with the wash-stand as though abstractedly.

Suddenly she fixed her dark violet eyes on my face.

"What exactly did my husband tell you, nurse?"

Well, one usually says the same thing to a question of that kind.

"I gathered you were a bit run-down and all that, Mrs. Leidner," I said glibly. "And that

you just wanted some one to look after you
and take any worries off your hands."

She bent her head slowly and thoughtfully.

"Yes," she said. "Yes—that will do very
well."

That was just a little bit enigmatic, but I
wasn't going to question it. Instead I said:

"I hope you'll let me help you with anything there is to do in the house. You
mustn't let me be idle."

She smiled a little.

"Thank you, nurse."

Then she sat down on the bed and, rather
to my surprise, began to cross-question me
rather closely. I say rather to my surprise
because, from the moment I set eyes on
her, I felt sure that Mrs. Leidner was a lady.
And a lady, in my experience, very seldom
displays curiosity about one's private affairs.

But Mrs. Leidner seemed anxious to
know everything there was to know about
me. Where I'd trained and how long ago.
What had brought me out to the East. How
it had come about that Dr. Reilly had recom-
mended me. She even asked me if I had
ever been in America or had any relations in

America. One or two other questions she asked me that seemed quite purposeless at the time, but of which I saw the significance later.

Then, suddenly, her manner changed. She smiled—a warm sunny smile—and she said, very sweetly, that she was very glad I had come and that she was sure I was going to be a comfort to her.

She got up from the bed and said:

"Would you like to come up to the roof and see the sunset? It's usually very lovely about this time."

I agreed willingly.

As we went out of the room she asked:

"Were there many other people on the train from Baghdad? Any men?"

I said that I hadn't noticed anybody in particular. There had been two Frenchmen in the restaurant-car the night before. And a party of three men whom I gathered from their conversation had to do with the Pipe line.

She nodded and a faint sound escaped her. It sounded like a small sigh of relief.

We went up to the roof together.

Mrs. Mercado was there, sitting on the parapet, and Dr. Leidner was bending over looking at a lot of stones and broken pottery that were laid out in rows. There were big things he called querns, and pestles and celts and stone axes, and more broken bits of pottery with queer patterns on them than I've ever seen all at once.

"Come over here," called out Mrs. Mercado. "Isn't it *too*, too beautiful?"

It certainly was a beautiful sunset. Hassanieh in the distance looked quite fairy-like with the setting sun behind it, and the River Tigris flowing between its wide banks looked like a dream river rather than a real one.

"Isn't it lovely, Eric?" said Mrs. Leidner.

The doctor looked up with abstracted eyes, murmured, "Lovely, lovely," perfunctorily and went on sorting potsherds.

Mrs. Leidner smiled and said:

"Archaeologists only look at what lies beneath their feet. The sky and the heavens don't exist for them."

Mrs. Mercado giggled.

"Oh, they're very queer people—you'll soon find *that* out, nurse," she said.

She paused and then added:

"We are all *so* glad you've come. We've

been so very worried about our dear Mrs. Leidner, haven't we, Louise?"

"Have you?"

Her voice was not encouraging.

"Oh, yes. She really has been *very* bad, nurse. All sorts of alarms and excursions. You know when anybody says to me of some one, 'It's just nerves,' I always say: But what could be *worse?* Nerves are the core and centre of one's being, aren't they?"

"Puss, puss," I thought to myself.

Mrs. Leidner said dryly:

"Well, you needn't be worried about me any more, Marie. Nurse is going to look after me."

"Certainly I am," I said cheerfully.

"I'm sure that will make all the difference," said Mrs. Mercado. "We've all felt that she ought to see a doctor or do *something*. Her nerves have really been all to pieces, haven't they, Louise dear?"

"So much so that I seem to have got on *your* nerves with them," said Mrs. Leidner. "Shall we talk about something more interesting than my wretched ailments?"

I understood then that Mrs. Leidner was the sort of woman who could easily make enemies. There was a cool rudeness in her tone (not that I blamed her for it) which brought a flush to Mrs. Mercado's rather sallow cheeks. She stammered out something, but Mrs. Leidner had risen and had joined her husband at the other end of the roof. I doubt if he heard her coming till she laid her hand on his shoulder, then he looked up quickly. There was affection and a kind of eager questioning in his face.

Mrs. Leidner nodded her head gently. Presently, her arm through his, they wandered to the far parapet and finally down the steps together.

"He's devoted to her, isn't he?" said Mrs. Mercado.

"Yes," I said. "It's very nice to see."

She was looking at me with a queer, rather eager sidelong glance.

"What do you think is really the matter with her, nurse?" she asked, lowering her voice a little.

"Oh, I don't suppose it's much," I said cheerfully. "Just a bit run down, I expect."

Her eyes still bored into me as they had done at tea. She said abruptly:

"Are you a mental nurse?"

"Oh, dear no!" I said. "What made you think that?"

She was silent for a moment, then she said:

"Do you know how queer she's been? Did Dr. Leidner tell you?"

I don't hold with gossiping about my cases. On the other hand, it's my experience that it's often very hard to get the truth out of the relatives, and until you know the truth you're often working in the dark and doing no good. Of course, when there's a doctor in charge, it's different. He tells you what it's necessary for you to know. But in this case there wasn't a doctor in charge. Dr. Reilly had never been called in professionally. And in my own mind I wasn't at all sure that Dr. Leidner had told me all he could have done. It's often the husband's instinct to be reticent—and more honour to him, I say. But all the same, the more I knew the better I could tell which line to take. Mrs. Mercado (whom I put down in my own mind as a thoroughly spiteful little cat) was clearly dying to talk. And frankly, on the human side as well as the professional, I wanted to hear what she had to say. You can put it that I was just every-day curious if you like.

I said, "I gather Mrs. Leidner's not been quite her normal self lately?"

Mrs. Mercado laughed disagreeably.

"Normal? I should say not. Frightening us to death. One night it was fingers tapping on her window. And then it was a hand without an arm attached. But when it came to a yellow face pressed against the window—and when she rushed to the window there was nothing there—well, I ask you, it *is* a bit creepy for all of us."

"Perhaps somebody was playing a trick on her," I suggested.

"Oh, no, she fancied it all. And only three days ago at dinner they were firing off shots in the village—nearly a mile away—and she jumped up and screamed out—it scared us all to death. As for Dr. Leidner, he rushed to her and behaved in the most ridiculous way. 'It's nothing, darling, it's nothing at all,' he kept saying. I think, you know, nurse, men sometimes *encourage* women in these hysterical fancies. It's a pity because it's a bad thing. Delusions shouldn't be encouraged."

"Not if they *are* delusions," I said dryly.

"What else could they be?"

I didn't answer because I didn't know what to say. It was a funny business. The shots and the screaming were natural enough—for any one in a nervous condition, that is. But this queer story of a spectral face and hand was different. It looked to me like one of two things—either Mrs. Leidner had made the story up (exactly as a child shows off by telling lies about something that never happened in order to make herself the centre of attraction) or else it was, as I had suggested, a deliberate practical joke. It was the sort of thing, I reflected, that an unimaginative hearty sort of young fellow like Mr. Coleman might think very funny. I decided to keep a close watch on him. Nervous patients can be scared nearly out of their minds by a silly joke.

Mrs. Mercado said with a sideways glance at me:

"She's very romantic-looking, nurse, don't you think so? The sort of woman things *happen* to."

"Have many things happened to her?" I asked.

"Well, her first husband was killed in the war when she was only twenty. I think that's very pathetic and romantic, don't you?"

"It's one way of calling a goose a swan," I said dryly.

"Oh! nurse. What an extraordinary remark!"

It was really a very true one. The amount of women you hear say, "If Donald—or Arthur—or whatever his name was—had *only* lived." And I sometimes think but if he had, he'd have been a stout, unromantic, short-tempered, middle-aged husband as likely as not.

It was getting dark and I suggested that we should go down. Mrs. Mercado agreed and asked if I would like to see the laboratory. "My husband will be there—working."

I said I would like to very much and we made our way there. The place was lighted by a lamp but it was empty. Mrs. Mercado showed me some of the apparatus and some copper ornaments that were being treated, and also some bones coated with wax.

"Where can Joseph be?" said Mrs. Mercado.

She looked into the drawing-office, where Carey was at work. He hardly looked up as we entered, and I was struck by the extraordinary look of strain on his face. It came to me suddenly: "This man is at the end of his tether. Very soon, something will snap." And I remembered somebody else had noticed that same tenseness about him.

As we went out again I turned my head for one last look at him. He was bent over his paper, his lips pressed very closely together, and that "death's head" suggestion of his bones very strongly marked. Perhaps it was fanciful, but I thought that he looked like a knight of old who was going into battle and knew he was going to be killed.

And again I felt what an extraordinary and quite unconscious power of attraction he had.

We found Mr. Mercado in the living-room. He was explaining the idea of some new process to Mrs. Leidner. She was sitting on a straight wooden chair, embroidering flowers in fine silks, and I was struck anew by her strange, fragile, unearthly appearance. She looked a fairy creature more than flesh and blood.

Mrs. Mercado said, her voice high and shrill:

"Oh, *there* you are, Joseph. We thought we'd find you in the lab."

He jumped up looking startled and confused, as though her entrance had broken a spell. He said stammeringly:

"I—I must go now. I'm in the middle of—middle of—"

He didn't complete the sentence but turned towards the door.

Mrs. Leidner said in her soft, drawling voice:

"You must finish telling me some other time. It was very interesting."

She looked up at us, smiled rather sweetly but in a faraway manner, and bent over her embroidery again.

In a minute or two, she said:

"There are some books over there, nurse. We've got quite a good selection. Choose one and sit down."

I went over to the bookshelf. Mrs. Mercado stayed for a minute or two, then, turning abruptly, she went out. As she passed me I saw her face and I didn't like the look of it. She looked wild with fury.

In spite of myself I remembered some of the things Mrs. Kelsey had said and hinted about Mrs. Leidner. I didn't like to think they were true because I liked Mrs. Leidner, but I wondered, nevertheless, if there mightn't perhaps be a grain of truth behind them.

I didn't think it was all her fault, but the fact remained that dear ugly Miss Johnson, and that common little spitfire Mrs. Mercado, couldn't hold a candle to her in looks or in attraction. And after all, men are men all over the world. You soon see a lot of that in my profession.

Mercado was a poor fish, and I don't suppose Mrs. Leidner really cared two hoots for his admiration—but his wife cared. If I wasn't mistaken, she minded badly and would be quite willing to do Mrs. Leidner a bad turn if she could.

I looked at Mrs. Leidner sitting there and sewing at her pretty flowers, so remote and far away and aloof. I felt somehow I ought to warn her. I felt that perhaps she didn't know how stupid and unreasoning and violent jealousy and hate can be—and how little it takes to set them smouldering.

And then I said to myself, "Amy Leatheran, you're a fool. Mrs. Leidner's no chicken. She's close on forty if she's a day, and she must know all about life there is to know."

But I felt that all the same perhaps she didn't.

She had such a queer untouched look.

I began to wonder what her life had been. I knew she'd only married Dr. Leidner two years ago. And according to Mrs. Mercado her first husband had died nearly twenty years ago.

I came and sat down near her with a book, and presently I went and washed my hands for supper. It was a good meal—some really excellent curry. They all went to bed early and I was glad for I was tired.

Dr. Leidner came with me to my room to see I had all I wanted.

He gave me a warm handclasp and said eagerly:

"She likes you, nurse. She's taken to you at once. I'm so glad. I feel everything's going to be all right now."

His eagerness was almost boyish.

I felt, too, that Mrs. Leidner had taken a liking to me, and I was pleased it should be so.

But I didn't quite share his confidence. I felt, somehow, that there was more to it all than he himself might know.

There was *something*—something I couldn't get at. But I felt it in the air.

My bed was comfortable, but I didn't sleep well for all that. I dreamt too much.

The words of a poem by Keats, that I'd had to learn as a child, kept running through my head. I kept getting them wrong and it worried me. It was a poem I'd always hated—I suppose because I'd had to learn it whether I wanted to or not. But somehow when I woke up in the dark I saw a sort of beauty in it for the first time.

"Oh, say what ails thee, knight at arms, alone—and (what was it?)—*palely loitering . . . ?"* I saw the knight's face in my mind for the first time—and it was Mr. Carey's face—a grim, tense, bronzed face like some of those poor young men I remembered as a girl during the war . . . and I felt sorry for him—and then I fell off to sleep again and I saw that the Belle Dame sans Merci was Mrs. Leidner and she was leaning sideways on a horse with an embroidery of flowers in her hands—and then the horse stumbled and everywhere there were bones coated in wax, and I woke up all goose-flesh and shivering, and told myself that curry never *had* agreed with me at night.

Chapter 7

The Man at the Window

I think I'd better make it clear right away that there isn't going to be any local colour in this story. I don't know anything about archaeology and I don't know that I very much want to. Messing about with people and places that are buried and done with doesn't make sense to me. Mr. Carey used to tell me that I hadn't got the archaeological temperament and I've no doubt he was quite right.

The very first morning after my arrival Mr. Carey asked if I'd like to come and see the palace he was—*planning* I think he called it. Though how you can plan for a thing that's happened long ago I'm sure I don't know! Well, I said I'd like to, and to tell the truth, I was a bit excited about it. Nearly three thousand years old that palace was, it appeared. I wondered what sort of palaces they had in those days, and if it would be like the pictures I'd seen of Tutankhamen's tomb furniture. But would you believe it, there was nothing to see but *mud!* Dirty mud walls about two feet high—and that's all there was to it. Mr. Carey took me here and there telling me things—how this was the great court, and there were some chambers here and an upper storey and various other rooms that opened off the central court. And all I thought was, "But how does he *know?*" though, of course, I was too polite to say so. I can tell you it *was* a disappointment! The whole excavation looked like nothing but mud to me—no marble or gold or anything handsome—my aunt's house in Cricklewood would have made a much more imposing ruin! And those old Assyrians or whatever they were called themselves *kings.* When Mr. Carey had shown me his old "palace," he handed me over to Father Lavigny, who showed me the rest of the mound. I was a little afraid of Father Lavigny, being a monk and a foreigner and having such a deep voice and all, but he was very kind—though rather vague. Sometimes I felt it wasn't much more real to him than it was to me.

Mrs. Leidner explained that later. She said that Father Lavigny was only interested in "written documents"—as she called them. They wrote everything on clay, these people, queer heathenish-looking marks too, but quite sensible. There were even school tablets—the teacher's lesson on one side and the pupil's effort on the back of it. I confess that that did interest me rather—it seemed so human, if you know what I mean.

Father Lavigny walked round the work with me and showed me what were temples or palaces and what were private houses, and also a place which he said was an early Akkadian cemetery. He spoke in a funny jerky way, just throwing in a scrap of information and then reverting to other subjects.

He said:

"It is strange that you have come here. Is Mrs. Leidner really ill, then?"

"Not exactly ill," I said cautiously.

He said:

"She is an odd woman. A dangerous woman, I think."

"Now what do you mean by that?" I said. "Dangerous? How dangerous?"

He shook his head thoughtfully.

"I think she is ruthless," he said. "Yes, I think she could be absolutely ruthless."

"If you'll excuse me," I said, "I think you're talking nonsense."

He shook his head.

"You do not know women as I do," he said.

And that was a funny thing, I thought, for a monk to say. But of course I suppose he might have heard a lot of things in confession. But that rather puzzled me, because I wasn't sure if monks heard confessions or if it was only priests. I supposed he *was* a monk with that long woollen robe—all sweeping up the dirt—and the rosary and all!

"Yes, she could be ruthless," he said musingly. "I am quite sure of that. And yet—though she is so hard—like stone, like marble—yet she is afraid. What is she afraid of?"

That, I thought, is what we should all like to know!

At least it was possible that her husband did know, but I didn't think any one else did.

He fixed me with a sudden bright, dark eye.

"It is odd here? You find it odd? Or quite natural?"

"Not quite natural," I said, considering. "It's comfortable enough as far as the arrangements go—but there isn't quite a comfortable feeling."

"It makes *me* uncomfortable. I have the idea"—he became suddenly a little more foreign—"that something prepares itself. Dr. Leidner, too, he is not quite himself. Something is worrying him also."

"His wife's health?"

"That perhaps. But there is more. There is—how shall I say it—an uneasiness."

And that was just it, there was an uneasiness.

We didn't say any more just then, for Dr. Leidner came towards us. He showed me a child's grave that had just been uncovered. Rather pathetic it was—the little bones— and a pot or two and some little specks that Dr. Leidner told me were a bead necklace.

It was the workmen that made me laugh. You never saw such a lot of scarecrows—all in long petticoats and rags, and their heads tied up as though they had toothache. And

every now and then, as they went to and fro
carrying away baskets of earth, they began
to sing—at least I suppose it was meant to
be singing—a queer sort of monotonous
chant that went on and on over and over
again. I noticed that most of their eyes were
terrible—all covered with discharge, and
one or two looked half blind. I was just
thinking what a miserable lot they were
when Dr. Leidner said, "Rather a fine-
looking lot of men, aren't they?" and I
thought what a queer world it was and how
two different people could see the same
thing each of them the other way round. I
haven't put that very well, but you can
guess what I mean.

After a bit Dr. Leidner said he was going
back to the house for a mid-morning cup of
tea. So he and I walked back together and
he told me things. When *he* explained, it
was all quite different. I sort of *saw* it all—
how it used to be—the streets and the
houses, and he showed me ovens where
they baked bread and said the Arabs used
much the same kind of ovens nowadays.

We got back to the house and found Mrs.
Leidner had got up. She was looking better
to-day, not so thin and worn. Tea came in

almost at once and Dr. Leidner told her what had turned up during the morning on the dig. Then he went back to work and Mrs. Leidner asked me if I would like to see some of the finds they had made up to date. Of course I said "Yes," so she took me through into the antika-room. There was a lot of stuff lying about—mostly broken pots it seemed to me—or else ones that were all mended and stuck together. The whole lot might have been thrown away, I thought.

"Dear, dear," I said, "it's a pity they're all so broken, isn't it? Are they really worth keeping?"

Mrs. Leidner smiled a little and she said:

"You mustn't let Eric hear you. Pots interest him more than anything else, and some of these are the oldest things we have— perhaps as much as seven thousand years old." And she explained how some of them came from a very deep cut on the mound down towards the bottom, and how, thousands of years ago, they had been broken and mended with bitumen, showing people prized their things just as much then as they do nowadays.

"And now," she said, "we'll show you something more exciting."

And she took down a box from the shelf and showed me a beautiful gold dagger with dark-blue stones in the handle.

I exclaimed with pleasure.

Mrs. Leidner laughed.

"Yes, everybody likes gold! Except my husband."

"Why doesn't Dr. Leidner like it?"

"Well, for one thing it comes expensive. You have to pay the workmen who find it the weight of the object in gold."

"Good gracious!" I exclaimed. "But why?"

"Oh, it's a custom. For one thing it prevents them from stealing. You see, if they *did* steal it wouldn't be for the archaeological value but for the intrinsic value. They could melt it down. So we make it easy for them to be honest."

She took down another tray and showed me a really beautiful gold drinking-cup with a design of rams' heads on it.

Again I exclaimed.

"Yes, it is beautiful, isn't it? These came from a prince's grave. We found other royal graves but most of them had been plundered. This cup is our best find. It is one of the most lovely ever found anywhere. Early Akkadian. Unique."

Suddenly, with a frown, Mrs. Leidner brought the cup up close to her eyes and scratched at it delicately with her nail.

"How extraordinary! There's actually wax on it. Some one must have been in here with a candle."

She detached the little flake and replaced the cup in its place.

After that she showed me some queer little terra-cotta figurines—but most of them were just rude. Nasty minds those old people had, I say.

When we went back to the porch Mrs. Mercado was sitting polishing her nails. She was holding them out in front of her admiring the effect. I thought myself that anything more hideous than that orange red could hardly have been imagined.

Mrs. Leidner had brought with her from the antika-room a very delicate little saucer broken in several pieces, and this she now proceeded to join together. I watched her for a minute or two and then asked if I could help.

"Oh, yes, there are plenty more." She fetched quite a supply of broken pottery and we set to work. I soon got into the hang of it and she praised my ability. I suppose most nurses are handy with their fingers.

"How busy everybody is," said Mrs. Mercado. "It makes me feel dreadfully idle. Of course I *am* idle."

"Why shouldn't you be if you like?" said Mrs. Leidner.

Her voice was quite uninterested.

At twelve we had lunch. Afterwards Dr. Leidner and Mr. Mercado cleaned some pottery, pouring a solution of hydrochloric acid over it. One pot went a lovely plum colour and a pattern of bulls' horns came out on another one. It was really quite magical. All the dried mud that no washing would remove sort of foamed and boiled away.

Mr. Carey and Mr. Coleman went out on the dig and Mr. Reiter went off to the photographic room.

"What will you do, Louise?" Dr. Leidner asked his wife. "I suppose you'll rest for a bit?"

I gathered that Mrs. Leidner usually lay down every afternoon.

"I'll rest for about an hour. Then perhaps I'll go out for a short stroll."

"Good. Nurse will go with you, won't you?"

"Of course," I said.

"No, no," said Mrs. Leidner. "I like going alone. Nurse isn't to feel so much on duty that I'm not allowed out of her sight."

"Oh, but I'd like to come," I said.

"No, really, I'd rather you didn't." She was quite firm—almost peremptory. "I must be by myself every now and then. It's necessary to me."

I didn't insist, of course. But as I went off for a short sleep myself it struck me as odd that Mrs. Leidner, with her nervous terrors, should be quite content to walk by herself without any kind of protection.

When I came out of my room at half-past three the courtyard was deserted save for a little boy with a large copper bath who was washing pottery, and Mr. Emmott, who was sorting and arranging it. As I went towards them Mrs. Leidner came in through the archway. She looked more alive than I had seen her yet. Her eyes shone and she looked uplifted and almost gay.

Dr. Leidner came out from the laboratory and joined her. He was showing her a big dish with bulls' horns on it.

"The prehistoric levels are being extraordinarily productive," he said. "It's been a good season so far. Finding that tomb right at the beginning was a real piece of luck. The only person who might complain is Father Lavigny. We've had hardly any tablets so far."

"He doesn't seem to have done very much with the few we have had," said Mrs. Leidner dryly. "He may be a very fine epigraphist but he's a remarkably lazy one. He spends all his afternoons sleeping."

"We miss Byrd," said Dr. Leidner. "This man strikes me as slightly unorthodox—though, of course, I'm not competent to judge. But one or two of his translations have been surprising to say the least of it. I can hardly believe, for instance, that he's right about that inscribed brick, and yet he must know."

After tea Mrs. Leidner asked me if I would like to stroll down to the river. I thought that perhaps she feared that her refusal to let me accompany her earlier in the afternoon might have hurt my feelings.

I wanted her to know that I wasn't the touchy kind, so I accepted at once.

It was a lovely evening. A path led be-

tween barley fields and then through some
flowering fruit trees. Finally we came to the
edge of the Tigris. Immediately on our left
was the Tell with the workmen singing in
their queer monotonous chant. A little to our
right was a big water-wheel which made a
queer groaning noise. It used to set my
teeth on edge at first. But in the end I got
fond of it and it had a queer soothing effect
on me. Beyond the water-wheel was the
village from which most of the workmen
came.

"It's rather beautiful, isn't it?" said Mrs.
Leidner.

"It's very peaceful," I said. "It seems
funny to me to be so far away from everywhere."

"Far from everywhere," repeated Mrs.
Leidner. "Yes. Here at least one might expect to be safe."

I glanced at her sharply, but I think she
was speaking more to herself than to me,
and I don't think she realized that her words
had been revealing.

We began to walk back to the house.

Suddenly Mrs. Leidner clutched my arm
so violently that I nearly cried out.

"Who's that, nurse? What's he doing?"

Some little distance ahead of us, just where the path ran near the expedition house, a man was standing. He wore European clothes and he seemed to be standing on tiptoe and trying to look in at one of the windows.

As we watched he glanced round, caught sight of us, and immediately continued on the path towards us. I felt Mrs. Leidner's clutch tighten.

"Nurse," she whispered. "Nurse . . ."

"It's all right, my dear, it's all right," I said reassuringly.

The man came along and passed us. He was an Iraqi, and as soon as she saw him near to, Mrs. Leidner relaxed with a sigh.

"He's only an Iraqi after all," she said.

We went on our way. I glanced up at the windows as I passed. Not only were they barred, but they were too high from the ground to permit of any one seeing in, for the level of the ground was lower here than on the inside of the courtyard.

"It must have been just curiosity," I said.

Mrs. Leidner nodded.

"That's all. But just for a minute I thought—"

She broke off.

I thought to myself, "You thought *what?* That's what I'd like to know. *What* did you think?"

But I knew one thing now—that Mrs. Leidner was afraid of a definite flesh and blood person.

Chapter 8
Night Alarm

It's a little difficult to know exactly what to note in the week that followed my arrival at Tell Yarimjah.

Looking back as I do from my present standpoint of knowledge I can see a good many little signs and indications that I was quite blind to at the time.

To tell the story properly, however, I think I ought to try and recapture the point of view that I actually held—puzzled, uneasy, and increasingly conscious of *something* wrong.

For one thing *was* certain, that curious sense of strain and constraint was *not* imagined. It was genuine. Even Bill Coleman the insensitive commented upon it.

"This place gets under my skin," I heard him say. "Are they always such a glum lot?"

It was David Emmott to whom he spoke, the other assistant. I had taken rather a fancy to Mr. Emmott; his taciturnity was not, I felt sure, unfriendly. There was something about him that seemed very steadfast and reassuring in an atmosphere where one was uncertain what any one was feeling or thinking.

"No," he said in answer to Mr. Coleman. "It wasn't like this last year."

But he didn't enlarge on the theme, or say any more.

"What I can't make out is what it's all about," said Mr. Coleman in an aggrieved voice.

Emmott shrugged his shoulders but didn't answer.

I had a rather enlightening conversation with Miss Johnson. I liked her very much. She was capable, practical and intelligent. She had, it was quite obvious, a distinct hero worship for Dr. Leidner.

On this occasion she told me the story of his life since his young days. She knew every site he had dug, and the results of the dig. I would almost dare swear she could quote from every lecture he had ever delivered. She considered him, she told me, quite the finest field archaeologist living.

"And he's so simple. So completely unworldly. He doesn't know the meaning of the word conceit. Only a really great man could be so simple."

"That's true enough," I said. "Big people don't need to throw their weight about."

"And he's so light-hearted too. I can't tell you what fun we used to have—he and Richard Carey and I—the first years we were out here. We were such a happy party. Richard Carey worked with him in Palestine, of course. Theirs is a friendship of ten years or so. Oh, well, I've known him for seven."

"What a handsome man Mr. Carey is," I said.

"Yes—I suppose he is."

She said it rather curtly.

"But he's just a little bit quiet, don't you think?"

"He usedn't to be like that," said Miss Johnson quickly. "It's only since—"

She stopped abruptly.

"Only since—?" I prompted.

"Oh, well." Miss Johnson gave a characteristic motion of her shoulders. "A good many things are changed nowadays."

I didn't answer. I hoped she would go on—and she did—prefacing her remarks with a little laugh as though to detract from their importance.

"I'm afraid I'm rather a conservative old fogy. I sometimes think that if an archaeologist's wife isn't really interested, it would be wiser for her not to accompany the expedition. It often leads to friction."

"Mrs. Mercado—" I suggested.

"Oh, her!" Miss Johnson brushed the suggestion aside. "I was really thinking of Mrs. Leidner. She's a very charming woman—and one can quite understand why Dr. Leidner 'fell for her'—to use a slang term. But I can't help feeling she's out of place here. She—it unsettles things."

So Miss Johnson agreed with Mrs. Kelsey that it was Mrs. Leidner who was responsible for the strained atmosphere. But then where did Mrs. Leidner's own nervous fears come in?

"It unsettles *him*," said Miss Johnson earnestly. "Of course, I'm—well, I'm like a faithful but jealous old dog. I don't like to see him so worn out and worried. His whole mind ought to be on the work—not taken up with his wife and her silly fears! If she's nervous of coming to out-of-the-way places, she ought to have stayed in America. I've no patience with people who come to a place and then do nothing but grouse about it!"

And then, a little fearful of having said more than she meant to say, she went on:

"Of course I admire her very much. She's a lovely woman and she's got great charm of manner when she chooses."

And there the subject dropped.

I thought to myself that it was always the same way—wherever women are cooped up together, there's bound to be jealousy. Miss Johnson clearly didn't like her chief's wife (that was perhaps natural) and unless I was much mistaken Mrs. Mercado fairly hated her.

Another person who didn't like Mrs. Leidner was Sheila Reilly. She came out once or twice to the dig, once in a car and twice with some young man on a horse—on two horses I mean, of course. It was at the back of my mind that she had a weakness for the silent young American, Emmott. When he was on duty at the dig she used to stay talking to him, and I thought, too, that *he* admired *her*.

One day, rather injudiciously, I thought, Mrs. Leidner commented upon it at lunch.

"The Reilly girl is still hunting David down," she said with a little laugh. "Poor David, she chases you up on the dig even! How foolish girls are!"

Mr. Emmott didn't answer, but under his tan his face got rather red. He raised his eyes and looked right into hers with a very curious expression—a straight, steady glance with something of a challenge in it.

She smiled very faintly and looked away.

I heard Father Lavigny murmur something, but when I said "Pardon?" he merely shook his head and did not repeat his remark.

That afternoon Mr. Coleman said to me:

"Matter of fact I didn't like Mrs. L. any too much at first. She used to jump down my throat every time I opened my mouth. But I've begun to understand her better now. She's one of the kindest women I've ever met. You find yourself telling her all the foolish scrapes you ever got into before you know where you are. She's got her knife into Sheila Reilly, I know, but then Sheila's been damned rude to her once or twice. That's the worst of Sheila—she's got no manners. And a temper like the devil!"

That I could well believe. Dr. Reilly spoilt her.

"Of course she's bound to get a bit full of herself, being the only young woman in the place. But that doesn't excuse her talking to Mrs. Leidner as though Mrs. Leidner were her great-aunt. Mrs. L's not exactly a chicken, but she's a damned good-looking woman. Rather like those fairy women who come out of marshes with lights and lure you away." He added bitterly, "You wouldn't find Sheila luring any one. All she does is to tick a fellow off."

I only remember two other incidents of any kind of significance.

One was when I went to the laboratory to fetch some acetone to get the stickiness off my fingers from mending the pottery. Mr. Mercado was sitting in a corner, his head was laid down on his arms and I fancied he was asleep. I took the bottle I wanted and went off with it.

That evening, to my great surprise, Mrs. Mercado tackled me.

"Did you take a bottle of acetone from the lab?"

"Yes," I said. "I did."

"You know perfectly well that there's a small bottle always kept in the antika-room."

She spoke quite angrily.

"Is there? I didn't know."

"I think you did! You just wanted to come spying round. I know what hospital nurses are."

I stared at her.

"I don't know what you're talking about, Mrs. Mercado," I said with dignity. "I'm sure I don't want to spy on any one."

"Oh, no! Of course not. Do you think I don't know what you're here for?"

Really, for a minute or two I thought she must have been drinking. I went away without saying any more. But I thought it was very odd.

The other thing was nothing very much. I was trying to entice a pi dog pup with a piece of bread. It was very timid, however, like all Arab dogs—and was convinced I meant no good. It slunk away and I followed it—out through the archway and round the corner of the house. I came round so sharply that before I knew I had cannoned into Father Lavigny and another man who were standing together—and in a minute I realized that the second man was the same one Mrs. Leidner and I had noticed that day trying to peer through the window.

I apologized and Father Lavigny smiled, and with a word of farewell greeting to the other man he returned to the house with me.

"You know," he said, "I am very ashamed. I am a student of Oriental languages and none of the men on the men work can understand me! It is humiliating, do you not think? I was trying my Arabic on that man, who is a townsman, to see if I got on better—but it still wasn't very successful. Leidner says my Arabic is too pure."

That was all. But it just passed through my head that it was odd the same man should still be hanging round the house.

That night we had a scare.

It must have been about two in the morning. I'm a light sleeper, as most nurses have to be. I was awake and sitting up in bed by the time that my door opened.

"Nurse, nurse!"

It was Mrs. Leidner's voice low and urgent.

I struck a match and lighted the candle.

She was standing by the door in a long blue dressing-gown. She was looking petrified with terror.

"There's some one—some one—in the room next to mine. . . . I heard him—scratching on the wall."

I jumped out of bed and came to her.

"It's all right," I said. "I'm here. Don't be afraid, my dear."

She whispered:

"Get Eric."

I nodded and ran out and knocked on his door. In a minute he was with us. Mrs. Leidner was sitting on my bed, her breath coming in great gasps.

"I heard him," she said. "I heard him—scratching on the wall."

"Some one in the antika-room?" cried Dr. Leidner.

He ran out quickly—and it just flashed across my mind how differently these two had reacted. Mrs. Leidner's fear was entirely personal, but Dr. Leidner's mind leaped at once to his precious treasures.

"The antika-room!" breathed Mrs. Leidner. "Of course! How stupid of me."

And rising and pulling her gown round

her, she bade me come with her. All traces of her panic-stricken fear had vanished.

We arrived in the antika-room to find Dr. Leidner and Father Lavigny. The latter had also heard a noise, had risen to investigate, and had fancied he saw a light in the antika-room. He had delayed to put on slippers and snatch up a torch and had found no one by the time he got there. The door, moreover, was duly locked, as it was supposed to be at night.

Whilst he was assuring himself that nothing had been taken, Dr. Leidner had joined him.

Nothing more was to be learned. The outside archway door was locked. The guard swore nobody could have got in from outside, but as they had probably been fast asleep this was not conclusive. There were no marks or traces of an intruder and nothing had been taken.

It was possible that what had alarmed Mrs. Leidner was the noise made by Father Lavigny taking down boxes from the shelves to assure himself that all was in order.

On the other hand, Father Lavigny himself was positive that he had (a) heard footsteps passing his window and *(b)* seen the flicker of a light, possibly a torch, in the antika-room.

Nobody else had heard or seen anything.

The incident is of value in my narrative because it led to Mrs. Leidner's unburdening herself to me on the following day.

Chapter 9
Mrs. Leidner's Story

We had just finished lunch. Mrs. Leidner went to her room to rest as usual. I settled her on her bed with plenty of pillows and her book, and was leaving the room when she called me back.

"Don't go, nurse, there's something I want to say to you."

I came back into the room.

"Shut the door."

I obeyed.

She got up from the bed and began to walk up and down the room. I could see that she was making up her mind to something and I didn't like to interrupt her. She was clearly in great indecision of mind.

At last she seemed to have nerved herself

to the required point. She turned to me and said abruptly:

"Sit down."

I sat down by the table very quietly. She began nervously:

"You must have wondered what all this is about?"

I just nodded without saying anything.

"I've made up my mind to tell you—everything! I must tell some one or I shall go mad."

"Well," I said. "I think really it would be just as well. It's not easy to know the best thing to do when one's kept in the dark."

She stopped in her uneasy walk and faced me.

"Do you know what I'm frightened of?"

"Some man," I said.

"Yes—but I didn't say whom—I said what."

I waited.

She said:

"I'm afraid of being killed!"

Well, it was out now. I wasn't going to show any particular concern. She was near enough hysterics as it was.

"Dear me," I said. "So that's it, is it?"

Then she began to laugh. She laughed

and she laughed—and the tears ran down her face.

"The way you said that!" she gasped. "The way you said it . . ."

"Now, now," I said. "This won't do." I spoke sharply. I pushed her into a chair, went over to the wash-stand and got a cold sponge and bathed her forehead and wrists.

"No more nonsense," I said. "Tell me calmly and sensibly all about it."

That stopped her. She sat up and spoke in her natural voice.

"You're a treasure, nurse," she said. "You make me feel as though I'm six. I'm going to tell you."

"That's right," I said. "Take your time and don't hurry."

She began to speak, slowly and deliberately.

"When I was a girl of twenty I married. A young man in one of our state departments. It was in 1918."

"I know," I said. "Mrs. Mercado told me. He was killed in the war."

But Mrs. Leidner shook her head.

"That's what she thinks. That's what everybody thinks. The truth is something quite different. I was a queer patriotic, enthusiastic girl, nurse, full of idealism. When I'd been married a few months I discovered—by a quite unforeseeable accident—that my husband was a spy in German pay. I learned that the information supplied by him had led directly to the sinking of an American transport and the loss of hundreds of lives. I don't know what most people would have done. . . . But I'll tell you what I did. I went straight to my father, who was in the War Department, and told him the truth. Frederick *was* killed in the war—but he was killed in America—shot as a spy."

"Oh, dear, dear!" I ejaculated. "How terrible!"

"Yes," she said. "It was terrible. He was so kind, too—so gentle. . . . And all the time . . . But I never hesitated. Perhaps I was wrong."

"It's difficult to say," I said. "I'm sure I don't know what one would do."

"What I'm telling you was never generally known outside the state departments. Ostensibly my husband had gone to the front and had been killed. I had a lot of sympathy and kindness shown me as a war widow."

Her voice was bitter and I nodded comprehendingly.

"Lots of people wanted to marry me, but I always refused. I'd had too bad a shock. I didn't feel I could ever *trust* any one again."

"Yes, I can imagine feeling like that."

"And then I became very fond of a certain young man. I wavered. An amazing thing happened! I got an anonymous letter—from Frederick—saying that if I ever married another man, he'd kill me!"

"From Frederick? From your dead husband?"

"Yes. Of course, I thought at first I was mad or dreaming. . . . At last I went to my father. He told me the truth. My husband hadn't been shot after all. He'd escaped—but his escape did him no good. He was involved in a train wreck a few weeks later and his dead body was found amongst others. My father had kept the fact of his escape from me, and since the man had died anyway he had seen no reason to tell me anything until now.

"But the letter I received opened up entirely new possibilities. Was it perhaps a fact that my husband was still alive?

"My father went into the matter as carefully as possible. And he declared that as far as one could humanly be sure the body that was buried as Frederick's *was* Frederick's. There had been a certain amount of disfiguration, so that he could not speak with absolute cast-iron certainty, but he reiterated his solemn belief that Frederick was dead and that this letter was a cruel and malicious hoax.

"The same thing happened more than once. If I seemed to be on intimate terms with any man, I would receive a threatening letter."

"In your husband's handwriting?"

She said slowly:

"That is difficult to say. I had no letters of his. I had only my memory to go by."

"There was no allusion or special form of words used that could make you sure?"

"No. There *were* certain terms—nicknames, for instance—private between us—if one of those had been used or quoted, then I should have been quite sure."

"Yes," I said thoughtfully. "That is odd. It looks as though it *wasn't* your husband. But is there any one else it could be?"

"There is a possibility. Frederick had a younger brother—a boy of ten or twelve at

the time of our marriage. He worshipped
Frederick and Frederick was devoted to
him. What happened to this boy, William his
name was, I don't know. It seems to me
possible that, adoring his brother as fanati-
cally as he did, he may have grown up re-
garding me as directly responsible for his
death. He had always been jealous of me
and may have invented this scheme by way
of punishment."

"It's possible," I said. "It's amazing the
way children do remember if they've had a
shock."

"I know. This boy may have dedicated his
life to revenge."

"Please go on."

"There isn't very much more to tell. I met
Eric three years ago. I meant never to marry.
Eric made me change my mind. Right up to
our wedding day I waited for another threatening letter. None came. I decided that
whoever the writer might be, he was either
dead, or tired of his cruel sport. *Two days
after our marriage I got this*."

Drawing a small attaché-case which was
on the table towards her, she unlocked it,
took out a letter and handed it to me.

The ink was slightly faded. It was written

in a rather womanish hand with a forward slant.

You have disobeyed. Now you cannot escape. You must be Frederick Bosner's wife only! You have got to die.

"I was frightened—but not so much as I might have been to begin with. Being with Eric made me feel safe. Then, a month later, I got a second letter."

I have not forgotten. I am making my plans. You have got to die. Why did you disobey?

"Does your husband know about this?"

Mrs. Leidner answered slowly.

"He knows that I am threatened. I showed him both letters when the second one came. He was inclined to think the whole thing a hoax. He thought also that it might be some one who wanted to blackmail me by pretending my first husband was alive."

She paused and then went on.

"A few days after I received the second letter we had a narrow escape from death by gas poisoning. Somebody entered our apartment after we were asleep and turned on the gas. Luckily I woke and smelled the gas in time. Then I lost my nerve. I told Eric how I had been persecuted for years, and I

told him that I was sure this madman, whoever he might be, did really mean to kill me.
I think that for the first time I really did think
it *was* Frederick. There was always something a little ruthless behind his gentleness.

"Eric was still, I think, less alarmed than I
was. He wanted to go to the police. Naturally I wouldn't hear of that. In the end we
agreed that I should accompany him here,
and that it might be wise if I didn't return to
America in the summer but stayed in London and Paris.

"We carried out our plan and all went well.
I felt sure that now everything would be all
right. After all, we had put half the globe between ourselves and my enemy.

"And then—a little over three weeks
ago—I received a letter—with an Iraq stamp
on it."

She handed me a third letter.

*You thought you could escape. You were
wrong. You shall not be false to me and live.
I have always told you so. Death is coming
very soon.*

"And a week ago—*this!* Just lying on the
table here. It had not even gone through the
post."

I took the sheet of paper from her. There was just one phrase scrawled across it.

I have arrived.

She stared at me.

"You see? You understand? He's going to kill me. It may be Frederick—it may be little William—*but he's going to kill me.*"

Her voice rose shudderingly. I caught her wrist.

"Now—now," I said warningly. "Don't give way. We'll look after you. Have you got any sal volatile?"

She nodded towards the wash-stand and I gave her a good dose.

"That's better," I said, as the colour returned to her cheeks.

"Yes, I'm better now. But oh, nurse, do you see why I'm in this state? When I saw that man looking in through my window, I thought: *He's come.* . . . Even when *you* arrived I was suspicious. I thought you might be a man in disguise—"

"The idea!"

"Oh, I know it sounds absurd. But you might have been in league with him perhaps—not a hospital nurse at all."

"But that's nonsense!"

"Yes, perhaps. But I've got beyond sense."

Struck by a sudden idea, I said:

"You'd *recognize* your husband, I suppose?"

She answered slowly.

"I don't even know that. It's over fifteen years ago. I mightn't recognize his face."

Then she shivered.

"I saw it one night—but it was a *dead* face. There was a tap, tap, tap on the window. And then I saw a face, a dead face, ghastly and grinning against the pane. I screamed and screamed. . . . And they said there wasn't anything there!"

I remembered Mrs. Mercado's story.

"You don't think," I said hesitatingly, "that you *dreamt* that?"

"I'm sure I didn't!"

I wasn't so sure. It was the kind of nightmare that was quite likely under the circumstances and that easily might be taken for a waking occurrence. However, I never contradict a patient. I soothed Mrs. Leidner as best I could and pointed out that if any stranger arrived in the neighbourhood it was pretty sure to be known.

I left her, I think, a little comforted, and I

went in search of Dr. Leidner and told him of our conversation.

"I'm glad she's told you," he said simply. "It has worried me dreadfully. I feel sure that all those faces and tappings on the window-pane have been sheer imagination on her part. I haven't known what to do for the best. What do you think of the whole thing?"

I didn't quite understand the tone in his voice, but I answered promptly enough.

"It's possible," I said, "that these letters may be just a cruel and malicious hoax."

"Yes, that is quite likely. But what are we to *do?* They are driving her mad. I don't know what to think."

I didn't either. It had occurred to me that possibly a woman might be concerned. Those letters had a feminine note about them. Mrs. Mercado was at the back of my mind.

Supposing that by some chance she had learnt the facts of Mrs. Leidner's first mar-riage. She might be indulging her spite by terrorizing the other woman.

I didn't quite like to suggest such a thing to Dr. Leidner. It's so difficult to know how people are going to take things.

"Oh, well," I said cheerfully, "we must hope for the best. I think Mrs. Leidner seems happier already from just talking about it. That's always a help, you know. It's bottling things up that makes them get on your nerves."

"I'm very glad she has told you," he repeated. "It's a good sign. It shows she likes and trusts you. I've been at my wits' end to know what to do for the best."

It was on the tip of my tongue to ask him whether he'd thought of giving a discreet hint to the local police, but afterwards I was glad I hadn't done so.

What happened was this. On the following day Mr. Coleman was going in to Hassanieh to get the workmen's pay. He was also taking in all our letters to catch the air mail.

The letters, as written, were dropped into a wooden box on the dining-room window-sill. Last thing that night Mr. Coleman took them out and was sorting them out into bundles and putting rubber-bands round them.

Suddenly he gave a shout.

"What is it?" I asked.

He held out a letter with a grin.

"It's our Lovely Louise—she really *is* going balmy. She's addressed a letter to some one at 42nd Street, Paris, France. I don't think that can be right, do you? Do you mind taking it to her and asking what she *does* mean? She's just gone off to bed."

I took it from him and ran off to Mrs. Leidner with it and she amended the address.

It was the first time I had seen Mrs. Leidner's handwriting, and I wondered idly where I had seen it before, for it was certainly quite familiar to me.

It wasn't till the middle of the night that it suddenly came to me.

Except that it was bigger and rather more straggling, *it was extraordinarily like the writing on the anonymous letters*.

New ideas flashed through my head.

Had Mrs. Leidner conceivably written those letters *herself?*

And did Dr. Leidner half suspect the fact?

Chapter 10
Saturday Afternoon

Mrs. Leidner told me her story on a Friday.

On Saturday morning there was a feeling of slight anti-climax in the air.

Mrs. Leidner, in particular, was inclined to be very off-hand with me and rather pointedly avoided any possibility of a *tête-à-tête*. Well, *that* didn't surprise me! I've had the same thing happen to me again and again. Ladies tell their nurses things in a sudden burst of confidence, and then, afterwards, they feel uncomfortable about it and wish they hadn't! It's only human nature.

I was very careful not to hint or remind her in any way of what she had told me. I purposely kept my conversation as matter-of-fact as possible.

Mr. Coleman had started in to Hassanieh

in the morning, driving himself in the lorry with the letters in a knapsack. He also had one or two commissions to do for the members of the expedition. It was pay-day for the men, and he would have to go to the bank and bring out the money in coins of small denominations. All this was a long business and he did not expect to be back until the afternoon. I rather suspected he might be lunching with Sheila Reilly.

Work on the dig was usually not very busy on the afternoon of pay-day as at three-thirty the paying-out began.

The little boy, Abdullah, whose business it was to wash pots, was established as usual in the centre of the courtyard, and again as usual, kept up his queer nasal chant. Dr. Leidner and Mr. Emmott were going to put in some work on the pottery until Mr. Coleman returned, and Mr. Carey went up to the dig.

Mrs. Leidner went to her room to rest. I settled her as usual and then went to my own room, taking a book with me as I did not feel sleepy. It was then about a quarter to one, and a couple of hours passed quite pleasantly. I was reading *Death in a Nursing Home*—really a most exciting story—though

I don't think the author knew much about the way nursing homes are run! At any rate I've never known a nursing home like that! I really felt inclined to write to the author and put him right about a few points.

When I put the book down at last (it was the red-haired parlourmaid and I'd never suspected her once!) and looked at my watch I was quite surprised to find it was twenty minutes to three!

I got up, straightened my uniform, and came out into the courtyard.

Abdullah was still scrubbing and still singing his depressing chant, and David Emmott was standing by him sorting the scubbed pots, and putting the ones that were broken into boxes to await mending. I strolled over towards them just as Dr. Leidner came down the staircase from the roof.

"Not a bad afternoon," he said cheerfully. "I've made a bit of a clearance up there. Louise will be pleased. She's complained lately that there's not room to walk about. I'll go and tell her the good news."

He went over to his wife's door, tapped on it and went in.

It must, I suppose, have been about a minute and a half later that he came out again. I happened to be looking at the door when he did so. It was like a nightmare. He had gone in a brisk, cheerful man. He came out like a drunken one—reeling a little on his feet, and with a queer dazed expression on his face.

"Nurse—" he called in a queer, hoarse voice. "Nurse—"

I saw at once something was wrong, and I ran across to him. He looked awful—his face was all grey and twitching, and I saw he might collapse any minute.

"My wife . . ." he said. "My wife . . . Oh, my God . . ."

I pushed past him into the room. Then I caught my breath.

Mrs. Leidner was lying in a dreadful huddled heap by the bed.

I bent over her. She was quite dead—must have been dead an hour at least. The cause of death was perfectly plain—a terrific blow on the front of the head just over the right temple. She must have got up from the bed and been struck down where she stood.

I didn't handle her more than I could help.

I glanced round the room to see if there was anything that might give a clue, but nothing seemed out of place or disturbed. The windows were closed and fastened, and there was no place where the murderer could have hidden. Obviously he had been and gone long ago.

I went out, closing the door behind me.

Dr. Leidner had collapsed completely now. David Emmott was with him and turned a white, inquiring face to me.

In a few low words I told him what had happened.

As I always suspected, he was a first-class person to rely on in trouble. He was perfectly calm and self-possessed. Those blue eyes of his opened very wide, but otherwise he gave no sign at all.

He considered for a moment and then said:

"I suppose we must notify the police as soon as possible. Bill ought to be back any minute. What shall we do with Leidner?"

"Help me to get him into his room."

He nodded.

"Better lock this door first, I suppose," he said.

He turned the key in the lock of Mrs. Leidner's door, then drew it out and handed it to me.

"I guess you'd better keep this, nurse. Now then."

Together we lifted Dr. Leidner and carried him into his own room and laid him on his bed. Mr. Emmott went off in search of brandy. He returned, accompanied by Miss Johnson.

Her face was drawn and anxious, but she was calm and capable, and I felt satisfied to leave Dr. Leidner in her charge.

I hurried out into the courtyard. The station wagon was just coming in through the archway. I think it gave us all a shock to see Bill's pink, cheerful face as he jumped out with his familiar "Hallo, 'allo, 'allo! Here's the oof!" He went on gaily, "No highway robberies—"

He came to a halt suddenly. "I say, is anything up? What's the matter with you all? You look as though the cat had killed your canary."

Mr. Emmott said shortly:

"Mrs. Leidner's dead—killed."

"*What?*" Bill's jolly face changed ludicrously. He stared, his eyes goggling. "Mother Leidner dead! You're pulling my leg."

"Dead?" It was a sharp cry. I turned to

see Mrs. Mercado behind me. "Did you say Mrs. Leidner had been *killed?*"

"Yes," I said. "Murdered."

"No!" she gasped. "Oh, no! I won't believe it. Perhaps she's committed suicide."

"Suicides don't hit themselves on the head," I said dryly. "It's murder all right, Mrs. Mercado."

She sat down suddenly on an upturned packing-case.

She said, "Oh, but this is horrible—*horrible* . . ."

Naturally it was horrible. We didn't need *her* to tell us so! I wondered if perhaps she was feeling a bit remorseful for the harsh feelings she had harboured against the dead woman, and all the spiteful things she had said.

After a minute or two she asked rather breathlessly:

"What are you going to do?"

Mr. Emmott took charge in his quiet way.

"Bill, you'd better get in again to Hassanieh as quick as you can. I don't know much about the proper procedure. Better get hold of Captain Maitland, he's in charge of the police here, I think. Get Dr. Reilly first. He'll know what to do."

Mr. Coleman nodded. All the facetiousness was knocked out of him. He just looked young and frightened. Without a word he jumped into the station wagon and drove off.

Mr. Emmott said rather uncertainly, "I suppose we ought to have a hunt round." He raised his voice and called:

"Ibrahim!"

"Na'am."

The house-boy came running. Mr. Emmott spoke to him in Arabic. A vigorous colloquy passed between them. The boy seemed to be emphatically denying something.

At last Mr. Emmott said in a perplexed voice:

"He says there's not been a soul here this afternoon. No stranger of any kind. I suppose the fellow must have slipped in without their seeing him."

"Of course he did," said Mrs. Mercado. "He slunk in when the boys weren't looking."

"Yes," said Mr. Emmott.

The slight uncertainty in his voice made me look at him inquiringly.

He turned and spoke to the little pot-boy, Abdullah, asking him a question.

The boy replied vehemently at length.

The puzzled frown on Mr. Emmott's brow increased.

"I don't understand it," he murmured under his breath. "I don't understand it at all."

But he didn't tell me what he didn't understand.

Chapter 11

An Odd Business

I'm adhering as far as possible to telling only my personal part in the business. I pass over the events of the next two hours, the arrival of Captain Maitland and the police and Dr. Reilly. There was a good deal of general confusion, questioning, all the routine business, I suppose.

In my opinion we began to get down to brass tacks about five o'clock when Dr. Reilly asked me to come with him into the office.

He shut the door, sat down in Dr. Leidner's chair, motioned me to sit down opposite him, and said briskly:

"Now, then, nurse, let's get down to it. There's something damned odd here."

I settled my cuffs and looked at him inquiringly.

He drew out a notebook.

"This is for my own satisfaction. Now, what time was it exactly when Dr. Leidner found his wife's body?"

"I should say it was almost exactly a quarter to three," I said.

"And how do you know that?"

"Well, I looked at my watch when I got up. It was twenty to three then."

"Let's have a look at this watch of yours."

I slipped it off my wrist and held it out to him.

"Right to the minute. Excellent woman. Good, that's *that* fixed. Now did you form any opinion as to how long she'd been dead?"

"Oh, really, doctor," I said, "I shouldn't like to say."

"Don't be so professional. I want to see if your estimate agrees with mine."

"Well, I should say she'd been dead at least an hour."

"Quite so. I examined the body at half-past four and I'm inclined to put the time of death between 1.15 and 1.45. We'll say half-past one at a guess. That's near enough."

He stopped and drummed thoughtfully with his fingers on the table.

"Damned odd, this business," he said. "Can you tell me about it—you were resting, you say? Did you hear anything?"

"At half-past one? No, doctor. I didn't hear anything at half-past one or at any other time. I lay on my bed from a quarter to one until twenty to three and I didn't hear anything except that droning noise the Arab boy makes, and occasionally Mr. Emmott shouting up to Dr. Leidner on the roof."

"The Arab boy—yes."

He frowned.

At that moment the door opened and Dr. Leidner and Captain Maitland came in. Captain Maitland was a fussy little man with a pair of shrewd grey eyes.

Dr. Reilly rose and pushed Dr. Leidner into his chair.

"Sit down, man. I'm glad you've come. We shall want you. There's something very queer about this business."

Dr. Leidner bowed his head. "I know." He looked at me. "My wife confided the truth to Nurse Leatheran. We mustn't keep anything back at this juncture, nurse, so please tell Captain Maitland and Dr. Reilly just what passed between you and my wife yesterday."

As nearly as possible I gave our conversation verbatim.

Captain Maitland uttered an occasional ejaculation. When I had finished he turned to Dr. Leidner.

"And this is all true, Leidner—eh?"

"Every word Nurse Leatheran has told you is correct."

"What an extraordinary story," said Dr. Reilly. "You can produce these letters?"

"I have no doubt they will be found amongst my wife's belongings."

"She took them out of the attaché-case on her table," I said.

"Then they are probably still there."

He turned to Captain Maitland and his usually gentle face grew hard and stern.

"There must be no question of hushing this story up, Captain Maitland. The one thing necessary is for this man to be caught and punished."

"You believe it actually is Mrs. Leidner's former husband?" I asked.

"Don't you think so, nurse?" asked Captain Maitland.

"Well, I think it is open to doubt," I said hesitatingly.

"In any case," said Dr. Leidner, "the man is a murderer—and I should say a dangerous lunatic also. He *must* be found, Captain Maitland. He must. It should not be difficult."

Dr. Reilly said slowly:

"It may be more difficult than you think . . . eh, Maitland?"

Captain Maitland tugged at his moustache without replying.

Suddenly I gave a start.

"Excuse me," I said, "but there's something perhaps I ought to mention."

I told my story of the Iraqi we had seen trying to peer through the window, and of how I had seen him hanging about the place two days ago trying to pump Father Lavigny.

"Good," said Captain Maitland, "we'll make a note of that. It will be something for the police to go on. The man may have some connection with the case."

"Probably paid to act as a spy," I suggested. "To find out when the coast was clear."

Dr. Reilly rubbed his nose with a harassed gesture.

"That's the devil of it," he said. "Supposing the coast wasn't clear—eh?"

I stared at him in a puzzled fashion.

Captain Maitland turned to Dr. Leidner.

"I want you to listen to me very carefully, Leidner. This is a review of the evidence we've got up to date. After lunch, which was served at twelve o'clock and was over by five and twenty to one, your wife went to her room accompanied by Nurse Leatheran, who settled her comfortably. You yourself went up to the roof, where you spent the next two hours, is that right?"

"Yes."

"Did you come down from the roof at all during that time?"

"No."

"Did any one come up to you?"

"Yes, Emmott did pretty frequently. He went to and fro between me and the boy, who was washing pottery down below."

"Did you yourself look over into the courtyard at all?"

"Once or twice—usually to call to Emmott about something."

"On each occasion the boy was sitting in the middle of the courtyard washing pots?"

"Yes."

"What was the longest period of time when Emmott was with you and absent from the courtyard?"

Dr. Leidner considered.

"It's difficult to say—perhaps ten minutes. Personally I should say two or three minutes, but I know by experience that my sense of time is not very good when I am absorbed and interested in what I am doing."

Captain Maitland looked at Dr. Reilly. The latter nodded. "We'd better get down to it," he said.

Captain Maitland took out a small notebook and opened it.

"Look here, Leidner, I'm going to read to you exactly what every member of your expedition was doing between one and two this afternoon."

"But surely—"

"Wait. You'll see what I'm driving at in a minute. First Mr. and Mrs. Mercado. Mr. Mercado says he was working in his laboratory. Mrs. Mercado says she was in her bedroom shampooing her hair. Miss Johnson says she was in the living-room taking impressions of cylinder seals. Mr. Reiter says he was in the dark-room developing plates. Father Lavigny says he was working in his bedroom. As to the two remaining members of the expedition, Carey and Coleman, the former was up on the dig and Coleman was in Hassanieh. So much for the members of the expedition. Now for the servants. The cook—your Indian chap—was sitting immediately outside the archway chatting to the guard and plucking a couple of fowls. Ibrahim and Mansur, the house-boys, joined him there at about 1.15. They both remained there laughing and talking until 2.30—*by which time your wife was already dead.*"

Dr. Leidner leaned forward.

"I don't understand—you puzzle me. What are you hinting at?"

"Is there any means of access to your wife's room except by the door into the courtyard?"

"No. There are two windows, but they are heavily barred—and besides, I think they were shut."

He looked at me questioningly.

"They were closed and latched on the inside," I said promptly.

"In any case," said Captain Maitland, "even if they had been open, no one could have entered or left the room that way. My fellows and I have assured ourselves of that.

It is the same with all the other windows giving on the open country. They all have iron bars and all the bars are in good condition. To have got into your wife's room, a stranger *must* have come through the arched doorway into the courtyard. But we have the united assurances of the guard, the cook and the house-boy that *nobody did so.*"

Dr. Leidner sprang up.

"What do you mean? What do you mean?"

"Pull yourself together, man," said Dr. Reilly quietly. "I know it's a shock, but it's got to be faced. *The murderer didn't come from outside*—so he must have come from *inside*. It looks as though Mrs. Leidner must have been murdered *by a member of your own expedition.*"

Chapter 12

"I Didn't Believe . . ."

"No. No!"

Dr. Leidner sprang up and walked up and down in an agitated manner.

"It's impossible what you say, Reilly. Absolutely impossible. One of *us*? Why, every single member of the expedition was devoted to Louise!"

A queer little expression pulled down the corners of Dr. Reilly's mouth. Under the circumstances it was difficult for him to say anything, but if ever a man's silence was eloquent his was at that minute.

"Quite impossible," reiterated Dr. Leidner. "They were all devoted to her. Louise had such wonderful charm. Every one felt it."

Dr. Reilly coughed.

"Excuse me, Leidner, but after all that's

only your opinion. If any member of the ex-pedition had disliked your wife they would naturally not advertise the fact to you."

Dr. Leidner looked distressed.

"True—quite true. But all the same, Reilly, I think you are wrong. I'm sure every one was fond of Louise."

He was silent for a moment or two and then burst out.

"This idea of yours is infamous. It's—it's frankly incredible."

"You can't get away from—er—the facts," said Captain Maitland.

"Facts? Facts? Lies told by an Indian cook and a couple of Arab house-boys. You know these fellows as well as I do, Reilly; so do you, Maitland. Truth as truth means nothing to them. They say what you want them to say as a mere matter of politeness."

"In this case," said Dr. Reilly dryly, "they are saying what we *don't* want them to say. Besides, I know the habits of your house-hold fairly well. Just outside the gate is a kind of social club. Whenever I've been over here in the afternoon I've always found most of your staff there. It's the natural place for them to be."

"All the same I think you are assuming too

much. Why shouldn't this man—this devil—
have got in earlier and concealed himself
somewhere?"

"I agree that that is not actually impossible," said Dr. Reilly coolly. "Let us assume
that a stranger *did* somehow gain admis-
sion unseen. He would have to remain concealed until the right moment (and he certainly couldn't have done so in Mrs.
Leidner's room, there is no cover there) and
take the risk of being seen entering the
room and leaving it—with Emmott and the
boy in the courtyard most of the time."

"The boy. I'd forgotten the boy," said Dr.
Leidner. "A sharp little chap. But surely,
Maitland, the boy *must* have seen the mur-
derer go into my wife's room?"

"We've elucidated that. The boy was
washing pots the whole afternoon with one
exception. Somewhere around half-past
one—Emmott can't put it closer than that—
he went up to the roof and was with you for
ten minutes—that's right, isn't it?"

"Yes. I couldn't have told you the exact
time but it must have been about that."

"Very good. Well, during that ten minutes,
the boy, seizing his chance to be idle,
strolled out and joined the others outside

the gate for a chat. When Emmott came down he found the boy absent and called him angrily, asking him what he meant by leaving his work. As far as I can see, *your wife must have been murdered during that ten minutes.*"

With a groan, Dr. Leidner sat down and hid his face in his hands.

Dr. Reilly took up the tale, his voice quiet and matter-of-fact.

"The time fits in with my evidence," he said. "She'd been dead about three hours when I examined her. The only question is— who did it?"

There was a silence. Dr. Leidner sat up in his chair and passed a hand over his forehead.

"I admit the force of your reasoning, Reilly," he said quietly. "It certainly *seems* as though it were what people call 'an inside job.' But I feel convinced that somewhere or other there is a mistake. It's plausible but there must be a flaw in it. To begin with, you are assuming that an amazing coincidence has occurred."

"Odd that you should use that word," said Dr. Reilly.

Without paying any attention Dr. Leidner went on:

"My wife receives threatening letters. She has reason to fear a certain person. Then she is—killed. And you ask me to believe that she is killed—not by that person—but by some one entirely different! I say that that is ridiculous."

"It seems so—yes," said Dr. Reilly meditatively.

He looked at Captain Maitland. "Coincidence—eh? What do you say, Maitland? Are you in favour of the idea? Shall we put it up to Leidner?"

Captain Maitland gave a nod.

"Go ahead," he said shortly.

"Have you ever heard of a man called Hercule Poirot, Leidner?"

Dr. Leidner stared at him, puzzled.

"I think I have heard the name, yes," he said vaguely. "I once heard a Mr. Van Aldin speak of him in very high terms. He is a private detective, is he not?"

"That's the man."

"But surely he lives in London, so how will that help us?"

"He lives in London, true," said Dr. Reilly, "but this is where the coincidence comes in.

He is now, not in London, but in Syria, and *he will actually pass through Hassanieh on his way to Baghdad to-morrow!*"

"Who told you this?"

"Jean Berat, the French consul. He dined with us last night and was talking about him. It seems he has been disentangling some military scandal in Syria. He's coming through here to visit Baghdad, and afterwards returning through Syria to London. How's that for a coincidence?"

Dr. Leidner hesitated a moment and looked apologetically at Captain Maitland.

"What do you think, Captain Maitland?"

"Should welcome co-operation," said Captain Maitland promptly. "My fellows are good scouts at scouring the countryside and investigating Arab blood feuds, but frankly, Leidner, this business of your wife's seems to me rather out of my class. The whole thing looks confoundedly fishy. I'm more than willing to have the fellow take a look at the case."

"You suggest that I should appeal to this man Poirot to help us?" said Dr. Leidner. "And suppose he refuses?"

"He won't refuse," said Dr. Reilly.

"How do you know?"

"Because I'm a professional man myself. If a really intricate case of say—cerebrospinal meningitis comes my way and I'm invited to take a hand, I shouldn't be able to refuse. This isn't an ordinary crime, Leidner."

"No," said Dr. Leidner. His lips twitched with sudden pain.

"Will you then, Reilly, approach this Hercule Poirot on my behalf?"

"I will."

Dr. Leidner made a gesture of thanks.

"Even now," he said slowly, "I can't realize it—that Louise is really dead."

I could bear it no longer.

"Oh! Dr. Leidner," I burst out. "I—I can't tell you how badly I feel about this. I've failed so badly in my duty. It was my job to watch over Mrs. Leidner—to keep her from harm."

Dr. Leidner shook his head gravely.

"No, no, nurse, you've nothing to reproach yourself with," he said slowly. "It's *I*, God forgive me, who am to blame. . . . *I didn't believe*—all along I didn't believe . . . I didn't dream for one moment that there was any *real* danger . . ."

He got up. His face twitched.

"*I let her go to her death.* . . . Yes, I let her go to her death—*not believing*—"

He staggered out of the room.

Dr. Reilly looked at me.

"I feel pretty culpable too," he said. "I thought the good lady was playing on his nerves."

"I didn't take it really seriously either," I confessed.

"We were all three wrong," said Dr. Reilly gravely.

"So it seems," said Captain Maitland.

Chapter 13
Hercule Poirot Arrives

I don't think I shall ever forget my first sight of Hercule Poirot. Of course, I got used to him later on, but to begin with it was shock, and I think every one else must have felt the same!

I don't know what I'd imagined—something rather like Sherlock Holmes—long and lean with a keen, clever face. Of course, I knew he was a foreigner, but I hadn't expected him to be *quite* as foreign as he was, if you know what I mean.

When you saw him you just wanted to laugh! He was like something on the stage or at the pictures. To begin with, he wasn't above five foot five, I should think—an odd plump little man, quite old, with an enormous moustache, and a head like an egg. He looked like a hairdresser in a comic play!

And this was the man who was going to find out who killed Mrs. Leidner!

I suppose something of my disgust must have shown in my face, for almost straight-away he said to me with a queer kind of twinkle:

"You disapprove of me, *ma sœur?* Re-member, the pudding proves itself only when you eat it."

The proof of the pudding's in the eating, I *suppose* he meant.

Well, that's a true enough saying, but I couldn't say I felt much confidence myself!

Dr. Reilly brought him out in his car soon after lunch on Sunday, and his first proce-dure was to ask us all to assemble together.

We did so in the dining-room, all sitting round the table. Mr. Poirot sat at the head of it with Dr. Leidner one side and Dr. Reilly the other.

When we were all assembled, Dr. Leidner cleared his throat and spoke in his gentle, hesitating voice.

"I dare say you have all heard of M. Her-cule Poirot. He was passing through Has-sanieh to-day, and has very kindly agreed to break his journey to help us. The Iraq police and Captain Maitland are, I am sure, doing their very best, but—but there are circumstances in the case"—he floundered and shot an appealing glance at Dr. Reilly— "there may, it seems, be difficulties. . . ."

"It is not all the square and overboard— no?" said the little man at the top of the table. Why, he couldn't even speak English properly!

"Oh, he *must* be caught!" cried Mrs. Mercado. "It would be unbearable if he got away!"

I noticed the little foreigner's eyes rest on her appraisingly.

"He? Who is *he*, madame?" he asked.

"Why, the murderer, of course."

"Ah! the murderer," said Hercule Poirot.

He spoke as though the murderer was of no consequence at all!

We all stared at him. He looked from one face to another.

"It is likely, I think," he said, "that you have none of you been brought in contact with a case of murder before?"

There was a general murmur of assent.

Hercule Poirot smiled.

"It is clear, therefore, that you do not understand the A.B.C. of the position. There are unpleasantnesses! Yes, there are a lot of unpleasantnesses. To begin with, there is *suspicion*."

"Suspicion?"

It was Miss Johnson who spoke. Mr. Poirot looked at her thoughtfully. I had an idea that he regarded her with approval. He looked as though he were thinking, "Here is a sensible, intelligent person!"

"Yes, mademoiselle," he said. "Suspicion! Let us not make the bones about it. *You are all under suspicion here in this house*. The cook, the house-boy, the scullion, the pot-boy—yes, and all the members of the expedition too."

Mrs. Mercado started up, her face working.

"How *dare* you? How dare you say such a thing! This is odious—unbearable! Dr. Leidner—you can't sit here and let this man—and let this man—"

Dr. Leidner said wearily:

"Please try and be calm, Marie."

Mr. Mercado stood up too. His hands were shaking and his eyes were bloodshot.

"I agree. It is an outrage—an insult—"

"No, no," said Mr. Poirot. "I do not insult

you. I merely ask you all to face facts. *In a house where murder has been committed, every inmate comes in for a certain share of suspicion.* I ask you what evidence is there that the murderer came from outside at all?"

Mrs. Mercado cried:

"But of course he did! It stands to reason! Why—" She stopped and said more slowly, "Anything else would be incredible!"

"You are doubtless correct, madame," said Poirot with a bow. "I explain to you only how the matter must be approached. First I assure myself of the fact that every one in this room is innocent. After that I seek the murderer elsewhere."

"Is it not possible that that may be a little late in the day?" asked Father Lavigny suavely.

"The tortoise, *mon père*, overtook the hare."

Father Lavigny shrugged his shoulders.

"We are in your hands," he said resignedly. "Convince yourself as soon as may be of our innocence in this terrible business."

"As rapidly as possible. It was my duty to make the position clear to you, so that you may not resent the impertinence of any questions I may have to ask. Perhaps, *mon père*, the Church will set an example?"

"Ask any questions you please of me," said Father Lavigny gravely.

"This is your first season, out here?"

"Yes."

"And you arrived—when?"

"Three weeks ago almost to a day. That is, on the 27th of February."

"Coming from?"

"The Order of the *Pères Blancs* at Carthage."

"Thank you, *mon père*. Were you at any time acquainted with Mrs. Leidner before coming here?"

"No, I had never seen the lady until I met her here."

"Will you tell me what you were doing at the time of the tragedy?"

"I was working on some cuneiform tablets in my own room."

I noticed that Poirot had at his elbow a rough plan of the building.

"That is the room at the south-west corner corresponding to that of Mrs. Leidner on the opposite side?"

"Yes."

"At what time did you go to your room?"

"Immediately after lunch. I should say at about twenty minutes to one."

"And you remained there until—when?"

"Just before three o'clock. I had heard the station wagon come back—and then I heard it drive off again. I wondered why, and came out to see."

"During the time that you were there did you leave the room, at all?"

"No, not once."

"And you heard or saw nothing that might have any bearing on the tragedy?"

"No."

"You have no window giving on the court-yard in your room?"

"No, both the windows give on the coun-tryside."

"Could you hear at all what was happen-ing in the courtyard?"

"Not very much. I heard Mr. Emmott passing my room and going up to the roof. He did so once or twice."

"Can you remember at what time?"

"No, I'm afraid I can't. I was engrossed in my work, you see."

There was a pause and then Poirot said:

"Can you say or suggest anything at all that might throw light on this business. Did you, for instance, notice anything in the days preceding the murder?"

Father Lavigny looked slightly uncomfortable.

He shot a half-questioning look at Dr. Leidner.

"That is rather a difficult question, monsieur," he said gravely. "If you ask me, I must reply frankly that in my opinion Mrs. Leidner was clearly in dread of some one or something. She was definitely nervous about strangers. I imagine she had a reason for this nervousness of hers—but I *know* nothing. She did not confide in me."

Poirot cleared his throat and consulted some notes that he held in his hand.

"Two nights ago I understand there was a scare of burglary."

Father Lavigny replied in the affirmative and retailed his story of the light seen in the antika-room and the subsequent futile search.

"You believe, do you not, that some unauthorized person was on the premises at that time?"

"I don't know what to think," said Father Lavigny frankly. "Nothing was taken or disturbed in any way. It might have been one of the house-boys—"

"Or a member of the expedition?"

"Or a member of the expedition. But in that case there would be no reason for the person not admitting the fact."

"But it *might* equally have been a stranger from outside?"

"I suppose so."

"Supposing a stranger *had* been on the premises, could he have concealed himself successfully during the following day and until the afternoon of the day following that?"

He asked the question half of Father Lavigny and half of Dr. Leidner. Both men considered the question carefully.

"I hardly think it would be possible," said Dr. Leidner at last with some reluctance. "I don't see where he could possibly conceal himself, do you, Father Lavigny?"

"No—no—I don't."

Both men seemed reluctant to put the suggestion aside.

Poirot turned to Miss Johnson.

"And you, mademoiselle? Do you consider such a hypothesis feasible?"

After a moment's thought Miss Johnson shook her head.

"No," she said. "I don't. Where could any one hide? The bedrooms are all in use and, in any case, are sparsely furnished. The dark-room, the drawing-office and the laboratory were all in use the next day—so were all these rooms. There are no cupboards or corners. Perhaps, if the servants were in collusion—"

"That is possible, but unlikely," said Poirot.

He turned once more to Father Lavigny.

"There is another point. The other day Nurse Leatheran here noticed you talking to a man outside. She had previously noticed that same man trying to peer in at one of the windows on the outside. It rather looks as though the man were hanging round the place deliberately."

"That is possible, of course," said Father Lavigny thoughtfully.

"Did you speak to this man first, or did he speak to you?"

Father Lavigny considered for a moment or two.

"I believe—yes, I am sure, that he spoke to me."

"What did he say?"

Father Lavigny made an effort of memory.

"He said, I think, something to the effect was this the American expedition house? And then something else about the Americans employing a lot of men on the work. I did not really understand him very well, but I endeavoured to keep up a conversation so as to improve my Arabic. I thought, perhaps, that being a townee he would understand me better than the men on the dig do."

"Did you converse about anything else?"

"As far as I remember, I said Hassanieh was a big town—and we then agreed that Baghdad was bigger—and I think he asked whether I was an Armenian or a Syrian Catholic—something of that kind."

Poirot nodded.

"Can you describe him?"

Again Father Lavigny frowned in thought.

"He was rather a short man," he said at last, "and squarely built. He had a very noticeable squint and was of fair complexion."

Mr. Poirot turned to me.

"Does that agree with the way you would describe him?" he asked.

"Not exactly," I said hesitatingly. "I should

have said he was tall rather than short, and very dark complexioned. He seemed to me of a rather slender build. I didn't notice any squint."

Mr. Poirot gave a despairing shrug of the shoulders.

"It is always so! If you were of the police how well you would know it! The description of the same man by two different people— never does it agree. Every detail is contradicted."

"I'm fairly sure about the squint," said Father Lavigny. "Nurse Leatheran may be right about the other points. By the way, when I said *fair*, I only meant fair for an *Iraqi*. I expect nurse would call that dark."

"Very dark," I said obstinately. "A dirty dark-yellow colour."

I saw Dr. Reilly bite his lip and smile.

Poirot threw up his hands.

"Passons!" he said. "This stranger hanging about, he may be important—he may not. At any rate he must be found. Let us continue our inquiry."

He hesitated for a minute, studying the faces turned towards him round the table, then, with a quick nod, he singled out Mr. Reiter.

"Come, my friend," he said. "Let us have your account of yesterday afternoon."

Mr. Reiter's pink, plumb face flushed scarlet.

"Me?" he said.

"Yes, you. To begin with, your name and your age?"

"Carl Reiter, twenty-eight."

"American—yes?"

"Yes, I come from Chicago."

"This is your first season?"

"Yes. I'm in charge of the photography."

"Ah, yes. And yesterday afternoon, how did you employ yourself?"

"Well—I was in the dark-room most of the time."

"*Most* of the time—eh?"

"Yes. I developed some plates first. Afterwards I was fixing up some objects to photograph."

"Outside?"

"Oh, no, in the photographic room."

"The dark-room opens out of the photographic room?"

"Yes."

"And so you never came outside the photographic room?"

"No."

"Did you notice anything that went on in the courtyard?"

The young man shook his head.

"I wasn't noticing anything," he explained. "I was busy. I heard the car come back, and as soon as I could leave what I was doing I came out to see if there was any mail. It was then that I—heard."

"And you began your work in the photographic room—when?"

"At ten minutes to one."

"Were you acquainted with Mrs. Leidner before you joined this expedition?"

The young man shook his head.

"No, sir. I never saw her till I actually got here."

"Can you think of *anything*—any incident—however small—that might help us?"

Carl Reiter shook his head.

He said helplessly:

"I guess I don't know anything at all, sir."

"Mr. Emmott?"

David Emmott spoke clearly and concisely in his pleasant soft American voice.

"I was working with the pottery from a quarter to one till a quarter to three—over-seeing the boy Abdullah, sorting it, and occasionally going up to the roof to help Dr. Leidner."

"How often did you go up to the roof?"

"Four times, I think."

"For how long?"

"Usually a couple of minutes—not more. But on one occasion after I'd been working a little over half an hour I stayed as long as ten minutes—discussing what to keep and what to fling away."

"And I understand that when you came down you found the boy had left his place?"

"Yes. I called him angrily and he reappeared from outside the archway. He had gone out to gossip with the others."

"That was the only time he left his work?"

"Well, I sent him up once or twice to the roof with pottery."

Poirot said gravely:

"It is hardly necessary to ask you, Mr. Emmott, whether you saw any one enter or leave Mrs. Leidner's room during that time?"

Mr. Emmott replied promptly.

"I saw no one at all. Nobody even came out into the courtyard during the two hours I was working."

"And to the best of your belief it was half-past one when both you and the boy were absent and the courtyard was empty?"

"It couldn't have been far off that time. Of course, I can't say *exactly*."

Poirot turned to Dr. Reilly.

"That agrees with your estimate of the time of death, doctor?"

"It does," said Dr. Reilly.

Mr. Poirot stroked his great curled moustaches.

"I think we can take it," he said gravely, "that Mrs. Leidner met her death during that ten minutes."

Chapter 14

One of Us?

There was a little pause—and in it a wave of horror seemed to float round the room.

I think it was at that moment that I first believed Dr. Reilly's theory to be right.

I *felt* that the murderer was in the room. Sitting with us—listening. *One of us* . . .

Perhaps Mrs. Mercado felt it too. For she suddenly gave a short sharp cry.

"I can't help it," she sobbed. "I—it's *so terrible!*"

"Courage, Marie," said her husband.

He looked at us apologetically.

"She is so sensitive. She feels things so much."

"I—I was so fond of Louise," sobbed Mrs. Mercado.

I don't know whether something of what I

felt showed in my face, but I suddenly found that Mr. Poirot was looking at me, and that a slight smile hovered on his lips.

I gave him a cold glance, and at once he resumed his inquiry.

"Tell me, madame," he said, "of the way you spent yesterday afternoon?"

"I was washing my hair," sobbed Mrs. Mercado. "It seems awful not to have known anything about it. I was quite happy and busy."

"You were in your room?"

"Yes."

"And you did not leave it?"

"No. Not till I heard the car. Then I came out and I heard what had happened. Oh, it was *awful!*"

"Did it surprise you?"

Mrs. Mercado stopped crying. Her eyes opened resentfully.

"What do you mean, M. Poirot? Are you suggesting—"

"What should I mean, madame? You have just told us how fond you were of Mrs. Leidner. She might, perhaps, have confided in you."

"Oh, I see. . . . No—no, dear Louise never told me anything—anything *definite*, that is.

Of course, I could see she was terribly worried and nervous. And there were those strange occurrences—hands tapping on the window and all that."

"Fancies, I remember you said," I put in, unable to keep silent.

I was glad to see that she looked momentarily disconcerted.

Once again I was conscious of Mr. Poirot's amused eye glancing in my direction.

He summed up in a business-like way.

"It comes to this, madame, you were washing your hair—you heard nothing and you saw nothing. Is there anything at all you can think of that would be a help to us in any way?"

Mrs. Mercado took no time to think.

"No, indeed there isn't. It's the deepest mystery! But I should say there is no doubt—no doubt *at all* that the murderer came from outside. Why, it stands to reason."

Poirot turned to her husband.

"And you, monsieur, what have you to say?"

Mr. Mercado stared nervously. He pulled at his beard in an aimless fashion.

"Must have been. Must have been," he said. "Yet how could any one wish to harm her? She was so gentle—so kind—" He shook his head. "Whoever killed her must have been a fiend—yes, a fiend!"

"And you yourself, monsieur, how did you pass yesterday afternoon?"

"I?" he stared vaguely.

"You were in the laboratory, Joseph," his wife prompted him.

"Ah, yes, so I was—so I was. My usual tasks."

"At what time did you go there?"

Again he looked helplessly and inquiringly at Mrs. Mercado.

"At ten minutes to one, Joseph."

"Ah, yes, at ten minutes to one."

"Did you come out in the courtyard at all?"

"No—I don't think so." He considered. "No, I am sure I didn't."

"When did you hear of the tragedy?"

"My wife came and told me. It was terrible—shocking. I could hardly believe it. Even now, I can hardly believe it is true."

Suddenly he began to tremble.

"It is horrible—horrible . . ."

Mrs. Mercado came quickly to his side.

"Yes, yes, Joseph, we all feel that. But we mustn't give way. It makes it so much more difficult for poor Dr. Leidner."

I saw a spasm of pain pass across Dr. Leidner's face, and I guessed that this emotional atmosphere was not easy for him. He gave a half glance at Poirot as though in appeal. Poirot responded quickly.

"Miss Johnson?" he said.

"I'm afraid I can tell you very little," said Miss Johnson. Her cultured well-bred voice was soothing after Mrs. Mercado's shrill treble. She went on:

"I was working in the living-room—taking impressions of some cylinder seals on plasticine."

"And you saw or noticed nothing?"

"No."

Poirot gave her a quick glance. His ear had caught what mine had—a faint note of indecision.

"Are you quite sure, mademoiselle? Is there something that comes back to you vaguely?"

"No—not really—"

"Something you saw, shall we say, out of the corner of your eye hardly knowing you saw it."

"No, certainly not," she replied positively.

"Something you *heard* then. Ah, yes, something you are not quite sure whether you heard or not?"

Miss Johnson gave a short vexed laugh.

"You press me very closely, M. Poirot. I'm afraid you are encouraging me to tell you what I am, perhaps, only imagining."

"Then there *was* something you—shall we say—imagined?"

Miss Johnson said slowly, weighing her words in a detached way:

"I have imagined—since—that at some time during the afternoon I heard a very faint cry. . . . What I mean is that I dare say I did hear a cry. All the windows in the living-room were open and one hears all sorts of sounds from people working in the barley fields. But you see—since—I've got the idea into my head that it was—that it was Mrs. Leidner I heard. And that's made me rather unhappy. Because if I'd jumped up and run along to her room—well, who knows? I might have been in time . . ."

Dr. Reilly interposed authoritatively.

"Now, don't start getting that into your head," he said. "I've no doubt but that Mrs. Leidner (forgive me, Leidner) was struck down almost as soon as the man entered the room, and it was that blow that killed her. No second blow was struck. Otherwise she would have had time to call for help and make a real outcry."

"Still, I might have caught the murderer," said Miss Johnson.

"What time was this, mademoiselle?" asked Poirot. "In the neighbourhood of half-past one?"

"It must have been about that time—yes." She reflected a minute.

"That would fit in," said Poirot thoughtfully. "You heard nothing else—the opening or shutting of a door, for instance."

Miss Johnson shook her head.

"No, I do not remember anything of that kind."

"You were sitting at a table, I presume. Which way were you facing? The courtyard? The antika-room? The verandah? Or the open countryside?"

"I was facing the courtyard."

"Could you see the boy Abdullah washing pots from where you were?"

"Oh, yes, if I looked up, but of course, I was very intent on what I was doing. All my attention was on that."

"If any one had passed the courtyard window, though, you would have noticed it?"

"Oh, yes, I am almost sure of that."

"And nobody did so?"

"No."

"But if any one had walked, say, across the middle of the courtyard, would you have noticed that?"

"I think—probably not—unless, as I said before, I had happened to look up and out of the window."

"You did not notice the boy Abdullah leave his work and go out to join the other servants?"

"No."

"Ten minutes," mused Poirot. "That fatal ten minutes."

There was a momentary silence.

Miss Johnson lifted her head suddenly and said:

"You know, M. Poirot, I think I have unintentionally misled you. On thinking it over, I do not believe that I could possibly have heard any cry uttered in Mrs. Leidner's room from where I was. The antika-room lay between me and her—and I understand her windows were found closed."

"In any case, do not distress yourself,

mademoiselle," said Poirot kindly. "It is not really of much importance."

"No, of course not. I understand that. But you see, it *is* of importance to me, because I feel I might have done something."

"Don't distress yourself, dear Anne," said Dr. Leidner with affection. "You must be sensible. What you heard was probably one Arab bawling to another some distance away in the fields."

Miss Johnson flushed a little at the kindliness of his tone. I even saw tears spring to her eyes. She turned her head away and spoke even more gruffly than usual.

"Probably was. Usual thing after a tragedy—start imagining things that aren't so at all."

Poirot was once more consulting his notebook.

"I do not suppose there is much more to be said. Mr. Carey?"

Richard Carey spoke slowly—in a wooden, mechanical manner.

"I'm afraid I can add nothing helpful. I was on duty at the dig. The news was brought to me there."

"And you know or can think of nothing

helpful that occurred in the days immediately preceding the murder?"

"Nothing at all."

"Mr. Coleman?"

"I was right out of the whole thing," said
Mr. Coleman with—was it just a shade of regret—in his tone. "I went into Hassanieh
yesterday morning to get the money for the
men's wages. When I came back Emmott
told me what had happened and I went
back in the bus to get the police and Dr.
Reilly."

"And beforehand?"

"Well, sir, things were a bit jumpy—but
you know that already. There was the
antika-room scare and one or two before
that—hands and faces at the window—you
remember, sir," he appealed to Dr. Leidner,
who bent his head in assent. "I think, you
know, that you'll find some Johnny *did* get
in from outside. Must have been an artful
sort of beggar."

Poirot considered him for a minute or two
in silence.

"You are an Englishman, Mr. Coleman?"
he asked at last.

"That's right, sir. All British. See the trade-
mark. Guaranteed genuine."

"This is your first season?"

"Quite right."

"And you are passionately keen on archaeology?"

This description of himself seemed to cause Mr. Coleman some embarrassment. He got rather pink and shot the side look of a guilty schoolboy at Dr. Leidner.

"Of course—it's all very interesting," he stammered. "I mean—I'm not exactly a brainy chap . . ."

He broke off rather lamely. Poirot did not insist.

He tapped thoughtfully on the table with the end of his pencil and carefully straightened an inkpot that stood in front of him.

"It seems then," he said, "that that is as near as we can get for the moment. If any one of you thinks of something that has for the time being slipped his or her memory do not hesitate to come to me with it. It will be well now, I think, for me to have a few words alone with Dr. Leidner and Dr. Reilly."

It was the signal for a breaking up of the party. We all rose and filed out of the door. When I was half-way out, however, a voice recalled me.

"Perhaps," said Mr. Poirot, "Nurse

Leatheran will be so kind as to remain. I think her assistance will be valuable to us."

I came back and resumed my seat at the table.

Chapter 15

Poirot Makes a Suggestion

Dr. Reilly had risen from his seat. When every one had gone out he carefully closed the door. Then, with an inquiring glance at Poirot, he proceeded to shut the window giving on the courtyard. The others were already shut. Then he, too, resumed his seat at the table.

"Bien!" said Poirot. "We are now private and undisturbed. We can speak freely. We have heard what the members of the expedition have to tell us and— But yes, *ma, sœur,* what is it you think?"

I got rather red. There was no denying that the queer little man had sharp eyes. He'd seen the thought passing through my mind—I suppose my face *had* shown a bit too clearly what I was thinking!

"Oh, it's nothing—" I said, hesitating.

"Come on, nurse," said Dr. Reilly. "Don't keep the specialist waiting."

"It's nothing really," I said hurriedly. "It only just passed through my mind, so to speak, that perhaps even if any one did know or suspect something it wouldn't be easy to bring it out in front of everybody else—or even, perhaps, in front of Dr. Leidner."

Rather to my astonishment, M. Poirot nodded his head in vigorous agreement.

"Precisely. Precisely. It is very just what you say there. But I will explain. That little reunion we have just had—it served a purpose. In England before the races you have a parade of the horses, do you not? They go in front of the grandstand so that every one may have an opportunity of seeing and judging them. That is the purpose of my little assembly. In the sporting phrase, I run my eye over the possible starters."

Dr. Leidner cried out violently, "I do not believe for one minute that *any* member of my expedition is implicated in this crime!"

Then, turning to me, he said authoritatively:

"Nurse, I should be much obliged if you

would tell M. Poirot here and now exactly what passed between my wife and you two days ago."

Thus urged, I plunged straightaway into my story, trying as far as possible to recall the exact words and phrases Mrs. Leidner had used.

When I had finished, M. Poirot said:

"Very good. Very good. You have the mind neat and orderly. You will be of great service to me here."

He turned to Dr. Leidner.

"You have these letters?"

"I have them here. I thought that you would want to see them first thing."

Poirot took them from him, read them, and scrutinized them carefully as he did so. I was rather disappointed that he didn't dust powder over them or examine them with a microscope or anything like that—but I realized that he wasn't a very young man and that his methods were probably not very up to date. He just read them in the way that any one might read a letter.

Having read them he put them down and cleared his throat.

"Now," he said, "let us proceed to get our facts clear and in order. The first of these letters was received by your wife shortly after her marriage to you in America. There had been others but these she destroyed. The first letter was followed by a second. A very short time after the second arrived you both had a near escape from coal gas poisoning. You then came abroad and for nearly two years no further letters were received. They started again at the beginning of your season this year—that is to say, within the last three weeks. That is correct?"

"Absolutely."

"Your wife displayed every sign of panic and, after consulting Dr. Reilly, you engaged Nurse Leatheran here to keep your wife company and allay her fears?"

"Yes."

"Certain incidents occurred—hands tapping at the window—a spectral face—noises in the antika-room. You did not witness any of these phenomena yourself?"

"No."

"In fact nobody did except Mrs. Leidner?"

"Father Lavigny saw a light in the antika-room."

"Yes, I have not forgotten that."

He was silent for a minute or two, then he said:

"Had your wife made a will?"

"I do not think so."

"Why was that?"

"It did not seem worth it from her point of view."

"Is she not a wealthy woman?"

"Yes, during her lifetime. Her father left her a considerable sum of money in trust. She could not touch the principal. At her death it was to pass to any children she might have—and failing children to the Pittstown Museum."

Poirot drummed thoughtfully on the table.

"Then we can, I think," he said, "eliminate one motive from the case. It is, you comprehend, what I look for first. *Who benefits by the deceased's death?* In this case it is a museum. Had it been otherwise, had Mrs. Leidner died intestate but possessed of a considerable fortune, I should imagine that it would prove an interesting question as to who inherited the money—you—or a former husband. But there would have been this difficulty, the former husband would have had to resurrect himself in order to claim it, and I should imagine that he would then be in danger of arrest, though I hardly fancy that the death penalty would be exacted so long after the war. However, these speculations need not arise. As I say, I settle first the question of money. For the next step I proceed always to suspect the husband or wife of the deceased! In this case, in the first place, you are proved never to have gone near your wife's room yesterday afternoon, in the second place, you lose instead of gain by your wife's death, and in the third place—"

He paused.

"Yes?" said Dr. Leidner.

"In the third place," said Poirot slowly. "I can, I think, appreciate devotion when I see it. I believe Dr. Leidner, that your love for your wife was the ruling passion of your life. It is so, is it not?"

Dr. Leidner answered quite simply:

"Yes."

Poirot nodded.

"Therefore," he said, "we can proceed."

"Hear, hear, let's get down to it," said Dr. Reilly with some impatience.

Poirot gave him a reproving glance.

"My friend, do not be impatient. In a case like this everything must be approached with order and method. In fact, that is my rule in every case. Having disposed of certain possibilities, we now approach a very important point. It is vital that, as you say— all the cards should be on the table—there must be nothing kept back."

"Quite so," said Dr. Reilly.

"That is why I demand the whole truth," went on Poirot.

Dr. Leidner looked at him in surprise.

"I assure you, M. Poirot, that I have kept nothing back. I have told you everything that I know. There have been no reserves."

"Tout de même, you have not told me *everything."*

"Yes, indeed. I cannot think of any detail that has escaped me."

He looked quite distressed.

Poirot shook his head gently.

"No," he said. *"You have not told me, for instance, why you installed Nurse Leatheran in the house."*

Dr. Leidner looked completely bewildered.

"But I have explained that. It is obvious. My wife's nervousness—her fears . . ."

Poirot leaned forward. Slowly and emphatically he wagged a finger up and down.

"No, no, no. There is something there that is not clear. Your wife is in danger, yes—she

is threatened with death, yes. You send—
not for the police—not for a private detective even—but for a *nurse!* It does not make
the sense, that!"

"I—I—" Dr. Leidner stopped. The colour
rose in his cheeks. "I thought—" He came
to a dead stop.

"Now we are coming to it," Poirot encouraged him. "You thought—what?"

Dr. Leidner remained silent. He looked
harassed and unwilling.

"See you," Poirot's tone became winning
and appealing, "it all rings true what you
have told me, except for that. Why a *nurse?*
There is an answer—yes. In fact, there can
be only one answer. *You did not believe
yourself in your wife's danger.*"

And then with a cry Dr. Leidner broke
down.

"God help me," he groaned. "I didn't. I
didn't."

Poirot watched him with the kind of attention a cat gives a mouse-hole—ready to
pounce when the mouse shows itself.

"What *did* you think then?" he asked.

"I don't know. I don't know . . ."

"But you do know. You know perfectly.
Perhaps I can help you—with a guess. *Did*

you, Dr. Leidner, suspect that these letters were all written by your wife herself?"

There wasn't any need for him to answer. The truth of Poirot's guess was only too apparent. The horrified hand he held up, as though begging for mercy, told its own tale.

I drew a deep breath. So I *had* been right in my half-formed guess! I recalled the curious tone in which Dr. Leidner had asked me what I thought of it all. I nodded my head slowly and thoughtfully, and suddenly awoke to the fact that M. Poirot's eyes were on me.

"Did you think the same, nurse?"

"The idea did cross my mind," I said truthfully.

"For what reason?"

I explained the similarity of the handwriting on the letter that Mr. Coleman had shown me.

Poirot turned to Dr. Leidner.

"Had you, too noticed that similarity?"

Dr. Leidner bowed his head.

"Yes, I did. The writing was small and cramped—not big and generous like Louise's, but several of the letters were formed the same way. I will show you."

From an inner breast pocket he took out

some letters and finally selected a sheet from one which he handed to Poirot. It was part of a letter written to him by his wife. Poirot compared it carefully with the anonymous letters.

"Yes," he murmured. "Yes. There are several similarities—a curious way of forming the letter *s*, a distinctive *e*. I am not a handwriting expert—I cannot pronounce definitely (and for that matter, I have never found two handwriting experts who agree on any point whatsoever)—but one can at least say this—the similarity between the two handwritings is very marked. It seems highly probable that they were all written by the same person. But it is not *certain*. We must take all contingencies into mind."

He leaned back in his chair and said thoughtfully:

"There are three possibilities. First, the similarity of the handwriting is pure coincidence. Second, that these threatening letters were written by Mrs. Leidner herself for some obscure reason. Third, that they were written by some one *who deliberately copies her handwriting*. Why? There seems no sense in it. One of these three possibilities must be the correct one."

He reflected for a minute or two and then, turning to Dr. Leidner, he asked, with a resumal of his brisk manner.

"When the possibility that Mrs. Leidner herself was the author of these letters first struck you, what theory did you form?"

Dr. Leidner shook his head.

"I put the idea out of my head as quickly as possible. I felt it was monstrous."

"Did you search for no explanation?"

"Well," he hesitated, "I wondered if worrying and brooding over the past had perhaps affected my wife's brain slightly. I thought she might possibly have written those letters to herself without being conscious of having done so. That is possible, isn't it?" he added, turning to Dr. Reilly.

Dr. Reilly pursed up his lips.

"The human brain is capable of almost anything," he replied vaguely.

But he shot a lightning glance at Poirot, and as if in obedience to it, the latter abandoned the subject.

"The letters are an interesting point," he said. "But we must concentrate on the case as a whole. There are, as I see it, three possible solutions."

"Three?"

"Yes. Solution one: the simplest. Your wife's first husband is still alive. He first threatens her and then proceeds to carry out his threats. If we accept this solution, our problem is to discover how he got in or out without being seen.

"Solution two: Mrs. Leidner, for reasons of her own (reasons probably more easily understood by a medical man than a layman), writes herself threatening letters. The gas business is staged by her (remember, it was she who roused you by telling you she smelt gas). But, *if Mrs. Leidner wrote herself the letters, she cannot be in danger from the supposed writer*. We must, therefore, look elsewhere for the murderer. We must look, in fact, amongst the members of your staff. Yes," in answer to a murmur of protest from Dr. Leidner, "that is the only logical conclusion. To satisfy a private grudge one of them killed her. That person, I may say, was probably aware of the letters—or was at any rate aware that Mrs. Leidner feared or was pretending to fear some one. That fact, in the murderer's opinion, rendered the murder quite safe for him. He felt sure it would be put down to a mysterious outsider—the writer of the threatening letters.

"A variant of this solution is that the murderer actually wrote the letters himself, being aware of Mrs. Leidner's past history. But in that case it is not quite clear *why* the criminal should have copied Mrs. Leidner's own handwriting since, as far as we can see, it would be more to his or her advantage that they should appear to be written by an outsider.

"The third solution is the most interesting to my mind. I suggest that the letters are genuine. They are written by Mrs. Leidner's first husband (or his younger brother), *who is actually one of the expedition staff.*"

Chapter 16

The Suspects

Dr. Leidner sprang to his feet.

"Impossible! Absolutely impossible! The idea is absurd!"

Mr. Poirot looked at him quite calmly but said nothing.

"You mean to suggest that my wife's former husband is one of the expedition *and that she didn't recognize him?*"

"Exactly. Reflect a little on the facts. Nearly twenty years ago your wife lived with this man for a few months. Would she know him if she came across him after that lapse of time? I think not. His face will have changed, his build will have changed—his voice may not have changed so much, but that is a detail he can attend to himself. And remember, *she is not looking for him amongst her own household.* She visualizes him as somewhere outside—a stranger. No, I do not think she would recognize him. And there is a second possibility. The young brother—the child of those days who was so passionately devoted to his elder brother. He is now a man. Will she recognize a child of ten or twelve years old in a man nearing thirty? Yes, there is young William Bosner to be reckoned with. Remember, his brother in his eyes may not loom as a traitor but as a patriot, a martyr for his own country—Germany. In his eyes *Mrs. Leidner* is the traitor—the monster who sent his beloved brother to death! A susceptible child is capable of great hero worship, and a young mind can easily be obsessed by an idea which persists into adult life."

"Quite true," said Dr. Reilly. "The popular view that a child forgets easily is not an accurate one. Many people go right through life in the grip of an idea which has been impressed on them in very tender years."

"*Bien.* You have these two possibilities. Frederick Bosner, a man by now of fifty odd, and William Bosner, whose age would be something short of thirty. Let us examine the members of your staff from these two points of view."

"This is fantastic," murmured Dr. Leidner. "*My* staff! The members of my own expedition."

"And consequently considered above suspicion," said Poirot dryly. "A very useful point of view. *Commençons!* Who could emphatically *not* be Frederick or William?"

"The women."

"Naturally. Miss Johnson and Mrs. Mercado are crossed off. Who else?"

"Carey. He and I have worked together for years before I even met Louise—"

"And also he is the wrong age. He is, I should judge, thirty-eight or nine, two young for Frederick, too old for William. Now for the rest. There is Father Lavigny and Mr. Mercado. Either of them might be Frederick Bosner."

"But, my dear sir," cried Dr. Leidner in a voice of mingled irritation and amusement, "Father Lavigny is known all over the world as an epigraphist and Mercado has worked for years in a well-known museum in New York. It is *impossible* that either of them should be the man you think!"

Poirot waved an airy hand.

"Impossible—impossible—I take no account of the word! The impossible, always I examine it very closely! But we will pass on for the moment. Who else have you? Carl Reiter, a young man with a German name, David Emmott—"

"He has been with me two seasons, remember."

"He is a young man with the gift of patience. *If* he committed a crime, it would not be in a hurry. All would be very well prepared."

Dr. Leidner made a gesture of despair.

"And lastly, William Coleman," continued Poirot.

"He is an Englishman."

"*Pourquoi pas?* Did not Mrs. Leidner say that the boy left America and could not be traced? He might easily have been brought up in England."

"You have an answer to everything," said Dr. Leidner.

I was thinking hard. Right from the beginning I had thought Mr. Coleman's manner rather more like a P. G. Wodehouse book than like a real live young man. Had he really been playing a part all the time?

Poirot was writing in a little book.

"Let us proceed with order and method," he said. "On the first count we have two names. Father Lavigny and Mr. Mercado. On the second we have Coleman, Emmott and Reiter.

"Now let us pass to the opposite aspect of the matter—means and opportunity. *Who amongst the expedition had the means and the opportunity of committing the crime?* Carey was on the dig, Coleman was in Hassanieh, you yourself were on the roof. That leaves us Father Lavigny, Mr. Mercado, Mrs. Mercado, David Emmott, Carl Reiter, Miss Johnson and Nurse Leatheran."

"Oh!" I exclaimed, and I bounded in my chair.

Mr. Poirot looked at me with twinkling eyes.

"Yes, I'm afraid, *ma sœur*, that you have got to be included. It would have been quite easy for you to have gone along and killed Mrs. Leidner while the courtyard was empty. You have plenty of muscle and strength, and she would have been quite unsuspicious until the moment the blow was struck."

I was so upset that I couldn't get a word

out. Dr. Reilly, I noticed, was looking highly amused.

"Interesting case of a nurse who murdered her patients one by one," he murmured.

Such a look as I gave him!

Dr. Leidner's mind had been running on a different tack.

"Not Emmott, M. Poirot," he objected. "You can't include him. He was on the roof with me, remember, during that ten minutes."

"Nevertheless we cannot exclude him. He could have come down, gone straight to Mrs. Leidner's room, killed her, and *then* called the boy back. Or he might have killed her on one of the occasions when he had *sent the boy up to you*."

Dr. Leidner shook his head, murmuring:

"What a nightmare! It's all so—fantastic."

To my surprise Poirot agreed.

"Yes, that is true. *This is a fantastic crime*. One does not often come across them. Usually murder is very sordid—very simple. But this is unusual murder . . . I suspect, Dr. Leidner, that your wife was an unusual woman."

He had hit the nail on the head with such accuracy that I jumped.

"Is that true, nurse?" he asked.

Dr. Leidner said quietly:

"Tell him what Louise was like, nurse. You are unprejudiced."

I spoke quite frankly.

"She was very lovely," I said. "You couldn't help admiring her and wanting to do things for her. I've never met any one like her before."

"Thank you," said Dr. Leidner and smiled at me.

"That is valuable testimony coming from an outsider," said Poirot politely. "Well, let us proceed. Under the heading of *means and opportunity* we have seven names. Nurse Leatheran, Miss Johnson, Mrs. Mercado, Mr. Mercado, Mr. Reiter, Mr. Emmott and Father Lavigny."

Once more he cleared his throat. I've always noticed that foreigners can make the oddest noises.

"Let us for the moment assume that our third theory is correct. That is, that the murderer is Frederick or William Bosner, and that Frederick or William Bosner is a member of the expedition staff. By comparing both lists we can narrow down our suspects on this count to four. Father Lavigny, Mr. Mercado, Carl Reiter and David Emmott."

"Father Lavigny is out of the question," said Dr. Leidner with decision. "He is one of the *Pères Blancs* in Carthage."

"And his beard's quite real," I put in.

"Ma sœur," said Poirot, "a murderer of the first class *never* wears a false beard!"

"How do you know the murderer is of the first class?" I asked rebelliously.

"Because if he were not, the whole truth would be plain to me at this instant—and it is not."

That's pure conceit, I thought to myself.

"Anyway," I said, reverting to the beard, "it must have taken quite a time to grow."

"That is a practical observation," said Poirot. Dr. Leidner said irritably:

"But it's ridiculous—quite ridiculous. Both he and Mercado are well-known men. They've been known for years."

Poirot turned to him.

"You have not the true vision. You do not appreciate an important point. *If Frederick Bosner is not dead—what has he been doing all these years?* He must have taken a different name. He must have built himself up a career."

"As a *Père Blanc?*" asked Dr. Reilly sceptically.

"It is a little fantastic that, yes," confessed Poirot. "But we cannot put it right out of court. Besides, there are other possibilities."

"The young 'uns?" said Reilly. "If you want my opinion, on the face of it there's only one of your suspects that's even plausible."

"And that is?"

"Young Carl Reiter. There's nothing actually against him, but come down to it and you've got to admit a few things—he's the right age, he's got a German name, he's new this year and he had the opportunity all right. He'd only got to pop out of his photographic place, cross the courtyard to do his dirty work and hare back again while the coast was clear. If any one were to have dropped into the photographic room while he was out of it, he can always say later that he was in the dark-room. I don't say he's your man but if you are going to suspect some one I say he's by far and away the most likely."

M. Poirot didn't seem very receptive. He nodded gravely but doubtfully.

"Yes," he said. "He is the most plausible, but it may not be so simple as all that."

Then he said:

"Let us say no more at present. I would like now if I may to examine the room where the crime took place."

"Certainly." Dr. Leidner fumbled in his pockets then looked at Dr. Reilly.

"Captain Maitland took it," he said.

"Maitland gave it to me," said Reilly. "He had to go off on that Kurdish business."

He produced the key.

Dr. Leidner said hesitatingly:

"Do you mind—if I don't— Perhaps, nurse—"

"Of course. Of course," said Poirot. "I quite understand. Never do I wish to cause you unnecessary pain. If you will be good enough to accompany me, *ma sœur*."

"Certainly," I said.

Chapter 17

The Stain by the Wash-stand

Mrs. Leidner's body had been taken to Hassanieh for the post-mortem, but otherwise her room had been left exactly as it was. There was so little in it that it had not taken the police long to go over it.

To the right of the door as you entered was the bed. Opposite the door were the two barred windows giving on the countryside. Between them was a plain oak table with two drawers that served Mrs. Leidner as a dressing-table. On the east wall there was a line of hooks with dresses hung up protected by cotton bags and a deal chest of drawers. Immediately to the left of the door was the wash-stand. In the middle of the room was a good-sized plain oak table with a blotter and inkstand and a small attaché-case. It was in the latter that Mrs. Leidner had kept the anonymous letters. The curtains were short strips of native material—white striped with orange. The floor was of stone with some goatskin rugs on it, three narrow ones of brown striped with white in front of the two windows and the wash-stand, and a larger better quality one of white with brown stripes lying between the bed and the writing-table.

There were no cupboards or alcoves or long curtains—nowhere, in fact, where any one could have hidden. The bed was a plain iron one with a printed cotton quilt. The only trace of luxury in the room were three pillows all made of the best soft and billowy down. Nobody but Mrs. Leidner had pillows like these.

In a few brief dry words Dr. Reilly explained where Mrs. Leidner's body had been found—in a heap on the rug beside the bed.

To illustrate his account, he beckoned me to come forward.

"If you don't mind, nurse?" he said.

I'm not squeamish. I got down on the floor and arranged myself as far as possible in the attitude in which Mrs. Leidner's body had been found.

"Leidner lifted her head when he found her," said the doctor. "But I questioned him closely and it's obvious that he didn't actually change her position."

"It seems quite straightforward," said Poirot. "She was lying on the bed, asleep or resting—some one opens the door, she looks up, rises to her feet—"

"And he struck her down," finished the doctor. "The blow would produce unconsciousness and death would follow very shortly. You see—"

He explained the injury in technical language.

"Not much blood, then?" said Poirot.

"No, the blood escaped internally into the brain."

"*Eh bien,*" said Poirot, "that seems straightforward enough—except for one thing. *If* the man who entered was a stranger, why did not Mrs. Leidner cry out at once for help? If she had screamed she would have been heard. Nurse Leatheran here would have heard her, and Emmott and the boy."

"That's easily answered," said Dr. Reilly dryly. "*Because it wasn't a stranger.*"

Poirot nodded.

"Yes," he said meditatively. "She may have been *surprised* to see the person—but she was not *afraid*. Then, as he struck, she *may* have uttered a half cry—too late."

"The cry Miss Johnson heard?"

"Yes, if she *did* hear it. But on the whole I doubt it. These mud walls are thick and the windows were closed."

He stepped up to the bed.

"You left her actually lying down?" he asked me. I explained exactly what I had done.

"Did she mean to sleep or was she going to read?"

"I gave her two books—a light one and a volume of memoirs. She usually read for a while and then sometimes dropped off for a short sleep."

"And she was—what shall I say—quite as usual?"

I considered.

"Yes. She seemed quite normal and in good spirits," I said. "Just a shade off-hand, perhaps, but I put that down to her having confided in me the day before. It makes people a little uncomfortable sometimes."

Poirot's eyes twinkled.

"Ah, yes, indeed, me, I know that well."

He looked round the room.

"And when you came in here after the murder, was everything as you had seen it before?"

I looked round also.

"Yes, I think so. I don't remember anything being different."

"There was no sign of the weapon with which she was struck?"

"No."

Poirot looked at Dr. Reilly.

"What was it in your opinion?"

The doctor replied promptly.

"Something pretty powerful of a fair size and without any sharp corners or edges. The rounded base of a statue, say—something like that. Mind you, I'm not suggesting that that *was* it. But that type of thing. The blow was delivered with great force."

"Struck by a strong arm? A man's arm?"

"Yes—unless—"

"Unless—what?"

Dr. Reilly said slowly:

"It is just possible that Mrs. Leidner might have been on her knees—in which case, the blow being delivered from above with a heavy implement, the force needed would not have been so great."

"On her knees," mused Poirot. "It is an idea—that."

"It's only an idea, mind," the doctor hastened to point out. "There's absolutely nothing to indicate it."

"But it's possible."

"Yes. And after all, in view of the circumstances, it's not fantastic. Her fear might have led her to kneel in supplication rather than to scream when her instinct would tell her it was too late—that nobody could get there in time."

"Yes," said Poirot thoughtfully. "It is an idea. . . ."

It was a very poor one, I thought. I couldn't for one moment imagine Mrs. Leidner on her knees to any one.

Poirot made his way slowly round the room. He opened the windows, tested the bars, passed his head through and satisfied himself that by no means could his shoulders be made to follow his head.

"The windows were shut when you found her," he said. "Were they also shut when you left her at a quarter to one?"

"Yes, they were always shut in the afternoon. There is no gauze over these windows as there is in the living-room and dining-room. They are kept shut to keep out the flies."

"And in any case no one could get in that way," mused Poirot. "And the walls are of the most solid—mud-brick—and there are no trap-doors and no sky-lights. No, there is only one way into this room—*through the door*. And there is only one way to the door—through the courtyard. And there is only one entrance to the courtyard—*through the archway*. And outside the archway there were five people and they all tell the same story, and I do not think, me, that they are lying. . . . No, they are not lying. They are not bribed to silence. The murderer was *here*. . . ."

I didn't say anything. Hadn't I felt the same thing just now when we were all cooped up round that table?

Slowly Poirot prowled round the room. He took up a photograph from the chest of drawers. It was of an elderly man with a white goatee beard. He looked inquiringly at me.

"Mrs. Leidner's father," I said. "She told me so."

He put it down again and glanced over the articles on the dressing-table—all of plain tortoiseshell—simple but good. He looked up at a row of books on a shelf, repeating the titles aloud.

"*Who Were the Greeks? Introduction to Relativity. Life of Lady Hester Stanhope. Crewe Train. Back to Methuselah. Linda Condon.* Yes, they tell us something, perhaps.

"She was not a fool, your Mrs. Leidner. She had a mind."

"Oh! she was a *very* clever woman," I said eagerly. "Very well read and up in everything. She wasn't a bit ordinary."

He smiled as he looked over at me.

"No," he said. "I've already realized that."

He passed on. He stood for some moments at the wash-stand where there was a big array of bottles and toilet creams.

Then, suddenly, he dropped on his knees and examined the rug.

Dr. Reilly and I came quickly to join him. He was examining a small dark brown stain, almost invisible on the brown of the rug. In fact it was only just noticeable where it impinged on one of the white stripes.

"What do you say, doctor?" he said. "Is that blood?"

Dr. Reilly knelt down.

"Might be," he said. "I'll make sure if you like?"

"If you would be so amiable."

Mr. Poirot examined the jug and basin. The jug was standing on the side of the wash-stand. The basin was empty, but beside the wash-stand there was an old kerosene tin containing slop water.

He turned to me.

"Do you remember, nurse? Was this jug *out* of the basin or *in* it when you left Mrs. Leidner at a quarter to one?"

"I can't be sure," I said after a minute or two. "I rather think it was standing in the basin."

"Ah?"

"But you see," I said hastily, "I only think so because it usually was. The boys leave it like that after lunch. I just feel that if it hadn't been in I should have noticed it."

He nodded quite appreciatively.

"Yes, I understand that. It is your hospital training. If everything had not been just so in the room, you would quite unconsciously have set it to rights hardly noticing what you were doing. And after the murder? Was it like it is now?"

I shook my head.

"I didn't notice then," I said. "All I looked for was whether there was any place any one could be hidden or if there were anything the murderer had left behind him."

"It's blood all right," said Dr. Reilly, rising from his knees. "Is it important?"

Poirot was frowning perplexedly. He flung out his hands with petulance.

"I cannot tell. How can I tell? It may mean nothing at all. I can say, if I like, that the murderer touched her—that there was blood on his hands—very little blood, but still blood—and so he came over here and washed them. Yes, it may have been like that. But I cannot jump to conclusions and say that it *was* so. That stain may be of no importance at all."

"There would have been very little blood," said Dr. Reilly dubiously. "None would have spurted out or anything like that. It would have just oozed a little from the wound. Of course, if he'd probed it at all . . ."

I gave a shiver. A nasty sort of picture came up in my mind. The vision of some-body—perhaps that nice pig-faced photographic boy, striking down that lovely woman and then bending over her probing the wound with his finger in an awful gloating fashion and his face, perhaps, quite different . . . all fierce and mad. . . .

Dr. Reilly noticed my shiver.

"What's the matter, nurse?" he said.

"Nothing—just goose-flesh," I said. "A goose walking over my grave."

Mr. Poirot turned round and looked at me.

"I know what you need," he said. "Presently when we have finished here and I go back with the doctor to Hassanieh we will take you with us. You will give Nurse Leatheran tea, will you not, doctor?"

"Delighted."

"Oh, no, doctor," I protested. "I couldn't think of such a thing."

M. Poirot gave me a little friendly tap on the shoulder. Quite an English tap, not a foreign one.

"You, *ma sœur*, will do as you are told," he said. "Besides, it will be of advantage to me. There is a good deal more that I want to discuss, and I cannot do it here where one must preserve the decencies. The good Dr. Leidner, he worshipped his wife and he is sure—oh, so sure—that everybody else felt the same about her! But that, in my opinion, would not be human nature! No, we want to discuss Mrs. Leidner with—how do you say—the gloves removed? That is settled then. When we have finished here, we take you with us to Hassanieh."

"I suppose," I said doubtfully, "that I ought to be leaving anyway. It's rather awkward."

"Do nothing for a day or two," said Dr. Reilly. "You can't very well go until after the funeral."

"That's all very well," I said. "And supposing I get murdered too, doctor?"

I said it half jokingly and Dr. Reilly took it in the same fashion and would, I think, have made some jocular response.

But M. Poirot, to my astonishment stood stock-still in the middle of the floor and clasped his hands to his head.

"Ah! if that were possible," he murmured. "It is a danger—yes—a great danger—and what can one do? How can one guard against it?"

"Why, M. Poirot," I said, "I was only joking! Who'd want to murder me, I should like to know?"

"You—or another," he said, and I didn't

like the way he said it at all. Positively creepy.

"But why?" I persisted.

He looked at me very straight then.

"I joke, mademoiselle," he said, "and I laugh. *But there are some things that are no joke*. There are things that my profession has taught me. And one of these things, the most terrible thing, is this:

"Murder is a habit . . ."

Chapter 18
Tea at Dr. Reilly's

Before leaving, Poirot made a round of the expedition house and the outbuildings. He also asked a few questions of the servants at second hand—that is to say, Dr. Reilly translated the questions and answers from English into Arabic and vice versa.

These questions dealt mainly with the appearance of the stranger Mrs. Leidner and I had seen looking through the window and to whom Father Lavigny had been talking on the following day.

"Do you really think that fellow had anything to do with it?" asked Dr. Reilly when we were bumping along in his car on our way to Hassanieh.

"I like all the information there is," was Poirot's reply.

And really, that described his methods very well. I found later that there wasn't any-thing—no small scrap of insignificant gos-sip—in which he wasn't interested. Men aren't usually so gossipy.

I must confess I was glad of my cup of tea when we got to Dr. Reilly's house. M. Poirot, I noticed, put five lumps of sugar in his.

Stirring it carefully with his teaspoon he said:

"And now we can talk, can we not? We can make up our minds who is likely to have committed the crime."

"Lavigny, Mercado, Emmott or Reiter?" asked Dr. Reilly.

"No, no—that was theory number three. I wish to concentrate now on theory number two—leaving aside all question of a mysteri-ous husband or brother-in-law turning up from the past. Let us discuss now quite sim-ply which member of the expedition had the means and opportunity to kill Mrs. Leidner, and who is likely to have done so."

"I thought you didn't think much of that theory."

"Not at all. But I have some natural deli-cacy," said Poirot reproachfully. "Can I dis-cuss in the presence of Dr. Leidner the motives likely to lead to the murder of his wife by a member of the expedition? That would not have been delicate at all. I had to sustain the fiction that his wife was adorable and that every one adored her!

"But naturally it was not like that at all. Now we can be brutal and impersonal and say what we think. We have no longer to consider people's feelings. And that is where Nurse Leatheran is going to help us. She is, I am sure, a very good observer."

"Oh, I don't know about that," I said.

Dr. Reilly handed me a plate of hot scones—"to fortify yourself," he said. They were very good scones.

"Come now," said M. Poirot in a friendly, chatty way. "You shall tell me, *ma sœur*, exactly what each member of the expedition felt towards Mrs. Leidner."

"I was only there a week, M. Poirot," I said.

"Quite long enough for one of your intelligence. A nurse sums up quickly. She makes her judgments and abides by them. Come, let us make a beginning. Father Lavigny, for instance?"

"Well, there now, I really couldn't say. He and Mrs. Leidner seemed to like talking together. But they usually spoke French and

I'm not very good at French myself though I learnt it as a girl at school. I've an idea they talked mainly about books."

"They were, as you might say, companionable together—yes?"

"Well, yes, you might put it that way. But, all the same, I think Father Lavigny was puzzled by her and—well—almost annoyed by being puzzled, if you know what I mean."

And I told him of the conversation I had had with him out on the dig that first day when he had called Mrs. Leidner a "dangerous woman."

"Now that is very interesting," M. Poirot said. "And she—what do you think she thought of him?"

"That's rather difficult to say, too. It wasn't easy to know what Mrs. Leidner thought of people. Sometimes, I fancy, *he* puzzled *her*. I remember her saying to Dr. Leidner that he was unlike any priest she had ever known."

"A length of hemp to be ordered for Father Lavigny," said Dr. Reilly facetiously.

"My dear friend," said Poirot. "Have you not, perhaps, some patients to attend? I would not for the world detain you from your professional duties."

"I've got a whole hospital of them," said Dr. Reilly.

And he got up and said a wink was as good as a nod to a blind horse, and went out laughing.

"That is better," said Poirot. "We will have now an interesting conversation *tête-à-tête*. But you must not forget to eat your tea."

He passed me a plate of sandwiches and suggested my having a second cup of tea. He really had very pleasant, attentive manners.

"And now," he said, "let us continue with your impressions. Who was there who in your opinion did *not* like Mrs. Leidner?"

"Well," I said, "it's only my opinion and I don't want it repeated as coming from me."

"Naturally not."

"But in my opinion little Mrs. Mercado fairly hated her!"

"Ah! And Mr. Mercado?"

"He was a bit soft on her," I said. "I shouldn't think women apart from his wife had ever taken much notice of him. And Mrs. Leidner had a nice kind way of being interested in people and the things they told her. It rather went to the poor man's head, I fancy."

"And Mrs. Mercado—she was not pleased?"

"She was just plain jealous—that's the truth of it. You've got to be very careful when there's a husband and wife about, and that's a fact. I could tell you some surprising things. You've no idea the extraordinary things women get into their heads when it's a question of their husbands."

"I do not doubt the truth of what you say. So Mrs. Mercado was jealous? And she hated Mrs. Leidner?"

"I've seen her look at her as though she'd have liked to kill her—oh, gracious!" I pulled myself up. "Indeed, M. Poirot, I didn't mean to say—I mean that is, not for one moment—"

"No, no. I quite understand. The phrase slipped out. A very convenient one. And Mrs. Leidner, was she worried by this animosity of Mrs. Mercado's?"

"Well," I said, reflecting, "I don't really think she was worried at all. In fact, I don't even know whether she noticed it. I thought once of just giving her a hint—but I didn't like to. Least said soonest mended. That's what I say."

"You are doubtless wise. Can you give me

any instances of how Mrs. Mercado showed her feelings?"

I told him about our conversation on the roof.

"So she mentioned Mrs. Leidner's first marriage," said Poirot thoughtfully. "Can you remember—in mentioning it—did she look at you as though she wondered whether you had heard a different version?"

"You think she may have known the truth about it?"

"It is a possibility. She may have written those letters—and engineered a tapping hand and all the rest of it."

"I wondered something of the same kind myself. It seemed the kind of petty revengeful thing she might do."

"Yes. A cruel streak, I should say. But hardly the temperament for cold-blooded brutal murder unless, of course—"

He paused and then said:

"It is odd, that curious thing she said to you. '*I know why you are here.*' What did she mean by it?"

"I can't imagine," I said frankly.

"She thought you were there for some ulterior reason apart from the declared one. What reason? And why should she be so concerned in the matter? Odd, too, the way you tell me she stared at you all through tea the day you arrived."

"Well, she's not a lady, M. Poirot," I said primly.

"That, *ma sœur*, is an excuse but not an explanation."

I wasn't quite sure for the minute what he meant. But he went on quickly.

"And the other members of the staff?"

I considered.

"I don't think Miss Johnson liked Mrs. Leidner either very much. But she was quite open and above-board about it. She as good as admitted she was prejudiced. You see, she's very devoted to Dr. Leidner and had worked with him for years. And of course, marriage does change things—there's no denying it."

"Yes," said Poirot. "And from Miss Johnson's point of view it would be an unsuitable marriage. It would really have been much more suitable if Dr. Leidner had married *her*."

"It would really," I agreed. "But there, that's a man all over. Not one in a hundred considers suitability. And one can't really blame Dr. Leidner. Miss Johnson, poor soul, isn't so much to look at. Now Mrs. Leidner was really beautiful—not young, of course—but oh! I wish you'd known her. There was something about her. . . . I remember Mr. Coleman saying she was like a thingummyjig that came to lure people into marshes. That wasn't a very good way of putting it but—oh, well—you'll laugh at me but there *was* something about her that was—well—unearthly."

"She could cast a spell—yes, I understand," said Poirot.

"Then I don't think she and Mr. Carey got on very well either," I went on. "I've an idea *he* was jealous just like Miss Johnson. He was always very stiff with her and so was she with him. You know—she passed him things and was very polite and called him Mr. Carey rather formally. He was an old friend of her husband's, of course, and some women can't stand their husband's old friends. They don't like to think that any one knew them before they did—at least that's rather a muddled way of putting it—"

"I quite understand. And the three young men? Coleman, you say, was inclined to be poetic about her."

I couldn't help laughing.

"It was funny, M. Poirot," I said. "He's much a matter-of-fact young man."

"And the other two?"

"I don't really know about Mr. Emmott. He's always so quiet and never says much. She was very nice to him always. You know—friendly—called him David and used to tease him about Miss Reilly and things like that."

"Ah, really? And did he enjoy that?"

"I don't quite know," I said doubtfully. "He'd just look at her. Rather funnily. You couldn't tell what he was thinking."

"And Mr. Reiter?"

"She wasn't always very kind to him," I said slowly. "I think he got on her nerves. She used to say quite sarcastic things to him."

"And did he mind?"

"He used to get very pink, poor boy. Of course, she didn't *mean* to be unkind."

And then suddenly, from feeling a little sorry for the boy, it came over me that he was very likely a cold-blooded murderer and had been playing a part all the time.

"Oh, M. Poirot," I exclaimed. "What do you think *really* happened?"

He shook his head slowly and thoughtfully.

"Tell me," he said. "You are not afraid to go back there to-night?"

"Oh, *no*," I said. "Of course, I remember

what you said, but who would want to murder *me?*"

"I do not think that any one could," he said slowly. "That is partly why I have been so anxious to hear all you could tell me. No, I think—I am sure—you are quite safe."

"If any one had told me in Baghdad—" I began and stopped.

"Did you hear any gossip about the Leidners and the expedition before you came here?" he asked.

I told him about Mrs. Leidner's nickname and just a little of what Mrs. Kelsey had said about her.

In the middle of it the door opened and Miss Reilly came in. She had been playing tennis and had her racquet in her hand.

I gathered Poirot had already met her when he arrived in Hassanieh.

She said how do you do to me in her usual off-hand manner and picked up a sandwich.

"Well, M. Poirot," she said. "How are you getting on with our local mystery?"

"Not very fast, mademoiselle."

"I see you've rescued nurse from the wreck."

"Nurse Leatheran has been giving me valuable information about the various members of the expedition. Incidentally I have learnt a good deal—about the victim. And the victim, mademoiselle, is very often the clue to the mystery."

Miss Reilly said:

"That's rather clever of you, M. Poirot. It's certainly true that if ever a woman deserved to be murdered Mrs. Leidner was that woman!"

"Miss Reilly!" I cried, scandalized.

She laughed, a short, nasty laugh.

"Ah!" she said. "I thought you hadn't been hearing quite the truth. Nurse Leatheran, I'm afraid, was quite taken in, like many other people. Do you know, M. Poirot, I rather hope that this case isn't going to be one of your successes. I'd quite like the murderer of Louise Leidner to get away with it. In fact, I wouldn't much have objected to putting her out of the way myself."

I was simply disgusted with the girl. M. Poirot, I must say, didn't turn a hair. He just bowed and said quite pleasantly:

"I hope, then, that you have an alibi for yesterday afternoon?"

There was a moment's silence and Miss Reilly's racquet went clattering down to the floor. She didn't bother to pick it up. Slack and untidy like all her sort! She said in a rather breathless voice:

"Oh, yes, I was playing tennis at the club. But, seriously, M. Poirot, I wonder if you know anything at all about Mrs. Leidner and the kind of woman she was?"

Again he made a funny little bow and said:

"You shall inform me, mademoiselle."

She hesitated a minute and then spoke with a callousness and lack of decency that really sickened me.

"There's a convention that one doesn't speak ill of the dead. That's stupid, I think. The truth's always the truth. On the whole it's better to keep your mouth shut about living people. You might conceivably injure them. The dead are past that. But the harm they've done lives after them sometimes. Not quite a quotation from Shakespeare but very nearly! Has nurse told you of the queer atmosphere there was at Tell Yarimjah? Has she told you how jumpy they all were? And how they all used to glare at each other like enemies? That was Louise Leidner's doing. When I was a kid out here three years ago they were the happiest, jolliest lot imaginable. Even last year they were pretty well all right. But this year there was a blight over them—and it was *her* doing. She was the kind of woman who won't let anybody else be happy! There *are* women like that and she was one of them! She wanted to break up things always. Just for fun—or for the sense of power—or perhaps just because she was made that way. And she was the kind of woman who had to get hold of every male creature within reach!"

"Miss Reilly," I cried, "I don't think that's true. In fact I *know* it isn't."

She went on without taking the least notice of me.

"It wasn't enough for her to have her husband adore her. She had to make a fool of that long-legged shambling idiot of a Mercado. Then she got hold of Bill. Bill's a sensible cove, but she was getting him all mazed and bewildered. Carl Reiter she just amused herself by tormenting. It was easy. He's a sensitive boy. And she had a jolly good go at David.

"David was better sport to her because he put up a fight. He felt her charm—but he wasn't having any. I think because he'd got sense enough to know that she didn't really care a damn. And that's why I hate her so. She's not sensual. She doesn't *want* affairs.

It's just cold-blooded experiment on her part and the fun of stirring people up and setting them against each other. She dabbled in that too. She's the sort of woman who's never had a row with any one in her life—but rows always happen where she is! She *makes* them happen. She's a kind of female Iago. She *must* have drama. But she doesn't want to be involved *herself*. She's always outside pulling strings—looking on—enjoying it. Oh, do you see *at all* what I mean?"

"I see, perhaps, more than you know, mademoiselle," said Poirot.

I couldn't make his voice out. He didn't sound indignant. He sounded—oh, well, I can't explain it.

Sheila Reilly seemed to understand for she flushed all over her face.

"You can think what you choose," she said. "But I'm right about her. She was a clever woman and she was bored and she experimented—with people—like other people experiment with chemicals. She enjoyed working on poor old Johnson's feelings and seeing her bite on the bullet and control herself like the old sport she is. She liked goading little Mercado into a white-hot frenzy. She liked flicking *me* on the raw—and she could do it too, every time! She liked finding out things about people and holding it over them. Oh, I don't mean crude blackmail—I mean just letting them know that she *knew*—and leaving them uncertain what she meant to do about it. My God, though, that woman was an artist! There was nothing crude about *her* methods!"

"And her husband?" asked Poirot.

"She never wanted to hurt him," said Miss Reilly slowly. "I've never known her anything but sweet to him. I suppose she was fond of him. He's a dear—wrapped up in his own world—his digging and his theories. And he worshipped her and thought her perfection. That might have annoyed some women. It didn't annoy her. In a sense he lived in a fool's paradise—and yet it wasn't a fool's paradise because to him she was what he thought her. Though it's hard to reconcile that with—"

She stopped.

"Go on, mademoiselle," said Poirot.

She turned suddenly on me.

"What have you said about Richard Carey?"

"About Mr. Carey?" I asked, astonished.

"About her and Carey?"

"Well," I said, "I've mentioned that they didn't hit it off very well—"

To my surprise she broke into a fit of laughter.

"Didn't hit it off very well! You fool! He's head over ears in love with her. And it's tearing him to pieces—because he worships Leidner too. He's been his friend for years. That would be enough for her, of course. She's made it her business to come between them. But all the same I've fancied—"

"*Eh bien?*"

She was frowning, absorbed in thought.

"I've fancied that she'd gone too far for once—that she was not only biter but bit! Carey's attractive. He's as attractive as hell. . . . She was a cold devil—but I believe she could have lost her coldness with him. . . ."

"I think it's just scandalous what you're saying," I cried. "Why, they hardly spoke to each other!"

"Oh, didn't they?" She turned on me. "A hell of a lot you know about it. It was 'Mr. Carey' and 'Mrs. Leidner' in the house, but they used to meet outside. She'd walk down the path to the river. And he'd leave the dig for an hour at a time. They used to meet among the fruit trees.

"I saw him once just leaving her, striding back to the dig, and she was standing, looking after him. I was a female cad, I suppose. I had some glasses with me and I took them out and had a good look at her face. If you ask me I believed she cared like hell for Richard Carey. . . ."

She broke off and looked at Poirot.

"Excuse my butting in on your case," she said with a sudden rather twisted grin, "but I thought you'd like to have the local colour correct."

And she marched out of the room.

"M. Poirot," I cried. "I don't believe one word of it all!"

He looked at me and he smiled, and he said (very queerly I thought):

"You can't deny, nurse, that Miss Reilly has shed a certain—illumination on the case."

Chapter 19
A New Suspicion

We couldn't say any more just then because Dr. Reilly came in, saying jokingly that he'd killed off the most tiresome of his patients.

He and M. Poirot settled down to a more or less medical discussion of the psychology and mental state of an anonymous letter-writer. The doctor cited cases that he had known professionally, and M. Poirot told various stories from his own experience.

"It is not so simple as it seems," he ended. "There is the desire for power and very often a strong inferiority complex."

Dr. Reilly nodded.

"That's why you often find that the author of anonymous letters is the last person in the place to be suspected. Some quiet inoffensive little soul who apparently can't say Boo to a goose—all sweetness and Christian meekness on the outside—and seething with all the fury of hell underneath!"

Poirot said thoughtfully:

"Should you say Mrs. Leidner had any tendency to an inferiority complex?"

Dr. Reilly scraped out his pipe with a chuckle.

"Last woman on earth I'd describe that way. No repressions about her. Life, life and more life—that's what she wanted—and got, too!"

"Do you consider it a possibility, psychologically speaking, that she wrote those letters?"

"Yes, I do. But if she did, the reason arose out of her instinct to dramatize herself. Mrs. Leidner was a bit of a film star in private life! She *had* to be the centre of things—in the limelight. By the law of opposites she married Leidner who's about the most retiring and modest man I know. He adored her—but adoration by the fireside wasn't enough for her. She had to be the persecuted heroine as well."

"In fact," said Poirot, smiling, "you don't

subscribe to his theory that she wrote them and retained no memory of her act?"

"No, I don't. I didn't turn down the idea in front of him. You can't very well say to a man who's just lost a dearly loved wife that that same wife was a shameless exhibitionist, and that she drove him nearly crazy with anxiety to satisfy her sense of the dramatic. As a matter of fact it wouldn't be safe to tell any man the truth about his wife! Funnily enough, I'd trust most women with the truth about their husbands. Women can accept the fact that a man is a rotter, a swindler, a drug-taker, a confirmed liar, and a general swine without batting an eyelash and without its impairing their affection for the brute in the least! Women are wonderful realists."

"Frankly, Dr. Reilly, what *was* your exact opinion of Mrs. Leidner?"

Dr. Reilly lay back in his chair and puffed slowly at his pipe.

"Frankly—it's hard to say! I didn't know her well enough. She'd got charm—any amount of it. Brains, sympathy. . . . What else? She hadn't any of the ordinary unpleasant vices. She wasn't sensual or lazy or even particularly vain. She was, I've always thought (but I've no proofs of it), a most accomplished liar. What I don't know (and what I'd like to know) is whether she lied to herself or only to other people. I'm rather partial to liars myself. A woman who doesn't lie is a woman without imagination and without sympathy. I don't think she was really a man-hunter—she just liked the sport of bringing them down 'with my bow and arrow.' If you get my daughter on the subject—"

"We have had that pleasure," said Poirot with a slight smile.

"H'm," said Dr. Reilly. "She hasn't wasted much time! Shoved her knife into her pretty thoroughly, I should imagine! The younger generation has no sentiment towards the dead. It's a pity all young people are prigs! They condemn the 'old morality' and then proceed to set up a much more hard and fast code of their own. If Mrs. Leidner had had half a dozen affairs Sheila would probably have approved of her as 'living her life fully'—or 'obeying her blood instincts.' What she doesn't see is that Mrs. Leidner was acting true to type—*her* type. The cat *is* obeying its blood instinct when it plays with the mouse! It's made that way. Men aren't little boys to be shielded and protected.

They've got to meet cat women—and faithful spaniel, yours-till-death adoring women,
and henpecking nagging bird women—and
all the rest of it! Life's a battlefield—not a
picnic! I'd like to see Sheila honest enough
to come off her high horse and admit that
she hated Mrs. Leidner for good old thor-
oughgoing personal reasons. Sheila's about
the only young girl in this place and she naturally assumes that she ought to have it all
her own way with the young things in
trousers. Naturally it annoys her when a
woman, who in her view is middle-aged and
who has already two husbands to her
credit, comes along and licks her on her
own ground. Sheila's a nice child, healthy
and reasonably good-looking and attractive
to the other sex as she should be. But Mrs.
Leidner was something out of the ordinary
in that line. She'd got just that sort of
calamitous magic that plays the deuce with
things—a kind of Belle Dame sans Merci."

I jumped in my chair. What a coincidence
his saying that!

"Your daughter—I am not indiscreet—she
has perhaps a *tendresse* for one of the
young men out there?"

"Oh, I don't suppose so. She's had Emmott and Coleman dancing attendance on her as a matter of course. I don't know that she cares for one more than the other. There are a couple of young Air Force chaps too. I fancy all's fish that comes to her net at present. No, I think it's age daring to defeat youth that annoys her so much! She doesn't know as much of the world as I do. It's when you get to my age that you really appreciate a schoolgirl complexion and a clear eye and a firmly knit young body. But a woman over thirty can listen with rapt attention and throw in a word here and there to show the talker what a fine fellow he is—and few young men can resist that! Sheila's a pretty girl—but Louise Leidner was beautiful. Glorious eyes and that amazing golden fairness. Yes, she was a beautiful woman."

Yes, I thought to myself, he's right. Beauty's a wonderful thing. She *had* been beautiful. It wasn't the kind of looks you were jealous of—you just sat back and admired. I felt that first day I met her that I'd do *anything* for Mrs. Leidner!

All the same, that night as I was being driven back to the Tell Yarimjah (Dr. Reilly made me stay for an early dinner) one or two things came back to my mind and made me rather uncomfortable. At the time I hadn't believed a word of all Sheila Reilly's outpouring. I'd taken it for sheer spite and malice.

But now I suddenly remembered the way Mrs. Leidner had insisted on going for a stroll by herself that afternoon and wouldn't hear of me coming with her. I couldn't help wondering if perhaps, after all, *she had* been going to meet Mr. Carey. . . . And of course, it *was* a little odd, really, the way he and she spoke to each other so formally. Most of the others she called by their Christian names.

He never seemed to look at her, I remembered. That might be because he disliked her—or it might be just the opposite. . . .

I gave myself a little shake. Here I was fancying and imagining all sorts of things— all because of a girl's spiteful outbursts! It just showed how unkind and dangerous it was to go about saying that kind of thing.

Mrs. Leidner *hadn't* been like that at all. . . .

Of course, *she* hadn't liked Sheila Reilly. She'd really been—almost catty about her that day at lunch to Mr. Emmott.

Funny, the way he'd looked at her. The

sort of way that you couldn't possibly tell what he was thinking. You never could tell what Mr. Emmott was thinking. He was so quiet. But very nice. A nice dependable person.

Now Mr. Coleman was a foolish young man if there ever was one!

I'd got to that point in my meditations when we arrived. It was just on nine o'clock and the big door was closed and barred.

Ibrahim came running with his great key to let me in.

We all went to bed early at Tell Yarimjah. There weren't any lights showing in the living-room. There was a light in the drawing-office and one in Dr. Leidner's office, but nearly all the other windows were dark. Every one must have gone to bed even earlier than usual.

As I passed the drawing-office to go to my room I looked in. Mr. Carey was in his shirtsleeves working over his big plan.

Terribly ill, he looked, I thought. So strained and worn. It gave me quite a pang. I don't know what there was about Mr. Carey—it wasn't what he *said* because he hardly said anything—and that of the most ordinary nature, and it wasn't what he *did*, for that didn't amount to much either—and yet you just couldn't help noticing him, and everything about him seemed to matter more than it would have about any one else. He just *counted*, if you know what I mean.

He turned his head and saw me. He removed his pipe from his mouth and said:

"Well, nurse, back from Hassanieh?"

"Yes, Mr. Carey. You're up working late. Everybody else seems to have gone to bed."

"I thought I might as well get on with things," he said. "I was a bit behind-hand. And I shall be out on the dig all to-morrow. We're starting digging again."

"Already?" I asked, shocked.

He looked at me rather queerly.

"It's the best thing, I think. I put it up to Leidner. He'll be in Hassanieh most of to-morrow seeing to things. But the rest of us will carry on here. You know it's not too easy all sitting around and looking at each other as things are."

He was right there, of course. Especially in the nervy, jumpy state every one was in.

"Well, of course you're right in a way," I said. "It takes one's mind off if one's got something to do."

The funeral, I knew, was to be the day after tomorrow.

He had bent over his plan again. I don't know why, but my heart just ached for him. I felt certain that he wasn't going to get any sleep.

"If you'd like a sleeping draught, Mr. Carey?" I said hesitatingly.

He shook his head with a smile.

"I'll carry on, nurse. Bad habit, sleeping draughts."

"Well, good-night, Mr. Carey," I said. "If there's anything I can do—"

"Don't think so, thank you, nurse. Good-night."

"I'm terribly sorry," I said, rather too impulsively I suppose.

"Sorry?" He looked surprised.

"For—for everybody. It's all so dreadful. But especially for you."

"For me? Why for me?"

"Well, you're such an old friend of them both."

"I'm an old friend of Leidner's. I wasn't a friend of hers particularly."

He spoke as though he had actually disliked her. Really, I wished Miss Reilly could have heard him!

"Well, good-night," I said and hurried along to my room.

I fussed around a bit in my room before undressing. Washed out some handkerchiefs and a pair of wash-leather gloves and wrote up my diary. I just looked out of my door again before I really started to get ready for bed. The lights were still on in the drawing-office and in the south building.

I supposed Dr. Leidner was still up and working in his office. I wondered whether I ought to go and say goodnight to him. I hesitated about it—I didn't want to seem officious. He might be busy and not want to be disturbed. In the end, however, a sort of uneasiness drove me on. After all, it couldn't do any harm. I'd just say good-night, ask if there was anything I could do and come away.

But Dr. Leidner wasn't there. The office itself was lit up but there was no one in it except Miss Johnson. She had her head down on the table and was crying as though her heart would break.

It gave me quite a turn. She was such a quiet, self-controlled woman. It was pitiful to see her.

"Whatever is it, my dear?" I cried. I put my

arm round her and patted her. "Now, now, this won't do at all. . . . You mustn't sit here crying all by yourself."

She didn't answer and I felt the dreadful shuddering sobs that were racking her.

"Don't, my dear, don't," I said. "Take a hold on yourself. I'll go and make you a cup of nice hot tea."

She raised her head and said:

"No, no, it's all right, nurse. I'm being a fool."

"What's upset you, my dear?" I asked.

She didn't answer at once, then she said: "It's all too awful. . . ."

"Now don't start thinking of it," I told her. "What's happened has happened and can't be mended. It's no use fretting."

She sat up straight and began to pat her hair.

"I'm making rather a fool of myself," she said in her gruff voice. "I've been clearing up and tidying the office. Thought it was best to *do* something. And then—it all came over me suddenly—"

"Yes, yes," I said hastily. "I know. A nice strong cup of tea and a hot-water bottle in your bed is what you want," I said.

And she had them too. I didn't listen to any protests.

"Thank you, nurse," she said when I'd settled her in bed, and she was sipping her tea and the hot-water bottle was in. "You're a nice kind sensible woman. It's not often I make such a fool of myself."

"Oh, anybody's liable to do that at a time like this," I said, "what with one thing and another. The strain and the shock and the police here, there and everywhere. Why, I'm quite jumpy myself."

She said slowly in rather a queer voice:

"What you said in there is true. What's happened has happened and can't be mended. . . ."

She was silent for a minute or two and then said—rather oddly, I thought:

"She was never a nice woman!"

Well, I didn't argue the point. I'd always felt it was quite natural for Miss Johnson and Mrs. Leidner not to hit it off.

I wondered if, perhaps, Miss Johnson had secretly had a feeling that she was pleased Mrs. Leidner was dead, and had then been ashamed of herself for the thought.

I said:

"Now you go to sleep and don't worry about anything."

I just picked up a few things and set the room to rights. Stockings over the back of the chair and coat and skirt on a hanger. There was a little ball of crumpled paper on the floor where it must have fallen out of a pocket.

I was just smoothing it out to see whether I could safely throw it away when she quite startled me.

"Give that to me!"

I did so—rather taken aback. She'd called out so peremptorily. She snatched it from me—fairly snatched it—and then held it in the candle flame till it was burnt to ashes.

As I say, I was startled—and I just stared at her.

I hadn't had time to see what the paper was—she'd snatched it so quick. But funnily enough, as it burned it curled over towards me and I just saw that there were words written in ink on the paper.

It wasn't till I was getting into bed that I realized why they'd looked sort of familiar to me.

It was the same handwriting as that of the anonymous letters.

Was *that* why Miss Johnson had given way to a fit of remorse? Had it been her all along who had written those anonymous letters?

Chapter 20
Miss Johnson, Mrs. Mercado, Mr. Reiter

I don't mind confessing that the idea came as a complete shock to me. I'd never thought of associating *Miss Johnson* with the letters. Mrs. Mercado, perhaps. But Miss Johnson was a real lady, and so self-controlled and sensible.

But I reflected, remembering the conversation I had listened to that evening between M. Poirot and Dr. Reilly, and that might be just *why*.

If it were Miss Johnson who had written the letters it explained a lot. Mind you, I didn't think for a minute Miss Johnson had had anything to do with the murder. But I *did* see that her dislike of Mrs. Leidner might have made her succumb to the temptation of well—putting the wind up her—to put it vulgarly.

She might have hoped to frighten away Mrs. Leidner from the dig.

But then Mrs. Leidner had been murdered and Miss Johnson had felt terrible pangs of remorse—first for her cruel trick and also, perhaps, because she realized that those letters were acting as a very good shield to the actual murderer. No wonder she had broken down so utterly. She was, I was sure, a decent soul at heart. And it explained, too, why she had caught so eagerly at my consolation of "what's happened's happened and can't be amended."

And then her cryptic remark—her vindication of herself—"She was never a nice woman!"

The question was, what was *I* to do about it?

I tossed and turned for a good while and in the end decided I'd let M. Poirot know about it at the first opportunity.

He came out next day but I didn't get a chance of speaking to him what you might call privately.

We had just a minute alone together and before I could collect myself to know how to begin, he had come close to me and was whispering instructions in my ear.

"Me, I shall talk to Miss Johnson—and others, perhaps, in the living-room. You have the key of Mrs. Leidner's room still?"

"Yes," I said.

"*Très bien*. Go there, shut the door behind you and give a cry—not a scream—a cry. You understand what I mean—it is alarm—surprise that I want you to express—not mad terror. As for the excuse if you are heard—I leave that to you—the stepped toe or what you will."

At that moment Miss Johnson came out into the courtyard and there was no time for more.

I understood well enough what M. Poirot was after. As soon as he and Miss Johnson had gone into the living-room I went across to Mrs. Leidner's room and, unlocking the door, went in and pulled the door to behind me.

I can't say I didn't feel a bit of a fool standing up in an empty room and giving a yelp all for nothing at all. Besides, it wasn't so easy to know just how loud to do it. I gave a pretty loud "Oh" and then tried it a bit higher and a bit lower.

Then I came out again and prepared my excuse of a stepped (stubbed I *suppose* he meant!) toe.

But it soon appeared that no excuse would be needed. Poirot and Miss Johnson were talking together earnestly and there had clearly been no interruption.

"Well," I thought, "that settles that. Either Miss Johnson imagined that cry she heard or else it was something quite different."

I didn't like to go in and interrupt them. There was a deck-chair on the porch so I sat down there. Their voices floated out to me.

"The position is delicate, you understand," Poirot was saying. "Dr. Leidner—obviously he adored his wife—"

"He worshipped her," said Miss Johnson.

"He tells me, naturally, how fond all his staff was of her! As for them, what can they say! Naturally they say the same thing. It is politeness. It is decency. It *may* also be the truth! But also it may *not!* And I am convinced, mademoiselle, that the key to this enigma lies in a complete understanding of Mrs. Leidner's character. If I could get the opinion—the honest opinion—of every member of the staff, I might, from the whole, build up a picture. Frankly, that is why I am here to-day. I knew Dr. Leidner would be in Hassanieh. That makes it easy for me to have a interview with each of you here in turn, and beg your help."

"That's all very well," began Miss Johnson and stopped.

"Do not make me the British *clichès*," Poirot begged. "Do not say it is not the cricket or the football, that to speak anything but well of the dead is not done—that—*enfin*—there is loyalty! Loyalty, it is a pestilential thing in crime. Again and again it obscures the truth."

"I've no particular loyalty to Mrs. Leidner," said Miss Johnson dryly. There was indeed a sharp and acid tone in her voice. "Dr. Leidner's a different matter. And, after all, she was his wife."

"Precisely—precisely. I understand that you would not wish to speak against your chief's wife. But this is not a question of a testimonial. It is a question of sudden and mysterious death. If I am to believe that it is a martyred angel who has been killed it does not add to the easiness of my task."

"I certainly shouldn't call her an angel,"

said Miss Johnson and the acid tone was even more in evidence.

"Tell me your opinion, frankly, of Mrs. Leidner—as a woman."

"H'm! To begin with, M. Poirot, I'll give you this warning. I'm prejudiced. I am—we all were—devoted to Dr. Leidner. And, I suppose, when Mrs. Leidner came along, we were jealous. We resented the demands she made on his time and attention. The devotion he showed her irritated us. I'm being truthful, M. Poirot, and it isn't very pleasant for me. I resented her presence here—yes, I did, though, of course, I tried never to show it. It made a difference to us, you see."

"Us? You say us?"

"I mean Mr. Carey and myself. We're the two old-timers, you see. And we didn't much care for the new order of things. I suppose that's natural, though perhaps it was rather petty of us. But it *did* make a difference."

"What kind of a difference?"

"Oh! to everything. We used to have such a happy time. A good deal of fun, you know, and rather silly jokes, like people do who work together. Dr. Leidner was quite light-hearted—just like a boy."

"And when Mrs. Leidner came she changed all that?"

"Well, I suppose it wasn't her *fault*. It wasn't so bad last year. And please believe, M. Poirot, that it wasn't anything she *did*. She's always been charming to me—quite charming. That's why I've felt ashamed sometimes. It wasn't her fault that little things she said and did seemed to rub me up the wrong way. Really nobody could be nicer than she was."

"But nevertheless things were changed this season? There was a different atmosphere."

"Oh, entirely. Really, I don't know what it was. Everything seemed to go wrong—not with the work—I mean with us—our tempers and our nerves. All on edge. Almost the sort of feeling you get when there is a thunderstorm coming."

"And you put that down to Mrs. Leidner's influence?"

"Well, it was never like that before she came," said Miss Johnson dryly. "Oh! I'm a cross-grained, complaining old dog. Conservative—liking things always the same. You really mustn't take any notice of me, M. Poirot."

"How would you describe to me Mrs. Leidner's character and temperament?"

Miss Johnson hesitated for a moment. Then she said slowly:

"Well, of course, she was temperamental. A lot of ups and downs. Nice to people one day and perhaps wouldn't speak to them the next. She was very kind, I think. And very thoughtful for others. All the same you could see she had been thoroughly spoilt all her life. She took Dr. Leidner's waiting on her hand and foot as perfectly natural. And I don't think she ever really appreciated what a very remarkable—what a really great—man she had married. That used to annoy me sometimes. And of course she was terribly highly strung and nervous. The things she used to imagine and the states she used to get into! I was thankful when Dr. Leidner brought Nurse Leatheran here. It was too much for him having to cope both with his work and with his wife's fears."

"What is your own opinion of these anonymous letters she received?"

I had to do it. I leaned forward in my chair till I could just catch sight of Miss Johnson's profile turned to Poirot in answer to his question.

She was looking perfectly cool and collected.

"I think some one in America had a spite against her and was trying to frighten or annoy her."

"Pas plus serieux que ça?"

"That's my opinion. She was a very handsome woman, you know, and might easily have had enemies. I think those letters were written by some spiteful woman. Mrs. Leidner being of a nervous temperament took them seriously."

"She certainly did that," said Poirot. "But remember—the last of them arrived by hand."

"Well, I suppose that *could* have been managed if any one had given their minds to it. Women will take a lot of trouble to gratify their spite, M. Poirot."

They will indeed, I thought to myself!

"Perhaps you are right, mademoiselle. As you say, Mrs. Leidner was handsome. By the way, you know Miss Reilly, the doctor's daughter?"

"Sheila Reilly? Yes, of course."

Poirot adopted a very confidential, gossipy tone.

"I have heard a rumour (naturally I do not

like to ask the doctor) that there was a *ten-dresse* between her and one of the members of Dr. Leidner's staff. Is that so, do you know?"

Miss Johnson appeared rather amused.

"Oh, young Coleman and David Emmott were both inclined to dance attendance. I believe there was some rivalry as to who was to be her partner in some event at the club. Both the boys went in on Saturday evenings to the club as a general rule. But I don't know that there was anything in it on her side. She's the only young creature in the place, you know, and so she's by way of being the belle of it. She's got the Air Force dancing attendance on her as well."

"So you think there is nothing in it?"

"Well—I don't know." Miss Johnson became thoughtful. "It is true that she comes out this way fairly often. Up to the dig and all that. In fact, Mrs. Leidner was chaffing David Emmott about it the other day—saying the girl was running after him. Which was rather a catty thing to say, I thought, and I don't think he liked it. . . . Yes, she was here a good deal. I saw her riding towards the dig on that awful afternoon." She nodded her head towards the open window.

"But neither David Emmott nor Coleman were on duty that afternoon. Richard Carey was in charge. Yes, perhaps she is attracted to one of the boys—but she's such a modern unsentimental young woman that one doesn't know quite how seriously to take her. I'm sure I don't know which of them it is. Bill's a nice boy, and not nearly such a fool as he pretends to be. David Emmott is a dear—and there's a lot to him. He is the deep, quiet kind."

Then she looked quizzically at Poirot and said:

"But has this any bearing on the crime, M. Poirot?"

M. Poirot threw up his hands in a very French fashion.

"You made me blush, mademoiselle," he said. "You expose me as a mere gossip. But what will you, I am interested always in the love affairs of young people."

"Yes," said Miss Johnson with a little sigh. "It's nice when the course of true love runs smooth."

Poirot gave an answering sigh. I wondered if Miss Johnson was thinking of some love affair of her own when she was a girl. And I wondered if M. Poirot had a wife, and if he went on in the way you always hear foreigners do, with mistresses and things like that. He looks so comic I couldn't imagine it.

"Sheila Reilly has a lot of character," said Miss Johnson. "She's young and she's crude, but she's the right sort."

"I take your word for it, mademoiselle," said Poirot.

He got up and said, "Are there any other members of the staff in the house?"

"Marie Mercado is somewhere about. All the men are up on the dig to-day. I think they wanted to get out of the house. I don't blame them. If you'd like to go up to the dig—"

She came out on the verandah and said, smiling to me:

"Nurse Leatheran won't mind taking you, I dare say."

"Oh, certainly, Miss Johnson," I said.

"And you'll come back to lunch, won't you, M. Poirot?"

"Enchanted, mademoiselle."

Miss Johnson went back into the living-room where she was engaged in cataloguing.

"Mrs. Mercado's on the roof," I said. "Do you want to see her first?"

"It would be as well, I think. Let us go up."

As we went up the stairs I said:

"I did what you told me. Did you hear anything?"

"Not a sound."

"That will be a weight off Miss Johnson's mind at any rate," I said. "She's been worrying that she might have done something about it."

Mrs. Mercado was sitting on the parapet, her head bent down, and she was so deep in thought that she never heard us till Poirot halted opposite her and bade her good-morning.

Then she looked up with a start.

She looked ill this morning, I thought, her small face pinched and wizened and great dark circles under her eyes.

"*Encore moi,*" said Poirot. "I come to-day with a special object."

And he went on much in the same way as he had done to Miss Johnson, explaining how necessary it was that he should get a true picture of Mrs. Leidner.

Mrs. Mercado, however, wasn't as honest as Miss Johnson had been. She burst into fulsome praise which, I was pretty sure, was quite far removed from her real feelings.

"Dear, *dear* Louise! It's so hard to explain her to some one who didn't know her. She was such an *exotic* creature. Quite different from any one else. You felt that, I'm sure, nurse? A martyr to nerves, of course, and full of fancies, but one put up with things in her one wouldn't from any one else. And she was so *sweet* to us all, wasn't she, nurse? And so *humble* about herself—I mean she didn't know anything about archæology, and she was so eager to learn. Always asking my husband about the chemical processes for treating the metal objects and helping Miss Johnson to mend pottery. Oh, we were all *devoted* to her."

"Then it is not true, madame, what I have heard, that there was a certain tenseness—an uncomfortable atmosphere—here?"

Mrs. Mercado opened her opaque black eyes very wide.

"Oh! who *can* have been telling you that? Nurse? Dr. Leidner? I'm sure *he* would never notice anything, poor man."

And she shot a thoroughly unfriendly glance at me.

Poirot smiled easily.

"I have my spies, madame," he declared gaily. And just for a minute I saw her eyelids quiver and blink.

"Don't you think," asked Mrs. Mercado with an air of great sweetness, "that after an event of this kind, every one always pretends a lot of things that never were? You know—tension, atmosphere, a 'feeling that something was going to happen'? I think people just *make up* these things afterwards."

"There is a lot in what you say, madame," said Poirot.

"And it really *wasn't* true! We were a thoroughly happy family here."

"That woman is one of the most utter liars I've ever known," I said indignantly, when M. Poirot and I were clear of the house and walking along the path to the dig. "I'm sure she simply hated Mrs. Leidner really!"

"She is hardly the type to whom one would go for the truth," Poirot agreed.

"Waste of time talking to her," I snapped.

"Hardly that—hardly that. If a person tells you lies with her lips she is sometimes telling you truth with her eyes. What is she afraid of, little Madame Mercado? I saw fear in her eyes. Yes—decidedly she is afraid of something. It is very interesting."

"I've got something to tell you, M. Poirot," I said.

Then I told him all about my return the night before and my strong belief that Miss Johnson was the writer of the anonymous letters.

"So *she's* a liar too!" I said. "The cool way she answered you this morning about these same letters!"

"Yes," said Poirot. "It was interesting that. *For she let out the fact that she knew all about those letters*. So far they have not been spoken of in the presence of the staff. Of course, it is quite possible that Dr. Leidner told her about them yesterday. They are old friends, he and she. But if he did not—well—then it is curious and interesting, is it not?"

My respect for him went up. It was clever the way he had tricked her into mentioning the letters.

"Are you going to tackle her about them?" I asked.

Mr. Poirot seemed quite shocked by the idea.

"No, no, indeed. Always it is unwise to

parade one's knowledge. Until the last minute I keep everything here." He tapped his forehead. "At the right moment—I make the spring—like the panther—and, *mon Dieu!* the consternation!"

I couldn't help laughing to myself at little M. Poirot in the rôle of a panther.

We had just reached the dig. The first person we saw was Mr. Reiter, who was busy photographing some walling.

It's my opinion that the men who were digging just hacked out walls wherever they wanted them. That's what it looked like anyway. Mr. Carey explained to me that you could feel the difference at once with a pick, and he tried to show me—but I never saw. When the man said *"Libn"*—mud-brick—it was just ordinary dirt and mud as far as I could see.

Mr. Reiter finished his photographs and handed over the camera and the plates to his boy and told him to take them back to the house.

Poirot asked him one or two questions about exposures and film packs and so on which he answered very readily. He seemed pleased to be asked about his work.

He was just tendering his excuses for

leaving us when Poirot plunged once more into his set speech. As a matter of fact it wasn't quite a set speech because he varied it a little each time to suit the person he was talking to. But I'm not going to write it all down every time. With sensible people like Miss Johnson he went straight to the point, and with some of the others he had to beat about the bush a bit more. But it came to the same in the end.

"Yes, yes, I see what you mean," said Mr. Reiter. "But indeed, I do not see that I can be much help to you. I am new here this season and I did not speak much with Mrs. Leidner. I regret, but indeed I can tell you nothing."

There was something a little stiff and foreign in the way he spoke, though, of course, he hadn't got any accent—except an American one, I mean.

"You can at least tell me whether you liked or disliked her?" said Poirot with a smile.

Mr. Reiter got quite red and stammered:

"She was a charming person—most charming. And intellectual. She had a very fine brain—yes."

"*Bien!* You liked her. And she liked you?"

Mr. Reiter got redder still.

"Oh, I—I don't know that she noticed me much. And I was unfortunate once or twice. I was always unlucky when I tried to do anything for her. I'm afraid I annoyed her by my clumsiness. It was quite unintentional . . . I would have done *anything*—"

Poirot took pity on his flounderings.

"Perfectly—perfectly. Let us pass to another matter. Was it a happy atmosphere in the house?"

"Please."

"Were you all happy together? Did you laugh and talk?"

"No—no, not exactly that. There was a little—stiffness."

He paused, struggling with himself, and then said:

"You see, I am not very good in company. I am clumsy. I am shy. Dr. Leidner always he has been most kind to me. But—it is stupid—I cannot overcome my shyness. I say always the wrong thing. I upset water jugs. I am unlucky."

He really looked like a large awkward child.

"We all do these things when we are

young," said Poirot, smiling. "The poise, the *savoir faire*, it comes later."

Then with a word of farewell we walked on.

He said:

"That, *ma sœur*, is either an extremely simple young man or a very remarkable actor."

I didn't answer. I was caught up once more by the fantastic notion that one of these people was a dangerous and cold-blooded murderer. Somehow, on this beautiful still sunny morning, it seemed impossible.

"They work in two separate places, I see," said Poirot, halting.

Mr. Reiter had been doing his photography on an outlying portion of the main excavation. A little distance away from us a second swarm of men were coming and going with baskets.

"That's what they call the deep cut," I explained. "They don't find much there, nothing but rubbishy broken pottery, but Dr. Leidner always says it's very interesting, so I suppose it must be."

"Let us go there."

We walked together slowly for the sun was hot.

Mr. Mercado was in command. We saw him below us talking to the foreman, an old man like a tortoise who wore a tweed coat over his long striped cotton gown.

It was a little difficult to get down to them as there was only a narrow path or stair and basket boys were going up and down it constantly, and they always seemed to be as blind as bats and never to think of getting out of the way.

As I followed Poirot down he said suddenly over his shoulder:

"Is Mr. Mercado right-handed or left-handed?"

Now that was an extraordinary question if you like!

I thought a minute, then:

"Right-handed," I said decisively.

Poirot didn't condescend to explain. He just went on and I followed him.

Mr. Mercado seemed rather pleased to see us.

His long melancholy face lit up.

M. Poirot pretended to an interest in archæology that I'm sure he couldn't have really felt, but Mr. Mercado responded at once.

He explained that they had already cut down through twelve levels of house occupation.

"We are now definitely in the fourth millennium," he said with enthusiasm.

I always thought a millennium was in the future—the time when everything comes right.

Mr. Mercado pointed out belts of ashes (how his hand did shake! I wondered if he might possibly have malaria) and he explained how the pottery changed in character, and about burials—and how they had had one level almost entirely composed of infant burials—poor little things—and about flexed position and orientation which seemed to mean the way the bones were lying.

And then suddenly, just as he was stooping down to pick up a kind of flint knife that was lying with some pots in a corner, he leapt into the air with a wild yell.

He spun round to find me and Poirot staring at him in astonishment.

He clapped his hand to his left arm.

"Something stung me—like a red-hot needle."

Immediately Poirot was galvanized into energy.

"Quick, *mon cher*, let us see. Nurse Leatheran!" I came forward.

He seized Mr. Mercado's arm and deftly rolled back the sleeve of his khaki shirt to the shoulder.

"There," said Mr. Mercado, pointing.

About three inches below the shoulder there was a minute prick from which the blood was oozing.

"Curious," said Poirot. He peered into the rolled-up sleeve. "I can see nothing. It was an ant, perhaps?"

"Better put on a little iodine," I said.

I always carry an iodine pencil with me, and I whipped it out and applied it. But I was a little absent-minded as I did so, for my attention had been caught by something quite different. Mr. Mercado's arm, all the way up the forearm to the elbow, was marked all over by tiny punctures. I knew well enough what *they* were—*the marks of a hypodermic needle.*

Mr. Mercado rolled down his sleeve again and recommenced his explanations. M. Poirot listened, but didn't try to bring the conversation round to the Leidners. In fact he didn't ask Mr. Mercado anything at all.

Presently we said good-by to Mr. Mercado and climbed up the path again.

"It was neat that, did you not think so?" my companion asked.

"Neat?" I asked.

M. Poirot took something from behind the lapel of his coat and surveyed it affectionately. To my surprise I saw that it was a long sharp darning needle with a blob of sealing wax making it into a pin.

"M. Poirot," I cried, "did *you* do that?"

"I was the stinging insect—yes. And very neatly I did it, too, do you not think so? You did not see me."

That was true enough. I never saw him do it. And I'm sure Mr. Mercado hadn't suspected. He must have been quick as lightning.

"But, M. Poirot, why?" I asked.

He answered me by another question.

"Did you notice anything, sister?" he asked.

I nodded my head slowly.

"Hypodermic marks," I said.

"So now we know something about Mr. Mercado," said Poirot. "I suspected—but I did not *know*. It is always necessary to *know*."

"And you don't care how you set about it!" I thought, but didn't say.

Poirot suddenly clapped his hand to his pocket.

"Alas, I have dropped my handkerchief down there. I concealed the pin in it."

"I'll get it for you," I said and hurried back.

I'd got the feeling, you see, by this time, that M. Poirot and I were the doctor and nurse in charge of a case. At least, it was more like an operation and he was the surgeon. Perhaps I oughtn't to say so, but in a queer way I was beginning to enjoy myself.

I remember just after I'd finished my training, I went to a case in a private house and the need for an immediate operation arose, and the patient's husband was cranky about nursing homes. He just wouldn't hear of his wife being taken to one. Said it had to be done in the house.

Well, of course it was just splendid for me! Nobody else to have a look in! I was in charge of everything. Of course, I was terribly nervous—I thought of everything conceivable that doctor could want, but even then I was afraid I might have forgotten something. You never know with doctors. They ask for absolutely anything sometimes! But everything went spendidly! I had each thing ready as he asked for it, and he actually told me I'd done first rate after it was over—and that's a thing most doctors wouldn't bother to do! The G.P. was very nice too. And I ran the whole thing myself!

The patient recovered, too, so everybody was happy.

Well, I felt rather the same now. In a way M. Poirot reminded me of that surgeon. *He* was a little man, too. Ugly little man with a face like a monkey, but a wonderful surgeon. He knew instinctively just where to go. I've seen a lot of surgeons and I know what a lot of difference there is.

Gradually I'd been growing a kind of confidence in M. Poirot. I felt that he, too, knew exactly what he was doing. And I was getting to feel that it was my job to help him— as you might say—to have the forceps and the swabs and all handy just when he wanted them. That's why it seemed just as natural for me to run off and look for his handkerchief as it would have been to pick up a towel that a doctor had thrown on the floor.

When I'd found it and got back I couldn't see him at first. But at last I caught sight of him. He was sitting a little way from the mound talking to Mr. Carey. Mr. Carey's boy was standing near with that great big rod thing with metres marked on it, but just at that moment he said something to the boy and the boy took it away. It seemed he had finished with it for the time being.

I'd like to get this next bit quite clear. You see, I wasn't quite sure what M. Piorot did or didn't want me to do. He might, I mean, have sent me back for that handkerchief *on purpose*. To get me out of the way.

It was just like an operation over again. You've got to be careful to hand the doctor just what he wants and not what he *doesn't* want. I mean, suppose you gave him the artery forceps at the wrong moment, and were late with them at the right moment! Thank goodness I know my work in the theatre well enough. I'm not likely to make mistakes there. But in this business I was really the rawest of raw little probationers. And so I had to be particularly careful not to make any silly mistakes.

Of course, I didn't for one moment imagine that M. Poirot didn't want me to hear what he and Mr. Carey were saying. But he might have thought he'd get Mr. Carey to talk better if I wasn't there.

Now I don't want anybody to get it into

their heads that I'm the kind of woman who goes about eavesdropping on private conversations. I wouldn't do such a thing. Not for a moment. Not however much I wanted to.

And what I mean is if it *had* been a private conversation I wouldn't for a moment have done what, as a matter of fact, I actually did do.

As I looked at it I was in a privileged position. After all, you hear many a thing when a patient's coming round after an anæsthetic. The patient wouldn't want you to hear it— and usually has no idea you *have* heard it— but the fact remains you *do* hear it. I just took it that Mr. Carey was the patient. He'd be none the worse for what he didn't know about. And if you think that I was just curious, well, I'll admit that I *was* curious. I didn't want to miss anything I could help.

All this is just leading up to the fact that I turned aside and went by a round-about way up behind the big dump until I was a foot from where they were, but concealed from them by the corner of the dump. And if any one says it was dishonourable I just beg to disagree. *Nothing* ought to be hidden from the nurse in charge of the case, though, of course, it's the doctor to say what shall be *done*.

I don't know, of course, what M. Poirot's line of approach had been, but by the time I'd got there he was aiming straight for the bull's eye, so to speak.

"Nobody appreciates Dr. Leidner's devotion to his wife more than I do," he was saying. "But it is often the case that one learns more about a person from their enemies than from their friends."

"You suggest that their faults are more important than their virtues?" said Mr. Carey. His tone was dry and ironic.

"Undoubtedly—when it comes to murder. It seems odd that as far as I know nobody has yet been murdered for having too perfect a character! And yet perfection is undoubtedly an irritating thing."

"I'm afraid I'm hardly the right person to help you," said Mr. Carey. "To be perfectly honest, Mrs. Leidner and I didn't hit it off particularly well. I don't mean that we were in any sense of the word enemies, but we were not exactly friends. Mrs. Leidner was, perhaps, a shade jealous of my old friendship with her husband. I, for my part, although I admired her very much and thought she was an extremely attractive woman, was just a shade resentful of her influence over Leidner. As a result we were quite polite to each other, but not intimate."

"Admirably explained," said Poirot.

I could just see their heads, and I saw Mr. Carey's turn sharply as though something in M. Poirot's detached tone struck him disagreeably.

M. Poirot went on:

"Was not Dr. Leidner distressed that you and his wife did not get on together better?"

Carey hesitated a minute before saying:

"Really—I'm not sure. He never said anything. I always hoped he didn't notice it. He was very wrapped up in his work, you know."

"So the truth, according to you, is that you did not really like Mrs. Leidner?"

Carey shrugged his shoulders.

"I should probably have liked her very much if she hadn't been Leidner's wife."

He laughed as though amused by his own statement.

Poirot was arranging a little heap of broken potsherds. He said in a dreamy, faraway voice:

"I talked to Miss Johnson this morning.

She admitted that she was prejudiced against Mrs. Leidner and did not like her very much, although she hastened to add that Mrs. Leidner had always been charming to her."

"All quite true, I should say," said Carey.

"So I believed. Then I had a conversation with Mrs. Mercado. She told me at great length how devoted she had been to Mrs. Leidner and how much she had admired her."

Carey made no answer to this, and after waiting a minute or two Poirot went on:

"That—I did not believe! Then I come to you and that which you tell me—well, again—*I do not believe* . . ."

Carey stiffened. I could hear the anger—repressed anger—in his voice.

"I really cannot help your beliefs—or your disbeliefs, M. Poirot. You've heard the truth and you can take it or leave it as far as I am concerned."

Poirot did not grow angry. Instead he sounded particularly meek and depressed.

"Is it my fault what I do—or do not believe? I have a sensitive ear, you know. And then—there are always plenty of stories going about—rumours floating in the air. One listens—and perhaps—one learns something! Yes, there *are* stories. . . ."

Carey sprang to his feet. I could see clearly a little pulse that beat in his temple. He looked simply splendid! So lean and so brown—and that wonderful jaw, hard and square. I don't wonder women fell for that man.

"What stories?" he asked savagely.

Poirot looked sideways at him.

"Perhaps you can guess. The usual sort of story—about you and Mrs. Leidner."

"What foul minds people have!"

"*N'est ce pas?* They are like dogs. However deep you bury an unpleasantness a dog will always root it up again."

"And you believe these stories?"

"I am willing to be convinced—of the truth," said Poirot gravely.

"I doubt if you'd know the truth if you heard it," Carey laughed rudely.

"Try me and see," said Poirot, watching him.

"I will then! You shall have the truth! I hated Louise Leidner—there's the truth for you! I hated her like hell!"

Chapter 22

David Emmott, Father Lavigny and a Discovery

Turning abruptly away, Carey strode off with long angry strides.

Poirot sat looking after him and presently he murmured:

"Yes—I see. . . ."

Without turning his head he said in a slightly louder voice:

"Do not come round the corner for a minute, nurse. In case he turns his head. Now it is all right. You have my handkerchief? Many thanks. You are most amiable."

He didn't say anything at all about my having been listening—and how he knew I *was* listening I can't think. He'd never once looked in that direction. I was rather relieved he didn't say anything. I mean, I felt all right with *myself* about it, but it might have been a little awkward explaining to him. So it was a good thing he didn't seem to want explanations.

"Do you think he did hate her, M. Poirot?" I asked.

Nodding his head slowly with a curious expression on his face, Poirot answered.

"Yes—I think he did."

Then he got up briskly and began to walk to where the men were working on the top of the mound. I followed him. We couldn't see any one but Arabs at first but we finally found Mr. Emmott lying face downwards blowing dust off a skeleton that had just been uncovered.

He gave his pleasant grave smile when he saw us.

"Have you come to see round?" he asked. "I'll be free in a minute."

He sat up, took his knife and began daintily cutting the earth away from round the bones, stopping every now and then to use either a bellows or his own breath. A very insanitary proceeding the latter, I thought.

"You'll get all sorts of nasty germs in your mouth, Mr. Emmott," I protested.

"Nasty germs are my daily diet, nurse," he said gravely. "Germs can't do anything to an

archæologist—they just get naturally dis-
couraged trying."

He scraped a little more away round the
thigh bone. Then he spoke to the foreman
at his side directing him exactly what he
wanted done.

"There," he said, rising to his feet. "That's
ready for Reiter to photograph after lunch.
Rather nice stuff she had in with her."

He showed us a little verdigrisy copper
bowl and some pins. And a lot of gold and
blue things that had been her necklace of
beads.

The bones and all the objects were
brushed and cleaned with a knife and kept
in position ready to be photographed.

"Who is she?" asked Poirot.

"First millennium. A lady of some consequence perhaps. Skull looks rather odd—I
must get Mercado to look at it. It suggests
death by foul play."

"A Mrs. Leidner of two thousand odd
years ago?" said Poirot.

"Perhaps," said Mr. Emmott.

Bill Coleman was doing something with a
pick to a wall face.

David Emmott called something to him

which I didn't catch and then started showing M. Poirot round.

When the short explanatory tour was over Emmott looked at his watch.

"We knock off in ten minutes," he said. "Shall we walk back to the house?"

"That will suit me excellently," said Poirot.

We walked slowly along the well-worn path.

"I expect you are all glad to get back to work again," said Poirot.

Emmott replied gravely:

"Yes, it's much the best thing. It's not been any too easy loafing about the house and making conversation."

"Knowing all the time *that one of you was a murderer.*"

Emmott did not answer. He made no gesture of dissent. I knew now that he had had a suspicion of the truth from the very first when he had questioned the house-boys.

After a few minutes he asked quietly:

"Are you getting anywhere, M. Poirot?"

Poirot said gravely:

"Will you help me to get somewhere?"

"Why, naturally."

Watching him closely, Poirot said:

"The hub of the case is Mrs. Leidner. I want to know about Mrs. Leidner."

David Emmott said slowly:

"What do you mean by knowing about her?"

"I do not mean where she came from and what her maiden name was. I do not mean the shape of her face and the colour of her eyes. I mean her—herself."

"You think that counts in the case?"

"I am quite sure of it."

Emmott was silent for a moment or two, then he said:

"Maybe you're right."

"And that is where you can help me. You can tell me what sort of a woman she was."

"Can I? I've often wondered about it myself."

"Didn't you make up your mind on the subject?"

"I think I did in the end."

"Eh bien?"

But Mr. Emmott was silent for some minutes, then he said:

"What did nurse think of her? Women are said to sum up other women quickly enough, and a nurse has a wide experience of types."

Poirot didn't give me any chance of speaking even if I had wanted to. He said quickly:

"What I want to know is what a *man* thought of her?"

Emmott smiled a little.

"I expect they'd all be much the same." He paused and said, "She wasn't young, but I think she was about the most beautiful woman I've ever come across."

"That's hardly an answer, Mr. Emmott."

"It's not so far off one, M. Poirot."

He was silent a minute or two and then he went on:

"There used to be a fairy story I read when I was a kid. A northern fairy story about the Snow Queen and Little Kay. I guess Mrs. Leidner was rather like that—always taking Little Kay for a ride."

"Ah, yes, a tale of Hans Andersen, is it not? And there was a girl in it. Little Gerda, was that her name?"

"Maybe. I don't remember much of it."

"Can't you go a little further, Mr. Emmott?"

David Emmott shook his head.

"I don't even know if I've summed her up correctly. She wasn't easy to read. She'd do a devilish thing one day, and a really fine one the next. But I think you're about right when you say that she's the hub of the case. That's what she always wanted to be—*at the centre of things*. And she liked to get *at* other people—I mean, she wasn't just satisfied with being passed the toast and the peanut butter, she wanted you to turn your mind and soul inside out for her to look at it."

"And if one did not give her that satisfaction?" asked Poirot.

"Then she could turn ugly!"

I saw his lips close resolutely and his jaws set.

"I suppose, Mr. Emmott, you would not care to express a plain unofficial opinion as to who murdered her?"

"I don't know," said Emmott. "I really haven't the slightest idea. I rather think that, if I'd been Carl—Carl Reiter, I mean—I would have had a shot at murdering her. She was a pretty fair devil to him. But, of course, he asks for it by being so darned sensitive. Just invites you to give him a kick in the pants."

"And did Mrs. Leidner give him—a kick in the pants?" inquired Poirot.

Emmott gave a sudden grin.

"No. Pretty little jabs with an embroidery needle—that was her method. He *was* irritating, of course. Just like some blubbering, poor-spirited kid. But a needle's a painful weapon."

I stole a glance at Poirot and thought I detected a slight quiver of his lips.

"But you don't really believe that Carl Reiter killed her?" he asked.

"No. I don't believe you'd kill a woman because she persistently made you look a fool at every meal."

Poirot shook his head thoughtfully.

Of course, Mr. Emmott made Mrs. Leidner sound quite inhuman. There was something to be said on the other side too.

There had been something terribly irritating about Mr. Reiter's attitude. He jumped when she spoke to him, and did idiotic things like passing her the marmalade again and again when he knew she never ate it. I'd have felt inclined to snap at him a bit myself.

Men don't understand how their mannerisms can get on women's nerves so that you feel you just have to snap.

I thought I'd just mention that to Mr. Poirot some time.

We had arrived back by now and Mr. Emmott offered Poirot a wash and took him into his room.

I hurried across the courtyard to mine.

I came out again about the same time they did and we were all making for the dining-room when Father Lavigny appeared in the doorway of his room and invited Poirot in.

Mr. Emmott came on round and he and I went into the dining-room together.

Miss Johnson and Mrs. Mercado were there already, and after a few minutes Mr. Mercado, Mr. Reiter and Bill Coleman joined us.

We were just sitting down and Mercado had told the Arab boy to tell Father Lavigny lunch was ready when we were all startled by a faint, muffled cry.

I suppose our nerves weren't very good yet, for we all jumped, and Miss Johnson got quite pale and said:

"*What was that?* What's happened?"

Mrs. Mercado stared at her and said:

"My dear, what *is* the matter with you? It's some noise outside in the fields."

But at that minute Poirot and Father Lavigny came in.

"We thought some one was hurt," Miss Johnson said.

"A thousand pardons, mademoiselle," cried Poirot.

"The fault is mine. Father Lavigny, he explains to me some tablets, and I take one to the window to see better—and, *ma foi*, not looking where I was going, I steb the toe, and the pain is sharp for the moment and I cry out."

"We thought it was another murder," said Mrs. Mercado, laughing.

"Marie!" said her husband.

His tone was reproachful and she flushed and bit her lip.

Miss Johnson hastily turned the conversation to the dig and what objects of interest had turned up that morning. Conversation all through lunch was sternly archæological.

I think we all felt it was the safest thing.

After we had had coffee we adjourned to the living-room. Then the men, with the exception of Father Lavigny, went off to the dig again.

Father Lavigny took Poirot through into the antika-room and I went with them. I was getting to know the things pretty well by now and I felt a thrill of pride—almost as though it were my own property—when Father Lavigny took down the gold cup and I heard Poirot's exclamation of admiration and pleasure.

"How beautiful! What a work of art!"

Father Lavigny agreed eagerly and began to point out its beauties with real enthusiasm and knowledge.

"No wax on it to-day," I said.

"Wax?" Poirot stared at me.

"Wax?" So did Father Lavigny.

I explained my remark.

"Ah, *je comprends*," said Father Lavigny. "Yes, yes, candle grease."

That led direct to the subject of the midnight visitor. Forgetting my presence they both dropped into French and I left them together and went back into the living-room.

Mrs. Mercado was darning her husband's socks and Miss Johnson was reading a book. Rather an unusual thing for her. She usually seemed to have something to work at.

After a while Father Lavigny and Poirot came out, and the former excused himself on the score of work. Poirot sat down with us.

"A most interesting man," he said, and asked how much work there had been for Father Lavigny to do so far.

Miss Johnson explained that tablets had been scarce and that there had been very few inscribed bricks or cylinder seals. Father Lavigny, however, had done his share of work on the dig and was picking up colloquial Arabic very fast.

That led the talk to cylinder seals, and presently Miss Johnson fetched from a cupboard a sheet of impressions made by rolling them out on plasticine.

I realized as we bent over them, admiring the spirited designs, that these must be what she had been working at on that fatal afternoon.

As we talked I noticed that Poirot was rolling and kneading a little ball of plasticine between his fingers.

"You use a lot of plasticine, mademoiselle?" he asked.

"A fair amount. We seem to have got through a lot already this year—though I can't imagine how. But half our supply seems to have gone."

"Where is it kept, mademoiselle?"

"Here—in this cupboard."

As she replaced the sheet of impressions she showed him the shelf with rolls of plasticine. Durofix, photographic paste and other stationery supplies.

Poirot stooped down.

"And this—what is this, mademoiselle?"

He had slipped his hand right to the back and had brought out a curious crumpled object.

As he straightened it out we could see that it was a kind of mask, with eyes and mouth crudely painted on in Indian ink and the whole thing roughly smeared with plasticine.

"How perfectly extraordinary," cried Miss Johnson. "I've never seen it before. How did it get there? And what is it?"

"As to how it got there, well, one hiding-place is as good as another, and I presume that this cupboard would not have been turned out till the end of the season. As to what it *is*—that, too, I think, is not difficult to say. *We have here the face that Mrs. Leidner described.* The ghostly face seen in the semi-dusk outside her window—without body attached."

Mrs. Mercado gave a little shriek.

Miss Johnson was white to the lips. She murmured:

"Then it was *not* fancy. It was a trick—a wicked trick! But who played it?"

"Yes," cried Mrs. Mercado. "Who could have done such a wicked, wicked thing?"

Poirot did not attempt a reply. His face was very grim as he went into the next room, returned with an empty cardboard box in his hand and put the crumpled mask into it.

"The police must see this," he explained.

"It's horrible," said Miss Johnson in a low voice. "Horrible!"

"Do you think everything's hidden here somewhere?" cried Mrs. Mercado shrilly. "Do you think perhaps the weapon—the club she was killed with—all covered with blood still, perhaps . . . Oh! I'm frightened—I'm frightened . . ."

Miss Johnson gripped her by the shoulder.

"Be quiet," she said fiercely. "Here's Dr. Leidner. We mustn't upset him."

Indeed, at that very moment the car had driven into the courtyard. Dr. Leidner got out of it and came straight across and in at the living-room door. His face was set in lines of fatigue and he looked twice the age he had three days ago.

He said in a quiet voice:

"The funeral will be at eleven o'clock to-morrow. Major Deane will read the service."

Mrs. Mercado faltered something, then slipped out of the room.

Dr. Leidner said to Miss Johnson:

"You'll come, Anne?"

And she answered:

"Of course, my dear, we'll all come. Naturally."

She didn't say anything else, but her face must have expressed what her tongue was powerless to do, for his face lightened up with affection and a momentary ease.

"Dear Anne," he said. "You are such a wonderful comfort and help to me. My dear old friend."

He laid his hand on her arm and I saw the red colour creep up in her face as she muttered, gruff as ever:

"That's all right."

But I just caught a glimpse of her expression and knew that, for one short moment, Anne Johnson was a perfectly happy woman.

And another idea flashed across my mind. Perhaps soon, in the natural course of things, turning to his old friend for sympathy, a new and happy state of things might come about.

Not that I'm really a matchmaker, and of course it was indecent to think of such a thing before the funeral even. But after all, it *would* be a happy solution. He was very fond of her, and there was no doubt she was absolutely devoted to him and would be perfectly happy devoting the rest of her life to him. That is, if she could bear to hear Louise's perfections sung all the time. But women can put up with a lot when they've got what they want.

Dr. Leidner then greeted Poirot, asking him if he had made any progress.

Miss Johnson was standing behind Dr. Leidner and she looked hard at the box in Poirot's hand and shook her head, and I realized that she was pleading with Poirot not to tell him about the mask. She felt, I was sure, that he had enough to bear for one day.

Poirot fell in with her wish.

"These things march slowly, monsieur," he said.

Then, after a few desultory words, he took his leave.

I accompanied him out to his car.

There were half a dozen things I wanted to ask him, but somehow, when he turned and looked at me, I didn't ask anything after all. I'd as soon have asked a surgeon if he thought he'd made a good job of an operation. I just stood meekly waiting for instructions.

Rather to my surprise he said:

"Take care of yourself, my child."

And then he added:

"I wonder if it is well for you to remain here?"

"I must speak to Dr. Leidner about leaving," I said. "But I thought I'd wait until after the funeral."

He nodded in approval.

"In the meantime," he said, "do not try and find out too much. You understand, I do not want you to be clever!" And he added with a smile, "It is for you to hold the swabs and for me to do the operation."

Wasn't it funny, his actually saying that?

Then he said quite irrelevantly:

"An interesting man, that Father Lavigny."

"A monk being an archæologist seems odd to me," I said.

"Ah, yes, you are a Protestant. Me, I

am a good Catholic. I know something of priests and monks."

He frowned, seemed to hesitate, then said:

"Remember, he is quite clever enough to turn you inside out if he likes."

If he was warning me against gossiping I felt that I didn't need any such warning!

It annoyed me and though I didn't like to ask him any of the things I really wanted to know, I didn't see why I shouldn't at any rate say one thing.

"You'll excuse me, M. Poirot," I said. "But it's 'stubbed your toe,' not *stepped* or *stebbed*."

"Ah? Thank you, *ma sœur*."

"Don't mention it. But it's just as well to get a phrase right."

"I will remember," he said—quite meekly for him.

And he got in the car and was driven away, and I went slowly back across the courtyard wondering about a lot of things.

About the hypodermic marks on Mr. Mercado's arm, and what drug it was he took. And about that horrid yellow smeared mask. And how odd it was that Poirot and Miss Johnson hadn't heard my cry in the living-room that morning, whereas we had all heard Poirot perfectly well in the dining-room at lunch time—and yet Father Lavigny's room and Mrs. Leidner's were just the same distance from the living-room and the dining-room respectively.

And then I felt rather pleased that I'd taught *Doctor* Poirot one English phrase correctly!

Even if he *was* a great detective he'd realize he *didn't* know *everything*!

Chapter 23
I Go Psychic

The funeral was, I thought, a very affecting affair.

As well as ourselves, all the English people in Hassanieh attended it. Even Sheila Reilly was there looking quiet and subdued in a dark coat and skirt. I hoped that she was feeling a little remorseful for all the unkind things she had said.

When we got back to the house I followed Dr. Leidner into the office and broached the subject of my departure. He was very nice about it, thanked me for what I had done (Done! I had been worse than useless) and insisted on my accepting an extra week's salary.

I protested because really I felt I'd done nothing to earn it.

"Indeed, Dr. Leidner, I'd rather not have any salary at all. If you'd just refund me my travelling expenses that's all I want."

But he wouldn't hear of that.

"You see," I said, "I don't feel I deserve it, Dr. Leidner. I mean, I've—well, I've failed. She—my coming didn't save her."

"Now don't get that idea into your head, nurse," he said earnestly. "After all, I didn't engage you as a female detective. I never dreamt my wife's life was in danger. I was convinced it was all nerves and that she'd worked herself up into a rather curious mental state. You did all any one could do. She liked and trusted you. And I think in her last days she felt happier and safer because of your being here. There's nothing for you to reproach yourself with."

His voice quivered a little and I knew what he was thinking. *He* was the only one to blame for not having taken Mrs. Leidner's fears seriously.

"Dr. Leidner," I said curiously. "Have you ever come to any conclusion about those anonymous letters?"

He said with a sigh:

"I don't know what to believe. Has M. Poirot come to any definite conclusion?"

"He hadn't yesterday," I said, steering rather neatly, I thought, between truth and fiction. After all, he hadn't until I told him about Miss Johnson.

It was on my mind that I'd like to give Dr. Leidner a hint and see if he reacted. In the pleasure of seeing him and Miss Johnson together the day before, and his affection and reliance on her, I'd forgotten all about the letters. Even now I felt it was perhaps rather mean of me to bring it up. Even if she had written them, she had had a bad time after Mrs. Leidner's death. Yet I did want to see whether that particular possibility had ever entered Dr. Leidner's head.

"Anonymous letters are usually the work of a woman," I said. I wanted to see how he'd take it.

"I suppose they are," he said with a sigh. "But you seem to forget, nurse, that these may be genuine. They may actually be written by Frederick Bosner."

"No, I haven't forgotten," I said. "But I can't believe somehow that that's the real explanation."

"I do," he said. "It's all nonsense his being one of the expedition staff. That is just an ingenious theory of M. Poirot's. I believe that the truth is much simpler. The man is a madman, of course. He's been hanging round the place—perhaps in disguise of some kind. And somehow or other he got in on that fatal afternoon. The servants may be lying—they may have been bribed."

"I suppose it's possible," I said doubtfully.

Dr. Leidner went on with a trace of irritability.

"It is all very well for M. Poirot to suspect the members of my expedition. I am perfectly certain *none* of them have anything to do with it! I have worked with them. I *know* them!"

He stopped suddenly, then he said:

"Is that your experience, nurse? That anonymous letters are usually written by women?"

"It isn't always the case," I said. "But there's a certain type of feminine spitefulness that finds relief that way."

"I suppose you are thinking of Mrs. Mercado?" he said.

Then he shook his head.

"Even if she were malicious enough to wish to hurt Louise she would hardly have the necessary knowledge," he said.

I remembered the earlier letters in the attaché-case.

If Mrs. Leidner had left that unlocked and Mrs. Mercado had been alone in the house one day pottering about, she might easily have found them and read them. Men never seem to think of the simplest possibilities!

"And apart from her there is only Miss Johnson," I said, watching him.

"That would be quite ridiculous!"

The little smile with which he said it was quite conclusive. The idea of Miss Johnson being the author of the letters had never entered his head! I hesitated just for a minute—but I didn't say anything. One doesn't like giving away a fellow woman, and besides, I had been a witness of Miss Johnson's genuine and moving remorse. What was done was done. Why expose Dr. Leidner to a fresh disillusion on top of all his other troubles?

It was arranged that I should leave on the following day, and I had arranged through Dr. Reilly to stay for a day or two with the matron of the hospital whilst I made arrangements for returning to England either via Baghdad or direct via Nissibin by car and train.

Dr. Leidner was kind enough to say that he would like me to choose a memento from amongst his wife's things.

"Oh, no, really, Dr. Leidner," I said. "I couldn't. It's much too kind of you."

He insisted.

"But I should like you to have something. And Louise, I am sure, would have wished it."

Then he went on to suggest that I should have her tortoiseshell toilet set!

"Oh, no, Dr. Leidner! Why, that's a most *expensive* set. I couldn't really."

"She had no sisters, you know—no one who wants these things. There is no one else to have them."

I could quite imagine that he wouldn't want them to fall into Mrs. Mercado's greedy little hands. And I didn't think he'd want to offer them to Miss Johnson.

He went on kindly:

"You just think it over. By the way, here is the key of Louise's jewel case. Perhaps you will find something there you would rather have. And I should be very grateful if you would pack up—all—all her clothes. I dare say Reilly can find a use for them amongst

some of the poor Christian families in Hassanieh."

I was very glad to be able to do that for
him, and I expressed my willingness.

I set about it at once.

Mrs. Leidner had only had a very simple
wardrobe with her and it was soon sorted
and packed up into a couple of suitcases. All
her papers had been in the small attaché-
case. The jewel case contained a few simple
trinkets—a pearl ring, a diamond brooch, a
small string of pearls and one or two plain
gold bar brooches of the safety-pin type,
and a string of large amber beads.

Naturally I wasn't going to take the pearls
or the diamonds, but I hesitated a bit between the amber beads and the toilet set. In
the end, however, I didn't see why I
shouldn't take the latter. It was a kindly
thought on Dr. Leidner's part, and I was sure
there wasn't any patronage about it. I'd take
it in the spirit it had been offered without any
false pride. After all, I *had* been fond of her.

Well, that was all done and finished with.
The suitcases packed, the jewel case
locked up again and put separate to give
to Dr. Leidner with the photograph of Mrs.

Leidner's father and one or two other personal little odds and ends.

The room looked bare and forlorn emp-
tied of all its accoutrements, when I'd finished. There was nothing more for me to
do—and yet somehow or other I shrank
from leaving the room. It seemed as though
there were something still to do there—
something I ought to *see*—or something I
ought to have *known*.

I'm not superstitious but the idea *did* pop
into my head that perhaps Mrs. Leidner's
spirit was hanging about the room and trying to get in touch with me.

I remember once at the hospital some of
us girls got a planchette and really it wrote
some very remarkable things.

Perhaps, although I'd never thought of
such a thing, I might be mediumistic.

As I say, one gets all worked up to imagine all sorts of foolishness sometimes.

I prowled round the room uneasily, touch-
ing this and that. But, of course, there
wasn't anything in the room but bare furniture. There was nothing slipped behind
drawers or tucked away. I couldn't hope for
anything of that kind.

In the end (it sounds rather batty, but as I

say, one gets worked up) I did rather a queer thing.

I went and lay down on the bed and closed my eyes.

I deliberately tried to forget who and what I was. I tried to think myself back to that fatal afternoon. I was Mrs. Leidner lying here resting, peaceful and unsuspicious.

It's extraordinary how you can work yourself up.

I'm a perfectly normal matter-of-fact individual—not the least little bit spooky, but I tell you that after I'd lain there about five minutes I began to *feel* spooky.

I didn't try to resist. I deliberately encouraged the feeling. I said to myself:

"I'm Mrs. Leidner. I'm Mrs. Leidner. I'm lying here—half asleep. Presently—very soon now—the door's going to open."

I kept on saying that—as though I were hypnotizing myself.

It's just about half-past one . . . it's just about the time. . . . The door is going to open . . . *the door is going to open*. . . . I shall see who comes in. . . ."

I kept my eyes glued on that door. Presently it was going to open. I should *see* it open. And I should see *the person who opened it*.

I must have been a little over-wrought that afternoon to imagine I could solve the mystery that way.

But I did believe it. A sort of chill passed down my back and settled in my legs. They felt numb—paralyzed.

"You're going into a trance," I said. "And in that trance you'll see . . ."

And once again I repeated monotonously again and again:

"The door is going to open—the door is going to open. . . ."

The cold numbed feeling grew more intense.

And then, slowly, *I saw the door just beginning to open*.

It was horrible.

I've never known anything so horrible before or since.

I was paralyzed—chilled through and through. I couldn't move. For the life of me I couldn't have moved.

And I was terrified. Sick and blind and dumb with terror.

That slowly opening door.

So noiseless.

In a minute I should see . . .

Slowly—slowly—wider and wider.

Bill Coleman came quietly in.

He must have had the shock of his life!

I bounded off the bed with a scream of terror and hurled myself across the room.

He stood stock-still, his blunt pink face pinker and his mouth opened wide with surprise.

"Hallo-allo-allo," he said. "What's up, nurse?"

I came back to reality with a crash.

"Goodness, Mr. Coleman," I said. "How you startled me!"

"Sorry," he said with a momentary grin.

I saw then that he was holding a little bunch of scarlet ranunculus in his hand. They were pretty little flowers and they grew wild on the sides of the Tell. Mrs. Leidner had been very fond of them.

He blushed and got rather red as he said:

"One can't get any flowers or things in Hassanieh. Seemed rather rotten not to have any flowers for the grave. I thought I'd just nip in here and put a little posy in that little pot thing she always had flowers in on her table. Sort of show she wasn't forgotten—eh? A bit asinine, I know, but—well—I mean to say—"

I thought it was very nice of him. He was all pink with embarrassment like Englishmen are when they've done anything sentimental. I thought it was a very sweet thought.

"Why, I think that's a very nice idea, Mr. Coleman," I said.

And I picked up the little pot and went and got some water in it and we put the flowers in.

I really thought much more of Mr. Coleman for this idea of his. It showed he had a heart and nice feelings about things.

He didn't ask me again what made me let out such a squeal and I'm thankful he didn't. I should have felt a fool explaining.

"Stick to common sense in future, woman," I said to myself as I settled my cuffs and smoothed my apron. "You're not cut out for this psychic stuff."

I bustled about doing my own packing and kept myself busy for the rest of the day.

Father Lavigny was kind enough to express great distress at my leaving. He said my cheerfulness and common sense had been such a help to everybody. Common sense! I'm glad he didn't know about my idiotic behaviour in Mrs. Leidner's room.

"We have not seen M. Poirot to-day," he remarked.

I told him that Poirot had said he was going to be busy all day sending off telegrams.

Father Lavigny raised his eyebrows.

"Telegrams? To America?"

"I suppose so. He said 'All over the world!' but I think that was rather a foreign exaggeration."

And then I got rather red, remembering that Father Lavingny was a foreigner himself.

He didn't seem offended though, just laughed quite pleasantly and asked me if there were any news of the man with the squint.

I said I didn't know but I hadn't heard of any.

Father Lavigny asked me again about the time Mrs. Leidner and I had noticed the man and how he had seemed to be standing on tiptoe and peering through the window.

"It seems clear the man had some overwhelming interest in Mrs. Leidner," he said thoughtfully. "I have wondered since whether the man could possibly have been a European got up to look like an Iraqi?"

That was a new idea to me and I considered it carefully. I had taken it for granted that the man was a native, but of course, when I came to think of it, I was really going by the cut of his clothes and the yellowness of his skin.

Father Lavigny declared his intention of going round outside the house to the place where Mrs. Leidner and I had seen the man standing.

"You never know, he might have dropped something. In the detective stories the criminal always does."

"I expect in real life criminals are more careful," I said.

I fetched some socks I had just finished darning and put them on the table in the living-room for the men to sort out when they came in, and then, as there was nothing much more to do, I went up on the roof.

Miss Johnson was standing there but she didn't hear me. I got right up to her before she noticed me.

But long before that I'd seen that there was something very wrong.

She was standing in the middle of the

roof staring straight in front of her, and there was the most awful look on her face. As though she'd seen something she couldn't possibly believe.

It gave me quite a shock.

Mind you, I'd seen her upset the other evening, but this was quite different.

"My dear," I said, hurrying to her, "whatever's the matter?"

She turned her head at that and stood looking at me—almost as if she didn't see me.

"What is it?" I persisted.

She made a queer sort of grimace—as though she were trying to swallow but her throat were too dry. She said hoarsely:

"I've just seen something."

"What have you seen? Tell me. Whatever can it be? You look all in."

She gave an effort to pull herself together, but she still looked pretty dreadful.

She said, still in that same dreadful choked voice.

"I've seen how some one could come in from outside—and no one would ever guess."

I followed the direction of her eyes but I couldn't see anything.

Mr. Reiter was standing in the door of the photographic room and Father Lavigny was just crossing the courtyard—but there was nothing else.

I turned back puzzled and found her eyes fixed on mine with the strangest expression in them.

"Really," I said, "I don't see what you mean. Won't you explain?"

But she shook her head.

"Not now. Later. We *ought* to have seen. Oh, we ought to have seen!"

"If you'd only tell me—"

But she shook her head.

"I've got to think it out first."

And pushing past me, she went stumbling down the stairs.

I didn't follow her as she obviously didn't want me with her. Instead I sat down on the parapet and tried to puzzle things out. But I didn't get anywhere. There was only the one way into the courtyard—through the big arch. Just outside it I could see the water-boy and his horse and the Indian cook talking to him. Nobody could have passed them and come in without their seeing him.

I shook my head in perplexity and went downstairs again.

Chapter 24

Murder Is a Habit

We all went to bed early that night. Miss Johnson had appeared at dinner and had behaved more or less as usual. She had, however, a sort of dazed look, and once or twice quite failed to take in what other people said to her.

It wasn't somehow a very comfortable sort of meal. You'd say, I suppose, that that was natural enough in a house where there'd been a funeral that day. But I know what I mean.

Lately our meals had been hushed and subdued, but for all that there had been a feeling of comradeship. There had been sympathy with Dr. Leidner in his grief and a fellow feeling of being all in the same boat amongst the others.

But to-night I was reminded of my first meal there—when Mrs. Mercado had watched me and there had been that curious feeling as though something might snap any minute.

I'd felt the same thing—only very much intensified—when we'd sat round the dining-room table with Poirot at the head of it.

To-night it was particularly strong. Every one was on edge—jumpy—on tenterhooks. If any one had dropped something I'm sure somebody would have screamed.

As I say, we all separated early afterwards. I went to bed almost at once. The last thing I heard as I was dropping off to sleep was Mrs. Mercado's voice saying goodnight to Miss Johnson just outside my door.

I dropped off to sleep at once—tired by my exertions and even more by my silly experience in Mrs. Leidner's room. I slept heavily and dreamlessly for several hours.

I awoke when I did awake with a start and a feeling of impending catastrophe. Some sound had woken me, and as I sat up in bed listening I heard it again.

An awful sort of agonized choking groan.

I had lit my candle and was out of bed in a twinkling. I snatched up a torch, too, in case the candle should blow out. I came out of my door and stood listening. I knew the sound wasn't far away. It came again—from the room immediately next to mine—Miss Johnson's room.

I hurried in. Miss Johnson was lying in bed, her whole body contorted in agony. As I set down the candle and bent over her, her lips moved and she tried to speak—but only an awful hoarse whisper came. I saw that the corners of her mouth and the skin of her chin were burnt a kind of greyish white.

Her eyes went from me to a glass that lay on the floor evidently where it had dropped from her hand. The light rug was stained a bright red where it had fallen. I picked it up and ran a finger over the inside, drawing back my hand with a sharp exclamation. Then I examined the inside of the poor woman's mouth.

There wasn't the least doubt what was the matter. Somehow or other, intentionally or otherwise, she'd swallowed a quantity of corrosive acid—oxalic or hydrochloric, I suspected.

I ran out and called to Dr. Leidner and he

woke the others, and we worked over her for all we were worth, but all the time I had an awful feeling it was no good. We tried a strong solution of carbonate of soda—and followed it with olive oil. To ease the pain I gave her a hypodermic of morphine sulphate.

David Emmott had gone off to Hassanieh to fetch Dr. Reilly, but before he came it was over.

I won't dwell on the details. Poisoning by a strong solution of hydrochloric acid (which is what it proved to be) is one of the most painful deaths possible.

It was when I was bending over her to give her the morphia that she made one ghastly effort to speak. It was only a horrible strangled whisper when it came.

"The window . . ." she said. *"Nurse . . . the window . . ."*

But that was all—she couldn't go on. She collapsed completely.

I shall never forget that night. The arrival of Dr. Reilly. The arrival of Captain Maitland. And finally with the dawn, Hercule Poirot.

He it was who took me gently by the arm and steered me into the dining-room where he made me sit down and have a cup of good strong tea.

"There, *mon enfant*," he said, "that is better. You are worn out."

Upon that, I burst into tears.

"It's too awful," I sobbed. "It's been like a nightmare. Such awful suffering. And her eyes . . . Oh, M. Poirot—her eyes . . ."

He patted me on the shoulder. A woman couldn't have been kinder.

"Yes, yes—do not think of it. You did all you could."

"It was one of the corrosive acids."

"It was a strong solution of hydrochloric acid."

"The stuff they use on the pots?"

"Yes. Miss Johnson probably drank it off before she was fully awake. That is—unless she took it on purpose."

"Oh, M. Poirot, what an awful idea!"

"It is a possibility, after all. What do you think?"

I considered for a moment and then shook my head decisively.

"I don't believe it. No, I don't believe it for a moment." I hesitated and then said, "I think she found out something yesterday afternoon."

"What is that you say? She found out something?"

I repeated to him the curious conversation we had had together.

Poirot gave a low soft whistle.

"*La pauvre femme!*" he said. "She said she wanted to think it over—eh? That is what signed her death warrant. If she had only spoken out—then—at once."

He said:

"Tell me again her exact words?"

I repeated them.

"She saw how some one could have come in from outside without any of you knowing? Come, *ma sœur*, let us go up to the roof and you shall show me just where she was standing."

We went up to the roof together and I showed Poirot the exact spot where Miss Johnson had stood.

"Like this?" said Poirot. "Now what do I see? I see half the courtyard—and the archway—and the doors of the drawing-office and the photographic room and the laboratory. Was there any one in the courtyard?"

"Father Lavigny was just going towards the archway and Mr. Reiter was standing in the door of the photographic room."

"And still I do not see in the least how any one could come in from outside and none of you know about it. . . . But *she* saw . . ."

He gave it up at last, shaking his head.

"*Sacré nom d'un chien—va!* What *did* she see?"

The sun was just rising. The whole eastern sky was a riot of rose and orange and pale, pearly grey.

"What a beautiful sunrise," said Poirot gently.

The river wound away to our left and the Tell stood up outlined in gold colour. To the south were the blossoming trees and the peaceful cultivation. The water-wheel groaned in the distance—a faint unearthly sound. In the north were the slender minarets and the clustering fairy whiteness of Hassanieh.

It was all incredibly beautiful.

And then, close at my elbow, I heard Poirot give a long deep sigh.

"Fool that I have been," he murmured. "When the truth is so clear—so clear."

Chapter 25

Suicide or Murder?

I hadn't time to ask Poirot what he meant, for Captain Maitland was calling up to us and asking us to come down.

We hurried down the stairs.

"Look here, Poirot," he said. "Here's another complication. The monk fellow is missing."

"Father Lavigny?"

"Yes. Nobody noticed it till just now. Then it dawned on somebody that he was the only one of the party not around, and we went to his room. His bed's not been slept in and there's no sign of him."

The whole thing was like a bad dream. First Miss Johnson's death and then the disappearance of Father Lavigny.

The servants were called and questioned,

but they couldn't throw any light on the mystery. He had last been seen at about eight o'clock the night before. Then he had said he was going out for a stroll before going to bed.

Nobody had seen him come back from that stroll.

The big doors had been closed and barred at nine o'clock as usual. Nobody, however, remembered unbarring them in the morning. The two house-boys each thought the other one must have done the unfastening.

Had Father Lavigny ever returned the night before? Had he, in the course of his earlier walk, discovered anything of a suspicious nature, gone out to investigate it later, and perhaps fallen a third victim?

Captain Maitland swung round as Dr. Reilly came up with Mr. Mercado behind him.

"Hallo, Reilly. Got anything?"

"Yes. The stuff came from the laboratory here. I've just been checking up the quantities with Mercado. It's HCl from the lab."

"The laboratory—eh? Was it locked up?"

Mr. Mercado shook his head. His hands

were shaking and his face was twitching. He looked a wreck of a man.

"It's never been the custom," he stammered. "You see—just now—we're using it all the time. I—nobody ever dreamt—"

"Is the place locked up at night?"

"Yes—all the rooms are locked. The keys are hung up just inside the living-room."

"So if any one had a key to that they could get the lot."

"Yes."

"And it's a perfectly ordinary key, I suppose?"

"Oh, yes."

"Nothing to show whether she took it herself from the laboratory?" asked Captain Maitland.

"She didn't," I said loudly and positively.

I felt a warning touch on my arm. Poirot was standing close behind me.

And then something rather ghastly happened.

Not ghastly in itself—in fact it was just the incongruousness that made it seem worse than anything else.

A car drove into the courtyard and a little man jumped out. He was wearing a sun helmet and a short thick trench coat.

He came straight to Dr. Leidner, who was standing by Dr. Reilly, and shook him warmly by the hand.

"Vous voilà, mon cher," he cried. "Delighted to see you. I passed this way on Saturday afternoon—en route to the Italians at Fugima. I went to the dig but there wasn't a single European about and alas! I cannot speak Arabic. I had not time to come to the house. This morning I leave Fugima at five—two hours here with you—and then I catch the convoy on. *Eh bien*, and how is the season going?"

It was ghastly.

The cheery voice, the matter-of-fact manner, all the pleasant sanity of an everyday world now left far behind. He just bustled in, knowing nothing and noticing nothing—full of cheerful bonhomie.

No wonder Dr. Leidner gave an inarticulate gasp and looked in mute appeal at Dr. Reilly.

The doctor rose to the occasion.

He took the little man (he was a French archaeologist called Verrier who dug in the Greek islands, I heard later) aside and explained to him what had occurred.

Verrier was horrified. He himself had been

staying at an Italian dig right away from civ-
ilization for the last few days and had heard
nothing.

He was profuse in condolences and
apologies, finally striding over to Dr. Leidner
and clasping him warmly by both hands.

"What a tragedy! My God, what a
tragedy! I have no words. *Mon pauvre col-
lègue*."

And shaking his head in one last ineffec-
tual effort to express his feelings, the little
man climbed into his car and left us.

As I say, that momentary introduction of
comic relief into tragedy seemed really more
gruesome than anything else that had happened.

"The next thing," said Dr. Reilly firmly, "is
breakfast. Yes, I insist. Come, Leidner, you
must eat."

Poor Dr. Leidner was almost a complete
wreck. He came with us to the dining-room
and there a funereal meal was served. I
think the hot coffee and fried eggs did us all
good, though no one actually felt they
wanted to eat. Dr. Leidner drank some coffee and sat twiddling his beard. His face
was grey, drawn with pain and bewilder-
ment.

After breakfast, Captain Maitland got down to things.

I explained how I had woken up, heard a queer sound and had gone into Miss Johnson's room.

"You say there was a glass on the floor?"

"Yes. She must have dropped it after drinking."

"Was it broken?"

"No, it had fallen on the rug. (I'm afraid the acid's ruined the rug, by the way.) I picked the glass up and put it back on the table."

"I'm glad you've told us that. There are only two sets of fingerprints on it, and one set is certainly Miss Johnson's own. The other must be yours."

He was silent for a moment, then he said: "Please go on."

I described carefully what I'd done and the methods I had tried, looking rather anxiously at Dr. Reilly for approval. He gave it with a nod.

"You tried everything that could possibly have done any good," he said. And though I was pretty sure I had done so, it was a relief to have my belief confirmed.

"Did you know exactly what she had taken?" Captain Maitland asked.

"No—but I could see, of course, that it was a corrosive acid."

Captain Maitland asked gravely:

"Is it your opinion, nurse, that Miss Johnson deliberately administered this stuff to herself?"

"Oh, no," I exclaimed. "I never thought of such a thing!"

I don't know why I was so sure. Partly, I think, because of M. Poirot's hints. His "murder is a habit" had impressed itself on my mind. And then one doesn't readily believe that any one's going to commit suicide in such a terribly painful way.

I said as much and Captain Maitland nodded thoughtfully.

"I agree that it isn't what one would choose," he said. "But if any one were in great distress of mind and this stuff were easily available it might be taken for that reason."

"*Was* she in great distress of mind?" I asked doubtfully.

"Mrs. Mercado says so. She says that Miss Johnson was quite unlike herself at dinner last night—that she hardly replied to anything that was said to her. Mrs. Mercado is quite sure that Miss Johnson was in terrible distress over something and that the idea of making away with herself had already occurred to her."

"Well, I don't believe it for a moment," I said bluntly.

Mrs. Mercado indeed! Nasty slinking little cat!

"Then what *do* you think?"

"I think she was murdered," I said bluntly.

He rapped out his next question sharply. I felt rather that I was in the orderly room.

"Any reasons?"

"It seems to me by far and away the most possible solution."

"That's just your private opinion. There was no reason why the lady should be murdered?"

"Excuse me," I said, "there was. She found out something."

"Found out something? What did she find out?"

I repeated our conversation on the roof word for word.

"She refused to tell you what her discovery was?"

"Yes. She said she must have time to think it over."

"But she was very excited by it?"

"Yes."

"A way of getting in from outside." Captain Maitland puzzled over it, his brows knit. "Had you no idea at all of what she was driving at?"

"Not in the least. I puzzled and puzzled over it but I couldn't even get a glimmering."

Captain Maitland said:

"What do you think, M. Poirot?"

Poirot said:

"I think you have there a possible motive."

"For murder?"

"For murder."

Captain Maitland frowned.

"She wasn't able to speak before she died?"

"Yes, she just managed to get out two words."

"What were they?"

"The window . . ."

"The window?" repeated Captain Maitland. "Did you understand to what she was referring?"

I shook my head.

"How many windows were there in her bedroom?"

"Just the one."

"Giving on the courtyard?"

"Yes."

"Was it open or shut? Open, I seem to remember. But perhaps one of you opened it?"

"No, it was open all the time. I wondered—"

I stopped.

"Go on, nurse."

"I examined the window, of course, but I couldn't see anything unusual about it. I wondered whether, perhaps, somebody changed the glasses that way."

"Changed the glasses?"

"Yes. You see, Miss Johnson always takes a glass of water to bed with her. I think that glass must have been tampered with and a glass of acid put there in its place."

"What do you say, Reilly?"

"If it's murder, that was probably the way it was done," said Dr. Reilly promptly. "No ordinary moderately observant human being would drink a glass of acid in mistake for one of water—if they were in full possession of their waking faculties. But if any one's accustomed to drinking off a glass of water in the middle of the night, that person might easily stretch out an arm, find the glass in the accustomed place, and still half asleep, toss off enough of the stuff to be fatal before realizing what had happened."

Captain Maitland reflected a minute.

"I'll have to go back and look at that window. How far is it from the head of the bed?"

I thought.

"With a very long stretch you could just reach the little table that stands by the head of the bed."

"The table on which the glass of water was?"

"Yes."

"Was the door locked?"

"No."

"So whoever it was could have come in that way and made the substitution?"

"Oh, yes."

"There would be more risk that way," said Dr. Reilly. "A person who is sleeping quite soundly will often wake up at the sound of a footfall. If the table could be reached from the window it would be the safer way."

"I'm not only thinking of the glass," said Captain Maitland absent-mindedly.

Rousing himself, he addressed me once again.

"It's your opinion that when the poor lady felt she was dying she was anxious to let you know that somebody had substituted acid for water through the open window? Surely the person's *name* would have been more to the point?"

"She mayn't have known the name," I pointed out.

"Or it would have been more to the point if she'd managed to hint what it was that she had discovered the day before?"

Dr. Reilly said:

"When you're dying, Maitland, you haven't always got a sense of proportion. One particular fact very likely obsesses your mind. That a murderous hand had come through the window may have been the principal fact obsessing her at the minute. It may have seemed to her important that she should let people know that. In my opinion she wasn't far wrong either. It *was* important! She probably jumped to the fact that you'd think it was suicide. If she could have used her tongue freely, she'd probably have said 'It wasn't suicide. I didn't take it myself. Somebody else must have put it near my bed *through the window.*' "

Captain Maitland drummed with his fingers for a minute or two without replying. Then he said:

"There are certainly two ways of looking at it. It's either suicide or murder. Which do you think, Dr. Leidner?"

Dr. Leidner was silent for a minute or two, then he said quietly and decisively:

"Murder. Anne Johnson wasn't the sort of woman to kill herself."

"No," allowed Captain Maitland. "Not in the normal run of things. But there might be circumstances in which it would be quite a natural thing to do."

"Such as?"

Captain Maitland stooped to a bundle which I had previously noticed him place by the side of his chair. He swung it on to the table with something of an effort.

"There's something here that none of you know about," he said. "We found it under the bed."

He fumbled with the knot of the covering, then threw it back revealing a heavy great quern or grinder.

That was nothing in itself—there were a dozen or so already found in the course of the excavations.

What riveted our attention on this particular specimen was a dull, dark stain and a fragment of something that looked like hair.

"That'll be your job, Reilly," said Captain Maitland. "But I shouldn't say that there's much doubt about this being the instrument with which Mrs. Leidner was killed!"

Chapter 26

Next It Will Be Me!

It was rather horrible. Dr. Leidner looked as though he were going to faint and I felt a bit sick myself.

Dr. Reilly examined it with professional gusto.

"No fingerprints, I presume?" he threw out.

"No fingerprints."

Dr. Reilly took out a pair of forceps and investigated delicately.

"H'm—a fragment of human tissue—and hair—fair blonde hair. That's the unofficial verdict. Of course, I'll have to make a proper test, blood group, etc., but there's not much doubt. Found under Miss Johnson's bed? Well, well—so *that's* the big idea. She did the murder, and then, God rest her, remorse came to her and she finished herself off. It's a theory—a pretty theory."

Dr. Leidner could only shake his head helplessly.

"Not Anne—not Anne," he murmured.

"I don't know where she hid this to begin with," said Captain Maitland. "Every room was searched after the first crime."

Something jumped into my mind and I thought, "In the stationery cupboard," but I didn't say anything.

"Wherever it was, she became dissatisfied with its hiding-place and took it into her own room, which had been searched with all the rest. Or perhaps she did that after making up her mind to commit suicide."

"I don't believe it," I said aloud.

And I couldn't somehow believe that kind nice Miss Johnson had battered out Mrs. Leidner's brains. I just couldn't *see* it happening! And yet it *did* fit in with some things—her fit of weeping that night, for instance. After all, I'd said "remorse" myself—only I'd never thought it was remorse for anything but the smaller more insignificant crime.

"I don't know what to believe," said Captain Maitland. "There's the French Father's disappearance to be cleared up too. My men are out hunting around in case he's been knocked on the head and his body rolled into a convenient irrigation ditch."

"Oh! I remember now—" I began.

Every one looked towards me inquiringly.

"It was yesterday afternoon," I said. "He'd been cross-questioning me about the man with a squint who was looking in at the window that day. He asked me just where he'd stood on the path and then he said he was going out to have a look round. He said in detective stories the criminal always dropped a convenient clue."

"Damned if any of my criminals ever do," said Captain Maitland. "So that's what he was after, was it? By jove, I wonder if he *did* find anything. A bit of a coincidence if both he and Miss Johnson discovered a clue to the identity of the murderer at practically the same time."

He added irritably, "Man with a squint? Man with a squint? There's more in this tale of that fellow with a squint than meets the eye. I don't know why the devil my fellows can't lay hold of him?"

"Probably because he hasn't got a squint," said Poirot quietly.

"Do you mean he faked it? Didn't know you could fake an actual squint."

Poirot merely said:

"A squint can be a very useful thing."

"The devil it can! I'd give a lot to know where that fellow is now, squint or no squint!"

"At a guess," said Poirot, "he has already passed the Syrian frontier."

"We've warned Tell Kotchek and Abu Kemal—all the frontier posts, in fact."

"I should imagine that he took the route through the hills. The route lorries sometimes take when running contraband."

Captain Maitland grunted.

"Then we'd better telegraph Deir ez Zor?"

"I did so yesterday—warning them to look out for a car with two men in it whose passports will be in the most impeccable order."

Captain Maitland favoured him with a stare.

"*You* did, did you? Two men—eh?"

Poirot nodded.

"There are two men in this."

"It strikes me, M. Poirot, that you've been keeping quite a lot of things up your sleeve."

Poirot shook his head.

"No," he said. "Not really. The truth came to me only this morning when I was watching the sun rise. A very beautiful sunrise."

I don't think that any of us had noticed that Mrs. Mercado was in the room. She must have crept in when we were all taken aback by the production of that horrible great blood-stained stone.

But now, without the least warning, she set up a noise like a pig having its throat cut.

"Oh, my God!" she cried. "I see it all. I see it all now. *It was Father Lavigny*. He's mad—religious mania. He thinks women are sinful. *He's killing them all*. First Mrs. Leidner—then Miss Johnson. And next it will be *me. . . .*"

With a scream of frenzy she flung herself across the room and clutched at Dr. Reilly's coat.

"I won't stay here, I tell you! I won't stay here a day longer. There's danger. There's danger all round. He's hiding somewhere—waiting his time. He'll spring out on me!"

Her mouth opened and she began screaming again.

I hurried over to Dr. Reilly, who had caught her by the wrists. I gave her a sharp slap on each cheek and with Dr. Reilly's help, I sat her down in a chair.

"Nobody's going to kill you," I said. "We'll see to that. Sit down and behave yourself."

She didn't scream any more. Her mouth closed and she sat looking at me with startled, stupid eyes.

Then there was another interruption. The door opened and Sheila Reilly came in.

Her face was pale and serious. She came straight to Poirot.

"I was at the post office early, M. Poirot," she said, "and there was a telegram there for you—so I brought it along."

"Thank you, mademoiselle."

He took it from her and tore it open while she watched his face.

It did not change, that face. He read the telegram, smoothed it out, folded it up neatly and put it in his pocket.

Mrs. Mercado was watching him. She said in a choked voice:

"Is that—from America?"

He shook his head.

"No, madame," he said. "It is from Tunis."

She stared at him for a moment as though she did not understand, then with a long sigh, she leant back in her seat.

"Father Lavigny," she said. "I *was* right. I've always thought there was something queer about him. He said things to me once . . . I suppose he's mad. . . ." She paused and then said, "I'll be quiet. But I *must* leave this place. Joseph and I can go in and sleep at the Rest House."

"Patience, madame," said Poirot. "I will explain everything."

Captain Maitland was looking at him curiously.

"Do you consider you've definitely got the hang of this business?" he demanded.

Poirot bowed.

It was a most theatrical bow. I think it rather annoyed Captain Maitland.

"Well," he barked. "Out with it, man."

But that wasn't the way Hercule Poirot did things. I saw perfectly well that he meant to make a song and dance of it. I wondered if he really *did* know the truth, or if he was just showing off.

He turned to Dr. Reilly.

"Will you be so good, Dr. Reilly, as to summon the others?"

Dr. Reilly jumped up and went off obligingly. In a minute or two the other members of the expedition began to file into the room.

First Reiter and Emmott. Then Bill Coleman. Then Richard Carey and finally Mr. Mercado.

Poor man, he really looked like death. I suppose he was mortally afraid that he'd get hauled over the coals for carelessness in leaving dangerous chemicals about.

Every one seated themselves round the table very much as we had done on the day M. Poirot arrived. Both Bill Coleman and David Emmott hesitated before they sat down, glancing towards Sheila Reilly. She had her back to them and was standing looking out of the window.

"Chair, Sheila?" said Bill.

David Emmott said in his low pleasant drawl, "Won't you sit down?"

She turned then and stood for a minute looking at them. Each was indicating a chair, pushing it forward. I wondered whose chair she would accept.

In the end she accepted neither.

"I'll sit here," she said brusquely. And she sat down on the edge of a table quite close to the window.

"That is," she added, "if Captain Maitland doesn't mind my staying?"

I'm not quite sure what Captain Maitland would have said. Poirot forestalled him.

"Stay by all means, mademoiselle," he said. "It is, indeed, necessary that you should."

She raised her eyebrows.

"Necessary?"

"That is the word I used, mademoiselle. There are some questions I shall have to ask you."

Again her eyebrows went up but she said nothing further. She turned her face to the window as though determined to ignore what went on in the room behind her.

"And now," said Captain Maitland, "perhaps we shall get at the truth!"

He spoke rather impatiently. He was essentially a man of action. At this very moment I feel sure that he was fretting to be out and doing things—directing the search for Father Lavigny's body, or alternatively sending out parties for his capture and arrest.

He looked at Poirot with something akin to dislike.

"If the beggar's got anything to say, why doesn't he say it?"

I could see the words on the tip of his tongue.

Poirot gave a slow appraising glance at us all, then rose to his feet.

I don't know what I expected him to say—something dramatic certainly. He was that kind of person.

But I certainly didn't expect him to start off with a phrase in Arabic.

Yet that is what happened. He said the words slowly and solemnly—and really quite religiously, if you know what I mean.

"Bismillahi ar rahman ar rahim."

And then he gave the translation in English.

"In the name of Allah, the Merciful, the Compassionate."

Chapter 27
Beginning of a Journey

"Bismillahi ar rahman ar rahim. That is the Arab phrase used before starting out on a journey. *Eh bien*, we too, start on a journey. A journey into the past. A journey into the strange places of the human soul."

I don't think that up till that moment I'd ever felt any of the so-called "glamour of the East." Frankly, what had struck me was the *mess* everywhere. But suddenly, with M. Poirot's words, a queer sort of vision seemed to grow up before my eyes. I thought of words like Samarkand and Ispahan—and of merchants with long beards—and kneeling camels—and staggering porters carrying great bales on their backs held by a rope round the forehead—and women with henna-stained hair and tattooed faces kneeling by the Tigris and washing clothes, and I heard their queer, wailing chants and the far-off groaning of the water-wheel. . . .

They were mostly things I'd seen and heard and thought nothing much of. But now, somehow they seemed *different*—like a piece of fusty old stuff you take into the light and suddenly see the rich colours of an old embroidery. . . .

Then I looked round the room we were sitting in and I got a queer feeling that what M. Poirot said was true—we *were* all starting on a journey. We were here together now, but we were all going our different ways.

And I looked at every one as though, in a sort of way, I were seeing them for the first time—*and* for the last time—which sounds stupid, but it was what I felt all the same.

Mr. Mercado was twisting his fingers nervously—his queer light eyes with their dilated pupils were staring at Poirot. Mrs. Mercado was looking at her husband. She had a strange watchful look like a tigress waiting to spring. Dr. Leidner seemed to have shrunk in some curious fashion. This last blow had just crumpled him up. You might almost say he wasn't in the room at all. He was somewhere far away in a place of his own. Mr. Coleman was looking straight at Poirot. His mouth was slightly open and his eyes protruded. He looked almost idiotic. Mr. Emmott was looking down at his feet and I couldn't see his face properly. Mr. Reiter looked bewildered. His mouth was pushed out in a pout and that made him look more like a nice clean pig then ever. Miss Reilly was looking steadily out of the window. I don't know what she was thinking or feeling. Then I looked at Mr. Carey, and somehow his face hurt me and I looked away. There we were, all of us. And somehow I felt that when M. Poirot had finished we'd all be somewhere quite different. . . .

It was a queer feeling. . . .

Poirot's voice went quietly on. It was like a river running evenly between its banks . . . running to the sea. . . .

"From the very beginning, I have felt that to understand this case one must seek not for external signs or clues, but for the truer clues of the clash of personalities and the secrets of the heart.

"And I may say that though I have now arrived at what I believe to be the true solution of the case. *I have no material proof of it.* I *know* it is so, because it *must* be so, because *in no other way* can every single fact fit into its ordered and recognized place.

"And that, to my mind, is the most satisfying solution there can be."

He paused and then went on:

"I will start my journey at the moment when I myself was brought into the case—when I had it presented to me as an accomplished happening. Now, every case, in my opinion, has a definite *shape* and *form*. The pattern of this case, to my mind, all revolved round the personality of Mrs. Leidner. Until I knew *exactly what kind of a woman Mrs. Leidner was* I should not be able to know why she was murdered and who murdered her.

"That, then, was my starting point—the personality of Mrs. Leidner.

"There was also one other psychological point of interest—the curious state of tension described as existing amongst the members of the expedition. This was attested to by several different witnesses—some of them outsiders—and I made a note that although hardly a starting point, it should nevertheless be borne in mind during my investigations.

"The accepted idea seemed to be that it was directly the result of Mrs. Leidner's influence on the members of the expedition, but for reasons which I will outline to you later this did not seem to me entirely acceptable.

"To start with, as I say, I concentrated solely and entirely on the personality of Mrs. Leidner. I had various means of assessing that personality. There were the reactions she produced in a number of people, all varying widely in character and temperament, and there was what I could glean by my own observation. The scope of the latter was naturally limited. But I *did* learn certain facts.

"Mrs. Leidner's tastes were simple and even on the austere side. She was clearly not a luxurious woman. On the other hand, some embroidery she had been doing was of an extreme fineness and beauty. That indicated a woman of fastidious and artistic taste. From the observation of the books in her bedroom I formed a further estimate. She had brains, and I also fancied that she was, essentially, an egoist.

"It had been suggested to me that Mrs. Leidner was a woman whose main preoccupation was to attract the opposite sex—that she was, in fact, a sensual woman. This I did not believe to be the case.

"In her bedroom I noticed the following books on a shelf: *Who Were the Greeks? Introduction to Relativity, Life of Lady Hester Stanhope, Back to Methuselah, Linda Condon, Crewe Train.*

"She had, to begin with, an interest in culture and in modern science—that is, a distinct intellectual side. Of the novels *Linda Condon*, and in a lesser degree *Crewe Train*, seemed to show that Mrs. Leidner had a sympathy and interest in the independent woman—unencumbered or entrapped by man. She was also obviously interested by the personality of Lady Hester Stanhope. *Linda Condon* is an exquisite study of the worship of her own beauty by a woman. *Crewe Train* is a study of a passionate individualist. *Back to Methuselah* is in sympathy with the intellectual rather than the emotional attitude to life. I felt that I was beginning to understand the dead woman.

"I next studied the reactions of those who

had formed Mrs. Leidner's immediate circle—and my picture of the dead woman
grew more and more complete.

"It was quite clear to me from the accounts of Dr. Reilly and others that Mrs.
Leidner was one of those women who are
endowed by Nature not only with beauty
but with the kind of calamitous magic which
sometimes accompanies beauty and can,
indeed, exist independently of it. Such
women usually leave a trail of violent hap-
penings behind them. They bring disaster—
sometimes on others—sometimes on themselves.

"I was convinced that Mrs. Leidner was a
woman who essentially worshipped *herself*
and who enjoyed more than anything else
the sense of *power*. Wherever she was, she
must be the centre of the universe. And
every one round her, man or woman, had
got to acknowledge her sway. With some
people that was easy. Nurse Leatheran, for
instance, a generous-natured woman with a
romantic imagination, was captured instantly and gave in ungrudging manner full
appreciation. But there was a second way in
which Mrs. Leidner exercised her sway—
the way of fear. Where conquest was too

easy she indulged a more cruel side to her nature—but I wish to reiterate emphatically that it was not what you might call *conscious* cruelty. It was as natural and unthinking as is the conduct of a cat with a mouse. Where consciousness came in, she was essentially kind and would often go out of her way to do kind and thoughtful actions for other people.

"Now of course the first and most important problem to solve was the problem of the anonymous letters. Who had written them and why? I asked myself: Had Mrs. Leidner written them *herself?*

"To answer this problem it was necessary to go back a long way—to go back, in fact, to the date of Mrs. Leidner's first marriage. It is here we start on our journey proper. The journey of Mrs. Leidner's life.

"First of all we must realize that the Louise Leidner of all those years ago is essentially the same Louise Leidner of the present time.

"She was young then, of remarkable beauty—that same haunting beauty that affects a man's spirit and senses as no mere material beauty can—and she was already essentially an egoist.

"Such women naturally revolt from the idea of marriage. They may be attracted by men, but they prefer to belong to themselves. They are truly *La Belle Dame sans Merci* of the legend. Nevertheless Mrs. Leidner *did* marry—and we can assume, I think, that her husband must have been a man of a certain force of character.

"Then the revelation of his traitorous activities occurs and Mrs. Leidner acts in the way she told Nurse Leatheran. She gave information to the Government.

"Now I submit that there was a psychological significance in her action. She told Nurse Leatheran that she was a very patriotic idealistic girl and that that feeling was the cause of her action. But it is a well-known fact that we all tend to deceive ourselves as to the motives for our own actions. Instinctively we select the best-sounding motive! Mrs. Leidner may have believed herself that it was patriotism that inspired her action, but I believe myself that it was really the outcome of an unacknowledged desire to get rid of her husband! She disliked domination—she disliked the feeling of belonging to some one else—in fact she disliked playing second fiddle. She took a patriotic way of regaining her freedom.

"But underneath her consciousness was a gnawing sense of guilt which was to play its part in her future destiny.

"We now come directly to the question of the letters. Mrs. Leidner was highly attractive to the male sex. On several occasions she was attracted by them—but in each case a threatening letter played its part and the affair came to nothing.

"Who wrote those letters? Frederick Bosner or his brother William or *Mrs. Leidner herself?*

"There is a perfectly good case for either theory. It seems clear to me that Mrs. Leidner was one of those women who do inspire devouring devotions in men, the type of devotion which can become an obsession. I find it quite possible to believe in a Frederick Bosner to whom Louise, his wife, mattered more than anything in the world! She had betrayed him once and he dared not approach her openly, but he was determined at least that she should be his or no one's. He preferred her death to her belonging to another man.

"On the other hand, if Mrs. Leidner had,

deep down, a dislike of entering into the marriage bond, it is possible that she took this way of extricating herself from difficult positions. She was a huntress who, the prey once attained, had no further use for it! Craving drama in her life, she invented a highly satisfactory drama—a resurrected husband forbidding the banns! It satisfied her deepest instincts. It made her a romantic figure, a tragic heroine, and it enabled her not to marry again.

"This state of affairs continued over a number of years. Every time there was any likelihood of marriage—a threatening letter arrived.

"But now we come to a really interesting point. Dr. Leidner came upon the scene— and no forbidding letter arrived! Nothing stood in the way of her becoming Mrs. Leidner. Not until *after* her marriage did a letter arrive.

"At once we ask ourselves—why?

"Let us take each theory in turn.

"*If* Mrs. Leidner wrote the letters herself the problem is easily explained. Mrs. Leidner really *wanted* to marry Dr. Leidner. And so she *did* marry him. But in that case, *why did she write herself a letter afterwards?*

Was her craving for drama too strong to be suppressed? And why only those two letters? After that no other letter was received until a year and a half later.

"Now take the other theory, that the letters were written by her first husband, Frederick Bosner (or his brother). Why did the threatening letter arrive *after* the marriage? Presumably Frederick could not have *wanted* her to marry Leidner. Why, then, did he not stop the marriage? He had done so successfully on former occasions. And why, *having waited till the marriage had taken place*, did he then resume his threats?

"The answer, an unsatisfactory one, is that he was somehow or other unable to protest sooner. He may have been in prison or he may have been abroad.

"There is next the attempted gas poisoning to consider. It seems extremely unlikely that it was brought about by an outside agency. The likely persons to have staged it were Dr. and Mrs. Leidner themselves. There seems no conceivable reason why *Dr.* Leidner should do such a thing, so we are brought to the conclusion that *Mrs.* Leidner planned and carried it out herself.

"Why? More drama?

"After that Dr. and Mrs. Leidner go abroad and for eighteen months they lead a happy, peaceful life with no threats of death to disturb it. They put that down to having successfully covered their traces, but such an explanation is quite absurd. In these days going abroad is quite inadequate for that purpose. And especially was that so in the case of the Leidners. He was the director of a museum expedition. By inquiry at the museum, Frederick Bosner could at once have obtained his correct address. Even granting that he was in too reduced circumstances to pursue the couple himself, there would be no bar to his continuing his threatening letters. And it seems to me that a man with his obsession would certainly have done so.

"Instead nothing is heard of him until nearly two years later when the letters are resumed.

"*Why* were the letters resumed?

"A very difficult question—most easily answered by saying that Mrs. Leidner was bored and wanted more drama. But I was not quite satisfied with that. This particular form of drama seemed to me a shade too vulgar and too crude to accord well with her fastidious personality.

"The only thing to do was to keep an open mind on the question.

"There were three definite possibilities: (1) the letters were written by Mrs. Leidner herself; (2) they were written by Frederick Bosner (or young William Bosner); (3) they might have been written *originally* by either Mrs. Leidner or her first husband, but they were now *forgeries*—that is, they were being written by a *third* person who was aware of the earlier letters.

"I now come to direct consideration of Mrs. Leidner's entourage.

"I examined first the actual opportunities that each member of the staff had had for committing the murder.

"Roughly, on the face of it, *any one* might have committed it (as far as opportunity went), with the exception of three persons.

"Dr. Leidner, by overwhelming testimony, had never left the roof. Mr. Carey was on duty at the mound. Mr. Coleman was in Hassanieh.

"But those alibis, my friends, were not *quite* as good as they looked. I except Dr. Leidner's. There is absolutely no doubt that he was on the roof all the time and did not come down until quite an hour and a quarter after the murder had happened.

"But was it *quite* certain that Mr. Carey was on the mound all the time?

"And had Mr. Coleman *actually been in Hassanieh* at the time the murder took place?"

Bill Coleman reddened, opened his mouth, shut it and looked round uneasily.

Mr. Carey's expression did not change.

Poirot went on smoothly.

"I also considered one other person who, I satisfied myself, would be perfectly capable of committing murder *if she felt strongly enough*. Miss Reilly has courage and brains and a certain quality of ruthlessness. When Miss Reilly was speaking to me on the subject of the dead woman, I said to her, jokingly, that I hoped she had an alibi. I think Miss Reilly was conscious then that she had had in her heart the desire, at least, to kill. At any rate she immediately uttered a very silly and purposeless lie. She said she had been playing tennis on that afternoon. The next day I learned from a casual conversation with Miss Johnson that far from playing tennis, Miss Reilly *had actually been near this house at the time of the murder*. It occurred to me that Miss Reilly, if not guilty of the crime, might be able to tell me something useful."

He stopped and then said quietly:

"Will you tell us, Miss Reilly, what you *did* see that afternoon?"

The girl did not answer at once. She still looked out of the window without turning her head, and when she spoke it was in a detached and measured voice.

"I rode out to the dig after lunch. It must have been about a quarter to two when I got there."

"Did you find any of your friends on the dig?"

"No, there seemed to be no one there but the Arab foreman."

"You did not see Mr. Carey?"

"No."

"Curious," said Poirot. "No more did M. Verrier when he went there that same afternoon."

He looked invitingly at Carey, but the latter neither moved nor spoke.

"Have you any explanation, Mr. Carey?"

"I went for a walk. There was nothing of interest turning up."

"In which direction did you go for a walk?"

"Down by the river."

"Not back towards the house?"

"No."

"I suppose," said Miss Reilly, "that you were waiting for some one who didn't come."

He looked at her but didn't answer.

Poirot did not press the point. He spoke once more to the girl.

"Did you see anything else, mademoiselle?"

"Yes. I was not far from the expedition house when I noticed the expedition lorry drawn up in a wadi. I thought it was rather queer. Then I saw Mr. Coleman. He was walking along with his head down as though he were searching for something."

"Look here," burst out Mr. Coleman. "I—"

Poirot stopped him with an authoritative gesture.

"Wait. Did you speak to him, Miss Reilly?"

"No, I didn't."

"Why?"

The girl said slowly:

"Because, from time to time, he started and looked round with an extraordinary furtive look. It—gave me an unpleasant feeling. I turned my horse's head and rode away. I don't think he saw me. I was not very near and he was absorbed in what he was doing."

"Look here," Mr. Coleman was not to be hushed any longer. "I've got a perfectly good explanation for what—I admit—looks a bit fishy. As a matter of fact, the day before I had slipped a jolly fine cylinder seal into my coat pocket instead of putting it in the antika-room—forgot all about it. And then I discovered I'd been and lost it out of my pocket—dropped it somewhere. I didn't want to get into a row about it so I decided I'd have a jolly good search on the quiet. I was pretty sure I'd dropped it on the way to or from the dig. I rushed over my business in Hassanieh. Sent a walad to do some of the shopping and got back early. I stuck the bus where it wouldn't show and had a jolly good hunt for over an hour. And didn't find the damn thing at that! Then I got into the bus and drove on to the house. Naturally, everyone thought I'd just got back."

"And you did not undeceive them?" asked Poirot sweetly.

"Well, that was pretty natural under the circumstances, don't you think?"

"I hardly agree," said Poirot.

"Oh, come now—don't go looking for trouble—that's *my motto!* But you can't fasten anything on me. I never went into the courtyard, and you can't find any one who'll say I did."

"That, of course, has been the difficulty," said Poirot. "The evidence of the servants that *no one entered the courtyard from outside*. But it occurred to me, upon reflection, that that was really *not* what they had said. They had sworn that *no stranger* had entered the premises. They had not been asked *if a member of the expedition* had done so."

"Well, you ask them," said Coleman. "I'll eat my hat if they saw me or Carey either."

"Ah! but that raises rather an interesting question. They would notice *a stranger* undoubtedly—but would they have even *noticed* a member of the expedition? The members of the staff are passing in and out all day. The servants would hardly notice their going and coming. It is possible, I think, that either Mr. Carey or Mr. Coleman *might* have entered and the servants' minds would have no remembrance of such an event."

"Bunkum!" said Mr. Coleman.

Poirot went on calmly:

"Of the two, I think Mr. Carey was the least likely to be noticed going or coming. Mr. Coleman had started to Hassanieh in the car that morning and he would be expected to return in it. His arrival on foot would therefore be noticeable."

"Of course it would!" said Coleman.

Richard Carey raised his head. His deep-blue eyes looked straight at Poirot.

"Are you accusing me of murder, M. Poirot?" he asked.

His manner was quite quiet but his voice had a dangerous undertone.

Poirot bowed to him.

"As yet I am only taking you all on a journey—my journey towards the truth. I had now established one fact—that all the members of the expedition staff, and also Nurse Leatheran, could in actual *fact* have committed the murder. That there was very little likelihood of some of them having committed it was a secondary matter.

"I had examined *means* and *opportunity*. I next passed to *motive*. I discovered that *one and all of you could be credited with a motive!"*

"Oh! M. Poirot," I cried. "Not *me!* Why, I was a stranger. I'd only just come."

"Eh bien, ma sœur, and was not that *just what Mrs. Leidner had been fearing? A stranger* from *outside?"*

"But—but—Why, Dr. Reilly knew all about me! He suggested my coming!"

"How much did he really know about you? *Mostly what you yourself had told him.* Impostors have passed themselves off as hospital nurses before now."

"You can write to St. Christopher's," I began.

"For the moment will you silence yourself. Impossible to proceed while you conduct this argument. I do not say I suspect you *now.* All I say is that, keeping the open mind, you might quite easily be some one other than you pretended to be. There are many successful female impersonators, you know. Young William Bosner might be something of that kind."

I was about to give him a further piece of my mind. Female impersonator indeed! But he raised his voice and hurried on with such an air of determination that I thought better of it.

"I am going now to be frank—brutally so. It is necessary. I am going to lay bare the underlying structure of this place.

"I examined and considered every single soul here. To begin with Dr. Leidner, I soon convinced myself that his love for his wife was the mainspring of his existence. He was a man torn and ravaged with grief. Nurse Leatheran I have already mentioned. If she were a female impersonator she was a most amazingly successful one, and I inclined to the belief that she was exactly what she said she was—a thoroughly competent hospital nurse."

"Thank you for nothing," I interposed.

"My attention was immediately attracted towards Mr. and Mrs. Mercado, who were both of them clearly in a state of great agitation and unrest. I considered first Mrs. Mercado. Was she capable of murder and if so for what reasons?

"Mrs. Mercado's physique was frail. At first sight it did not seem possible that she could have had the physical strength to strike down a woman like Mrs. Leidner with a heavy stone implement. If, however, Mrs.

Leidner had been on her knees at the time, the thing would at least be *physically possible*. There are ways in which one woman can induce another to go down on her knees. Oh! not emotional ways! For instance, a woman might be turning up the hem of a skirt and ask another woman to put in the pins for her. The second woman would kneel on the ground quite unsuspectingly.

"But the motive? Nurse Leatheran had told me of the angry glances she had seen Mrs. Mercado direct at Mrs. Leidner. Mr. Mercado had evidently succumbed easily to Mrs. Leidner's spell. But I did not think the solution was to be found in mere jealousy. I was sure Mrs. Leidner was not in the least interested really in Mr. Mercado—and doubtless Mrs. Mercado was aware of the fact. She might be furious with her for the moment, but for *murder* there would have to be greater provocation. But Mrs. Mercado was essentially a fiercely maternal type. From the way she looked at her husband I realized, not only that she loved him, but that she would fight for him tooth and nail—and more than that—*that she envisaged the possibility of having to do so*.

She was constantly on her guard and uneasy. The uneasiness was for him—not for herself. And when I studied Mr. Mercado I could make a fairly easy guess at what the trouble was. I took means to assure myself of the truth of my guess. Mr. Mercado was a drug addict—in an advanced stage of the craving.

"Now I need probably not tell you all that the taking of drugs over a long period has the result of considerably blunting the moral sense.

"Under the influence of drugs a man commits actions that he would not have dreamed of committing a few years earlier before he began the practice. In some cases a man has committed murder—and it has been difficult to say whether he was wholly responsible for his actions or not. The law of different countries varies slightly on that point. The chief characteristic of the drug-fiend criminal is overweening confidence in his own cleverness.

"I thought it possible that there was some discreditable incident, perhaps a criminal incident, in Mr. Mercado's past which his wife had somehow or other succeeded in hushing up. Nevertheless his career hung on a thread. If anything of this past incident were bruited about, Mr. Mercado would be ruined. His wife was always on the watch. But there was Mrs. Leidner to be reckoned with. She had a sharp intelligence and a love of power. She might even induce the wretched man to confide in her. It would just have suited her peculiar temperament to feel she knew a secret which she could reveal at any minute with disastrous effects.

"Here, then, was a possible motive for murder on the part of the Mercados. To protect her mate, Mrs. Mercado, I felt sure, would stick at nothing! Both she and her husband had had the opportunity—during that ten minutes when the courtyard was empty."

Mrs. Mercado cried out, "It's not *true!*"

Poirot paid no attention.

"I next considered Miss Johnson. Was *she* capable of murder?

"I thought she was. She was a person of strong will and iron self-control. Such people are constantly repressing themselves— and one day the dam bursts! But if Miss Johnson had committed the crime it could only be for some reason connected with Dr.

Leidner. If in any way she felt convinced that Mrs. Leidner was spoiling her husband's life, then the deep unacknowledged jealousy far down in her would leap at the chance of a plausible motive and give itself rein.

"Yes, Miss Johnson was distinctly a possibility.

"Then there were the three young men.

"First Carl Reiter. If, by any chance, one of the expedition staff was William Bosner, then Reiter was by far the most likely person. But if he *was* William Bosner, then he was certainly a most accomplished actor! If he were merely *himself*, had he any reason for murder?

"Regarded from Mrs. Leidner's point of view, Carl Reiter was far too easy a victim for good sport. He was prepared to fall on his face and worship immediately. Mrs. Leidner despised undiscriminating adoration—and the door-mat attitude nearly always brings out the worst side of a woman. In her treatment of Carl Reiter Mrs. Leidner displayed really deliberate cruelty. She inserted a gibe here—a prick there. She made the poor young man's life a hell to him."

Poirot broke off suddenly and addressed

the young man in a personal, highly confidential manner.

"*Mon ami*, let this be a lesson to you. You are a *man*. Behave, then, like a *man!* It is against Nature for a man to grovel. Women and Nature have almost exactly the same reactions! Remember it is better to take the largest plate within reach and fling it at a woman's head than it is to wriggle like a worm whenever she looks at you!"

He dropped his private manner and reverted to his lecture style.

"Could Carl Reiter have been goaded to such a pitch of torment that he turned on his tormentor and killed her? Suffering does queer things to a man. I could not be *sure* that it was *not so!*

"Next, William Coleman. His behaviour, as reported by Miss Reilly, is certainly suspicious. If he was the criminal it could only be because his cheerful personality concealed the hidden one of William Bosner. I do not think William Coleman, as William Coleman, has the temperament of a murderer. His faults might lie in another direction. Ah! perhaps Nurse Leatheran can guess what they would be?"

How *did* the man do it? I'm sure I didn't look as though I was thinking anything at all.

"It's nothing really," I said, hesitating. "Only if it's to be all truth, Mr. Coleman *did* say once himself that he would have made a good forger."

"A good point," said Poirot. "Therefore if he had come across some of the old threatening letters, he could have copied them without difficulty."

"Oy, oy, oy!" called out Mr. Coleman. "This is what they call a frame-up."

Poirot swept on.

"As to his being or not being William Bosner such a matter is difficult of verification. But Mr. Coleman has spoken of a *guardian*—not of a father—and there is nothing definitely to veto the idea."

"Tommyrot," said Mr. Coleman. "Why all of you listen to this chap beats me."

"Of the three young men there remains Mr. Emmott," went on Poirot. "He again might be a possible shield for the identity of William Bosner. Whatever *personal* reasons he might have for the removal of Mrs. Leidner I soon realized that I should have no means of learning them from him. He could keep his own counsel remarkably well, and there was not the least chance of provoking him nor of tricking him into betraying himself on any point. Of all the expedition he seemed to be the best and most dispassionate judge of Mrs. Leidner's personality. I think that he always knew her for exactly what she was—but what impression her personality made on him I was unable to discover. I fancy that Mrs. Leidner herself must have been provoked and angered by his attitude.

"I may say that of all the expedition, *as far as character and capability were concerned*, Mr. Emmott seemed to me the most fitted to bring a clever and well-timed crime off satisfactorily."

For the first time Mr. Emmott raised his eyes from the toes of his boots.

"Thank you," he said.

There seemed to be just a trace of amusement in his voice.

"The last two people on my list were Richard Carey and Father Lavigny.

"According to the testimony of Nurse Leatheran and others, Mr. Carey and Mrs. Leidner disliked each other. They were both civil with an effort. Another person, Miss Reilly, propounded a totally different theory to account for their attitude of frigid politeness.

"I soon had very little doubt that Miss Reilly's explanation was the correct one. I acquired my certitude by the simple expedient of provoking Mr. Carey into reckless and unguarded speech. It was not difficult. As I soon saw, he was in a state of high nervous tension. In fact he was—and is—very near a complete nervous breakdown. A man who is suffering up to the limit of his capacity can seldom put up much of a fight.

"Mr. Carey's barriers came down almost immediately. He told me, with a sincerity that I did not for a moment doubt, that he hated Mrs. Leidner.

"And he was undoubtedly speaking the truth. He *did* hate Mrs. Leidner. But *why* did he hate her?

"I have spoken of women who have calamitous magic. But men have that magic too. There are men who are able without the least effort to attract women. What they call in these days *le sex appeal!* Mr. Carey had this quality very strongly. He was to begin with devoted to his friend and employer, and indifferent to his employer's wife. That did not suit Mrs. Leidner. She *must* dominate—and she set herself out to capture Richard Carey. But here, I believe, something entirely unforeseen took place. She herself, for perhaps the first time in her life, fell a victim to an over-mastering passion. She fell in love—really in love—with Richard Carey.

"And he—was unable to resist her. Here is the truth of the terrible state of nervous tension that he has been enduring. He has been a man torn by two opposing passions. He loved Louise Leidner—yes, but he also hated her. He hated her for undermining his loyalty to his friend. There is no hatred so great as that of a man who has been made to love a woman against his will.

"I had here all the motive that I needed. I was convinced that *at certain moments* the most natural thing for Richard Carey to do would have been to strike with all the force of his arm at the beautiful face that had cast a spell over him.

"All along I had felt sure that the murder of Louise Leidner was a *crime passionnel*. In Mr. Carey I had found an ideal murderer for that type of crime.

"There remains one other candidate for the title of murderer—Father Lavigny. My attention was attracted to the good Father straightaway by a certain discrepancy between his description of the strange man who had been seen peering in at the window and the one given by Nurse Leatheran. In all accounts given by different witnesses there is usually *some* discrepancy, but this was absolutely glaring. Moreover, Father Lavigny insisted on a certain characteristic—a squint—which ought to make identification much easier.

"But very soon it became apparent that *while Nurse Leatheran's description was substantially accurate*, Father Lavigny's was *nothing of the kind*. It looked almost as though Father Lavigny was deliberately misleading us—as though he did *not want the man caught*.

"But in that case *he must know something about this curious person*. He had been seen talking to the man but we had only his word for what they had been talking about.

"What had the Iraqi been doing when Nurse Leatheran and Mrs. Leidner saw him? Trying to peer through the window— Mrs. Leidner's window, so they thought, but I realized when I went and stood where they had been, that it might equally have been *the antika-room window*.

"The night after that an alarm was given. Some one was in the antika-room. Nothing proved to have been taken, however. The interesting point to me is that when Dr. Leidner got there he found *Father Lavigny there before him*. Father Lavigny tells his story of seeing a light. *But again we have only his word for it*.

"I begin to get curious about Father Lavigny. The other day when I make the suggestion that Father Lavigny may be Frederick Bosner Dr. Leidner pooh-poohs the suggestion. He says Father Lavigny is a well-known man. I advance the supposition that Frederick Bosner, who has had nearly twenty years to make a career for himself, under a new name, may very possibly *be* a well-known man by this time! All the same, I do not think that he has spent the intervening time in a religious community. A very much simpler solution presents itself.

"Did any one at the expedition know Father Lavigny by sight before he came? Apparently not. Why then should not it be *some one impersonating the good Father?* I found out that a telegram had been sent to Carthage on the sudden illness of Dr. Byrd, who was to have accompanied the expedition. To intercept a telegram, what could be easier? As to the work, there was no other epigraphist attached to the expedition. With a smattering of knowledge a clever man *might* bluff his way through. There had been very few tablets and inscriptions so far, and already I gathered that Father Lavigny's pronouncements had been felt to be somewhat unusual.

"It looked very much as though Father Lavigny were an *impostor*.

"But was he Frederick Bosner?

"Somehow affairs did not seem to be shaping themselves that way. The truth seemed likely to lie in quite a different direction.

"I had a lengthy conversation with Father Lavigny. I am a practising Catholic and I know many priests and members of religious communities. Father Lavigny struck me as not ringing quite true to his rôle. But he struck me, on the other hand, as familiar in quite a different capacity. I *had* met men of his type quite frequently—but they were not members of a religious community. Far from it!

"I began to send off telegrams.

"And then, unwittingly, Nurse Leatheran gave me a valuable clue. We were examining the gold ornaments in the antika-room and she mentioned a trace of wax having been found adhering to a gold cup. Me, I say, 'Wax?' and Father Lavigny, he said 'Wax?' and his tone was enough! I knew in a flash what he was doing here."

Poirot paused and addressed himself directly to Dr. Leidner.

"I regret to tell you, monsieur, that the gold cup in the antika-room, the gold dagger, the hair ornaments and several other things *are not the genuine articles found by you*. They are very clever electrotypes. Father Lavigny, I have just learned by this last answer to my telegrams, is none other than Raoul Menier, one of the cleverest thieves known to the French police. He specializes in thefts from museums of *objets d'art* and such like. Associated with him is Ali Yusuf, a semi-Turk, who is a first-class working jeweller. Our first knowledge of Menier was when certain objects in the Louvre were found not to be genuine—in every case it was discovered that a distinguished archæologist *not known pre-viously by sight to the director* had recently had the handling of the spurious articles when paying a visit to the Louvre. On inquiry all these distinguished gentlemen denied having paid a visit to the Louvre at the times stated!

"I have learned that Menier was in Tunis preparing the way for a theft from the Holy Fathers when your telegram arrived. Father Lavigny, who was in ill-health, was forced to refuse, but Menier managed to get hold of the telegram and substitute one of accep-tance. He was quite safe in doing so. Even if the monks should read in some paper (in itself an unlikely thing) that Father Lavigny was in Iraq they would only think that the newspapers had got hold of a half truth as so often happens.

"Menier and his accomplice arrived. The latter is seen when he is reconnoitering the antika-room from outside. The plan is for Father Lavigny to take wax impressions. Ali then makes clever duplicates. There are al-ways certain collectors who are willing to pay a good price for genuine antiques and will ask no embarrassing questions. Father Lavigny will effect the substitution of the fake for the genuine article—preferably at night.

"And that is doubtless what he was doing when Mrs. Leidner heard him and gave the alarm. What can he do? He hurriedly makes up a story of having seen a light in the antika-room.

"That 'went down,' as you say, very well. But Mrs. Leidner was no fool. She may have remembered the trace of wax she had noticed and then put two and two together. And if she did, what will she do then? Would it not be *dans son caractère* to do nothing at once, but to enjoy herself by letting hints slip to the discomfiture of Father Lavigny. She will let him see that she suspects—but not that she *knows*. It is, perhaps, a dangerous game, but she enjoys a dangerous game.

"And perhaps she plays that game too long. Father Lavigny sees the truth, and strikes before she realizes what he means to do.

"Father Lavigny is Raoul Menier—a thief. Is he also—a *murderer*?"

Poirot paced the room. He took out a handkerchief, wiped his forehead and went on:

"That was my position this morning. There were eight distinct possibilities and I did not know which of these possibilities was the right one. I still did not know *who was the murderer*.

"But murder is a habit. The man or woman who kills once will kill again.

"And by the second murder, the murderer was delivered into my hands.

"All along it was ever present in the back of my mind that some one of these people might have knowledge that they had kept back—knowledge incriminating the murderer.

"If so, that person would be in danger.

"My solicitude was mainly on account of Nurse Leatheran. She had an energetic personality and a brisk inquisitive mind. I was terrified of her finding out more than it was safe for her to know.

"As you all know, a second murder did take place. But the victim was not Nurse Leatheran—it was Miss Johnson.

"I like to think that I should have reached the correct solution anyway by pure reasoning, but it is certain that Miss Johnson's murder helped me to it much quicker.

"To begin with, one suspect was eliminated—Miss Johnson herself—for I did not for a moment entertain the theory of suicide.

"Let us examine now the facts of this second murder.

"Fact one: On Sunday evening Nurse Leatheran finds Miss Johnson in tears, and that same evening Miss Johnson burns a fragment of a letter which nurse believes to be in the same handwriting as that of the anonymous letters.

"Fact two: The evening before her death Miss Johnson is found by Nurse Leatheran standing on the roof in a state that Nurse describes as one of incredulous horror. When nurse questions her she says, 'I've seen how some one could come in from outside—and no one would ever guess.' She won't say any more. Father Lavigny is crossing the courtyard and Mr. Reiter is at the door of the photographic room.

"Fact three: Miss Johnson is found dying. The only words she can manage to articulate are 'the window—the window—'

"Those are the facts, and these are the problems with which we are faced:

"What is the truth of the letters?

"What did Miss Johnson see from the roof?

"What did she mean by 'the window—the window'?

"*Eh bien*, let us take the second problem first as the easiest of solution. I went up with Nurse Leatheran and I stood where Miss Johnson had stood. From there she could see the courtyard and the archway and the north side of the building and two members of the staff. Had her words anything to do with either Mr. Reiter or Father Lavigny?

"Almost at once a possible explanation leaped to my brain. If a stranger came in from *outside* he could only do so in *disguise*. And there was only *one* person whose general appearance lent itself to such an impersonation. Father Lavigny! With a sun helmet, sun glasses, black beard and a monk's long woollen robe, a stranger could pass in without the servants *realizing* that a stranger had entered.

"Was *that* Miss Johnson's meaning? Or had she gone further? Did she realize that Father Lavigny's whole *personality* was a disguise. That he was some one other than he pretended to be?

"Knowing what I did know about Father

Lavigny I was inclined to call the mystery solved. Raoul Menier was the murderer. He had killed Mrs. Leidner to silence her before she could give him away. Now *another person lets him see that she has penetrated his secret*. She, too, must be removed.

"And so everything is explained! The second murder. Father Lavigny's flight—minus robe and beard. (He and his friend are doubtless careering through Syria with excellent passports as two commercial travellers.) His action in placing the blood-stained quern under Miss Johnson's bed.

"As I say, I was almost satisfied—but not quite. For the perfect solution must explain *everything*—and this does not do so.

"It does not explain, for instance, why Miss Johnson should say 'the window—the window,' as she was dying. It does not explain her fit of weeping over the letter. It does not explain her mental attitude on the roof—her incredulous horror and her refusal to tell Nurse Leatheran what it was that *she now suspected or knew*.

"It was a solution that fitted the *outer* facts, but it did not satisfy the *psychological* requirements.

"And then, as I stood on the roof, going

over in my mind those three points: the letters, the roof, the window, I *saw*—just as Miss Johnson had seen!

"And this time what I saw explained everything!"

Chapter 28
Journey's End

Poirot looked round. Every eye was now fixed upon him. There had been a certain relaxation—a slackening of tension. Now the tension suddenly returned.

There was something coming . . . something . . .

Poirot's voice, quiet and unimpassioned, went on:

"The letters, the roof, 'the window' . . . Yes, everything was explained—everything fell into place.

"I said just now that three men had alibis for the time of the crime. Two of those alibis I have shown to be worthless. I saw now my great—my amazing mistake. The third alibi was worthless too. Not only *could* Dr. Leidner have committed the murder—but I was convinced that he *had* committed it."

There was a silence, a bewildered un-comprehending silence. Dr. Leidner said nothing. He seemed lost in his faraway world still. David Emmott, however, stirred uneasily and spoke.

"I don't know what you mean to imply, M. Poirot. I told you that Dr. Leidner never left the roof until at least a quarter to three. That is the absolute truth. I swear it solemnly. I am not lying. And it would have been quite impossible for him to have done so without my seeing him."

Poirot nodded.

"Oh, I believe you. *Dr. Leidner did not leave the roof*. That is an undisputed fact. But what I saw—and what Miss Johnson had seen—was *that Dr. Leidner could murder his wife from the roof without leaving it*."

We all stared.

"The *window*," cried Poirot. "Her window! That is what I realized—just as Miss Johnson realized it. Her window was directly underneath, on the side away from the courtyard. And Dr. Leidner was alone up there with no one to witness his actions. And those heavy stone querns and grinders were up there all ready to his hand. So simple, so very simple, granted one thing—*that the murderer had the opportunity to move the body before any one else saw it.* . . . Oh, it is beautiful—of an unbelievable simplicity!

"Listen—it went like this:

"Dr. Leidner is on the roof working with the pottery. He calls you up, Mr. Emmott, and while he holds you in talk he notices that, as usually happens, the small boy takes advantage of your absence to leave his work and go outside the courtyard. He keeps you with him ten minutes, then he lets you go and as soon as you are down below shouting to the boy he sets his plan in operation.

"He takes from his pocket the plasticine-smeared mask with which he has already scared his wife on a former occasion and dangles it over the edge of the parapet till it taps on his wife's window.

"That, remember, is the window giving on the countryside facing the opposite direction to the courtyard.

"Mrs. Leidner is lying on her bed half asleep. She is peaceful and happy. Suddenly the mask begins tapping on the window and attracts her attention. But it is not dusk now—it is broad daylight—there is nothing terrifying about it. She recognizes it for what it is—a crude form of trickery! She is not frightened but indignant. She does what any other woman would do in her place. Jumps off the bed, opens the window, passes her head through the bars and turns her face upwards to see who is playing the trick on her.

"Dr. Leidner is waiting. He has in his hands, poised and ready, a heavy quern. At the psychological moment *he drops it*. . . .

"With a faint cry (heard by Miss Johnson) Mrs. Leidner collapses on the rug underneath the window.

"Now there is a hole in this quern, and through that Dr. Leidner had previously passed a cord. He has now only to haul in the cord and bring up the quern. He replaces the latter neatly, blood-stained side down, amongst the other objects of that kind on the roof.

"Then he continues his work for an hour or more till he judges the moment has come for the second act. He descends the stairs, speaks to Mr. Emmott and Nurse Leatheran, crosses the courtyard and enters his wife's room. This is the explanation he himself gives of his movements there.

" '*I saw my wife's body in a heap by the bed. For a moment or two I felt paralyzed as though I couldn't move. Then at last I went and knelt down by her and lifted up her head. I saw she was dead. . . . At last I got up. I felt dazed and as though I were drunk. I managed to get to the door and call out.*'

"A perfectly possible account of the actions of a grief-dazed man. Now listen to what I believe to be the truth. Dr. Leidner enters the room, hurries to the window, and having pulled on a pair of gloves, closes and fastens it, then picks up his wife's body and transports it to a position between the bed and the door. Then he notices a slight stain on the window-side rug. He cannot change it with the other rug, they are a different size, but he does the next best thing. He puts the stained rug in front of the wash-stand and the rug from the wash-stand under the window. *If* the stain is noticed, it will be connected with the *wash-stand—not with the window*—a very important point. There must be no suggestion that the window played any part in the business. Then he comes to the door and acts the part of the overcome husband, and that, I imagine, is not difficult. For he *did* love his wife."

"My good man," cried Dr. Reilly impatiently, "if he loved her, why did he kill her? Where's the motive? Can't you speak, Leidner? Tell him he's mad."

Dr. Leidner neither spoke nor moved.

Poirot said:

"Did I not tell you all along that this was a *crime passionnel*? Why did her first husband, Frederick Bosner, threaten to kill her? Because he loved her. . . . And in the end, you see, he made his boast good. . . .

"Mais oui—mais oui—once I realized that it is Dr. Leidner who did the killing everything falls into place. . . .

"For the second time I recommence my journey from the beginning—Mrs. Leidner's first marriage—the threatening letters—her second marriage. The letters prevented her marrying any other man—but they did not prevent her marrying Dr. Leidner. How simple that is—*if Dr. Leidner is actually Frederick Bosner*.

"Once more let us start our journey—from the point of view this time of young Frederick Bosner.

"To begin with he loves his wife Louise

with an overpowering passion, such as only a woman of her kind can evoke. She betrays him. He is sentenced to death. He escapes. He is involved in a railway accident but he manages to emerge with a second personality—*that of a young Swedish archæologist, Eric Leidner*, whose body is badly disfigured and who will be conveniently buried as Frederick Bosner.

"What is the new Eric Leidner's attitude to the woman who was willing to send him to his death? First and most important, *he still loves her*. He sets to work to build up his new life. He is a man of great ability, his profession is congenial to him and he makes a success of it. *But he never forgets the ruling passion of his life*. He keeps himself informed of his wife's movements. Of one thing he is cold-bloodedly determined (remember Mrs. Leidner's own description of him to Nurse Leatheran—gentle and kind but ruthless), *she shall belong to no other man*. Whenever he judges it necessary he despatches a letter. He imitates some of the peculiarities of her handwriting in case she should think of taking his letters to the police. Women who write sensational anonymous letters to themselves are such a common phenomenon that the police will be sure to jump to that solution given the likeness of the handwriting. At the same time he leaves her in doubt as to whether he is really alive or not.

"At last, after many years, he judges that the time has arrived; he re-enters her life. All goes well. His wife never dreams of his real identity. He is a well-known man. The upstanding, good-looking young fellow is now a middle-aged man with a beard and stooping shoulders. And so we see history repeating itself. As before, Frederick is able to dominate Louise. For the second time she consents to marry him. *And no letter comes to forbid the banns*.

"But *afterwards* a letter *does* come. Why?

"I think that Dr. Leidner was taking no chances. The intimacy of marriage *might* awaken a memory. He wishes to impress on his wife, once and for all, *that Eric Leidner and Frederick Bosner are two* different people. So much so that a threatening letter comes from the former on account of the latter. The rather puerile gas poisoning business follows—arranged by Dr. Leidner, of course. Still with the same object in view.

"After that he is satisfied. No more letters

need come. They can settle down to happy married life together.

"And then, after nearly two years, *the letters recommence*.

"*Why? Eh bien*, I think I know. *Because the threat underlying the letters was always a genuine threat*. (That is why Mrs. Leidner has always been frightened. She *knew* her Frederick's gentle but ruthless nature.) *If she belongs to any other man but him he would kill her. And she has given herself to Richard Carey*.

"And so, having discovered this, cold-bloodedly, calmly, Dr. Leidner prepares the scene for murder.

"You see now the important part played by Nurse Leatheran? Dr. Leidner's rather curious conduct (it puzzled me at the very first) in securing her services for his wife is explained. It was vital that a reliable professional witness should be able to state incontrovertibly that Mrs. Leidner had been dead *over an hour* when her body was found—that is, that she had been killed at a time when *everybody could swear her husband was on the roof*. A suspicion *might* have arisen that he had killed her when he entered the room and found the body—but that was out of the question when a trained hospital nurse would assert positively that she had already been dead an hour.

"Another thing that is explained is the curious state of tension and strain that had come over the expedition this year. I never from the first thought that that could be attributed solely to *Mrs.* Leidner's influence. For several years this particular expedition had had a reputation for happy good-fellowship. In my opinion the state of mind of a community is always directly due to the influence of the man at the top. Dr. Leidner, quiet though he was, was a man of great personality. It was due to his tact, to his judgment, to his sympathetic manipulation of human beings that the atmosphere had always been such a happy one.

"If there was a change, therefore, the change must be due to the man at the top—in other words, to *Dr.* Leidner. It was Dr. Leidner, not Mrs. Leidner, who was responsible for the tension and uneasiness. No wonder the staff felt the change without understanding it. The kindly genial Dr. Leidner, outwardly the same, was only playing the part of himself. The real man was an obsessed fanatic plotting to kill.

"And now we will pass on to the second murder—that of Miss Johnson. In tidying up Dr. Leidner's papers in the office (a job she took on herself unasked, craving for something to do) she must have come on some unfinished draft of one of the anonymous letters.

"It must have been both incomprehensible and extremely upsetting to her! Dr. Leidner has been deliberately terrorizing his wife! She cannot understand it—but it upsets her badly. It is in this mood that Nurse Leatheran discovers her crying.

"I do not think at the moment that she suspects Dr. Leidner of being the murderer, but my experiments with sounds in Mrs. Leidner's and Father Lavigny's rooms are not lost upon her. She realizes that if it *was* Mrs. Leidner's cry she heard, *the window in her room must have been open, not shut*. At the moment that conveys nothing vital to her, *but she remembers it*.

"Her mind goes on working—ferreting its way towards the truth. Perhaps she makes some reference to the letters which Dr. Leidner understands and his manner changes. She may see that he is, suddenly, afraid.

"But Dr. Leidner *cannot* have killed his wife! He was on the *roof* all the time.

"And then, one evening, as she herself is on the roof puzzling about it, the truth comes to her in a flash. Mrs. Leidner has been killed from up *here*, through the open window.

"It was at that minute that Nurse Leatheran found her.

"And immediately, her old affection re-asserting itself, she puts up a quick camouflage. Nurse Leatheran must not guess the horrifying discovery she has just made.

"She looks deliberately in the opposite direction (towards the courtyard) and makes a remark suggested to her by Father Lavigny's appearance as he crosses the courtyard.

"She refuses to say more. She has got to 'think things out.'

"And Dr. Leidner, who has been watching her anxiously, *realizes that she knows the truth*. She is not the kind of woman to conceal her horror and distress from him.

"It is true that as yet she has not given him away—but how long can he depend upon her?

"Murder is a habit. That night he substitutes a glass of acid for her glass of water. There is just a chance she may be believed to have deliberately poisoned herself. There is even a chance she may be considered to have done the first murder and has now been overcome with remorse. To strengthen the latter idea he takes the quern from the roof and puts it under her bed.

"No wonder that poor Miss Johnson, in her death agony, could only try desperately to impart her hard-won information. Through 'the window,' *that* is how Mrs. Leidner was killed, *not* through the door—through the *window*. . . .

"And so thus, everything is explained, everything falls into place. . . . Psychologically perfect.

"But there is no proof. No proof at all. . . ."

None of us spoke. We were lost in a sea of horror. . . . Yes, and not only horror. Pity, too.

Dr. Leidner had neither moved nor spoken. He sat just as he had done all along. A tired, worn, elderly man.

At last he stirred slightly and looked at Poirot with gentle tired eyes.

"No," he said, "there is no proof. But that does not matter. You knew that I would not deny truth. . . . I have never denied truth . . . I think—really—I am rather glad . . . I'm so tired . . ."

Then he said simply:

"I'm sorry about Anne. That was bad—senseless—it wasn't *me!* And she suffered, too, poor soul. Yes, that wasn't me. It was fear. . . ."

A little smile just hovered on his pain-twisted lips.

"You would have made a good archæologist, M. Poirot. You have the gift of re-creating the past.

"It was all very much as you said.

"I loved Louise and I killed her . . . If you'd known Louise you'd have understood. . . . No, I think you understand anyway. . . ."

Chapter 29
L'Envoi

There isn't really any more to say about things.

They got "Father" Lavigny and the other man just as they were going on board a steamer at Beyrouth.

Sheila Reilly married young Emmott. I think that will be good for her. He's no door-mat—he'll keep her in her place. She'd have ridden roughshod over poor Bill Coleman.

I nursed him, by the way, when he had appendicitis a year ago. I got quite fond of him. His people were sending him out to farm in South Africa.

I've never been out East again. It's funny—sometimes I wish I could. I think of the noise the water-wheel made and the women washing, and that queer haughty look that camels give you—and I get quite a homesick feeling. After all, perhaps dirt isn't really so unhealthy as one is brought up to believe!

Dr. Reilly usually looks me up when he's in England, and as I said, it's he who's got me into this. "Take it or leave it," I said to him. "I know the grammar's all wrong and it's not properly written or anything like that—but there it is."

And he took it. Made no bones about it. It will give me a queer feeling if it's ever printed.

M. Poirot went back to Syria and about a week later he went home on the Orient Express and got himself mixed up in another murder. He was clever, I don't deny it, but I shan't forgive him in a hurry for pulling my leg the way he did. Pretending to think I might be mixed up in the crime and not a real hospital nurse at all!

Doctors are like that sometimes. Will have their joke, some of them will, and never think of *your* feelings!

I've thought and thought about Mrs. Leidner and what she was really like. . . . Sometimes it seems to me she was just a terrible woman—and other times I remember how nice she was to me and how soft her voice was—and her lovely fair hair and everything—and I feel that perhaps, after all, she was more to be pitied than blamed. . . .

And I can't help but pity Dr. Leidner. I know he was a murderer twice over, but it doesn't seem to make any difference. He was so dreadfully fond of her. It's awful to be fond of any one like that.

Somehow, the more I get older, and the more I see of people and sadness and illness and everything, the sorrier I get for every one. Sometimes, I declare, I don't know what's become of the good strict principles my aunt brought me up with. A very religious woman she was, and most particular. There wasn't one of our neighbours whose faults she didn't know backwards and forwards. . . .

Oh, dear, it's quite true what Dr. Reilly said. How does one stop writing? If I could find a really good telling phrase.

I must ask Dr. Reilly for some Arab one.

Like the one M. Poirot used.

In the name of Allah, the Merciful, the Compassionate . . .

Something like that.

Dame Agatha Christie is the most widely published author of all time. In a career that spanned more than fifty years, Christie wrote eighty novels and short story collections, nineteen plays—one of which, *The Mousetrap*, is the longest-running play in history—and five nonfiction books, including her autobiography. In addition, she wrote six romantic novels under the pseudonym Mary Westmacott. Two of the characters she created, the ingenious Belgian Hercule Poirot and the irrepressible and relentless Miss Jane Marple, became world-famous detectives. Poirot was immortalized on television by David Suchet, and Miss Marple by both Joan Hickson and Geraldine McEwan.

Agatha Christie achieved Britain's highest honor when she was made a Dame of the British Empire. She died in 1976.